Prai
THRE

"Dark, dangerous, ... im-
possible to put down!"
—GENA SHOWALTER,
New York Times bestselling author of
Seduce the Darkness

"Action-packed, edgy, and thrilling, *Three Days to
Dead* is a fabulous debut! Kelly Meding's world and
characters will grab you from the first page. You won't
want to miss this one."
—JEANIENE FROST,
New York Times bestselling author of
the Night Huntress series

"*Three Days to Dead* is gritty, imaginative and a terrific
read. Debut author Kelly Meding is a real storyteller
and I look forward to reading more of her work."
—PATRICIA BRIGGS,
New York Times bestselling author of *Bone Crossed*

"*Three Days to Dead* is one of the best books I've read.
Ever. Evy Stone is a heroine's heroine, and I rooted for
her from the moment I met her. Kelly Meding has written a phenomenal story, one that's fast-paced, gritty, and
utterly addictive. Brava! More! More! *More!*"
—JACKIE KESSLER, co-author of *Black and White*

"Meding delivers a thrilling urban fantasy full of desperate humans and menacing evil. Especially impressive
are her worldbuilding skills, which she uses to deftly
paint a portrait of a city on the edge of disaster."
—*Romantic Times* (four and a half stars)

"A fun, fast-paced book, with a likable lead and a lot of energy."

—CHARLES DELINT, *F&SF*

"I read *Three Days to Dead* in about four hours because it was just that good [and] Meding has shown that she isn't afraid of breaking her readers' hearts."

—*The Good, The Bad and The Unread*

"A fast-paced, immensely readable novel . . . There's a lot of potential for a great series here."

—*The Book Smugglers*

"A fabulous read and a great addition to the urban fantasy genre."

—*Literary Escapism*

"From beginning to end, I was completely absorbed in Evy's story . . . I wanted to savor each word . . . Everything, from the plot to the description and fabulous action scenes, is sharp and original . . . *Three Days to Dead* is a gritty, action-packed, fabulous urban fantasy novel by an author that has become an absolutely autobuy for me!"

—*The Book Lush*

Praise for AS LIE THE DEAD

"Rising star Meding returns to the ominous world and gutsy heroine first introduced in her exceptional debut . . . Evy is an unforgettable heroine and Meding an author to watch!"

—*Romantic Times* (four stars)

"Fabulous . . . One outstanding feature of this excellent series is the author's ability to mix her fantastical,

astounding paranormal world with the grime and typical troubles we all experience in our everyday mundane lives—and both feel completely real . . . The Dreg City series remains a must for all urban fantasy fans."
—*Bitten by Books*

"After reading *Three Days to Dead* my expectations for *As Lie the Dead* were really high and I'm happy to say that I was not disappointed at all. *As Lie the Dead* is an action packed read with a thrilling story and a heart-breakingly sweet romance."
—*Book Lovers, Inc.*

"After reading the first book in this new series, *Three Days to Dead*, I was in awe of the author and I was glad to have found a book that I had *really* enjoyed reading. After reading *As Lie the Dead*, I am again in awe of the author and now I know for sure that I have found a series that has me hooked."
—*Yummy Men and Kick Ass Chicks*

"Wow! I LOVED Kelly's debut novel, *Three Days to Dead* . . . *As Lie the Dead* is even better."
—*Hoosblog*

"Meding is definitely an author to add to your must-read piles."
—*The Phantom Paragrapher*

"Great non-stop action with fun characters and twists you won't see coming . . . This is a great book."
—*My world . . . in words and pages*

"Kelly Meding continues to make me a happy reader, and once again I couldn't put her book down until I finished it."
—*The Good, The Bad and The Unread*

Books published by The Random House Publishing Group
are available at quantity discounts on bulk purchases for
premium, educational, fund-raising, and special sales use.
For details, please call 1-800-733-3000.

WRONG SIDE
OF DEAD

KELLY MEDING

BANTAM BOOKS
NEW YORK

Sale of this book without a front cover may be unauthorized. If this book is coverless, it may have been reported to the publisher as "unsold or destroyed" and neither the author nor the publisher may have received payment for it.

Wrong Side of Dead is a work of fiction. Names, characters, places, and incidents either are the product of the author's imagination or are used fictitiously. Any resemblance to actual persons, living or dead, events, or locales is entirely coincidental.

A Bantam Mass Market Original

Copyright © 2012 by Kelly Meding

All rights reserved.

Published in the United States by Dell, an imprint of The Random House Publishing Group, a division of Random House, Inc., New York.

BANTAM BOOKS and the rooster colophon are registered trademarks of Random House, Inc.

ISBN 978-0-345-52579-6
eISBN 978-0-345-52580-2

Cover illustration: Cliff Nielson

Printed in the United States of America

www.bantamdell.com

9 8 7 6 5 4 3 2 1

Bantam Books mass market edition: February 2012

Acknowledgments

Writing is a solitary endeavor, but no book is written in a vacuum, so there are lots of terrific folks to thank. My fabulous agent, Jonathan Lyons, for your patience with those flashbacks and for always believing in me. My tireless editor, Anne Groell, whose advice and suggestions always lead to a better book. Also David Pomerico, Mike Braff, and all the good folks at Bantam/Random House.

Lots of love to Nancy for entertaining all of those crazy emails, for cheering when things are good, and for being there when things are bad. Thanks to my friends and family for loving me no matter what, even when I'm being a pain.

Most important, thank you to my readers for your love and support, and for following Evy's adventures through the wild, wonderful, terrifying world of Dreg City. I wouldn't be here without you.

WRONG SIDE
OF DEAD

Chapter One

The rave was already in full swing by the time Phineas and I showed up dressed to blend, even though we weren't there for a party. Illegal raves full of drunk college students and twentysomethings were the ideal hunting ground for half-Blood vampires, which made the transformed warehouse the perfect place for our little stakeout. But while any Halfie would do, I was hoping to see one particular target show up.

The music vibrated in my chest, loud enough for me to know my ears would be ringing by the time I left. We paused just inside, and Phineas el Chimal, my squad leader and partner for the night, closed his eyes to orient his more sensitive were-hearing to the din. Ravers jostled past us, ignorant of the partygoers around them, caught up in their own narrow little worlds. They had no clue why we were there, or that death was mingling among the kegs, glow sticks, and gyrating bodies.

No clue and no fucking manners. I was ready to turn around and slap the next person who elbowed me.

Phin saved them by opening his clear blue eyes and smiling. "Ready to have some fun?" he asked.

"Definitely." I draped myself onto his arm so we'd look like the happy couple we were pretending to be, and his fingers laced through mine. We both knew we'd have to do some acting, and I trusted him to watch my back. He'd been doing it without fail since the day we met nearly three months ago.

I stumbled a little in my knee-high boots, not used to the three-inch heels. My default shoes of choice were sneakers or combat boots—better for running and kicking. But the black leather boots I had on now matched my black leather miniskirt, and their knee-high length carefully hid a pair of serrated blades. The boots were the only place where my skimpy outfit could easily camouflage weapons, so I suffered the indignity of stumbling around in them. Anyway, it was also a good excuse to lean on Phin and put on a lovey-dovey show.

At least Phin had the benefit of jeans and a black wife-beater, which showed off his toned physique and earned him appreciative smiles from a few female gawkers. I shot them possessive glares as we wove our way into the dancing, gyrating crowd. The air was thick with the distinctive odors of smoke, beer, and sweat.

Phin tilted his head, pretended to nuzzle my neck, and whispered, "Team one, six o'clock."

I spotted them easily, dancing amid a tight cluster near the DJ's stage. Gina Kismet and Marcus Dane were team one to our team two, and even from a distance they made quite the convincing (if mismatched) couple—Gina's five-foot-two, pale-skinned, red-haired goth girl to his six-foot-one, black-haired, copper-eyed pirate.

Okay, so I never actually called him a pirate to his face, but the long hair in a ponytail, the ruddy complexion, and the tendency toward scruffy facial hair gave that impression. Even if I hadn't known that the man was actually Felia—a were-jaguar, to be precise—I would have suspected he wasn't quite what he appeared.

They were burning it up on the dance floor, completely into each other—at least to the untrained eye. And besides our two pairs, we had two single plants mingling around the rave, on the lookout for shimmering eyes and silver-streaked hair, or even a set of fangs that hadn't been filed down. Half-Blood vampires have certain telltale signs that can be covered up with contacts and hair dye, but members of the newest crop of Halfies were bolder and smarter, and they weren't as afraid of us as they used to be, back when an organization called the Triads existed and just our name sent them fleeing in fear. God, I miss those days.

It didn't really help that one of our own was now one of these bolder Halfies and seemed to be using our hard-learned tactics against us.

Phin swept me through the crowd, and we ended up near the makeshift bar, where two guys with silver rings in their noses were filling cups from dozens of different kegs. Phin collected a beer for each of us to complete the fitting-in image. Beer wasn't my favorite, but I'd guzzled worse in the line of duty.

At least a hundred people were in the main part of the warehouse, and I imagined dozens more wandered around, getting into any unlocked rooms they could find. Initial surveillance told us that the place had a section of offices on the north side of the warehouse, as well as roof access from the main floor.

Although I had officially returned to the field last week, after spending almost three weeks training and recovering from being nearly tortured to death (again) last month, this was my first big mission since . . . well, since my time with the Triads.

And a lot was riding on finding the guy we were looking for.

"Time to play," I said.

Phin grinned. The strobe lights lit his angular face in a way that accentuated the fact that he was a were-osprey—a predator in every sense of the word, but also a very loyal ally. Our relationship had its share of ups (me saving his life twice in the first two weeks we knew each other) and downs (him stabbing me in the stomach the first day we knew each other), but I wouldn't want anyone else by my side for tonight's operation. Except maybe the one man who no longer wanted to be there.

We moved with the crowd, creating an easy dance of grinding and groping, while carefully observing the other dancers and sipping slowly at our beers. Gina and Marcus had disappeared. I spotted one of our single plants, a full-Blood vampire named Quince, dancing it up with a pair of girls in slinky dresses. He'd dyed his white hair dark blond and wore blue contact lenses to cover his glimmering purple eyes. That color was a very distinctive vampire attribute. The other was his long, lean frame, which he carried like a male model.

Quince had joined our organization two weeks ago and proved, right from the start, to be eager and very trainable. Phin immediately asked to have him assigned to his squad.

Before separating for the night's mission, our working sextet had come up with a handful of signals, since using earbuds would be useless with the noise levels. Quince caught me looking at him and tugged hard on his left earlobe—shorthand for "I might have something."

I scratched my forehead along the hairline, motioning that I understood. "Come on," I said to Phineas.

We leaned on each other, pretending to be more tipsy than we were, as we threaded our way to the opposite wall, which was painted with Day-Glo stripes and splatters. Quince extricated himself from his dance partners and met us there, slapping Phin on the shoulder as if greeting an old buddy.

"Rumors are circulating about a private party at midnight," Quince said, his tone serious even as his expression remained playful. "It promises a narcotic experience that is both mind-altering and life-changing."

It definitely sounded like what happens when humans are infected with the vampire parasite, which turns them into half-Bloods. Vampires are a species unto themselves; they aren't made and they were never human. Their saliva, however, is highly infectious to humans, and a single bite alters a human being's brain functions and physical nature. Many infected humans go insane from the change, but some adapt and are able to function with relative ease—relative given that they're still driven by bloodlust and are at risk of infecting more humans. Which is why all Halfies are on our "kill first, don't ask questions" list.

But the functional Halfies were our target tonight. During the last two weeks, we'd stumbled across several places where a dozen or more Halfie corpses had been dumped after being beheaded. Word on the street said several functioning Halfies were looking to create an army of similarly functioning Halfies to take us on. And since two in three went bat shit crazy from the infection, they seemed to be building their ranks by trial and error.

Which meant the bodies of the once innocent were piling up, and their makers had to be stopped. Of all the minor disasters plaguing the city, this was our most pressing. And the most personal, given the former Hunter who was helping to organize it.

"Where's the party?" I asked.

"Meeting on the roof," he replied. "For a brief inspection, I assume, before reporting the location to the chosen candidates."

"Awesome. What time is it?"

Phin checked his cell phone. "Eleven-twenty."

Good, we had a little time. "Quince, I want you and the other plants to stay down here just in case things get rowdy. Phin and I will let team one know, then head up to the roof."

Quince nodded, laughed like I'd just told the funniest

joke ever, then melted back into the crowd. He was a damned good actor, for a vampire.

Phin crowded in and pressed his forehead to mine, like a lover going in for a kiss. His familiar scent, wild and clean like a raging mountain river, settled around me. "Think he'll show for the roof meet?" he asked, mouth mere inches from mine.

"Hope so," I replied, "but I'm not counting on it." I was keenly aware of Phin's warmth and of every place our skin touched. I missed this kind of contact with a man—one man in particular, who made me crazy in the best and worst ways. But I couldn't waste time missing Wyatt, or mourning our broken relationship. I had a damned job to do.

"I'll go tell Marcus," Phin said. "Meet me by the roof access."

"Okay."

I lingered against the wall for the length of a song. That should be enough time for Phin to track down Marcus and Kismet and let them in on the new plan. The music changed. I eyed a path toward the far end of the warehouse where the stairwell (according to the blueprints) was located, aware of the pulsing throng between me and it.

Which was why I didn't notice my shadow until he'd sidled up next to me, leaning casually against the wall like he belonged there. I shifted sideways, prepared to tell him to get lost, and froze. *Shit.*

"Hey, Evy."

He'd taken care to dye his hair back to its natural shade of brown, and donned a pair of lavender-tinted sunglasses to obscure the new shimmer to his eyes, but the face was the same. Felix Diggory, former Hunter and two-week-old half-Blood, grinned at me, his unfiled fangs gleaming brightly under the constantly shifting lights.

I wasn't sure how I'd react when I saw him again. I

expected anger, grief, maybe even a little bit of shame, since I was there the night Felix got infected. Instead, all I felt was relief. Relief that he was here and I had the chance to correct my mistake. The mistake that allowed him to run free in the first place.

I'd been cooped up for weeks, training to gain back what I'd lost when Thackery tortured me. All I'd wanted was a few hours in the city to kick back, eat a hamburger with Milo and Felix, and enjoy a conversation that didn't revolve around tactics, weapons, or interspecies peace. Then we three made the idiotic decision to follow some Halfies onto a bus—no weapons, no plan, no backup.

It was no wonder only two of us got off that bus still human.

"Hey, Felix," I said.

"You look good. Still training?"

"Yeah, getting back into fighting form."

He dragged his tongue along the front teeth between his fangs, as if he thought I hadn't noticed them. "Saw you with Phineas earlier. You two on a date or are you working?"

I considered lying—for about three seconds. "Working. Looking for you, actually."

"Me?" He tilted his head. "I'm flattered."

"Don't be. You know why we're here."

His mouth quirked at the corners. "Because I'm a big, bad Halfie now, and therefore must be slaughtered with extreme prejudice?"

"Bingo."

"Good luck with that."

"You don't think I can take you?"

"The last time I saw you, you couldn't take a house cat."

Okay, it was a challenge, then. Good. I needed to get him out of the warehouse and away from hundreds of potential human shields—or victims. Rumors were circulating. The newspapers were printing stories full of incomplete information, speculating on mutilated bodies and the extraordinary number of missing persons. People weren't stupid, no matter what we did to try to convince them it was business as usual. I couldn't kill Felix in front of so many witnesses without causing a huge mess—and not just of the spilled-blood variety.

I shifted my stance and pulled back my shoulders. "I might surprise you. I killed three Halfies just last week, all by my little old self."

He chuckled. "Good for you, Evy," he said, then let his gaze scan the crowd. "So who's here with you? I know you and Phineas can't be out hunting by yourselves."

"Marcus and Gina are here, and some new guys you don't know."

His attention snapped back to me. Eyebrows arched and lips slightly parted, he was caught somewhere between surprise and excitement. "Gina's here? Really?"

The eagerness in those words broke my heart a little bit. Gina Kismet had been his boss, his Handler, for a little over two years. Their entire Triad had been very close, and losing Felix to infection had devastated all of them—Gina, Tybalt Monahan, and especially Milo Gant, whose feelings for Felix had once extended far beyond simple friendship.

"Yeah, she's here somewhere," I said. I didn't bother trying to be casual as I scanned the crowd myself, looking for familiar faces. But we were tucked against a wall with a sea of people in front of us, and the lights made it difficult to see far or well.

"I wish I had time to say hello, since I never got the chance to say good-bye."

The last thing Gina needed was to see him like this,

but I kept my disagreement to myself. "Someplace else you need to be?"

"Yep."

"Okay, but you do realize that's not going to happen, yeah?"

In an instant, the predatory intensity was back. His nostrils flared, and he parted his lips just enough to let the tips of his fangs show. "You couldn't kill me the last time."

"I wasn't myself the last time."

"So what do you propose? We duke it out right here on the dance floor?"

He was playing along nicely. "I was thinking the roof. You and me."

Felix cocked his head. His curious expression was so much like his old self that my heart hurt, and it made it difficult to remember this was no longer a man, but a monster. "Let me guess," he said. "I win, and I get bragging rights on finally killing the unkillable Evy Stone."

I shrugged one shoulder. "As long as you promise to kill me and not infect me."

"You survived infection once before."

True, and I would probably survive it again. A unique healing ability, gifted to me by a gnome, helped me battle the vampire parasite, which infects humans and turns them into Halfies. The ability also helped me survive too many near-fatal wounds in the three months since I died and was magically resurrected into my current body. An ability that part of me wished had been physical—something that could be duplicated and used to help others who were wounded or dying.

Because sometimes being the one who always survives when your friends die all around you really sucks. "Then I guess we're both fighting to kill," I said.

He ran his tongue along his front teeth, between his fangs. He didn't seem particularly pleased by our inevitable throw-down. "Guess so. And I kind of still owe you."

"For what?"

"For punching me in the head the night of the factory fire."

I snorted. "Somehow I think getting blown up in that fire is payback enough."

"Maybe." He checked his wristwatch. "Well, let's do this so I can still make my appointment."

The utter normalcy of the statement took me momentarily aback. For the majority of Halfies, the infection makes them go mad. They can't think about anything except blood and death, and they rarely run around making plans and speaking about appointments. The normal conversation (so to speak) I was having with Felix was an anomaly. The insane Halfies were the ones we most often encountered and killed. It made me wonder again just how many other lucid Halfies were out there—and how many more Felix had made in the two weeks since he was infected.

I just nodded.

"Ladies first?"

"You're fucking out of your mind if you think I'm turning my back on you."

Felix smiled. "That's the Evy I remember."

He pushed off the wall and strolled past me. Other partygoers, tired of the grind, slid quickly into our places. I kept my attention on Felix as I followed him through the smoke-and-liquor-scented throng, barely an arm's reach between us. As much as I wanted to look for someone in my group, to signal them about my destination, I couldn't risk Felix disappearing into the crowd. Now that I had him, I wasn't about to let him get away.

His path wound us in and out of clusters of dancers and groups of drinkers, but his goal always seemed to be the roof access door at the opposite end of the warehouse. Three-quarters of the way there, I spotted Quince. His attention was on Felix, who he knew on sight from photographs. If Felix sensed the full-Blood vampire nearby, he made no indication. But if Felix was signaling anyone else, I couldn't tell.

I passed into Quince's line of sight and pretended to adjust one of my clip-on earrings—the signal that I had engaged the target.

Felix reached the access door. It was partially hidden behind a stack of old wooden pallets, in what was a pretty lame attempt at keeping people from opening the door. The door itself was large and metal, but he opened it easily with one hand and slipped into the stairwell. I grabbed the door handle before it could slam shut and nearly wrenched my arm from its socket. The fucking thing was *heavy*.

The stairwell itself was dark and stifling. I stopped inside and let my eyes adjust to the murky shadows. Felix's pale skin came into focus, several steps up the first flight. He beckoned, and I followed the sound of his echoing footfalls.

He could have attacked at any time, using his extra-sensitive night vision to gain the upper hand and kill me, but he didn't. He just kept going until he reached the roof door. It didn't open right away, probably rusted shut from disuse. I waited one step below the landing while he slammed his shoulder into the door.

It squealed open, and he stumbled out onto the roof. I followed, maintaining distance and caution as I stepped into the humid night air. The roof was tar and metal, longer than it was wide, and dotted with dozens of vents. It sagged in places. We'd probably missed a sign warning that it wasn't safe to walk on, but it was too late now.

The noise of the rave was muffled, bass vibrations occasionally dancing up through my feet and ankles. The sounds of the city seemed far away, even though we were still in her midst. Maybe three blocks from here was the old potato chip factory where I'd nearly died.

The rush of air clued me in to duck, and I narrowly missed the fist aimed at my skull. I slammed my right shoulder forward and up, hitting muscle and ribs, and ejected an "oof!" of air from Felix. I drove my left fist sideways and landed a perfect kidney shot. A regular human male might have dropped to the roof in pain. Felix only stumbled, and then returned the favor by driving his elbow down into the middle of my back.

Bolts of fire blossomed from the point of contact, searing all the way to my toes. I dropped to my knees, saw his knee coming at my face, and rolled with the blow. It glanced off my cheekbone, a flash of pain, and I tumbled sideways. I used the momentum to keep rolling, and also to reach into my boot.

I came up in a crouch a few feet away, one blade curled backward against my wrist, ready to slash at anything that came at me. My cheek smarted, and something warm dripped down my neck.

Felix grinned, fangs gleaming brightly. "First blood," he said, as if it were some sort of accomplishment. And maybe in some ways it was. Prior to his infection, he'd spent weeks battling chronic pain and poor mobility, courtesy of old injuries. He never thought he'd walk without a limp, much less draw first blood in a fistfight with an ex-Hunter. But he was still a half-Blood, and far worse (and far better) men had made me bleed.

"Lucky shot," I said. The open wound concerned me. If he managed to get saliva into the wound (gross, yeah, but possible), it could spread the parasite. Fighting the infection would hurt like hell, and I'd much rather avoid the agony.

"I wish I could make this last, Evy, but we'll be interrupted pretty soon."

I didn't know if he meant by my people, or by his. "Come and get me, big boy," I drawled.

He lunged, and I leapt up to meet him.

Chapter Two

I seriously overestimated my leaping abilities.

We slammed together in an awkward tangle and hit the roof with a dull thud, thrashing and seeking purchase. I slashed with my blade and felt it cut skin and cloth. Warm blood slicked my fingers, making my grip on the knife less certain. Felix clawed with his hands and kicked with his knees, landing blows on my thighs and upper arms. We probably looked like a pair of angry chicks in a catfight, for all the grace either of us was showing.

Pretty sad for a pair of former Hunters.

He snapped at my face with his fangs, and I rewarded him with a head butt that cracked his nose. He howled and reeled back, even as his grip on my arms tightened, fingernails digging into skin. It exposed his throat, but I couldn't get my hand up. I couldn't get the blade across his windpipe to put him out of his fucking misery.

I did get my right knee up and between us (not a small feat, considering the leather miniskirt), and used it as a brace to keep him out of biting distance. My knife hand was stuck making shallow stabs at his ribs, but I was not close enough to cause real damage. We were at an awkward impasse that neither one of us was going to win.

Interruption was inevitable. The only question was by his people, or by mine?

It turned out to be both simultaneously. An explosion of activity stole Felix's attention first, and it loosened his grip on my arms just enough. I shoved my knee against his chest, broke his hold, and rolled away. Someone slammed into me sideways, and we went tumbling across the tarred roof, my arms and legs scraping against what felt like a lifetime's accumulation of grit. I ended up on top of my attacker, my back to his chest, and slammed my left elbow backward. Bone connected with bone and sent a jolt through my arm from wrist to shoulder.

Plan B. I lifted up my head and crashed it back down. A nose crunched and the person below me—male, from the serious lack of breasts pressing in my shoulders—screeched and shoved. I lunged and came up in a crouch. He tried to scuttle away. I scrambled up behind him and slit his throat. As he slumped to the ground, gurgling out purplish blood, I observed the chaos.

Kismet and Phineas were going two against five with some teenage Halfies about fifteen feet away. Neither of them had drawn guns. So close to the rave and hundreds of innocents, gunshots would be too damned loud. They fought with blades, and with as much skill as any Hunter I'd ever seen. Especially Phin. He moved like liquid, dancing out of arm's reach, lunging in to draw blood, then back out before the Halfie could bite.

I'd seen him fight before, several times. The very first time, though, he'd been in bi-shift form—still human, but with man-sized osprey wings protruding from his back that made him look like a dark-haired angel. He told me once that his people had been fierce warriors, and he proved it each time he went into battle.

His wings weren't out this time, but he was no less intense. He caught me watching, and gave me a wink and a grin. Uh-oh.

Phin grabbed a Halfie by the neck and sent him at me

like a bowling ball down a lane. I stopped the male Halfie's progress with the sharp heel of my boot, crouched, and cleanly snapped his neck. He thudded to the roof. Kismet and Phin dispatched the other Halfies with only a bit more effort. The front of Kismet's dress was ripped, nearly exposing her breasts, and her skin was spattered with Halfie blood. Phin, meanwhile, barely looked disheveled.

He gave me another wicked grin, battle lust shining in his eyes. Eyes that flickered past me, then blinked. In surprise, not in warning. I turned, curious, and nearly burst out laughing.

Marcus had shifted into jaguar form—a big black thing of beauty and power—but that wasn't what was so funny. He was sitting on top of Felix, front paws pinning down the thrashing man's shoulders like a giant paperweight. The fact that Felix was struggling to remove the two-hundred-pound immovable object threatened to give me a bad case of the giggles. It was just so ridiculous.

I stared. Marcus yawned. Behind me, Phin laughed.

Kismet appeared by my shoulder. She hadn't seen Felix since the day he was infected. Her jaw was set, her expression hard. She had mourned him, just as Milo and Tybalt had, but that didn't mean much when the "dead" person was still alive and being held down by a were-cat.

She looked up at me, and I held her gaze without blinking. I'd been where she was—about to end the suffering of a loved one because of vampire infection. I didn't know exactly what she felt, but I could damned well guess. She blinked, then inhaled a deep breath. Let it out. Palmed a blade.

Felix had stopped struggling. As Kismet walked toward him, he twisted his head around to look at her. He offered a sad smile. "Hey, Kis. We had a good couple years, huh?"

She froze. Even with her back to me, I saw muscles tense and could just imagine her expression—ice and anger flashing in wide green eyes. "No," she said in a voice full of cold fury, "we didn't. You have his memories and body, but you aren't Felix. Felix died the moment he was infected."

"Maybe. Probably. Shit."

He seemed so sane, so completely in his right mind that my curiosity bubbled over. I closed the distance between me and Kismet. "How did you not go insane from the infection?" I asked before I could censor myself.

His iridescent eyes flickered from her to me. "This wasn't supposed to happen." He went on before I could ask for clarification. "I can smell your blood, Evy. It smells so sweet. I want to taste it. That's really disgusting, right?"

Marcus growled.

"It's partially impulse control," Felix said as if he hadn't even mentioned wanting to taste my blood. "The desire is there, but it doesn't have to be. I want to hunt and feed, but I don't do it."

"You just don't?" I asked. "Bullshit."

He shrugged—or at least he tried to shrug. "It's an addiction, a craving. I was a Hunter, so I know it's wrong. I know I'm a monster, and I don't want to be." He sounded so . . . resigned. Almost sad. With the shimmering eyes and the fangs, it was pretty damned eerie.

Half-Bloods were abominations. They weren't controllable, hence the entire reason for our open execution policy. Even if Felix hadn't run the night he was infected, we couldn't have risked keeping him alive. You can feed and tame a wild animal, but you live with the constant risk of being turned on and attacked. The kindest thing you can do is set them free—and for Halfies, that means death.

Marcus made a noise not unlike a bored grunt. His bright copper eyes shifted from me to Phin, then down to his trapped prey. He bared long, deadly teeth, silently asking if it was time to end this. Therians were not prone to infection, so he could crush Felix's throat with those powerful jaws and not risk turning, but I knew that Kismet wouldn't allow that.

She squatted next to his head.

"Tell Milo and Tybalt I'm sorry," Felix said.

She nodded, turning the blade in her hand.

"Wait a moment," Phineas said. He passed me to stand on the other side of Felix, then looked straight down. "Who's organizing this?"

Felix frowned. "Organizing what?"

"Who sent you here tonight recruiting? Who's turning young people into half-Bloods?"

His eyes widened like a child caught in a lie, then hardened just as quickly. "You're going to kill me anyway."

"Yes."

"Then I think I'd rather not tell you."

"Why not?"

He looked away, focusing on one of the big black paws holding him down. I turned it over in my mind for a moment. He seemed stuck, as though he wanted to tell us something but couldn't. And I could only guess at the reasons. Glimpses of the old Felix kept peeking through, winking at us, while the monster remained in charge. Felix deserved release from that monster, but he did have information we needed. *Hell.*

"Marcus, can you keep sitting on him for a minute?" I asked. "Phin, Kis, a word?"

They followed me to a safe distance, far enough that

with the pulse of the rave beneath us, Felix shouldn't be able to hear.

"What?" Kismet asked.

"I think we should truss him up and take him back to the Watchtower with us," I said. Before either could reply, I held up a silencing hand and kept talking. "He's half-sane, and he knows a lot more than he's saying about who's organizing this. That's valuable information that we might be able to get out of him."

"You trust him?"

"Absolutely not, but I think it's worth the risk. He's been out there for two weeks. He knows exactly where the Watchtower is, but we've yet to see an open attack, or even spies sniffing around. It's possible there's enough of the old Felix inside him to keep him from completely betraying us."

"You want him interrogated?" Phin said.

"Yes."

"We cannot offer him freedom in exchange for information."

"I know that, and I wouldn't even consider it. But maybe he'll take something else."

"Such as?"

I glanced at Kismet. "A chance to say good-bye to his friends." She glared, but I didn't relent. "Felix told me once about how much it hurt to lose Lucas, because they didn't get to say good-bye. Maybe we can use that to reason with him."

Kismet flinched. Almost eighteen months ago, Milo had been Lucas Moore's replacement in Kismet's Triad. Lucas and Felix had been best friends, and Lucas's sudden death from a brain aneurysm had devastated Felix. Hunters lived every day with the risk of dying on any patrol, but no one expects to lose a loved one while he's watching a baseball game at home in your apartment.

It was kind of a low blow, though, since Kismet and

Lucas had been secretly, madly in love for most of his tenure in her Triad.

"That might actually work," she said. But she looked anything but happy about it.

Goodie. "Phin?"

"I think it's worth trying."

"Awesome. Prisoner it is."

Halfway back, the roof door swung open and Quince stepped out with Kyle Jane, another Therian team member, close behind. They both stopped and surveyed the scene.

"It seems we missed the party," Quince said.

Marcus couldn't reasonably sit on Felix in the car, so he stayed put until Phin returned with enough restraints to bind a raging rhinoceros. The end package wasn't pretty, but everyone seemed satisfied that Felix could neither get loose nor bite anyone on the drive back. He was dumped into the SUV's rear compartment with jaguar-Marcus and Quince as guards. Kyle drove, with Kismet riding shotgun.

I wasn't sure if the mission was a success or not. Sure, we prevented other innocent (drunken idiot) bystanders from being infected and potentially executed. I'd kicked a little ass and had the bruises and an itchy, healing cheekbone to prove it. We got our hands on Felix, who'd been rogue for two weeks. We were one step closer to knowing who was organizing this and why, but it still felt . . . incomplete. I mulled on it during the drive back to the Watchtower.

Carved out of the bones of the abandoned Capital City Mall, situated on the East Side near the Black River, our headquarters was more a small city than a tower of any sort. Individual stores were now rooms with designated uses—weapons storage, a central Operations room, a small infirmary, a gymnasium and training room, as well as converted showers and sleeping quarters. About two hundred humans, Therians, and vampires lived here full-time, including me.

Its conversion began six weeks ago, after the vampire Families made a deal with the Assembly of Clan Elders. The mall was protected by the vampires, because it had a Sanctuary—a magical hot spot where the power of the Break bled through—and it was offered as a headquarters for their joint efforts in protecting their people.

Humans were invited to play after Boot Camp was destroyed last month. The Watchtower was run by a Triumvirate—one representative of each of the three races, and all major decisions needed a unanimous vote. Astrid, a were-cat and Marcus's sister, stood for the Therians, my kind-of friend Isleen for the vampires, and former-Handler Adrian Baylor for the humans.

Tensions were high and for good reason, but everyone mostly got along. We all had the same goals now: protect the city and protect our people. At all costs.

Kyle followed a well-worn path through the weedy parking lot toward the interior of the U-shaped mall's curve, which created a sort of canyon. The entire lot and structure were protected by a barrier spell, which urged anyone outside of it to look away. And that was only the first security measure in place.

Kyle drove through the illusion of a wall and into a parking lot made of two hollowed-out former restaurants. The lot held an array of vehicles, mostly trucks, vans, and sport utility vehicles of various makes, models, and colors. No sense in being predictable.

Quince and Kyle hauled Felix out of the back and carried him by the ropes like a trussed-up Christmas tree. He didn't struggle or protest. Marcus followed, a silent sentinel. Something occurred to me as I shut my door.

"Hey, did anyone pick up Marcus's clothes at the rave?" I asked.

Blank looks. Marcus snuffled, and if a jaguar could act annoyed, he did.

Kyle chuckled. Therians had to remove their clothing in order to shift. And, likewise, they shifted back to human form completely nude. I've learned that most have little issue with nudity—at least, in small groups. But I imagined Marcus had no intention of walking the length of the mall to his sleeping quarters in just his bare skin.

The parking lot led into a short, tiled corridor, which intersected with the main length of the mall's interior. The old fountain in the center now held a thriving herb garden—not all the plants meant for spicing food. Left and right, the corridor stretched down about a hundred yards in either direction before sharply turning again. Each end of the mall was capped by an old department store. The structure on the right/east was being converted into larger living quarters. The old store on the left/west would eventually be a training facility, not unlike the obstacle course we ran at Boot Camp.

Operations was straight ahead, with weapons storage right next door. To the right of weapons was our brand-new jail, complete with restraint cells and an interrogation room. I despised that place more than any other part of the Watchtower, and I avoided it as much as possible. My initial look at the completed design had lasted exactly ninety seconds, and I'd left shaking.

Three familiar faces emerged from Ops. Astrid Dane was my height, with long, straight black hair and the same exotic looks as her brother, Marcus. She led the charge, hands balled into fists, clearly unhappy with our gift. Behind her trailed Milo Gant and Wyatt Truman, both studies in shock. Rightfully so, I guess. We hadn't left with the intention of bringing home a prisoner. It just worked out that way.

My heart went out to Milo for the horror he must have felt at the sight of someone he'd once loved so much reduced to so little. Milo had been there with me the night Felix was infected. He'd been shot in the abdomen and hadn't actually seen it happen, but that had only added to his guilt. Neither of us had been able to save Felix.

"Hey," Kismet said. "Did Dr. Vansis say you could be up and around like this?" When it came to her former Hunters, she was a mother hen to the end.

"Yeah, as long as I don't overdo it and pull my stitches," Milo replied. His voice was rough, weighed down with emotion. He met my gaze, and I couldn't even muster a supportive smile for the young man who'd once tried to kill me and who I now counted as one of my best friends.

"I take it *that* has information," Astrid said, pointing at Felix.

Back to business. Curiosity was drawing a small crowd that wisely kept its distance.

"He knows who's creating and organizing the Halfies, and why," Phineas said.

"Is it sane?"

"Mostly, yes. And self-aware."

"And it tells us in exchange for what?"

"Good-byes to old friends before he's executed."

Astrid glanced at Milo, who looked slightly ill—whether at the idea of talking to Felix or the mention of his execution, I didn't know. But my money was on the latter. She turned back to our little group. "Who's responsible?" *If he gets loose and bites someone* dangled at the end of the question.

"I am," Kismet and I said in stereo.

Behind Astrid, Wyatt frowned, eyebrows furrowing.

The silent disapproval irritated me, just as most of our interactions over the last few weeks had irritated me. Irrationally, maybe, but not entirely my fault. He was in the room, yelling right back, during the argument two weeks ago that fractured us down the middle.

"Fine," Astrid said. "Lock him up. We'll debrief in the conference room in fifteen minutes, then see what the prisoner has to say." She eyeballed everyone in our little cluster, nostrils flaring. "Who's bleeding?"

I touched my cheek. The cut had already scabbed over, the blood around it drying to a flaky mess on my skin.

"I am," Phin said.

"What?" I rounded on him, planting both hands on my hips, all of my irritation firmly directed at him now. I couldn't see any wounds, but with his black clothes that meant nothing. "How?"

"The scuffle on the roof. One of the half-Bloods had a switchblade. It isn't deep." From his tone of voice, you'd think it was just a mosquito bite. And considering that two months ago he'd been kidnapped and cut open while fully conscious, a minor stab wound probably didn't seem very important. But it still made me want to slap him.

"Get it treated," Astrid said.

"But—"

"Stone, make sure he gets it looked at."

I opened my mouth to argue, then clamped it shut. It didn't matter that my feet hurt from those fucking boots, or that I desperately wanted to shower blood and bits of roof grit off my skin and maybe put on some real clothes. Astrid wasn't a large woman, but her word was law. Especially in that impatient voice.

"Fine," I said.

The infirmary was to the left of Operations, about halfway down the length of the mall. Why so far down? It never made sense to me, but I didn't design the place.

Maybe because it was closer to the training rooms, where injuries tended to happen on a regular basis. I still felt ridiculous, click-clacking my way down the hall.

Partway there, I grabbed Phin's arm. "Hold on for a second." I balanced on my left foot and yanked down the zipper on the right boot. Cool air hit my legs, and I peeled the offending leather away from sweaty, red-marked skin. My ankle protested being bent back to its normal angle, and again when I put my weight on it. Blissful pain. I moaned.

Phin made a sound somewhere between a snort and a laugh. "Better?"

"Almost." My left leg soon joined my right in boot freedom. I let go of Phin, then threw the offending objects against the nearest wall. They hit the floor with a clattering thud. I bounced on the balls of my feet, stretching my calf muscles, smoothing out the aches. "Yeah, much better."

"You're going to leave them there?"

I eyed the boots. "I borrowed the damned things for this rave. If someone wants them, they're welcome to them. Knee-high leather boots with three-inch heels are torture devices."

He chuckled and continued walking. I padded behind, the ceramic tile floor cool on my bare feet. A familiar buzz of power tickled over my skin as we passed the Sanctuary. A vampire was always standing guard at the hall entrance leading down to what had once been a set of the mall's public bathrooms. The women's restroom was the last place anyone would think to find a Sanctuary. Its location had certainly surprised the hell out of me.

The infirmary was a few stores down, in what I'm told was once an electronics outlet. Not that it mattered much, since the entire thing was gutted, outfitted with an emergency surgical suite (not that we had a surgeon yet, but it was on the To Do list), a fully stocked closet of supplies, an exam room, and four private patient rooms. The adjacent store was under construction as an expansion. We were in a pretty dangerous and injury-prone line of work, after all.

The infirmary wasn't a doctor's office, so there was no waiting room. Just a desk, some filing cabinets, and the curtained exam room. All of our Boot Camp medical staff had been slaughtered last month. The Assembly brought in an Ursia (were–grizzly bear) physician they trusted, and who was familiar with human, Therian, and vampire anatomy. Dr. Reid Vansis was good, and he knew it. He also had the grumpy personality of most Ursia I'd met, which made him someone I preferred to avoid. But he'd saved Milo's life when he was shot, and I respected him for it.

But Vansis also wasn't in. As the only doctor in residence, he had a large whiteboard on the wall behind his desk where he wrote his location when he wasn't in the office. In large black letters he'd scrawled "SLEEPING." Which meant we were not to disturb him except for emergencies. Which this clearly wasn't.

Terrific.

"Take off your shirt," I said.

Phin yanked the hem of his shirt out of his jeans and up over his shoulders, and whipped it off in one smooth motion. He wasn't fast enough to hide his wince, though. A long, pale line divided his chest from sternum to belly button—a terrible reminder of the hell he'd been through because of me.

"Turn around," I said.

He did, presenting a lean, perfectly muscled back. Hiding just above the waist of his jeans was a four-inch gash, still oozing blood. This close, I could see the dark, damp patch where the blood had soaked into his pants. I could also see more meat than I was comfortable with.

"Damn, Phin, that might need stitches."

"It does?" He twisted his torso in a vain attempt to see his own lower back, and only managed to make the wound gape wider. He hissed, then quit trying to see it and felt around with his fingers. "It'll heal, Evy. Use those butterfly bandages to keep it together until it can mend."

I eyeballed the gash. "Are you sure?"

"Yes."

"Okay."

Therians healed faster than the average human, but it would still be several days before that wound was completely gone. And it would likely scar. Small lines and imperfections dotted his back and shoulders—scars I never had the guts to ask about. I still didn't.

We moved our little production into the curtained exam area and assembled a tray of useful items—bandages, medical tape, alcohol, gauze, scissors. He turned, once again presenting his back. I wetted some gauze with the alcohol and paused to assess the playing field. This wasn't going to work.

"Okay, Phin," I said, "I need you to drop your pants."

"I—pardon me?"

Chapter Three

Phin turned his head far enough to see me over his shoulder. "Drop my pants?"

"Yes, please. The wound is too low and your jeans are in the way."

"I was uncertain if I would have to shift this evening." I frowned. "Okay. And?"

"In the interest of expediency, I wore as few layers as possible."

What the hell was he—? Oh. "You're not wearing underwear?"

"Correct."

"I've seen you naked, you know."

He turned completely around, his face a question mark. As a general rule, Therians weren't shy about nudity, but he was always more careful than most about exposing himself. In front of me, at any rate. "You have?" he asked.

"Well, I was half-delirious from smoke inhalation and it was hard to see through the inferno."

"I don't— Oh, the factory fire." Understanding dawned, and he smiled. It was a warm, friendly smile. "I suppose that's only fair, as I've seen you naked, as well."

I forced a grin, even as my heart pounded against my ribs. Neither of our situations had been ideal; however, the reason he saw me naked nearly two months ago was one of the worst memories of my life. I shoved it away, not wanting to ponder the circumstances of that day and what that fucking pùca had done. Mimicking Wyatt's body and face so perfectly, then knocking me out and stealing syringes of my blood. Driven by an instinctive need to leave chaos in its wake, the pùca made me believe, for the merest fraction of an instant, that Wyatt was actually hurting me.

I looked at the floor, the ceiling, anywhere but at Phin.

Warm palms cupped my cheeks. "Evy, I am so sorry. That was a callous thing to say."

I swallowed against the acid creeping into my throat. Met his gaze and found myself staring into intense twin pools of concern. "It's okay."

He pursed his lips, eyebrows furrowed, his sharp features displaying every bit of the predatory bird he shifted into. "No, it isn't. It was meant in jest and it caused you pain, which wasn't my intention."

"I know, Phin. I'm fine."

"I'm still sorry."

"Apology accepted." I pressed gently into his hands, appreciating the gesture. The joy of simply being touched in a nonviolent manner. I curled my fingers around his right wrist and squeezed, marveling again at the hard muscle beneath feather-soft skin. "Thank you. Now turn around and drop your pants."

His eyebrows arched, and then he laughed. He undid his belt and shoved his jeans down to his knees. With the field clear (and my eyes firmly on the wound) I cleaned the skin around the slice, then put a clean gauze pad over it.

"Hold this down hard," I said.

He reached around and pressed the pad against the cut while I opened a few butterfly bandages. I still thought it needed stitches, and I didn't trust myself to apply the liquid bandage stuff to anyone besides myself.

"Have you spoken to Wyatt recently?" he asked, breaking a perfectly good nonawkward silence.

I swatted his hand away and peeled off the bloody gauze pad. The bleeding had slowed, but it was still oozing. "You mean besides him telling our squad to not get killed tonight as we left a few hours ago? No." Two of the butterflies adhered easily. The third was refusing to stick, so I opened another.

"Evy, may I ask you a personal question?"

"Sure. Just remember your bare ass is at my mercy."

He chuckled, and I had an irrational urge to poke him in the ribs. I tore strips of medical tape instead. "What changed?"

"You're going to have to narrow that down." I covered the butterflied wound with a clean gauze pad. Taped it down, creating a rectangle of white against tan skin.

Phin hauled his pants back up, turning to face me as he buttoned them. His eyes searched my face, genuinely curious. "I know things were difficult after Thackery hurt you, and you told me that you and Wyatt were giving each other space to figure things out. But something changed between you two the night Felix was infected."

My heart ached at the memory of that awful night two weeks ago. The evening began so normally, but had devolved into blood and violence, and ended with heartbreak. It was the night Wyatt and I realized just how much we'd both been changed by those three weeks I was with Thackery. Wyatt and I both said some things that night that had needed to be said for a while. The fight broke us both; there was no going back to how things used to be.

"A lot changed that night, Phin."

"I know. I've seen you every day since. You've thrown yourself into your training and you rarely interact with anyone outside our squad except for Milo. You make it a point to avoid Wyatt, and when you do see him—"

"What?"

"The temperature in the room drops twenty degrees."

"Weather control isn't one of my gifts, Phin."

"Do you still love him?"

If anyone else had asked me that, I'd have told them to fuck off. "I'll always love him," I said as I leaned my unbruised hip against a supply cabinet and crossed my arms over my stomach. "But the way you love someone can change, especially if you hurt them badly enough. And what if—?" I froze, the thought stuck in my throat. Something I'd never voiced out loud, much less to another person.

"What if?" Phin asked. He took a step toward me, hands tucked loosely in his jeans pockets. Intent.

"Nothing." I reached for the small pile of bandage wrappers and shoved them into the nearest waste can. As I turned to leave the cubicle, Phin blocked my way without (wisely) grabbing me.

"What if what?"

I heaved a defeated sigh. He wasn't letting it go. "What if, despite all the pain and heartache we've endured, Wyatt and I really aren't meant to be together? What if that's why we can't seem to make this work?"

Phin tilted his head to the side, considering me, my words, probably both. "What if you're wrong?" he finally said.

"But what if I'm right, Phin?"

He went silent again, his mouth pressing into a thin line. I could almost see the wheels turning, the gears clicking away as he made connections. Weighed his words. "Evangeline, may I present the Therian's perspective on this?"

"Go for it." The human perspective wasn't doing me much good.

"Shit or get off the pot."

My jaw unhinged. I think my brain fuzzed out for a moment, because I couldn't have possibly heard him say what I thought. I finally squawked out a garbled, "Huh?"

"Granted, that's a human expression, but it sums up my perspective very simply. Therian lives are relatively short compared to humans. You have the luxury of waffling on matters of the heart and on choosing a mate. We don't. We must follow our instincts, make our choices, and then live with them." He paused, eyes searching mine. "Therefore, if you are not willing to follow your gut, to choose Wyatt, and to live with the consequences of that choice, then get off the metaphorical pot and move on."

A small amount of time must have passed with me simply staring at him. At some point, I realized my mouth was really dry and I clamped it shut. Swallowed. I wasn't used to being called to the mat, especially over my love life. But everything he'd said was true, and it also set my own wheels turning. Curiosity overcame shock.

Phin and I had been friends for several months, and yet I knew very little about him. His Clan's slaughter was still a sore subject, and I could never broach it without feeling guilty—not just for the painful reminder, but for my own role in so many deaths. Deaths of the people he loved.

"May I ask *you* a personal question?" I said.

His face went blank, and his hands pressed deeper into his pockets—as if he could make himself smaller and that would somehow lessen the impact of whatever I was about to ask. "Yes."

"Have you ever been in love?"

Blue fire danced in his eyes. His nostrils flared and, just for an instant, I swore he looked ready to attack.

Then his expression softened, grief tempering the fury. "Yes, I have. I was very much in love with my wife, Jolene."

Jolene. Wife. My insides ached for him. Tears tightened my throat, wanting to spill for a woman I hadn't known. I swallowed hard, grasping for my voice. "She loved you?"

"Yes." He smiled, but though his expression was gentle, a hint of ferocity still lingered. "I'm ten years old, Evy. I have lived half my lifetime and loved well for three of those years. You're twice as old as I, and all you've experienced is heartache and betrayal. It grieves me to know this."

"I've experienced love."

"The love of your teammates, yes. The love of a man who moved Heaven and Earth to bring you back to life, certainly. But have you ever loved with your whole heart? Offered it to someone with no expectations in return, because you loved him so deeply you could do nothing less?"

Tears blurred my vision, and I blinked them away. The answer to Phin's question was so easy, and I hated him for asking. Hated myself just as much for the answer. "No. No, I haven't."

I'd wanted to with Wyatt. Wanted him to be the one I gave my heart to, and I knew he'd have accepted me with compassion, desire, and love. Before Thackery broke me. Before I told Wyatt the whole truth about how Felix got away the night he was infected.

It didn't matter anymore. I'd lived my entire life tormented by the stupid, storybook notion of true love, and I'd be damned if I'd mourn something I didn't need. "People like me don't get that one true love, Phin," I said with more conviction in my voice than in my heart. "We get a few flings along the way to an early grave."

"Perhaps. But is that what you want, Evy?"

"Does it matter?"

"It matters to me."

"Why?"

He blinked rapidly, as if my question surprised him. "Because I've seen your heart. You show it every day in the way you fight to protect those you care about. You have so much love hiding inside of you. Please don't deny yourself the chance to share it."

Those damned tears were back, choking me. I fought them, unwilling to cry. There was too much to do and no time for an emotional breakdown. Still, I couldn't let it go. "And what happens when I die again and break Wyatt's heart for the third time?"

"No one can predict the future, Evy, not even the wisest of mages. Lovers die and hearts break. Losing my wife was the worst agony I have ever endured, but even knowing our short time together, I'd gladly suffer it again. Because now, with time between us, I can think of her and remember the joy."

He pulled his hands from his pockets and cupped my cheek in his palm. His thumb brushed away a stray tear. The warm touch and sweet gesture undid me. I flung my arms around his shoulders and held on. Emotions churned and burned in my chest, but I couldn't force out that first sob. The dam wouldn't break.

Phin held me close, solid muscle beneath skin as soft as air. His heart beat nearly twice as fast as mine—its natural pace. He had so many reasons to hate me. Over three hundred, to be perfectly frank. And yet he didn't. It would be easier to hate myself if he wasn't so forgiving of my worst sins.

I pressed my cheek to his shoulder and just held on, waiting for the world to stop spinning out of control. Allowing my emotions time to right themselves once more, so I could step outside the infirmary and do my job. The night was far from over. Depending on what we got from Felix, it may have only just begun.

"Please, Evangeline," he whispered. "Please don't harden your heart before you've allowed it to truly love."

The dam began to crack. And then the sound of an old-fashioned bell ringing filled the room. I pulled away, confused, until Phin pulled his cell phone out of his jeans pocket. His expression sharpened.

"Emergency page," he said. "Come on."

Operations was in a state of minor chaos when we arrived. Created from the skeletons of three different stores, the combined space was full of computer workstations, whiteboards, a map of the city, and a few cubicles. Half a dozen volunteers were always on duty, manning the computers and an intricate switchboard setup that connected more than a hundred different cell phones to one another on a private network. It often reminded me of a police station bull pen, where all the major activity occurred. Just like now.

At least thirty people—human, Therian, and vampire—were in Operations. It was the busiest I'd ever seen it, and that simple fact settled a cold knot right into the middle of my already upset stomach.

Astrid, Marcus, and Wyatt were hunched over a desk, listening to the same phone conversation. Adrian Baylor and Kismet were at one of the computers. Kyle had taken over a chair near the partitioned conference area, phone clutched in his hand; he looked absolutely panicked. Milo, Tybalt, and Quince all showed signs of distress. As if sensing our arrival, Astrid spun around, her copper eyes flashing with fury.

"What's going on?" Phin asked.

"We have disappearances," she replied. "Civilian and actives, all within the last two hours."

Internal alarms clanged in my head. Attention was shifting in our direction.

Phin marched right into her personal space. "Who's missing?"

"Lynn Neil. She isn't answering her phone, and a neighbor says the front door of the apartment is ajar. Sharpe's squad is closest. They're checking it out."

Shit. Lynn was Felia and had been connected to me before we ever actually met. She and her then-boyfriend Kiefer had lived together in an apartment that Wyatt and I had once used as a hiding place during the first day of my resurrection. A few days later, Kiefer threw in with another were-cat named Belle, defied the Assembly, and helped kidnap Joseph and a still-pregnant Aurora from my Parkside East apartment. I'd stabbed Kiefer with a nail file and then Leo Forrester shot him to death.

Lynn hadn't known about her boyfriend's extracurricular activities, and I was unclear on how she and Kyle ended up together. Theirs was the only mixed-Clan relationship I knew about, and I doubted everyone approved. But I met Lynn once, and she was the very definition of sweet—even after I told her I'd borrowed and ruined some of her clothes.

I glanced at Kyle; he had to be a wreck inside.

"Michael and Dawn Jenner," Astrid continued. "One of them hit a panic button seven minutes ago. The nearest squad just reported their house has been broken into and both are missing."

Double shit. Michael Jenner was the voice of the Assembly of Clan Elders, and he often did their business for them. He'd proved a valuable ally and had helped save my life once. Even gave me a place to stay while I healed from injuries obtained during a factory explosion. Wait—

"Dawn?" I asked.

"His daughter," Phin replied. "Equi children live with their mothers. Why was she—?"

"Probably visiting," Astrid said. "She just reached the age of maturity and is free to travel as she likes."

Equi shifted into various wild horses, zebras, donkeys, and tarpans, but I didn't know enough about this particular Clan to understand the intricacies of who raised the kids. At the moment, it didn't matter.

"Leah is also missing," Marcus said, his deep voice dripping with anger.

"Seriously?" I said. "Does Jackson know?"

"Not yet."

A member of the Ursia Clan, Leah de Loew was one of the founding members of the Watchtower, as well as a good friend of both Astrid and Marcus. She led one of the squads, and her mate, Jackson, was a member of another. Given the fact that Leah shifted into a three-hundred-pound black bear, whoever took her didn't do it randomly.

"Someone is kidnapping Therians?" Phin asked.

Astrid nodded, her expression pensive. "All Therians connected to the Watch in some manner."

Phin paled. "Aurora and Joseph?"

"I called the house. No one answered, so I sent out a squad."

He turned and bolted out of Operations faster than I'd ever seen him move. I didn't wait for permission—I simply followed him, tamping down my own growing sense of dread. Aurora, her daughter Ava, and Joseph were the only surviving members of Phin's Clan. They lived in a small country house twenty miles outside the city and stayed far away from Clan politics. I had been named Ava's *Aluli*—the Therian equivalent of a godmother—and although I'd seen the rapidly growing child only twice since her birth, she meant a great deal to me.

And she meant even more to Phin, which was why I was chasing him down the mall corridor in my bare feet, well aware of people staring at us.

"Phineas, wait!" I mustered a burst of speed and caught up to him in the parking area. He'd stripped off his shirt, and he stopped to unbuckle his belt. "Phin—"

"I can fly the distance faster than anyone can drive," he said, his voice as cold as I'd ever heard it.

"Take me with you."

"Evy—"

"Ava is my goddaughter, Phin, and if anyone is still there you'll need backup."

He seemed poised to argue. Instead, brown and white mottled wings unfolded from his back, stretching to an impressive width. "All right."

The moon was out, its accompanying stars hidden behind a haze of light pollution. Flying out of the city like this wasn't as dangerous in the middle of the night, but we would still be open targets the entire way—and neither of us cared. All that mattered was getting to our destination.

I crossed my arms just below my breasts in a familiar position we'd used several times in the past. Phin pressed against me from behind, his chest to my back, and looped his arms around my waist, just under mine. And then up we went in a rush of air, his powerful wings lifting us into the sky.

The city passed in a blur of lights, and then metal gave way to greenery as the forested mountains rose up around us. The air cooled a bit and reminded me I was still in my rave getup and still barefoot. Our hasty departure hadn't left much time for finding shoes or strapping on extra weapons—two things I regretted. But my regret didn't overshadow my fear.

Fear that we were already too damned late.

We didn't talk. Phin flew too fast, and my extra weight had him working twice as hard. His perspiration dampened the back of my tank top, despite the constant whir of wind around us. His arms had developed a very faint tremor. He'd once flown me like this for a mile and a half, but never for twenty.

A seed of guilt burrowed into my guts. I was slowing him down, using up his strength, because I hadn't wanted to be left behind. But it was more than just needing to be there to protect Ava. Phin and I were so much alike when people we loved were in danger—we both proceeded with a very narrow focus, danger be damned. Nothing put Phin's blinders on faster than his family. If they *had* been taken, I couldn't allow him to lose control.

The excuse made me feel a little better about my decision to go with him, but it didn't erase the fear that he'd arrive too tired to defend himself.

The occasional light peeked out from the trees below us, and Phin altered his direction slightly until we were following a mountain road. He descended rapidly, and I clutched at his wrist, half-afraid we were actually falling. Then he beat his wings hard and we slowed. Down through trees and into unexpected darkness.

It was the least graceful landing ever. He was exhausted and breathing hard, and he stumbled as his feet hit the driveway. We both pitched ass over teakettle into the dirt. Phin twisted around at the last moment and took the brunt of the fall.

His arms loosened, and I rolled off his chest, giving him as much room as possible. He hadn't pulled his wings back in whatever way he does when he bi-shifts (a gift only a few of the Clans possessed), and I realized I was kneeling on one. I scrambled away on my knees, about to apologize.

"Go," he said, flapping one hand at me even as he gasped for air. "I'll be right there."

I didn't argue, just squashed down that seed of guilt, rolled to my feet, and ran toward the house.

It was a two-story log cabin style, with a wide front porch and lots of windows. It was also completely dark, not a single light on in the house or the yard. The moon provided a bit of illumination, but I didn't have super sight or even very good night vision. I grabbed a large, smooth stone out of the row lining the flower beds, and then crept up onto the porch.

My heart thundered in my chest, so loud in my ears that I swore anyone within a hundred feet could hear it. Boards creaked beneath my feet. The front door was ajar. I inched closer. Toed it open a bit farther.

A brown blur flew in past me—Phin in osprey form. *Dammit.*

I busted in behind him, one hand holding the rock back and ready to swing, and the other reaching for a light switch I knew was there somewhere. The house was nearly silent, save the whispery sounds of flapping wings. Phineas was usually the epitome of caution. The fact that he'd barreled inside like this spoke volumes about his state of mind.

My questing fingers finally found the damned switch. A table lamp blazed to life, casting a yellow glow on the cozy front room. A rocking chair was knocked onto its side, and several books were scattered around on the floor as though shoved there. Nothing else seemed out of place.

The downstairs held the living room, kitchen, and a bathroom, and I checked them quickly. Then I hit the stairs, taking them two at a time, confident that if anyone was lurking upstairs to attack, Phin would have let me know. The second floor was basically a short hallway with four open doors. I went into the first on the left—Ava's room—and froze.

It was a mess. The crib lay on its side, bedding and stuffed toys scattered about. A framed picture of a dancing princess had fallen, and its glass littered the pale yellow carpet. A curtain was ripped off the rod. Toys spilled out of an upset basket. Aurora had been so proud of this room . . .

"Phin?" I said.

"Here."

I followed the sound across the hall to Joseph's room. Phin had shifted back and stood stark naked in the middle of the bedroom, staring down at the floor. The bandage was gone, and his cut from the rave fight had healed a bit; it was still red and puffy, but no longer bleeding. I couldn't tell if anything in the room had been disturbed, because it looked like a monk's cell—single bed, single piece of framed art, a few books on a side table, nothing else.

"They're gone," Phin said. The utter heartbreak in his voice chilled me. He turned his head to look at me, devastated blue eyes glittering in the semidark.

Furious tears stung my eyes. As I approached, my nose told me what he'd been staring at on the floor before I made out the stain. I squatted. Touched it. Cool, but still damp. "We didn't miss them by much," I said. "Blood's fresh. Not Halfie blood." I hadn't even realized Halfies were my top suspects for this until I said it.

It made a horrific kind of sense, and Felix had been the perfect distraction.

"It's Therian," Phin said.

"You can smell that?"

"Yes. Our blood is . . . earthier."

I touched his shoulder. "We'll find them, Phin. I swear to you, we'll find them. Alive."

He met my gaze. Blinked. A single tear tracked down his cheek. His wings were back—another mark of his absolute fury. "Ava is the future of our race. I will kill whoever took them."

"And I'll help you."

Chapter Four

Eleri's squad showed up ten minutes later. A vampire ally from before the Watch's inception, Eleri was one of the few vampires I trusted with my unprotected back. Her squad was an interesting mix of ex-Handler Conrad Morgan, ex-Hunter Paul Ryan, a Cania named Crow, and a Felia named Sanchez Drake. With the squad was a Gifted human named Brett Lewis. Never officially a Hunter, Brett was often brought in to do freelance work for the Triads and had, likewise, been recruited into the Watch as a floater—not assigned to any single squad.

Like Wyatt and me, Brett had a tap to the Break, and his particular ability was a kind of telepathy called post-cognition. He could sense recent events in a particular area, usually as a series of images and flashes, especially if high levels of emotion were involved.

I was damned glad to see him.

Phin offered clipped answers to Eleri's questions while observing Brett, who had squatted next to the over-turned books in the living room. Brett closed his eyes. I felt the snap-pop of his tap as he accessed the magic of the Break. Lately my ability to sense when others were using their Gifts had increased—a development no other Gifted could explain.

Just one more quirk of being me.

"A woman with curly hair was asleep here," Brett

said. "A noise startled her. A red feather. She fell, knocked over the books." He was silent for several long seconds, then stood up. "That's all I sense here."

"A red feather could be a tranquilizer dart," Eleri said. "I imagine that sedation is the only method by which so many Therians were captured so quickly."

"You're probably right," Phin said.

"Where else?" Brett asked.

Phin led the way upstairs to Ava's room. Brett was quiet for a long while as he examined the room, touching toys and the crib. He shook his head.

"Nothing," he said.

"Are you sure?" I asked.

He quirked an eyebrow at me, the message clear—was I an idiot for questioning him? "Yes. The child was probably asleep and didn't feel anything."

"But the room's a mess."

"Probably for show. To freak you out, which it's obviously doing."

Okay, so I was starting to really hate this guy. Even if he did have a good point. The sight of this room had horrified me, and I couldn't stop imagining the dreadful things that might have happened to Ava. It made the entire kidnapping that much more personal.

"Across the hall," Phin said. "There's blood in that room."

Brett nodded. We followed him out. He took two steps into Joseph's room and stopped. Gazed around. He shivered—nearly imperceptibly, but perfectly timed with a slight Break snap-pop sensation. Two more steps, closer to the bloodstain. He angled slightly, giving me a view of his partial profile, and closed his eyes.

"An elderly man wakes. He seems startled. Concerned. He moves"—Brett's eyebrows arched—"very quickly out of bed. A red feather hits the pillow. He's fighting someone smaller, younger. He's struck. Falls. There." He pointed straight at the stain.

"Who's fighting him?" Phin asks.

"They're unclear. I can't decipher faces, but they're likely Halfies." He opened his eyes and turned. "Half-Bloods are difficult to detect with my ability, because their emotions are radically altered from what they ought to be. They're harder to pinpoint and therefore harder to see clearly."

It made sense. It was an annoying handicap, but it made sense.

"Thank you for your assistance, Mr. Lewis," Eleri said.

"You're welcome. Was anyone else in the house during the incident?"

Phin shook his head, lips pressed tight, as unhappy with the results of Brett's visions as I was. "At this hour?" he said. "No, it should have been just the three of them."

"All right." Brett hesitated. "With your permission, Mr. el Chimal, I'll check the other rooms."

"Feel free."

Brett excused himself from the room. Phin's cell phone rang. He made no move to answer it, so I yanked it out of his back pocket. Astrid's name was on the caller I.D.

"This is Stone," I said.

"Stone?" Astrid replied. "Why—?"

"He's preoccupied."

Phin shot me a grateful smile. He was struggling to remain outwardly calm, and I could easily imagine the inferno churning beneath. Although his Clan had lived peacefully in the city for decades, they were a warrior race. Sitting still and waiting were not in his nature. He wanted his family back.

"What's your status?" she asked.

"Brett Lewis just confirmed that Halfies were involved. Joseph is wounded, but we don't know how badly."

"Halfies seem to be a common thread in all the disappearances, and I don't think it's a coincidence—"

"That we ran into Felix and crew tonight?"

"Yeah."

"I had the same thought. Has he said anything?"

"No." She hesitated. "We're about to begin interrogating him."

A tiny part of me wanted to be there; the rest of me was glad to be far away from it. Interrogating Halfies used to be one of my favorite pastimes, but seeing the face of someone I used to consider a friend staring back at me from the other side of the table . . . no.

"Who's interrogating him?" I asked.

"Marcus and Wyatt."

I flinched. "Does Kismet know?"

"Yes. I've forbidden both her and Gant from watching."

Not a bad idea. She and Milo did not need to see their old teammate tortured for information. And if Felix did know anything about these kidnappings, Marcus wasn't going to be kind. I'd seen the were-cat in battle, and I'd seen his jaguar form rip throats out of Halfie teenagers.

"Has anyone else gone missing?"

"No. Everyone connected to a member of the Watch has been taken to a safe location, and the Assembly has been informed. The Clan Elders are seeing to their people."

"Good."

"How's Phineas?" she asked in a voice so quiet I almost didn't hear her.

I glanced at the man in question—glaring out the bedroom window—then slipped into the hallway. I was halfway downstairs before I replied. "He's pretty close to the breaking point," I whispered. "I'm damned close to snapping, myself."

"I know what they mean to him."

"Yeah, just the future of his entire race."

Astrid sighed, and in the sound I detected . . . sadness? "The Felia and the Coni are not natural allies, but we all grieved for his Clan's destruction. We want them back, Stone. All of them."

"Me, too."

"If Felix gives us anything, we'll let you know."

"Okay, thanks."

I turned at the bottom of the stairs and nearly crashed into Brett. He stood by the living room wall, eyes closed, one hand touching a framed photo hanging at eye level. It was a candid shot of myself holding a squirming Ava, with Phin and Aurora in the background. I remembered the day it was taken. As Ava's godparents, Phin and I had been invited to dinner so we could perform the official "bonding" ceremony. It mostly involved making a solemn promise to protect Ava and see to her future, and drinking a cup of stinky tea.

Looking at her apple-cheeked face, with the same dark curly hair as her mother, my stomach ached for her safety.

"Stone?" Astrid said.

"One sec." I pulled the phone away from my face. "Brett?"

His eyelids flew up, and he blinked hard, eyes dilated so wide that only a thin circle of brown lined the irises. "Someone else was here," he said.

My heart thudded. "With the half-Bloods?"

"At the same time, yes."

"Who?"

"His face seems familiar, but I don't know who he is. He's human, though."

Little icy fingers danced up my spine. "Are you sure?"

"Not one hundred percent, but close. He stood here and looked at this photo. He watched everything that happened."

"Did he speak? Interact? Anything to tell you who he is?"

Brett shook his head. "I don't get the soundtrack, just the blurry highlight reels."

The simple fact that this mystery man had looked at that particular photo creeped me the hell out. "What did he look like?"

"Tall, thin, dark hair. Quite handsome, but sad."

The world grayed out at the edges, and I blinked hard to keep from falling over from a sudden wave of vertigo. "Was he wearing a long black duster?"

Brett frowned, eyes narrowing. "That's an odd detail to guess in the middle of summer."

"Shit." My stomach dropped to my feet. I put the phone back to my ear. "Astrid?"

"What's happening?" she asked.

"I need you to send a photo of Walter Thackery to Phin's phone right now."

"On it. Why?"

"Because I think he was here tonight. I think the bastard's involved."

The best photo we had of Thackery was six years old, but that didn't matter. Brett identified him as the special guest star in the kidnapping as soon as the image appeared on Phin's phone.

I don't remember moving or sitting, only realizing that Phineas was crouched in front of me, holding my hands and saying something, and that I was now on the living room sofa. Walter-fucking-Thackery had held me captive for twenty days, tortured me in order to watch me heal, and cut off my goddamned pinkie finger—all in the name of science. Those twenty days left me a very different person from the one who went with him in order to prevent him from releasing dangerous beasts on an unsuspecting city.

To stop him from murdering Phineas in cold blood.

A coven of gargoyles on the hunt for one of their own had attacked the mobile lab where Thackery had stashed me. Max, a former ally of mine, had been among the gargoyles who rescued me, and he brought me back to the city. Thackery had been at large ever since—just over a month now.

Someone put a glass of water in my hand. I sipped without tasting it. Everything felt distant, not quite real, not even Phin's constant, comforting presence. He squeezed my knee. The near-ticklish sensation shocked some sense back into me, and I met his steady gaze.

"There you are," he said. "With me?"

"Yeah." I forced my hand to loosen its grip on the frosted glass before it shattered. "I think so. Did I pass out?"

"Not exactly. You seemed to go catatonic for a moment, though."

I groaned. "Awesome."

"No one is judging you, Evangeline. They know what Thackery did."

I waved my left hand in front of his face. "Because I walk around with the evidence every single day. God, I can't believe I freaked out just now."

"I'm more disinclined to believe he's involved, but Mr. Lewis insists Thackery is the man in his vision."

"It doesn't make any sense. Thackery despises vampires. He wants to see them all dead. Hell, he thought he could use my blood to *cure* the infected, so why would he align with half-Bloods?"

"One of many questions we'll ask when we find him."

I only wished I had Phin's confidence. We'd had no previous luck locating Thackery—not while he was blackmailing me, and not after I was taken. The man wasn't stupid. In fact, he was pretty much a genius, especially when it came to his genetic meddling. He had a plan, and he had an endgame in mind. Finding him would not be easy.

No, *finding him will be fucking impossible—unless he wants to be found.*

"Everyone makes mistakes," Phin said.

It took me a moment to realize I'd said that "fucking impossible" thought out loud. "He hasn't made one yet."

"Then he's due."

"Maybe."

Everyone missing was connected to me in some way. They were also all Therian. No humans had been taken, and I could think of several who would have been easy targets. "Why all Therians? If Thackery is really involved in this, why would he want them?"

Phin shifted positions so he was sitting next to me on the couch, one hand still on my knee. "He wouldn't have been so precise with his choices if it was merely for experimentation."

"True." But it didn't make me feel any better about the idea of a small child in the hands of a madman. Or anyone else at his mercy. "He can do his experiments and fuck with me at the same time."

"You believe this is personal?"

"Don't you? Thackery chose people connected to me, connected to the Watch, when he could have snatched any of hundreds of other Therians in this city. The bastard doesn't do anything randomly."

Phin nodded, thoughtful. "Another bargain, perhaps?"

I shuddered at the thought. His last two bargains hadn't gone well for any of us. The first had been the trade of inanimate objects—two of his experimental serums for the crystal housing a demon. The second had been me for the safety of the city. "Both times, Thackery contacted us almost immediately to make his demands," I said.

Eleri entered the living room, her expression impassive. "We followed two imprints of new tire tracks down the lane," she said, "but they disappeared once the vehicles reached the main road. Depth and spacing indicate a van or a utility vehicle, but we cannot ascertain more than that."

A van or a utility vehicle was used to spirit away three kidnapped Therians—duh. If ever information could be more useless . . . "Thank you," I said.

"You are welcome. My squad is returning to the Watchtower. Do you require transportation?"

"Yes, thanks," Phin said.

I didn't want to leave, but we'd do no good here. Aurora, Ava, and Joseph were gone, and we weren't likely to find them unless Walter Thackery wished it. Two months into her life and I'd already managed to fail Ava, just as I've failed almost everyone else I've been responsible for.

Some fucking *Aluli* I turned out to be.

On the trip back, I somehow got stuck in the rear bench seat of the SUV between the window and Paul Ryan. Phineas had shifted into osprey form—to save seating space, he said, but I was jealous of his clever way of avoiding conversation—and was perched in the small rear compartment with his pants and shoes.

I gazed out the window at the passing mountains, and then the outskirts of the city, trying to ignore Paul. We'd managed to mostly avoid each other these last few months, and for good reason. He'd been a one-week rookie in the Triads when I was first resurrected, and his twitchy trigger finger had gotten Wyatt killed. Granted, a gnome healing crystal had brought Wyatt back, but that wasn't the point. And he'd helped out at Parker's Palace and fought hard at the Boot Camp slaughter, but I still wanted to dislike Ryan on principle.

And he was still twitchy. He shifted on the crowded seat, hands tapping on his thighs, like someone in the middle of a sugar high. Or someone who wanted to say something and kept changing his mind. I resisted the urge to elbow him in the ribs. Hard.

Lucky for him, I dozed off for the last half of the trip. I jerked awake as we pulled into the parking area. As soon as the side door slid open, Phineas flew out and away. I was the last one out of the SUV. The cold cement floor sent a shock through my bare feet, reminding me that I needed to find shoes and a change of clothes.

"Stone?" Paul's voice stopped me short.

I turned and shot him an impatient look.

"I'm real sorry about your friends," he said. "Not just Felix, but the Therians, too."

"Um, thanks." I didn't know what else to say. We were in no danger of becoming BFFs or anything, but the sentiment was a pleasant surprise.

He nodded, and then followed the rest of his squad out of the lot.

I cast around for Phin. He'd gone off on his own, probably to calm down before going back to work. I kind of liked the idea. I could use a little relaxation, too, so I didn't take my temper out on someone who didn't deserve it. The gym was a good place to do that.

My room, alas, was on the opposite end of the mall from the gymnasium rooms. We always kept extra sweats around, though, so I forewent a trip for clothes and headed the other way. My path took me past Operations. A buzz of conversation drifted through the open doors, and I slipped by quickly.

"Stone!"

Shit. I stopped, looked over my shoulder. Baylor had poked his head out of Ops.

"What?" I asked.

"You reporting in?"

"I already reported to Astrid," I replied. "Eleri can report the rest of it. Unless Walter Thackery happens to call with ransom demands, I don't want to talk to anyone for at least half an hour. Okay?"

Fortunately, Baylor was used to my snappish tendencies. "Okay. Where's Phineas?"

"Around, probably blowing off steam."

He nodded, then went back into Operations. The entire mall was outfitted with heat sensors in order to keep track of the two hundred–plus people who came and went on a daily basis. If Baylor needed to locate Phin, an osprey-sized heat signature would be easy to spot on the internal security system.

I made it to the gym without further incident. Some of the free weights were being used. I ignored the funny looks my outfit earned me, snatched a pair of sweatpants and a cotton T-shirt out of the community locker, and put them on with practiced ease. The sticky leather skirt came off as the sweatpants went up. Tank top off after the T-shirt was on. All skills I learned in Juvie, when privacy was at a minimum and you wanted to flash as little skin as possible in a room full of others.

The adjoining workout room was empty. Blue mats lined the floor, with two specific wrestling areas taped out. The opposite side of the room had several suspended heavy bags and three speed bags. Throwing some punches at sand-filled leather was a better alternative to taking my anger out on someone's softer flesh, so I found a pair of gloves that fit.

My first punch sent a shock up my right shoulder. I hadn't done this in a while. The majority of my physical training these last few weeks had been about endurance.

Getting my cardio stamina back up, getting my joints loose and flexible again, and putting back on some useful muscles—all lost during those weeks of torture.

I spread my feet, corrected my stance, tried again. Better.

Left hand, right hand. Jabs, upper cuts, crosses. Sweat slicked my back and face and trickled down my neck. It felt great. I imagined Thackery's face on that heavy bag. A face I'd looked up at from a metal gurney for twenty days, always calculating and earnest, a zealot to his own research. A face I longed to beat into a bloody, broken mess and then watch as it took its last breath.

My arms and back muscles burned from exertion. My legs felt like jelly, and it was getting harder and harder to breathe. I just couldn't stop. Stopping was giving up, and I wasn't giving up on this. Wouldn't stop until I had Ava, Aurora, Joseph, Leah, Michael Jenner, and all the missing others back.

Back from wherever they'd been taken.

Back from someone who'd kill without hesitation.

I should have done more to protect them.

Sweat trickled down my cheeks—no, not sweat. Tears. My throat closed, making it almost impossible to breathe. The dam I'd been slamming against all night finally broke, and I fell to my knees sobbing. For Felix. For Ava. For my own pent-up frustration and anger. For everyone whose loved ones were missing.

I couldn't stop the torrent of tears or stifle the choking gasps. Couldn't do anything but let it out. And then someone's arms were around me, pulling me close. I let him drag me against a firm chest, held tight by those strong, warm arms. I pressed my face into the crook of his shoulder, awareness breaking through with a single thought—Wyatt.

The realization just deepened my sobs. I wrapped my arms around his waist and held on. One hand cupped my neck while the other stroked my back in gentle circles. I let him hold me, let him rock me, like he hadn't for so long.

"I should have died, Wyatt." I barely choked out the words. "He should have killed me. They'd all be safe if I was dead."

"You don't know that," he replied. His voice rumbled in his chest, a soothing sound beneath my cheek.

"Everyone else dies, but not me. Not even when I give up and ask."

He tensed. My words were the source of our most recent argument. An argument that had split us down the center. One I didn't care to repeat. Not now, not ever. In my lowest moment, I told Walter Thackery I wouldn't resist his experiments if he promised to kill me when he was done. I'd been convinced I wouldn't mentally survive being tortured again.

I'd been wrong—so fucking wrong—but it didn't change the fact that I'd given up. More than the memories of the torture, it was my own cowardice that haunted me, that had changed me, and I was terrified that it had forever altered the way Wyatt saw me. That he'd never again look at me the way he had a month ago at Boot Camp, with wonder and need and love.

"It's okay, Evy," he said softly.

It wasn't, but I loved that he'd said it anyway, and that he held me without judgment while I cried.

Chapter Five

Sunday, June 29
Boot Camp

I launch myself at Wyatt and throw my arms around his neck in a choking hug. His arms snake around my waist, painfully tight. I press my face into his neck, inhaling his scent, feeling his sandpapery skin on my face. He twirls us in a circle, and I laugh out loud—I didn't feel him lift me off the ground.

He sets me back down and crushes his lips to mine. I open for him and groan under the bruising, possessive force of a kiss tinged with desperation and joy. I don't want it to end, but I'm sore and tired and the adrenaline rush is almost gone. It's way too easy to collapse against Wyatt's chest; he doesn't let me fall.

His hand strokes my neck, tangles in the thick waves of my ponytail. "When?"

I understand his shorthand. "Yesterday morning. Max and his coven attacked the truck the day before, but he brought me back to the city yesterday before sunrise."

"Truck?"

I explain what I can stand to remember. How Walter Thackery kept me in a tractor-trailer laboratory for almost three weeks, kept us on the move, kept those twenty days an endless cycle of hellish pain. I gloss over the details; Wyatt has a pretty good imagination, and he's seen some of the injuries I've healed from with his own eyes.

Wyatt's walkie crackles to life with a stranger's voice: "Marcus to Truman. You alive, pal?"

Wyatt grabs the walkie off his impressively weaponed belt. "Yeah, I'm alive. There's a Pit behind the main building. Meet me there."

He puts the device back without waiting for a response from this Marcus person, and I can't help wondering if he has something to do with Wyatt's new look. The Black Ops outfit and rigging, especially.

"Stone!" echoes down into the Pit before I can question him.

I look up, shielding my eyes with one hand. A tall, slim figure descends the bleachers, heading quickly for our position. As soon as he's within reach, I let go of Wyatt and throw my arms around Tybalt. I surprise myself and him, too, because it takes a few seconds for him to hug back.

"How many lives are you down to?" he asks.

I snort laughter. "Might be on my last one after this. Heard you killed something today."

He pulls back, one hand still gripping my left elbow, and I glance down. His missing forearm has been replaced by . . . well, it looks robotic and a little bit deadly. "Yeah, I did," he says, not hiding the pride in that statement. "Guess I'm not useless after all." He gives a pointed look at Wyatt as he speaks, which reminds me of all the questions I have for both of them.

Wyatt beats me to it. "How'd you get out here?"

"Rode in with Baylor's team," Tybalt replies. "Carly and I stayed in touch after Felix got hurt, and since I'm not a Hunter anymore, there are no rules against us being friends."

Carly—I vaguely recall meeting her the night the hounds attacked us at the cabin in the woods. Good for Tybalt, too, for doing everything he can to help. I twist my wrist to give his arm a squeeze. He looks down and both eyebrows shoot to his hairline. Crap.

Tybalt takes my left hand in his and lifts it up, anger etching deep lines in his forehead. "Jesus Christ, Stone. Did Thackery do that to you?"

"Yep." I wrench my hand out of his grip and take a step backward, away from both men and their angry, confused looks. "He thought my healing powers made great nighttime entertainment. Thought if he could prove it was physical and not magical, he could re-create it somehow."

"And he cut off your finger to prove that?"

"At the end."

Wyatt shudders. There's a deadly anger radiating from him, so strong it's almost a physical force.

"We looked for you," Tybalt says.

"I know. Thackery kept us on the move."

He nods, quiet misery in his expression. Coming from someone who tried to kill me only a few weeks ago, the emotion is both touching and overwhelming. His gaze flickers beyond my head, and he blinks hard. "What the hell is that?"

I don't have to look to know what he's talking about. The corpse of Wolf Boy is baking in the mid-morning sun, my knife still buried in its mouth. In its half-transformed state, it looks like some hybrid beast that Walter Thackery might have cooked up, only I'm sure it's not a hybrid. It's something else.

"Whoever he was, he worked for Thackery," I reply. "I've seen him before, both as a huge wolf and as a teen-age boy."

"A shape-shifter?"

"If so, he's not from a Clan I've ever heard of."

A low feline growl raises the hair on the back of my neck, and I pivot with a complete lack of grace. An unfamiliar man dressed in clothes identical to Wyatt's is crouched over the wolf-thing's body. I didn't even hear him descend the bleachers. Felia. Has to be.

He looks up, copper eyes going past me, right to Wyatt. "Well, it seems like we finally found the source of the smell," he says in a voice as smooth and rich as gourmet coffee.

"Smell?" I ask.

"It was detected in the parking garage where Thackery left Phineas," Wyatt says. His voice is strained, tight, as though he's struggling to not scream the words. "And a few other places around the city, including the old train station."

"Detected by who?"

"Myself," the Felia says as he stands, "as well as several other of our brethren. Our sense of smell is more developed than yours."

"And you are?"

He flashes a predatory smile. "My name is Marcus Dane, and you must be the infamous Evangeline Stone. I've heard quite a lot about you."

"I really can't say the same."

"And for good reason."

I hold his stare, unsure if I like his candor or find it annoying. Probably a little of both. His information only enforces my suspicion that Thackery used Wolf Boy to do quite a bit of his dirty work. And wherever Thackery is now, he'll be super-fucking-pissed to find out his teenage sidekick is a corpse. I break the stare-off first.

"I want to take him back with us," Marcus says, jacking his thumb at said corpse. And he isn't talking to me.

"Agreed," Wyatt says. "Do you know what he is?"

"Perhaps, yes. The Assembly must be told about this."

I glance at Tybalt, whose confusion mirrors my own. We're both completely lost in the conversation.

"All right." Wyatt shifts his attention to me. "Evy, I know you have a lot of questions—"

"Most of my questions can wait," I reply. If I start asking them now, we'll be in this Pit all damned day. "I need to see what's happening topside, and there are still a lot of wounded to tend to." Such as Greg, the Hunter I didn't know at all until half an hour ago and am now curious about—his arm and leg were bleeding heavily the last time I saw him.

"Yourself included," Marcus says, gesturing at my ankle and forearm.

My ankle is a mass of itchy-healing sensations. My arm isn't bleeding as it was, but it does hurt like a bastard. The skin is swollen and hot, but I ignore it in favor of getting the hell out of the Pit. I'm just lucky Wolf Boy never got a better angle with his teeth. "I'll heal."

He tilts his head. "Indeed."

I'm winded by the time we reach the top of the Pit and am doing my best to not pant or gasp. Though frustrating, my lack of energy doesn't really surprise me. I haven't eaten properly in weeks, and my stamina wouldn't let me go two rounds with a toddler right now, even after sleeping most of yesterday and all night. One hour's battle has completely exhausted me. I need to rest.

I also need answers, and the latter seriously trumps the former.

Wyatt stays close without actually touching—hovering yet still giving me space. I can't read his face and that worries me. He's always been so open with me, so blunt and honest, that this invisible wall around his emotions is jarring, almost painful.

Understandable, though. It's not every day your girlfriend comes back to life for the second time.

Our group heads for the front of the Admin building, where I left Kismet and company earlier, with Marcus in the lead and Tybalt behind us. As we round the smoking remains of Boot Camp's most important building, two things are immediately clear.

First, a triage area is already under way, with Adrian Baylor shouting orders to both the injured and able-bodied trainees. The teens are tense, most of them pale-faced but stoically doing as they're told by someone whose sheer size and voice command their attention. They're setting up in the parking lot next to Admin. Someone's already raided the infirmary for supplies. The only thing I don't see is any of the medical staff.

Second, the few non-wounded Hunters and a handful of brave trainees have gathered around one of the Jeeps in a tense cluster. Gina Kismet is standing on the hood next to a raven-haired woman in Black Ops gear identical to Wyatt's. I locate Phineas in the crowd, as well as Milo and a handful of other familiar faces, both Hunters and Handlers.

Two more Black Ops strangers, male and female, break away from the group and head over to intercept us.

"What the hell is Astrid doing?" Marcus asks. The angle of his head suggests he means the woman with Kismet.

The new female has the palest green eyes I've ever seen, and short, spiky hair in numerous shades of brown. "Volunteering our help with cleanup, apparently," she replies. "Preliminary death count is twenty-six, but that will probably go up."

Twenty-six. Jesus Christ. Anywhere from twenty to thirty teens are at Boot Camp training at any given time, plus the trainers, medical staff, and people employed at R&D, which totals maybe fifteen more. That's more than half of our numbers dead.

"Are they all trainees?" Tybalt asks.

The female shakes her head. "It appears the beasts rampaged through your Admin building before they made their presence known outside. Your staff is dead.

Many of your trainees are wounded and several more may die."

I shudder. "What about Hunters?"

"Several injuries, but I believe they are all alive." She gives me a once-over with her creepy pale eyes. My instincts scream she's Therian; I'm just not sure which Clan. "Evangeline Stone, I presume?"

Does everyone know who I am? "Yep. Who are you?"

"Leah de Loew. You're prettier than I imagined you'd be."

"Um, thanks?" I'm too exhausted to put more thought into a response or wonder just exactly what she's heard about me, other than the obvious. Died and rose again; died again and rose one more time. Okay, so less "rose one more time" and more "didn't actually die the second time." Or if you count the factory fire from last month, it's the third time . . . oh forget it. Trying to make sense of my second life is going to give me migraines.

"Leah, Kyle," Marcus says. "I want to show you something."

They wander back toward the Pit with Marcus. Knowing their names doesn't make me trust them, even though Wyatt seems to, and I hate being left out of the conversation about Wolf Boy. Sooner or later, though, I expect Marcus will confirm my werewolf theory.

"You went and got some new friends," I say to Wyatt.

"Well, I needed to keep busy after the brass fired me and forbade Gina, Adrian, and the rest of the Triads from helping me look for you." He's so matter-of-fact about something that shocks me. Not so much the part about the brass forbidding Kismet and Baylor from searching for me—it's the fact that they wanted to look for me at all that trips me up.

"Some of them looked anyway, when they could," Tybalt says. "Milo and I went out when he wasn't on patrol or sitting with Felix."

"I heard about Felix," I say, oddly touched by Tybalt's admission. It's been so long since anyone except Jesse, Ash, and Wyatt cared if I lived or died that I don't quite know how to accept the idea of new friendships. Or that others care. It's equally odd to care so much that a Hunter who once tried to kill me is now permanently disabled and will probably never walk without serious pain again. "I'm sorry."

"Us, too."

"So how come you're not dressed like you're about to rob a high-security vault?"

"I wasn't invited. Conflict of interest."

A look is exchanged by Wyatt and Tybalt, and I don't have the first clue how to interpret it. Amazing how much people and circumstances can change in three weeks. The thought makes me kind of dizzy. Everything feels ten degrees hotter. My arm seems twenty pounds heavier, the Wolf Boy bite on my arm throbbing and achy.

"Which means what, exactly?" I ask.

"Evangeline?" Phin's voice is a welcome sound, and his attention flickers to my swollen arm as he approaches. "That's newly acquired."

"What can I say? I collect injuries everywhere I go." I curl my left hand into a fist and hide it behind my hip, not in the mood for more shock over my missing pinkie. The heat and humidity of the June morning are adding to my exhaustion, as is my painful forearm. A bead of sweat trickles down my forehead and into my eye—when did I start sweating so badly? "Oh, and sorry. I lost your gun in the Pit somewhere."

"We'll find it." He touches my shoulder, but his face is fuzzy and I'm not sure if he's frowning or smiling. "Evy?"

Vertigo hits. "I think I'm gonna pass out."

Someone catches me.

Waking up in a nice, soft bed surrounded by air-conditioning and the wonderful scent of coffee is too much to hope for. It's still damned hot, but at least I'm horizontal on something moderately comfortable. My head's pounding, and I consider sleeping awhile longer. At least until the pounding goes away.

Then someone screams and I jerk upright. Every muscle in my back aches, and the world fuzzes out for a few seconds as everything spins in circles. My stomach grumbles, demanding food. Or a gulp of water, at the very least. I try to recall where my weapons are as my vision clears.

The interior of a high-tech-looking helicopter comes into focus. The sliding doors on both sides are open, allowing a moderate flow of air into the stuffy interior. It's powered down on the lawn opposite the parking lot, where someone has erected a kind of tent to protect the wounded. Did one of them scream?

Someone had wrapped my forearm in gauze. Faint spots of blood have oozed through the white, as well as a few pale streaks of yellow. It's itchy, though, instead of achy, so I know it's finally healing.

I climb out of the helicopter, more than a little embarrassed at having passed out. A black body bag is outside, waiting to be loaded, and my money's on Wolf Boy being in it. Going wherever the hell it is that Marcus and company want to take it. It occurs to me to warn them that the corpse might be tagged somehow, but they seem like a smart bunch. They'll think to check. I don't know if Thackery's even still alive, much less in possession of any equipment capable of tracking his little wolf toy.

People come and go, moving in pairs and trios. Some carry bodies, others equipment. It reminds me of a moving crew. I scan the crowd for someone who can give me answers.

"Evy, hey." Milo jogs over from the far side of the helicopter. His clothes are smeared with drying blood of various colors, and his nose is a little swollen. He holds out a bottle of water. "It's warm, but it's wet."

"Thanks." I untwist the cap and indulge in a few sips, which immediately sit uneasily in my stomach. "You okay?"

"Yeah, I got pretty lucky. How do you feel?"

"Nothing a good meal and a few aspirin can't cure. What the hell's going on?"

"We're evacuating Boot Camp."

I blink. "What? Why? I mean, I know it's a mess here, but—what?" The fear and unease in his expression stop me short.

"Baylor got a call a few minutes ago."

"Orders from the brass?"

He snorts, and it's not a pleasant sound. "No. The brass are all dead."

I cannot have heard him correctly. "What do you mean they're dead?"

"Dead, as in no longer alive."

"Were they murdered?"

"No. Apparently, while we were here fighting creatures from hell, they walked into an interrogation room in Major Cases and blew their brains out."

It feels like an awful joke. The brass are our bosses, in the loosest sense of the word—three higher-ups in the ranks of the Metro Police Department, who give orders to the Handlers and make sure they work independently from the police. They provide protection for the Hunters and answer to the Fey Council. No one knows who they are.

Until now, apparently.

"We're sure it was the brass?" I ask.

"Yeah."

"How?"

"The timing's no coincidence," Wyatt says. He's with Marcus, who gives Milo a curious look. "Three cops, one a captain, don't just kill themselves out of the blue, and all our calls to the brass have gone unanswered since this began."

"But why? Why would they do that?"

"I don't know, Evy. I really don't."

I swallow hard against rising fear and uncertainty. Without us, the city has no defense against the Dregs. "So what happens to the Triads now?"

"They'll pack up and head out. Marcus knows of an abandoned motel a few miles off the bypass where they can stay for a while until things get sorted out."

"They," I repeat. "So that's it? You're really done with the Triads, Wyatt? Just like that?"

His eyes narrow. "Don't think this is easy for me, Evy. I've been part of the Triads for ten goddamned years, and it physically hurts to see it all reduced to this. But they're not my responsibility anymore, and I haven't really been a Handler since the night Jesse and Ash were killed."

I ball my fists and plant them on both hips, indignation on the rise. "So you get fired and you turn your back on people who need you? That's not like you, Wyatt."

"The Triads are over, Evy. Over. I can't turn on something that no longer exists." A flush creeps into his neck, his own anger boiling up from the inside. "If I actually thought for a second that they could be saved . . . But they can't. Boot Camp is practically destroyed, and the staff is dead. The brass is dead. Half the trainees are dead, and the active Triad forces, minus rookies, are down to half."

On paper, the numbers sound awful. Apocalyptic, even. But this cannot be the end of it all. The city won't survive without us fighting against the darker species who want to dominate and destroy. "So what then?" I snap. "We pack up, go home, and let the fucking goblins and Halfies take over the city? We let them win?"

"No, that's not what I'm saying."

"Really? Because that's what it sounds like, Wyatt."

It's as close to a real fight as we've ever had, and a pretty damned loud one, too. Occasional evacuees stop and take notice before scurrying on their way. Even Milo has taken a step back, out of the line of verbal fire.

"Just tell her, Truman," Marcus says.

"It's Astrid's call."

"She'll get over it."

I glare at both of them. "Tell me what?"

Wyatt looks like he'd rather stick his head in a viper's nest than say whatever it is that Marcus is goading him on about. More than anything else, it's Wyatt's lack of trust that hurts me the most. He should have just shot me in the head and gotten it over with.

"You know, screw it," I say. "Keep your fucking secrets, both of you."

"Evy," Wyatt says, reaching for me.

I dodge away from his hand. "Don't. Tell you what, Wyatt, you run into the guy I fell in love with? Send him to come talk to me." I walk away. After six steps I stop and angle back. "By the way, make sure that thing"—I point at the bundled corpse—"isn't being traced."

I don't look back this time, just walk, careful to maintain a steady pace and not run like I want to. To get away as quickly as possible. Utter fury boils inside my chest, fueled by confusion and fatigue.

The Triads are broken, but they're not unfixable. They can't be.

The city won't survive without us.

Chapter Six

Greg's dead. He bled out from his leg wound, and while I know it isn't my fault, I still feel like I should apologize to him. He's just one more body among dozens of others, carefully arranged in respectful rows beneath a haphazardly erected tent. The smell of death is suffocating in the summer heat, but no one's bothering me so I stay put, comfortable here among the dead.

I think Greg is one of Sharpe's Hunters, and he's also the first to die from today's engagement. Some are wounded, and they're being tended to under another tent. I'm not sure what's become of Bastian—if he's alive or dead—and I'm not sure I care. Others are taking care of things, so I allow myself the luxury of just sitting and thinking, drumming up enough energy to walk to one of the Jeeps later when we evacuate.

Evacuate. It's a foreign word to me, and one I just can't assign to Boot Camp. We've always been here. Okay, realistically, we've been here about eight years, but for every Hunter currently active, it's always been here. It's been our heart, the lifeblood of the Triads. Leaving it all behind feels like walking away from a funeral—fully aware that what I'm walking away from is never coming back, no matter how much I want it to.

We have a city to protect. We have able-bodied Hunters and Handlers who need someone to guide them. If all the brass are truly dead, someone has to step up and make decisions. Maybe Kismet or Baylor, I don't know.

Wyatt's obviously turned his back on everything he once believed in.

No, not going there. Just thinking Wyatt's name infuriates me all over again, and makes me second-guess returning, coming back into his life when he's managed to accept that I was gone. I should have stayed away, for both of our sakes.

Phineas is smart to approach from a wide angle, giving me plenty of time to see him. I am so not in the mood to be startled. He has a bottle of water and a banana, and he's stripped out of his black shirt and shoulder holsters. Given the heat, I kind of wish I could strip down a little more. I might have, too, if I wasn't so embarrassed about my starved and tortured appearance.

"They're bringing food out of the cafeteria," Phin says as he stoops under the tent. He squats in front of me and holds out the banana. "Hungry?"

"Famished. Thank you." I start to peel the banana, more grateful than I can properly convey. The first bite is too sweet, too sticky, but I force it down anyway, glad it's solid. It isn't a milkshake. And it isn't lemon.

My stomach clenches and twirls at the memory of those awful protein smoothies, and I choke on the second bite. Spit it out. Phin takes the banana away and presses the bottle of water into my hand. I manage a few sips. Much more and I'll probably vomit for real.

"I'm sorry, Evy."

"Not your fault. You have no idea how much I want to be able to eat that." Almost as much as I want a cold shower. I rinsed my hands before hiding in the tent of death, but my body is sticky with blood, sweat, and a layer of grime that looks like a second skin. If I look half as gross as I feel . . .

"Perhaps something blander."

"Something tells me the kitchen isn't taking orders."

His mouth quirks. "Once we leave, then. It shouldn't be much longer."

"I have nowhere to go, Phin." The words eject themselves before I can self-edit, and a pang of sadness sits heavily in my chest. It isn't completely true—I still have the old apartment on Cottage Place. I just don't want to go back there. And so far, no one has offered me an alternative. Or asked for my help.

He frowns, eyebrows furrowing. "You assume Wyatt won't ask you to accompany him?"

"Well, he didn't seem too keen on the idea the last time we talked."

"Wyatt is used to being in control, to making his own decisions. He's now part of something over which he does not have complete control."

I snort, then sip more water. Still hot, still queasy, but definitely less likely to barf at any moment. "So who is in control? This Astrid chick?"

"Please don't call her 'chick' to her face. And yes, Astrid was the leader of the Assembly's private security force. She helped clean up Belle's mess last month. She also delivered punishment to Snow."

Impressive résumé. "Felia?"

"Correct."

So eye color really does run in Clans, as every copper-eyed were I've met so far has been Felia. Phin shares bright blue eyes with Joseph, Aurora, and Ava—the last of his own Clan of birds-of-prey shifters. "How about the others?"

"Marcus is Felia, as well. Leah is Ursia and Kyle is Cania."

"Leah is a bear?" I can't help the brief bubble of laughter at the idea of the slight woman with multicolored hair shifting into a bear—grizzly, black, panda, or teddy. It seems too ridiculous.

As if I have room to judge.

"So how'd Wyatt get mixed up in the Assembly's little task force?" I ask.

"He was invited, same as I."

"By Astrid?"

"Yes."

"So she decides who to let in?"

"Mostly, but Marcus is her second, and his opinion carries a lot of weight."

Terrific. "Any other humans?"

Phin hesitates. "Not at present. Tybalt was considered, but his loyalty to Gina Kismet and her team made him too great a risk."

"Uh-huh."

"Please understand, Evy, this isn't personal. The Assembly has long seen a need to protect itself and its Clans, and now we have the means and the outside support to do so."

"Outside support."

He presses his lips together, an indeterminate emotion passing across his face like a shadow. "I can't promise anything except this: you will have somewhere to go. When you were—when you went with Thackery, the Assembly was . . . honored by your sacrifice."

"Phin—"

"Please, Evy." He takes my hand and squeezes it tight. "The other Elders saw a human Hunter trade herself for a Dreg whom she called a friend. Astrid was assigned to look for you. Wyatt was out of touch these past few days because he was in the mountains with her and Marcus, following a scent trail. Wyatt may have let you go, but he never gave up hope of punishing Thackery for taking you away."

A bubble of emotion settles in my throat and makes it difficult to breathe. *He may have let you go.* I can't argue the truth in Phin's statement. It's too late to fix what Thackery helped us break. Wyatt and I both changed dramatically, and I doubt for the better. All we can do—all of us, I realize, as I glance at the activity beyond the tent—is to start over.

"It feels like such a small thing to say thank you," Phin adds. "You saved many lives that day, Evy, but you saved mine as well. Again."

I put down the bottle of water and cover our clasped hands with my other, holding tight. His touch is cotton and steel—something so unique to him and comfortingly familiar. "I don't have many friends, Phin, but I'll always fight for the ones I have."

"As will I." His eyes burn with a fierce truth.

"Just stop getting kidnapped, okay?"

He smiles. "I'll do my best."

"Good."

Movement outside the tent catches my attention. A young man, probably a trainee, is standing in a patch of sunlight. His gray sweats are stained red and black, and his face is pale beneath a mop of thick brown hair. His wide eyes look around without seeming to really see. He's scared, if his trembling hands are any indication, and more than a little lost. I don't know him, but I can guess his story—this was his last chance to make a life, to matter. And he's watching it burn to the ground.

My heart aches for him, and for the dozen or so others like him who have nowhere to go. And more than that, my chest burns with anger.

For the first time since waking up in Chalice Frost's body and realizing I had a second chance at this life thing, I feel like I have a choice. A choice about my next step and where I want to go from here.

"I want to speak with Astrid," I say.

Phin blinks. "I'm sure I can find her for you."

"Not right this minute. I want an official meeting with the head of your Assembly task force."

"Are you applying for a job?"

"Maybe. Does she book appointments for that?"

"There's a first time for everything. I'll speak with her and let you know."

"Thank you."

"You're welcome. And I meant what I said, Evy, about you having a place to go, even if only for a few days. You're more than welcome in the condo I share with Rufus."

I nod, acknowledging without committing. Phin and Wyatt haven't been there in several days; however, they may both return tonight, and I don't have the strength for another fight with Wyatt. "So, any word on our evacuation progress?"

"Several large trucks are en route to assist in removing all salvageable equipment," he replies. "I don't think a decision has been made on the structures."

The main building, which housed Research and Development, is a smoldering mess. The dormitory in the rear of the grounds and the entire gymnasium complex are in various states of disaster, but neither has serious structural problems. Still, if we're really evacuating for good, everything needs to be leveled.

"Some well-placed explosives will take care of the problem, I'd think," I say, only half-serious.

"It's being considered."

"Problem is, it's too damned noisy," Kismet says from somewhere behind us.

I twist my head to look at her, as sweaty and blood-smeared as the rest of us. "Fire?"

"Harder to control. We don't want the whole mountain to go. Normally, we'd ask the Fey for help, but—"

A little hard to do with the brass dead, the entire Council ignoring us, and very little left in the way of magical allies. "Right," I say. "Any news on Bastian's condition?"

Kismet takes a few steps forward. She's short enough

to not have to stoop beneath the low tent. "Morgan's taking him and two others to the hospital. Their injuries are serious and we can't treat them here."

It's a risky move. Without our contacts in the police department, those medical records will be hard to hide. Operating as Triads depended upon secrecy and the ability to move around without being bothered by the real police. It's an advantage we've lost in a most spectacular manner.

"We'll take the other injured out of here in waves," she continues, speaking to me like an equal. It's unsettling. "Some of the rooms in this motel will be for our little MASH unit, and the others for living in until we come up with something more permanent. The equipment can be stored in the trucks for now."

Good plan, all around. "What kind of help is Astrid offering?" I ask.

"Assistance with transportation and any medical personnel we require."

When she doesn't continue, I say, "And?"

"That's it."

I glance at Phin, whose expression is blank. Our hands are still entwined, and I'm sure Kismet's noticed, but I don't give a shit. "Gee, that's generous."

Kismet shrugs. "She didn't have to help us at all, Stone. Her team showing up today helped immensely. A lot more people could have been hurt or killed."

"True." Annoying, but true.

"And she wants to meet with us. Officially meet."

"Meet, huh?" Looking up at Kismet is starting to hurt my neck, so I let go of Phin and carefully stand. The tarp brushes the top of my head. No dizziness, no vertigo. Score one for me. "Who's us?"

"Me, Adrian Baylor, and you."

I hear Phin stand up behind me, tenting the tarp upward. "Why me?" I ask. "I'm not in charge of anything."

"Wyatt wants you included in this."

So Wyatt spoke to Astrid about me. I can't help wondering if it's because of our little fight, or in spite of it. Or which makes me less crazy. "Now?"

"Tonight, after we've moved out and settled in."

"I guess you and Baylor are in charge now, huh?"

A haze of grief steals briefly across her face, chased just as quickly by uncertainty. "Looks that way," she says. "Which means you're welcome to come with us, Stone." Her gaze flickers over my shoulder. "Unless you have a better offer?"

"Depends on your definition." I can't explain why I'm leery of returning to Phin's shared condo. Especially if Wyatt shows up.

I can't tell her the secret that Rufus confessed to me about his involvement in the death of Wyatt's family ten years ago, and if I'm put in the same room with both of them, I won't be able to keep my mouth shut. Maybe that's what Rufus wants, and maybe the chance to unload his guilt is what he hoped for when he told me, because I don't like lying to Wyatt.

God, I don't want to be responsible for this secret.

"This works out, though," I say, my way of redirecting the conversation. "I wanted to speak with Astrid anyway. Right now, the Assembly is our best chance."

Kismet nods, understanding without further clarification. The future of the Triads and the safety of the city are foremost in her mind, as well. "The vampires, too. They've helped us in the past. They don't want to see the goblins or Halfies overrun the city any more than we do. Your contacts would be useful."

"Contacts?" I snort. Can't help it. "Isleen and I didn't exactly exchange phone numbers. She just has this odd habit of showing up."

Kismet arches a slim eyebrow at me.

"Okay, fine," I say. "You call her, I'll kiss her ass."

Behind me, Phin chokes to hide laughter. "It's very likely a vampire representative will be at your audience with Astrid," he says.

I pivot on my heel, hands going to my hips. "Why's that?"

He smiles, the enigmatic bastard. "A lot's happened in the past three weeks, Evy."

A series of sarcastic barbs die on my tongue as I comprehend the hidden meaning in his words. "Like unexpected alliances?" His expression remains neutral. "I'll take that as a yes. Awesome." I spin to face Kismet again, whose mouth is open in an O. "Looks like we'll get to talk to the vampires tonight, too."

Her expression shifts from surprise to annoyance. "Secret alliances between the Assembly and the Families? When were we going to hear about this?"

Phin steps around me, closer to Kismet. "When the Assembly chose to disclose it. We work with your Triads, not for them. We no longer answer to you." It's not quite a threat, but it's close enough.

And I don't know how I feel about it.

Someone had the good sense to empty out Boot Camp's stash of sweats and spare clothes and distribute them to the motel rooms housing the refugees. Changing into clean sweat-shorts and a T-shirt makes my shower so much sweeter, and I'm almost energized as I exit the bathroom.

The four female trainees assigned to the room clam up the moment I step out. They're a little intimidated by me, and I hate it. Okay, so I came back from the dead, have nearly died enough times to make any cat cash in its nine lives, and I can be pretty scary when I yell. Which I did ten minutes ago to gain access to their shower.

"Thanks," I say as I glide through the small room,

straight to the door. Summer humidity hits like a soggy blanket the moment I step outside onto a cracked sidewalk, facing a weed-pocked parking lot and the side of a mountain. Many of the room doors are open, creating a beehive effect of people going in and out at random, passing messages or delivering supplies. Three hours here and things are running smoothly, thanks to Baylor and Kismet.

The Green Acres Lodge office has become our modified command center, so I head around to the front. The motel is L shaped, the inside of the L facing the mountains, and the office on the short end, along with an old diner. I'm on the long end, so it's a hefty walk. My poor stomach is tied up in unhappy knots, an awful combination of nerves and lack of food.

I still have no idea where I stand in all this. My brain wants to help the remaining Triads in whatever way I can. My heart wants to find Wyatt, haul him into the nearest empty room, and demand to know what he's thinking. What he's feeling. To have him tell me everything that happened while I was missing.

But I don't even know if he's still here, or if he left with his new playmates.

A familiar Cadillac is parked in front of the office, next to a red sports car with heavily tinted windows. Looks like I'm the last one to the party, so I pick up my pace. Instead of the office, I find them assembled in the diner, chairs clustered around a few pushed-together tables. The entire place is spotless, and the retro chrome gleams under fresh lightbulbs in overhead fixtures. It reminds me a little of the diner where Phineas and I almost had lunch one day.

All of the usual suspects are here: Kismet, Baylor, Phineas, Astrid, Marcus, and Wyatt. The three less-expected faces offer pleased smiles at my entrance. Michael Jenner, despite the heat, is wearing one of his customary suits. As representative of the Assembly, he always shows up to speak for the best interests of the fourteen were-Clans. For a lawyer, he's not half-bad.

I don't know why I'm surprised to see Isleen and Eleri, but I am. Isleen has been an ally and a tentative friend since my resurrection—as much a friend as any vampire can be to a human. She stands and walks to me, extending her hand for a firm shake.

"It pleases me that you are alive, yet again," she says, her voice a familiar, lilting cadence that most vampires possess.

"I'm pretty pleased about it, too," I reply. My smile is forced. I'm too damned tired for witty banter. I just want to know what's happening. I shake Jenner's hand, too, then pull a chair into the circle between him and Baylor. Wyatt is directly across from me, staring intently.

"I was just expressing the Assembly's sincere condolences," Jenner says, "on the loss of so many of your people today."

"I'd think the Assembly would be doing backflips over it," I say, unable to censor myself.

Astrid makes a startled noise, but Jenner just chuckles. "I admit, there are a few Elders who expressed a sense of justice over the news. However, they're also intelligent enough to see how this can be a devastating blow to lasting peace. The Triads were far from perfect, but they were effective in their efforts to quell the larger uprisings of the darker races."

"Effective until now," Astrid says.

"We might still surprise you," Kismet retorts.

Astrid folds her hands in her lap, copper eyes flashing. "Your forces are at half strength, the Fey Council is ignoring you, and your protection within the Police Department has apparently committed group suicide. You'd be lucky to manage surprising a house cat."

Wow. All eyes are on Kismet, who's in her seat only

because Baylor's hand is on her shoulder. Color rises high in her cheeks. Marcus nudges Astrid in the ribs, and she shifts her glare to him.

"This bickering is unproductive," Isleen says. She stands, drawing up to her full, lean height. Long white hair cascades down her back, a familiar and stark contrast to her black clothes. Lavender eyes take their turn sending silent messages to various people in our circle. "And if there are no objections, I will begin."

No one objects.

"After the events at Parker's Palace, Mr. Jenner approached the royal Fathers of the ruling Families with an offer from the Assembly. Although neither the Assembly nor the Fathers condoned the actions of the man named Leonard Call, we could also not ignore the implications of their organization and their ability to attract members of both our races. We also could not continue ignoring the host of internal problems that have been plaguing the Triads for months."

Baylor grunts—the only sound in an otherwise silent room. I glance at Wyatt, who's giving Isleen his full attention. I have no doubt he's heard all this before; he just doesn't want to make eye contact with those of us who haven't.

No one else is asking, so I do. "What was the offer?"

Isleen tilts her head in my direction without actually looking at me. "An alliance between our peoples."

This time it's Kismet who makes a noise. "Really? Since when have the vampires and the Clans ever gotten along?"

"Necessity creates strange bedfellows," Jenner replies.

I glance at Phineas, on Jenner's right, and he's staring straight at me.

"This alliance was not offered lightly," Phin says, addressing the group. "Fourteen Elders means that many opinions were heard and many concerns still remain.

However, what Call and Snow managed to do at Parker's Palace is only one illustration of how ineffective the Triads have become. There are simply not enough of you, and your methods of control through fear no longer work."

It's a conversation that Phin and I had weeks ago—words I didn't want to hear then but am hearing now. I hate that he's right and that the remains of the Triads are being pressed between a rock and a fucking hard place.

"The Clans and the Families are not your enemies," Isleen says. "But we can be your allies, and we are offering humans a partnership in this."

"What is this, exactly?" Kismet asks. The fact that she doesn't say no outright gives me hope. I don't know Astrid or Marcus, but I do know Phin and Isleen. And I trust them.

"A multirace security force," Astrid says, unfolding from her chair. She isn't a tall woman, but she ripples with the power of her animal half, and it makes her presence in the room that much larger.

Kismet stands as well. "Run by you?"

"No," Isleen says. "Run by a trifecta, a representative from each of our races. Final decisions go through them."

"Then let me guess. You and Astrid represent your people?"

"Correct."

"So who represents ours?"

"That is a choice you will have to discuss if you choose to accept our offer."

Kismet and Baylor exchange a look I can't see, then both turn to face me. Asking or deferring, I have no idea, so I shrug and tilt my head. Their call. I'm not against the idea, but I won't speak for them or the other Handlers and Hunters. It won't be easy convincing them that this is a good idea, and it won't go over any better coming from me. In fact, some of the Handlers might nix it outright just because I said it.

"What specifically is this partnership about?" Baylor asks as Kismet sits back down.

"It's about protecting our peoples and this city from those who would destroy it," Isleen says. She gives Astrid a look I can't see—I'm starting to really hate the chair I chose—and Astrid sits. "As you well know, the Families and the Clans have remained mostly neutral in the actions taken by the Triads these past ten years. We do our best to present no threat, and we expect to not be threatened in return, save the most extreme of cases."

Cases such as Snow—a were-fox—or Kitsune, who helped organize Halfies, vampires, and other shifters in a rally against humans, and who murdered more than sixty of them at an arts benefit last month. Cases such as the occasional rogue vampire who thinks biting and infecting humans is a good idea.

"We wish to see the half-Blood problem wiped out, as well as the goblins permanently disabled as a threat," she continues. "Humans have their flaws, but evolution has given you this world, and I have no desire to see the dark races reclaim it."

"Do the Clans feel the same way?" Baylor asks.

"The majority do, yes," Jenner says. "This city allows the Clans something that does not exist in many other places. It gives us a chance to interact freely with humans, to be part of your world, your culture, and your technology. Because we age more rapidly than humans, it's difficult for us to establish ourselves in urban areas. It's why so many of us have chosen to live here, rather than hiding in tiny towns scattered across the country. Or, as some have done, choosing to live as animals."

He's laying it on the table, and I respect Michael Jenner more than ever. I've never considered how rapid aging must interfere with a Therian's ability to interact with humans, to create and establish relationships without revealing their inhumanity. Sure, in the two years I knew Danika, I saw the were-falcon age from a skinny preadolescent to a mature young woman. Physically, at any rate. She wasn't even five years old when she died.

"Neither of our peoples want to see humans crushed or removed from power in this city," Jenner continues. "Because if the city falls to the rule of goblins, Fey, or others, they will spread beyond the valley and across this state and into others. Fear and violence will become a way of life, and that way leads to destruction."

"The Fey don't want to rule; they've been our allies," Kismet says.

Wyatt laughs. It's a low, terrible sound that skitters worms of fear down my spine. All eyes are on him, but he says nothing. Arms crossed over his chest, he gives his full attention to Isleen.

She takes the stage again. "You assume the Fey are your friends because they came to you ten years ago and pushed you to create the Triads. You assume the Fey are on your side because they've fed you information and occasionally patted you on the head when you've done a good job. You assume too much, and you forget that the creatures helping you are not human, care nothing for humans, and are as old as the rivers dividing this city."

The fear in my spine settles icy cold in my gut. My mind whirls with information. Things I know about the creation of the Triads—Amalie approached Wyatt and the first trained Hunters; Amalie made contact with the officers who became the brass; Amalie set everything about the Triads in motion.

"I don't get it," I say, startling myself by speaking at all. "Why would the Fey Council put so much time and effort into the Triads? Just to control us?"

"That," Isleen replies, "and to amuse themselves."

"Amuse themselves?"

"Human literature is often incorrect in its records of the ancient races, but humans did manage to capture one aspect of the Fey. They see other races, lesser races, as playthings. They delight in interfering and creating chaos. And, although not immortal, most live an exceptionally long time."

"So you're saying that Amalie's been playing us this whole time? That everything she's done for the Triads is the setup for some sort of ten-year practical joke?" I can't reconcile the notion with everything I know, and a quick glance at Baylor and Kismet suggests the same on their end.

"Ten years is half my lifetime," Jenner says, "and an eighth of the average human's. But it's merely a moment to a sprite or a faerie."

"Or an elf," Wyatt says. Speaking for the first time, and his words make my stomach twist. He hasn't changed his posture or taken the floor. His expression is flat, but his eyes blaze with anger even from a distance.

I catch his gaze and hold it. "What are you saying?" I ask.

"That I've been a fool. A fool and a puppet, and I've been those things for a long, long time."

Chapter Seven

Wyatt holds me captive with his eyes and his voice, and it's as though we're having this conversation alone. "The system that we put in place has been rotting at its core for years, Evy. Call and Snow were just symptoms of a larger problem—one that I couldn't see until recently. It took losing everything I'd once lived for to see just how broken things are."

"The Triads?"

"Mostly. Whatever purpose Amalie ultimately had in mind for us, she chose well when she picked the first Hunters. I was so blinded by grief and rage against the bounty hunters who killed my family that I'd have listened to anyone who pointed me in a direction and said to kill. Most of us had the same grudge against a Halfie or a goblin. We did everything she told us to do."

An image of Rufus flashes in my mind and with it the secret I'm keeping for him. He didn't ask me to keep it, sure, but how can I tell Wyatt that one of his oldest, dearest friends helped slaughter his family ten years ago and put him on this path?

"We never questioned an order from the Fey Council or the brass, not once in ten years," Wyatt continues. "Even the orders that didn't make sense, that we found difficult to live with."

I know him. I can see in his eyes and the slight down-turn of his mouth that he's thinking about Rain, the Kitsune he shot in cold blood for the simple crime of loving a human.

"Thinking back on some of them, they made sense as political moves. They drove a big damned wedge between humans and potential ally races."

"Sunset Terrace," I say, choking on the words.

Next to Wyatt, Phineas nods and doesn't bother hiding a flash of grief. Several days before I died the first time, I'd hidden in the Sunset Terrace Apartments with my friend Danika, in order to escape the Hunters who wanted me dead. She helped me escape before the Triads descended and, upon orders from the brass, burned the complex to the ground with all inhabitants trapped within its walls. More than three hundred members of the Coni and Stri Clans—all birds of prey of one variety or another—died that night. The order never made sense, even as a scare tactic to keep the Clans in line, and it was directly responsible for the retaliatory attack on humans at Parker's Palace.

The brass had to know there'd be a response of some sort, Assembly sanctioned or not, and Parker's Palace was it.

"You don't think the Fey Council simply condoned the attack on Sunset Terrace," I say. "You think they ordered it through the brass?"

"Yes."

"And I gave them a convenient excuse?"

"Yes."

"But why—oh fuck." It comes crashing down like a tidal wave, and everything seems fuzzy and far away for a moment. Weeks ago I accused the brass of purposely murdering the Coni and Stri because they were one of the oldest, most powerful of the Clans. The Coni are bi-shifters, able to maintain human form while still bearing wings strong enough to allow them to fly—like angels, creatures of legend. I tried to expose the brass, to make them accountable for Sunset Terrace, so the Assembly wouldn't demand Rufus's life in return. After circumstances secured a stay of execution on Rufus, I'd let the whole thing go.

Goddammit!

"Stone was right," Kismet says. She sounds like she'd rather chew glass than admit it. Kismet knew what I was after back then, and she nearly killed me for it.

"She was," Phineas says. "But had she known then, she still couldn't have gotten to them. They never would have allowed it."

"How could they have stopped it?"

I have a funny feeling I know what he's going to say.

"Because the three men you called the brass were no longer human. They were full-time avatars for three of Amalie's sprites. You were always being given her orders, protected by her whims. She's been manipulating you. All of you."

The room tips a little and I drop my head into my hands, elbows braced on my knees. It's too much, too fast. Everything is falling apart, spinning out of control. And yet it all makes a perfect kind of sense, even down to this morning's group suicide. The Fey Council has been silent for weeks. They didn't help look for me when Thackery had me. They hid behind pacifism and refused to get involved when an elf tried to bring a demon into our world. Their invisible fingerprints cover everything. All signs point to the Council.

Wyatt and I had stood in Amalie's presence in First Break, the underground home of the Fair Ones, and I had felt at peace there. Protected. Did she actually lie to our faces that day, or were her words chosen so carefully that it was all truth hiding behind falsehoods? I don't know. It seems so long ago. Another lifetime.

Baylor shifts forward in his seat, angling toward Wyatt.

"You're absolutely convinced of this? That the Fey Council has been fucking with us all along?"

"Yes," Wyatt replies without hesitation. "Amalie has been playing everyone like her own private chess set, but there was one thing she didn't count on and it screwed up her carefully laid plans."

"And what's that?"

"Evy."

I jerk upright. "Huh?"

"You," Wyatt says. "You have consistently defied her expectations, so she's had to improvise. And for a creature who's been planning this for decades, improvisation doesn't come easily. It's probably why she's withdrawn completely and ceased contact."

"Why? Because she's frustrated that I haven't laid down and died yet?"

"Pretty much. I think that night in First Break she fully expected us to stay there until your clock ran out, so we wouldn't interfere with Tovin's plan."

Okay, this makes absolutely no sense whatsoever. Amalie told us how to stop Tovin from bringing the demon across the Break. "What are you talking about?"

"You were there, Evy, when Tovin summoned the Tainted. He was going to do it whether he had me to host the thing or not. He had those hounds in the room, and he had you at the end. If we'd stayed in First Break like Amalie wanted, Tovin would have summoned the Tainted anyway and no one would have been there to stop him."

"Why, though? Why would Amalie have wanted the Tainted loose and uncontrollable?"

"Chaos," Kismet says.

Wyatt nods. "The Tainted would have destroyed everything in its path. Tovin may have even gone further and loosed those caged hounds, as well as the hybrids locked in the lab. The goblins would have swarmed the streets, along with the Halfies. The city—" He stops, looks away, his temper simmering.

"Chaos," I repeat.

"But she gave you that spell to turn the Tainted into a crystal," Kismet said. "Why?"

"To keep playing the part of the benevolent ruler?"

"I have another theory on that," Wyatt said. "I don't think she intended that spell to work."

I frown at him. "But it did."

"Do you remember what Jaron said before she died?"

"Betrayal." We've just never known what she meant.

"What happened directly before she showed up on our doorstep?"

He can't possibly mean Alex's funeral, so . . . "The earthquake. Thackery stole the crystal from the Nerei. The trolls were fighting, and some were attacking Boot Camp."

"Exactly."

"The Fey aren't united," Kismet says, catching on faster than I am. "Someone made sure the containment spell worked. You think Jaron was working against Amalie?"

"Yes," Wyatt says. "That's my theory."

I struggle to maintain some semblance of composure when all I want to do is scream. In some ways, I always knew what might happen if we failed at Olsmill. While Tovin summoned the Tainted across First Break, the crystal containing the captured Tainted is currently contained and hidden far away from the Fey. A lead-lined box in the back of one of the trucks parked outside isn't the best of places, but we're keeping it close.

Hearing all this said out loud and knowing it's what Amalie wanted spears my chest with a dull pain. I do not suffer betrayal well, and this . . . there isn't even a word for what this is.

"But why?" Kismet asks. "What does the Fey Council gain by that sort of chaos and destruction?"

"Well, that should be obvious," Astrid says. "The extinction of the human race."

"Evy?"

Wyatt's voice carries up the side of the hill long after I hear his approach through the underbrush. The sun is setting, casting the forest in shadows, and as hungry and exhausted as I am, I can't bring myself to leave the comfort of these woods. It isn't quiet—activity from the motel below prevents that. But it seems isolated. A private place to muddle through my thoughts.

"If you ask if I'm okay, I may have to punch you," I say.

He laughs. I've missed that sound. I shift sideways on the fallen log that's my chair. He stands a few feet away, leaning against a tree trunk, hands in the pockets of his cargo pants, a black smudge slowly melting into twilight. I want to run to him, throw my arms around his neck, and let him hold me.

Instead, I ask, "Any word from the hospital?"

"Yeah."

"And?"

"Bastian died a few minutes ago."

I feel nothing at the news—just the same numbness around my heart that has been there since the meeting. "So what did they decide?"

"Gina and Adrian are talking to the other Handlers right now," he replies. "It'll take some time, but I think they'll come around."

"And if they don't?"

"Then they don't. We can't force anyone to accept the idea of working alongside the very creatures they've been taught to hate and hunt. No one changes their mind-set overnight, Evy. You know that."

"Yeah, I do." My tentative friendship with Danika

planted the seeds of change that Phin's influence forced into growing. Seeing individuals rather than an entire race, and judging each one separately. "So I guess this is what we were fighting over earlier?"

"For the most part, yes."

"For the most part?"

He picks a path through the fallen branches and brush, each step careful and deliberate. He sits on the log without upsetting its balance, an arm's reach of distance between us. Up close and without the lens of recent battle, I see the shadows under his eyes, the new wrinkles at the corners. The weight he's lost and the way he's aged. He's not even thirty, and yet he looks close to fifty now.

"You know, part of me feels like I betrayed you," he says, "by accepting that you'd died."

"Wyatt, don't."

"No, Evy, please." He's speaking to me, but his attention is on the ground in front of us. "Part of me does think so. I never should have doubted you'd find a way back, and that part is so happy to have been wrong."

"What's the other part think?"

He draws his fingers through his hair, down his chin to scratch at his throat where his dark beard has shadowed the skin. He still won't look at me. "The other part of me is angry and scared of getting his heart broken a third time."

The words hit like a punch to the gut, all the more powerful because they're honest. For Wyatt I've died twice, and both times I broke his heart. And I cannot guarantee it won't happen again. Loss is part of our lives; we both know and accept this. But how do you lose the same person over and over, and still find the strength to return for more?

Do I even have the right to expect him to? I wouldn't be here at all if Max hadn't interfered. I told Thackery to kill me when he was finished with me, and he swore he would. Consistently defying expectations by not dying is fun when it confounds the bad guy, but not when it hurts the people I care about. Coming back ripped open a healing wound.

Again.

"I get it," I say.

"Do you? Because I'm not even sure I get it. Everything is so—"

"Different?"

He finally looks at me with utter devastation in his eyes. Glimmering with unshed tears, full of confusion and love and fear and so many things that both thrill and hurt me. "I still love you. That hasn't changed."

"It's okay, Wyatt." It isn't okay, not one bit, but I say it anyway. I say it like I mean it because I have to. He needs this. He deserves this.

"Is it?"

"Of course." I scoot closer and rest one hand on his knee. "I still love you, too, and even though I've said it only a few times, I do mean it. And you're right. Everything is different now and we can't pretend it isn't. We can't go back. We can't fix it. We can only be who we are now."

He turns his hand so we're palm to palm, fingers curling tight. "And who are we?"

"I don't know." My throat's tight, clogging with tears. "But I think we both need time to figure that out for ourselves before we can think about us again." The hand around mine squeezes tighter. "A part of me died in that trailer, Wyatt, in Thackery's lab, and I'm not entirely sure who's still left. I've been free less than two days, and now everything I thought was true isn't. I don't know where I go from here."

"I know the feeling." His voice is low, raspy with emotion. "Before this morning, I was ready to turn my back on the Triads and everything I'd help build. On the people who used to count on me and call me a friend. We'd learned all of these things about the Fey, and then the Assembly and the Families came together, and I needed what they were offering me. I wanted a fresh start. Everything about the Triads reminded me of you.

"But then I heard about Boot Camp being attacked and . . . I can't even explain how I felt. It was beyond personal. And then I got there and saw those kids fighting. They were so brave, and then Gina told me you were alive, and I didn't believe her. Even when I saw you fighting that wolf, I didn't believe it. But you were real. Everything I'd abandoned was real. The people I hurt were real, and they needed me more than ever."

"Wyatt," I say, drawing out his name, unsure if I even want to ask this. "If the attack hadn't happened this morning, would Astrid and Isleen still have invited the Triads into this little task force?"

He flinches. "Not this soon, no. I've brought it up, but we had no way of exposing the brass and no guarantee that anyone, even Gina, would listen to me. But now—"

"Now we don't really have a choice."

"There's always a choice, Evy, but I do think that joining us is the lesser of many evils. And we'll be five times stronger than we ever were before. Not only in numbers, but in abilities and knowledge and political power. Instead of bullying the Families and Clans, we'll be working with them. Cooperating instead of ordering around. And if Amalie really is trying to instigate some sort of surface civil war, we'll have a much stronger position from which to fight back."

"You're right."

"But?"

"No buts." I poke him in the shoulder. "I can't say you're right without adding a but?"

"You can. You just rarely do."

We smile, and it feels so normal. So much like us—here, alone in the woods, with the problems of the world seeming so far away, as if the last three weeks never happened. Only they did, and we'll remember that as soon as we rejoin the others. So many things still need to be said before either of us can heal.

"I'm not sorry I went with Thackery." It's the first thing that comes to mind. I don't think I can ever tell Wyatt that I asked Thackery to kill me, but I can tell him about this.

He flinches. "I know. It was the right decision."

"The right decision for everyone else."

"Well, it was a Bigger Picture kind of moment."

"It always is, and that's okay. This is the life we chose." Dusky shadows lengthen on the ground as twilight wanes. "Do you ever think about how different things would have turned out if you'd gotten Tybalt instead of me four years ago?"

Wyatt arches both eyebrows, expression going thoughtful. "Well, for one thing, I wouldn't have kissed him that night I came over to your place drunk off my ass."

"You remember that?"

"Parts of it."

"You never said anything."

"I was embarrassed, Evy. I never should have gone over there, much less kissed you."

"Well, now that I know more about the anniversary in question, I'm glad you did." My thoughts jump back to Rufus and his part in the reason behind that particular anniversary. It isn't my secret to tell, and yet I feel like I'm lying to Wyatt simply by keeping my mouth shut.

"You've been part of my life, blonde or brunette, for the last four years, Evy Stone," he says. "I can't imagine my life without you in it. And for a while you weren't, and I hated it. I hated the guy I was, and I hated you for leaving me." He seems to realize just how tightly he's been squeezing my hand and relaxes his grip. "You said that a part of you died in that trailer, and you aren't sure what's left."

I nod, positive I know what's coming.

"Part of me died with you," he says, voice tight. Near the breaking point. "Died when I accepted you were gone. And I don't know who's left, either."

"Maybe, um." I swallow against the lump in my throat. "Maybe we both need time to figure that out. Time to just . . . make sense of the world again."

"Apart." It isn't a question.

I laugh, and it's a hollow sound. "Well, we're going to be working together, I think, so 'apart' is a relative term."

"Right."

"We're not going anywhere, Wyatt, but no pressure, no expectations. For a while. I think we both need this." I tell myself it's for him as much as me, but I'm being selfish. Incredibly selfish with the two hardest secrets I've ever kept from him.

"For a while," he says. His voice cracks.

He opens his arms and I fall against his chest, clinging to his warmth despite the heat of the evening. I rest my cheek against his heart and listen to it beat for a while, as his free hand strokes my back, his chin a comfortable weight on the top of my head.

We're still sitting like that a while later when Kismet finds us and delivers good news: our three-way alliance among humans, Therians, and vampires is a go.

Chapter Eight

Funny how it's possible to both feel better and feel like utter crap at the exact same time. My nose was stuffed, my eyes were swollen, and my head felt twenty pounds heavier, but all in all I was okay. The minor breakdown over the Therian abductions and Thackery's involvement was over. I leaned against Wyatt's chest, comfortable there on the floor of the gym, content to be held until I had collected myself enough to ask a coherent question.

"What are you doing here?"

He stiffened. "I can go if you're uncomfortable."

He could—what? I sat up and twisted my somewhat-stiff neck to stare at him. He looked startled. I shook my head, confused. Then I got it and laughed. "No, you idiot, not that. I thought you and Marcus were interrogating Felix."

"We had to stop for a bit. The only thing he'd say was 'I can't' and 'it's for them,' and it was getting"—he blanched—"messy."

"Oh." Ugh. I tried to get Felix's words to make sense, but a fog had settled around my reasoning skills, and it wasn't going away.

"You okay?"

"Yeah, I think so." I touched my face. I really wanted to blow my nose. "When did I become such a weepy mess?"

"When you died and got a new body complete with new emotional imbalances?"

"Oh. Yeah." I smiled.

So did he. "Get it out of your system?"

"I think so. Although the punching bag may never forgive me."

"It might surprise you."

The teasing banter was so normal, so *us*, that it was easy to forget we weren't *us* anymore. Hadn't been for weeks. I sat up straighter and got my first good look at Wyatt. Flecks of blood dotted his gray T-shirt and the skin of his bare arms. Some stuck to his neck. If any had made it to his face, he'd taken the time to wipe it off. He was smiling, but it didn't hide the hint of concern in his expression or the shadows haunting his eyes.

"I'm so sorry about Ava," he said.

"Don't be sorry yet." A brief flare of annoyance shut out any lingering threads of grief. "I plan on getting her back alive, along with the rest of them."

"I didn't mean—"

"I know, Wyatt, but saying you're sorry feels like a condolence, and I don't want it."

He lifted his hand and brushed a damp strand of hair off my forehead. "What do you want, then?"

Boy, that was a loaded question, and it had nothing to do with the missing Therians. For once, I didn't know what to say because I didn't have a clue what I wanted from him. We'd been keeping each other at arm's length for two weeks, getting the space we both needed. I just didn't know if I was ready for the heart-to-heart that would finally lay it all on the table.

"I want a shower," I said.

"Well, you are kind of a mess."

"No kidding." I had dirt on my arms and legs from both of my tumbles (the roof of the rave and the driveway landing), drying sweat everywhere from my battle with the heavy bag, not to mention tears, snot, and probably a little bit of blood from any number of sources. I couldn't smell very good, either. "No, I think 'mess' is kind. I'm downright disgusting."

"Come on, then, Stinky." Wyatt stood up, then offered his hand. I waved my boxing glove at him. He laughed, then grabbed my wrist and helped lever me to my feet. He unstrapped the gloves—for which I was eternally grateful, as my fingers were stiff and refusing to work properly—and tossed them aside.

"Thank you for this," I said.

"Of course. I'll do everything I can to help you get the Coni back. You know that."

"I do." I flexed my fingers, wincing at the sharp twinges in my joints. The soreness would fade quickly, thanks to my healing ability, so in some bizarre way I wanted to enjoy the pain while it existed.

We headed for the door. I grabbed his arm before we reached it, and he stopped short.

"One favor after my shower?" I asked.

"Depends on the favor."

Smart man. "I want to speak with Felix."

"Think you can make him talk?"

"Probably not, but if he isn't talking, then Astrid won't keep him alive much longer. I just want a minute before his neck gets snapped."

"Why?"

"Because he never finished answering a question I asked him on the roof."

The shower felt wonderful. A little bit of steamy, wet heaven after a nightmarish few hours. I almost felt normal again as I left the bathrooms in fresh jeans, a navy blue tank top, and the latest in heavy-duty sneakers. My hair was left to dry in whichever manner it chose.

Wyatt was lingering outside of the jail. "Astrid said you could have five minutes."

"Generous of her."

"Play nice, Evy."

"With Astrid or Felix?"

"Astrid. She's taking these disappearances more personally than you are. Clan protection is her job."

True, and a great point. Except for Phineas (and, to an extent, Kyle), I hadn't given consideration to the feelings of the Therians we worked with. Before creating the Watch, Astrid had headed up an elite security team for the Assembly of Clan Elders. Losing so many people at once had to hurt.

"Okay," I said. "Five minutes."

We went inside. The first room was large, with a center desk and three observation windows, one on each wall. The rooms to the immediate left and center were both specialty jail cells—the walls created with alternating strips of silver bars (anti-Therian) and raw pine (anti-vampire) to keep the majority of potential prisoners from staging a breakout. To the right was the interrogation room, its walls a similar composition. Two different chairs were bolted to the floor at intervals, also of different materials depending on who was being questioned. A rack of tools hung on the back wall of that room next to an industrial sink.

Seth Nevada stood behind the desk, arms crossed over his chest. I didn't know him well; he'd been a Handler in a different part of the city and had volunteered here as the equivalent of town sheriff. Three others worked under him, and the quartet manned the jail. Humans were chosen because of the wall materials—to prevent accidental injury. Nevada was smart, fair, and fond of snacking on hard-boiled eggs.

"Truman. Stone," he said.

I gave an impolite half nod in his general direction, too horrified by what I saw in the interrogation room. Felix was slumped over in the wooden chair, bare arms and thighs bearing weeping blisters at every point of contact. Blood oozed from several parts of his body, and he was having trouble breathing. It took me a moment to spot the reason—a small head of garlic was hanging around his neck. Vampires and Halfies are allergic to all plants in the allium family, but garlic and onions had the worst effect.

And we knew all the tricks.

My stomach twisted. *He's not your friend, Felix died, he's not your friend, Felix is dead.* Seeing him like that made it harder to remember.

It also made it impossible to forget Alex Forrester. A kind young man who was once the best friend of Chalice, my new body, he'd volunteered to help me after my resurrection. He lost his life for his generosity, ending up in a position very similar to the one Felix was in now—a half-Blood tied to a wooden chair, tortured for information.

A warm hand squeezed my shoulder. I knew it was Wyatt without looking. "You sure you want to do this?" he whispered.

"Yes." *No. Fuck.*

Nevada punched a code into the digital lock, and the interrogation door clicked. I pulled it open, stepped inside, and pulled it shut.

The odors of garlic and blood stung my nose and watered my eyes. Felix didn't move, head down, arms and ankles shackled to the chair. He seemed to have passed out, but I knew better.

"I hear you haven't been very cooperative," I said.

His head snapped up, iridescent eyes blinking through a sheen of tears. "You brought me here and assumed I'd trade info for good-byes," he said, voice hoarse, bitter.

"Not interested?"

"Anything I agree to ends with me being executed anyway, so what's the point?"

I lifted one shoulder in a half shrug, struggling to keep an air of nonchalance when all I wanted to do was look away. "One final good deed before you die? For old time's sake?"

Felix snorted, then winced. "What the hell do I owe the Triads?"

"I don't know. Most of us were heading toward early death, jail, or a pretty fucked-up adult life before we were recruited. You think you'd have lasted this long without the Triads?"

He looked away, as if actually considering the question. I was barely eighteen and on my way to jail for assault and B&E when the Triads made me an offer. In some ways, Boot Camp was like jail, but I have no doubts that a prison full of women who were a lot tougher than I'd been back then would have killed me. Or at least broken my spirit. Four years as a Triad Hunter had broken a lot of my bones, but so far my spirit was intact and still fighting.

I didn't know Felix's story. Hell, I barely knew anyone's story—even Tybalt's and Milo's, who were the closest Hunter friends I had now. Talking about the past wasn't a particularly favorite subject of conversation for anyone.

"I was a street hustler," Felix said.

It took me a moment to process that. I was afraid to interrupt or react in any way, just in case I shut him up.

"It was fast money, and it kept me from starving and freezing in the streets. Hated it, though, every fucking second. I guess Gina knew, because our Handlers got all the dirt on us, right? But if so, she never said anything. When the guys found out, no one cared. I hated it so much that I couldn't believe they didn't care." He was babbling a bit, saying whatever his muddled memory pulled out of storage.

"They were your partners," I said. "They loved you."

Felix hung his head. A tear splashed into the leg of his jeans. When he looked up again, his face was a mask of misery and fear. "I just want it all to stop hurting, like before."

My heart beat a little faster. "Soon." Damn, I hated to play this card. "Felix, if you ever cared about Milo, or Tybalt, or Gina, you'll be honest with us."

He snarled, baring his fangs, and lunged. He didn't get far enough to make me jump—the restraints were too tight. "Fuck you, Stone. Don't tell me who I care about."

"You're a half-Blood, Felix. The depth of your feelings now means shit to me, but the man you were? The Hunter who died on that bus? He'd help us. You wanna die a monster or a man?"

He settled back in the chair, miserable. And also potentially pondering my words. He flexed his fingers, weeping palms leaving damp streaks on the wood arms, then curled his hands around the ends, as though he enjoyed the agony of the blisters.

"It's for them," I said, repeating the words he'd said to Wyatt. "You meant Kismet, Tybalt, and Milo, didn't you?"

Felix dropped his chin to his chest, shoulders tensing. It was as good as a verbal confirmation.

"Someone's threatening them if you don't keep your mouth shut about this Halfie collection. Am I right?"

"He promised they'd be safe."

Ding! "Who did?"

"I can't—"

"They're here in the Watchtower, Felix. We can protect them, but you have to tell me from who." He was so close to giving me the confirmation I needed but didn't want to hear. He just had to say Thackery's name. "Please, Felix."

A tear splashed onto his shirt, adding another damp spot to the muddle of fluids already present. "Two conditions?" he finally said.

"Ask."

"You finish what you started on the bus."

I jerked, startled by the request. Angry, agonized eyes met mine, and I could only stare back at him.

"I want *you* to kill me," he said.

My mouth felt like sand, and my stomach dropped to the floor. Son of a bitch. It was Alex's death all over again. He'd begged me to set him free and I put a bullet in the back of his head. *Fuck!*

"Fine. What's the other condition?"

"I'll only talk to you and Milo."

I balled my right hand into a fist and pressed it hard against my thigh to stave off an irrational need to punch something. "Has Milo come to see you?"

"No, none of them have."

"You think there's a good reason for that?"

"Yeah, but I . . . I need to say good-bye. I owe Milo that."

There it was—the reason we'd brought him back here in the first place. And now that he'd caught on, I was uncertain if the others would follow through. Milo had been incredibly hurt by Felix's infection for very personal reasons. Seeing him earlier in the corridor must have ripped the scab off a healing wound—if it had even scabbed over in the first place.

"I can't promise Milo," I said.

"Then anything I know about Walter Thackery dies with me."

Ding ding ding! We have a winner, ladies and gentle-

men! It was almost too easy, and now that Felix was talking, I needed to tread carefully. "What do you know about Thackery?" I asked.

"He's the one organizing us."

Cold fingers crept up my spine. "He threatened to kill Gina, Milo, and Tybalt so you wouldn't run to us and spill your guts?"

"Yes."

It made sense, but it also . . . didn't. We had the resources to keep them safe from Thackery, and yet the recent Therian kidnappings seemed to prove otherwise. I just couldn't help thinking there was more to it. A second, more powerful reason that Felix would be Thackery's lapdog. "What else does Thackery have on you?"

He glared. "Don't forget the price of admission."

Dammit.

The door clicked open. "Evy?" Wyatt asked. "Outside a minute?"

I followed him out, my mind reeling with the confirmation of Thackery's involvement in this. In the outer office, I asked, "Did either you or Marcus mention Thackery or the missing Therians to him?"

"No, we didn't," Wyatt said. "He knew on his own."

"Which means he was at the rave on purpose, as a distraction."

"Almost definitely, but that's not why—"

"Phineas is missing," Astrid said as she stormed into the jail's office. Every muscle rippled with annoyance. She looked like a prowling cat ready to pounce on the first prey that moved.

"Missing?" My heart nearly burst out of my chest. "How—?"

"He left the Watchtower without informing anyone. We've been watching his heat signature since his return from the country house, and not five minutes ago he flew off the grid."

"He left?"

"I just said that."

"Where the hell would he go?"

"Would he search on his own?" Wyatt asked.

"Maybe," I said, "but he'd tell someone first."

"Are you certain?" Astrid asked.

I threw my hands up, exasperated. "No, I'm not, Astrid. I'm his friend, not a telepath. He's angry and he feels responsible, and even Phineas isn't above doing something stupid when his emotions are running high." I glanced at Wyatt. "Would he go back to the condo?"

Phin owned a condo in Uptown. It was a lovely three-bedroom place in a private community. For a time, he'd shared it with Wyatt and Rufus St. James. Rufus was wounded badly several months ago, and those injuries left him with a great deal of pain and unable to walk without assistance, so he opted to use a wheelchair for ease of mobility. He'd also turned down several offers to join the Watch, so he continued living at the condo. Wyatt now lived here at the Watchtower, and Phin shuttled between the two.

"Maybe," Wyatt replied. "But if he did, I'm sure Rufus would—" As if on cue, Wyatt's cell phone rang. He pulled it out of his pocket, then showed me the I.D. Rufus. He flipped it open. "Is he there?"

I almost pinched Wyatt for not putting the call on speaker.

He nodded an affirmation—Phin was at the condo. "What's he doing?" A pause. "Try to keep him there. His family has been kidnapped and I don't—" He fell silent, listening. "Walter Thackery's involved, but we don't know why yet. Just try to keep him—Rufus?"

"What?" I asked, unable to stay silent any longer. This was a ridiculous way to manage a conversation.

Wyatt held up a shushing hand. "Rufus, what just

happened?" I was nearly reduced to tapping my foot by the time Wyatt said, "Okay, thanks" and hung up.

"Well?" Astrid and I said in stereo.

"He showed up on the condo balcony," Wyatt said. "Rufus let him in, and he went straight to his room, didn't say a word. Rufus called when he heard a lot of noise, like he was shoving stuff around, searching for something. Said Phin came out with a wooden box about the size of a loaf of bread, went back to the balcony, opened up the box, shifted back into an osprey, and flew off clutching whatever was inside the box in his talons."

"Rufus didn't see what he took out of the box?" I asked, shocked by the described actions.

Wyatt shook his head. "Said it was long and shiny. The inside of the box was lined with satin, and he said the construction looked old. No nails, just wooden joints. Could have held a knife or something similar."

We both looked at Astrid, who shrugged. "If that box's contents hold significance for Phineas or his Clan, I'm not aware of it," she said.

"Awesome." Wait. Significance for his Clan? It could very well be a waste of time, but . . . "I think I know where Phin went."

Wyatt insisted I not go alone or without weapons, so it was a good ten minutes later before we were in a Jeep and driving north. It was less than an hour until dawn, the streets quiet and thick with summer heat. We'd taken a real Jeep with the removable plastic roof and windows, and the hot air blasted us. I twisted my hair around one hand, wishing I'd thought to grab a rubber band or something.

We were crossing the Lincoln Street Bridge toward downtown when Wyatt asked, "Did you get to ask your question?"

"Huh?"

"Felix. You said you had to ask him something."

"Oh, no. I didn't." The conversation had abruptly changed when he brought Thackery into it. The kidnapped Therians and the Halfie army had to be connected somehow, and knowing Thackery's hatred of vampires and penchant for scientific experimentation, it probably wasn't good. We also knew that Thackery had been threatening Felix's loved ones to ensure his cooperation. In some ways, that spoke to Felix's level of sanity and control, but there had to be more.

"What was the question?"

I almost commented on curiosity and cats, but it would have been funny only if Marcus was around. Still, talking was better than awkward silences. "Back on the roof of the rave, I asked Felix how he was able to maintain his sanity, despite the infection."

"And?"

"He said he just did, but that's bullshit. There's something else, and I want to know what."

Wyatt turned onto Atlantic Avenue, which would take us north into the heart of Mercy's Lot. Our ultimate destination was just a bit farther south, on the border of the Lot and the rest of downtown. A place I used to know very, very well.

"Shit," Wyatt suddenly said.

I gave him a sharp look, but he didn't seem alarmed. "What is it?"

He glanced at me, a peculiar expression on his face. "What if Thackery developed some sort of serum that helps half-Bloods maintain their sanity? Like a Halfie Prozac or something? What if that's the other thing he's holding over Felix?"

A chill wrapped around my heart and squeezed. "If Thackery did that, he'd have loyal and sane Halfies at his disposal." And it made a horrific kind of sense, considering Thackery's need to be crowned World's Maddest Mad Scientist. "But why the body dumps?"

"Maybe they're failed experiments. Maybe the serum didn't work, so he killed them. We didn't collect samples from those body dumps. We'll never know if there was anything unusual in their physiology." He tapped his fingers against the steering wheel. "It's also possible that some of them refused to enlist in Thackery's private army, serum or not, so he had them disposed of."

"That's an awful lot of maybes and ifs, Wyatt."

"You know, that's usually my line."

"I'm serious."

"So am I." He reached out with his right hand and squeezed my arm. "The idea of it scares the shit out of me, too, Evy, but we both know what Thackery is capable of scientifically. We can't disregard the possibility."

I hated that he knew me so well. Walter Thackery and his experiments had been haunting my afterlife since the first time I ran into one of his hounds. His fingerprints covered every major event since my resurrection, and he'd been as difficult to capture as an eel in an oil slick. We were no match for him intellectually, and so far he'd had all kinds of hybrid monsters doing his physical dirty work. The Halfies were just another in a long line of victims.

Just like Wolf Boy had been. Discovering that an actual werewolf had been alive and well and moving freely in the city had thrown the Assembly into a tizzy. As a Clan, werewolves had supposedly gone extinct in the early sixteenth century. No one would tell me why ("It's Clan business, Stone, and it's need to know" was a favorite statement from Michael Jenner); they'd say only that werewolves had been bloodthirsty, nasty creatures with no desire to adapt and live among humans. They preferred wolf form, preferred the hunt, and offered no mercy to their prey.

That Thackery had one in his employ until I killed the kid during the destruction of Boot Camp . . . Well, it had the Assembly on the alert for signs of others popping up. So far, none had. But that didn't mean Wolf Boy was the only one Thackery knew about. Thackery never showed all his cards at once.

Wolf Boy, the hounds, the hybrids, his never-ending experiments—all served to remind me that Thackery was little more than a sociopath. And that he terrified me on the most basic of levels.

I squared my shoulders, more for me than Wyatt, because he couldn't really see it anyway. "I'm not disregarding the theory. Hiding from something until it goes away isn't my style, Wyatt."

"I know that. Just making sure you didn't forget."

The temptation to knuckle him in the arm was almost too strong to resist. Childish, maybe, but dammit, he still knew how to bring that out in me. He knew my buttons better than anyone. "So Thackery knows how to make Halfies less crazy, and he's now recruiting an army of them to do what?"

"The last six years of his life have been dedicated to curing vampirism in humans. He thought your blood would help."

"Yeah, I was there, thanks," I deadpanned.

He slowed for a left turn. "But it didn't, is my point. What if Thackery got to a place where he decided if you can't beat them, join them?"

"Fight fire with fire?"

"Whichever metaphor you want, yes. He could theoretically use those Halfies to attack the vampires. Look at how those Halfies fought for Tovin at Olsmill. They almost match full-Blood vampires in strength and speed. Their biggest flaw was being mostly bat shit insane."

"Which Thackery has taken care of."

"Exactly."

I dropped my face into the palms of my hands, mind racing. This was bad on so many levels. Granted, it was all fucking theory, but it was a damned good theory. All of the pieces fit, and it did make an awful kind of sense.

Wyatt's hand slid up my arm to squeeze my shoulder. "We're almost there."

I sat up. Familiar row homes and middle-class apartment buildings lined the rolling streets of this small slice of city halfway between the bustle of downtown and the desperate poverty of Mercy's Lot. Wyatt parked near a familiar telephone booth, within view of my destination.

"Hang here while I go look," I said.

He nodded, surprising me with his lack of protest at my wanting to go alone. "I'll call Astrid and let her in on our new theory."

"Okay."

I grabbed a spare pair of sweatpants from the backseat and climbed out. I walked up the inclined sidewalk toward an empty lot half a block long and nearly as deep. The last time I was here, the blackened rubble of a major apartment building fire still lay scattered in heaps and piles. In the intervening months, someone had cleared the lot of debris, leaving behind a cement foundation and an asphalt parking lot. All other evidence of the Sunset Terrace Apartments was gone, bulldozed away. Forgotten.

But not by everyone.

A familiar figure was sitting cross-legged a few dozen yards away, back to me, easy to spot even in the gloom of faraway streetlights. I approached slowly, taking noisy steps, allowing the gentle breeze to carry my scent to him. Phin turned his head when I closed in to less than ten feet, then looked away. It wasn't an invitation. It also wasn't a "get the hell away from me," so I took it as permission to come closer.

I sat next to him on the warm concrete, noting the knife-shaped object in his lap.

"Rufus called you," Phineas said.

"Yes."

"He's concerned."

"We all are, Phin. You left without telling anyone where you were going, and right now, we can't afford to let you out of our sight."

"Lest we lose the last of the Coni?"

"We haven't lost the others yet. They're just misplaced."

The corner of his mouth quirked. He looked at me full-on, and the simmering hatred in his blue eyes startled me. "Three stories up from this spot is where Jolene and I lived. After she died, I left Sunset Terrace and moved east, closer to the river. Remaining with the Clan only reminded me of the pain. I survived the massacre because I had turned my back on my people."

"If you'd been here, you'd have died, too, Phineas. And who would have protected Aurora and Joseph when they needed you?"

His nostrils flared. He looked away, over the landscape of cement.

"What is this?" I asked. "I've never seen you play the self-pity card."

"I prefer to think of it as self-reflection." He lifted the object in his lap—a knife. Fourteen inches from hilt to tip, it gleamed a reflective gold. The blade curved to both sides, divided like a trident missing its center prong. Intricate patterns and swirls decorated the base of the blade where both halves came together, and the handle appeared to be some sort of smooth bone carved with similar patterns.

It looked deadly.

"I told you once that the Coni were a warrior race," he said. "Centuries ago, we left behind our savage ways and embraced peace. We chose a life among humans rather than as mythical beings apart from others. We were one of the first Clans to integrate. One of the first to propose what is now the Assembly."

"Do you think the Fey are punishing you for that?" I asked.

"They punished us for being powerful, and because it played well with their other plans. Two hundred and twelve of us were Coni, Evy. We were a force to reckon with, even against the Fey's magic. To anger all of the bi-shifting Clans at once? The Fey would stand no chance in a direct battle." He snorted. "As if they would dirty themselves to fight their own battles."

He had a point. I'd never seen a sprite outside First Break without the use of a human avatar. A few faeries, yes, but they were less powerful than their fellow Fey. Demanding that the Triads destroy the Coni and Stri Clans could have ended with humans and Therians at each others' metaphorical throats, on the edge of open war. It hadn't (by some miracle), which threw a lovely monkey wrench into the sprites' plans. Left them scrambling and improvising, which they don't do well.

"What's the knife for, Phin?" I asked.

"Until about five centuries ago, our elite guard carried them as symbols of their status. Only a few survived, and one has been passed through my line. The others were destroyed during the fire."

I studied the gold knife and its twin blades—one for each branch of the Clan. Coni and Stri, separate and together. Its age surprised me.

"For me, this is no longer about the Watchtower or the city's best interests," Phin said, his voice cold. "It's about my Clan. I will do whatever it takes to find them and bring them home."

"I know you will. So will I."

"Walter Thackery will die by this blade."

As much as I wanted to argue and lay claim to killing Thackery, I didn't. Phin hadn't said who would wield that blade, after all, which left all sorts of things open for interpretation. "We have to find him first," I said.

"Something tells me we won't have to wait long."

"Oh yeah?"

"Yes." He turned his head slightly, giving me three-quarters of his profile. "Don't react, but we are being watched."

I tensed. "Wyatt's in the car."

"The opposite direction, about two o'clock."

Damn him and his Therian eyesight. All I made out in the shadows between two faraway streetlights was a dark blob. "What is it?"

"A wolf."

Terrific.

Chapter Nine

I tried swallowing, only my mouth had gone dry. "Just one?"

"So far," Phin replied. "He's upwind and making no effort to disguise his presence. Larger than your average wolf." His nostrils flared. "I know that scent."

"Wolf Boy?"

"Yes."

"Shit." I still couldn't make it out, and really, really hoped that Wyatt stayed put inside the Jeep. Werewolves moved damned fast; it could cross the distance between us in seconds. I had a pair of knives strapped one to each ankle and a switchblade in my rear pocket. I'd also been up close and personal with a werewolf, and I remembered its thick, sturdy muscles. Killing one with a single knife hadn't been easy.

"I'm going to stand up. Stay put."

"Okay."

He handed me his knife, then drew up slowly. I kept my eyes far away from his naked ass as he did so, then held up the sweats when he asked for them. He got them on without incident or warning, which I took as a good sign. Maybe the new wolf was just there to spy on us.

"Slowly now," Phin whispered, extending his hand. I took it.

We both heard the low growl—from the opposite direction.

"It's at your seven o'clock," he said.

The Jeep. I looked. I couldn't fucking help it. The Jeep was barely visible, a good thirty yards away, and in between the circles of light. Smack in the middle of the light nearest the Jeep was the second werewolf, its gray coat glistening, hackles raised, attention fixed—on a Jeep with zero protection in the form of a roof or windows. Wyatt sat perfectly still behind the wheel, though I had no doubt he was preparing to summon some sort of weapon.

"Can you teleport over there?" Phin asked.

"Yes." Easily.

"Weapons?"

"Got 'em."

I was standing now. A third growl, distinctly different from the first two, echoed behind us. Three of them, and they had us surrounded. *Fan-fucking-tastic.*

"Can you teleport to safety?"

"Not the way they're spread out," I said. No matter which way I went, I'd be too close to one of the wolves.

"I can fly you out."

"Then they'll just attack Wyatt."

The first wolf stepped into a pool of light. Its black-and-white pelt gleamed and its eyes seemed to wink. It came a few steps forward, head low, no longer showing teeth. I calculated how quickly I could pull out the switchblade. As the wolf drew closer, Phin's wings appeared. He kept them tucked close to his back, prepared without showing outward aggression.

The other two wolves hadn't moved; Wyatt remained still.

At less than ten feet away, the black-and-white wolf shifted. The familiar, faint tingle of Break power crawled over my skin. I passed the fancy Coni blade back to

Phin, who held it loosely by his thigh. Any direct threat from us would get someone killed quickly.

A teenage boy continued walking toward us, a mirror image of Wolf Boy—same narrow build, blond hair, and flashing silver eyes, right down to the straight point of his nose. Hatred hung around him like a bad smell, almost a physical presence. He stopped an arm's length from Phin. He had no weapons in his hands and was completely naked—but I had no doubt he was the most dangerous person in our threesome.

The two males sized each other up, observing and assessing in such a blatantly alpha, testosterone-coated manner that I wanted to crack their heads together. I couldn't check on the other two wolves without taking my attention away from the boy in front of us, and I desperately wanted to make sure that Wyatt was okay.

"Coni." The boy's maturing voice cracked despite his attempt to appear menacing, and he spoke as if those four letters tasted foul in his mouth.

"Lupa," Phin replied, his voice just as frigid.

"Surprised to see us alive?"

"I was surprised last month when the first Lupa showed his ugly face, but like most vermin, where there's one—"

The teen growled deep in his chest—a God-awful sound from someone who looked so young. So human. "Your ancestors failed to destroy us centuries ago, and their failure will be your undoing."

I laughed out loud; I couldn't help it. The spy-movie villain dialogue was just too much. The slip earned me a nasty snarl from Teen Wolf, as well as a flash of elongated canine teeth.

"You," he said. "You killed our brother. You will bleed for that."

"I've bled enough for both my lifetimes, thanks." Okay, so sassing him was probably not the best use of my time, but the entire thing felt ridiculous. Until a few weeks ago, werewolves didn't exist, and here I was having a big, bad showdown with one who looked like the Before side of an acne cream commercial.

Then the rest of what he'd said caught up to me. *Your ancestors failed to destroy us.* The Coni had been an elite guard. A warrior race. The Coni destroyed the Lupa Clan.

"How did you survive?" Phin asked.

Teen Wolf grinned, showing off those nasty teeth. "By the mercy of the Great People. We have been protected these centuries, prepared for a time when the Great People will retake this world and the Lupa can claim their place in it."

"The Great People?"

"Yes."

My heart slammed against my ribs as one more awful puzzle piece clicked into place. A puzzle we'd started to put together mere hours after the massacre at Boot Camp last month. "He means the Fey," I said.

Phin gave no reaction to my statement. "How many of you are there?"

The boy laughed. "You are truly arrogant to believe I'd reveal such a thing. It would ruin the grand surprise."

"Is Walter Thackery working directly for the Fey Council?" I asked.

"Not to his knowledge."

It was an evasive answer, which led me to believe that Thackery didn't know where his assistance was coming from. But whether or not he knew or cared mattered little to me. Thackery's Halfie army had to be stopped, just as the potential legion of werewolves had to be found and contained before a real war broke out. A big, bloody war that would encompass the entire city.

"Why are you here?" I asked. "To gloat before you kill us?"

"Unfortunately, our orders are not to kill you," Teen Wolf replied with real regret in his voice.

"Let me guess, then. We have one chance to accept an offer to join you or else suffer the consequences?"

"Hardly. We neither need nor want your partnership."

Huh. "What, then?"

"I wanted to look you both in the eye before we met on the battlefield. I want you both to know the face of the man who will kill you."

"Oh yeah?" I made a show of looking around. "Is he here?"

Teen Wolf snapped his teeth at me.

Phin touched my elbow. "And when shall we meet on this battlefield?" he asked.

"Soon enough," Teen Wolf replied. "The world stands balanced on the edge of a razor blade. All it requires is one final push to change everything."

I flexed my right hand and shifted my stance—just enough to get his attention. "Why wait? Let's throw down, kid."

He tensed, eyes glimmering with bloodlust. He was considering it, and if it wasn't for some confounding loyalty to his master, he probably would have. Instead, he quirked a cocky eyebrow at me. "Soon. Enjoy your final days."

"Uh-huh."

Teen Wolf backed up several steps. He shifted quickly, brown and silver hair coating once-pink skin, back bending, arms and legs changing shape. Only his silver eyes seemed to stay the same—angry, intelligent, hungry. He snarled, and the wolf behind us made an answering sound. I hazarded a look; it was moving away.

Instinct yelled at me to not let them escape. They were enemies, and enemies had to be dealt with before they became a problem later. And these three wolves (plus any others that they had hidden away) were sure to be a huge problem in the near future. Walter Thackery did not make idle threats, and if something was about to happen, I had to believe it would. Something huge.

And werewolves existed. Holy shit.

"When they're out of sight—" I started, whispering.

"I'll follow them," Phin finished.

Teen Wolf was nearly to the far edge of the vacant lot. He paused and dipped his head low to the ground. Only then did I think to check on the third wolf—just in time to hear the shout.

The third wolf leapt onto the hood of the Jeep and springboarded right over the windshield. I was already running when Wyatt yelled. A cold splash of panic overrode my ability to properly access my tether to the Break and teleport. All I saw was the furry back hunched in the front seat of the Jeep. Wyatt hadn't made another sound and, more than anything else, that terrified me. I opened the switchblade as I ran.

The wolf squealed and leapt out of the Jeep. It stumbled on the pavement, turned, and raced down the street in the same direction the other wolves had gone. I paused long enough to shift my hold on the switchblade, hoping to throw it, but the damned wolf was too fucking fast.

"Wyatt!"

At first, all I saw was the blood. It drenched the front seat, as well as Wyatt's face and clothes. He was folded into the floor, moderately protected by the steering wheel, a red-coated knife still clutched in his hand. My nose told me that the majority of the blood in the Jeep wasn't human—it was darker, had a heavy, earthy odor—but the rest of me took a bit longer to catch up.

I yanked open the passenger door and climbed inside, hands shaking, adrenaline a bitter taste in my mouth. "Wyatt? Where are you hurt?"

"Fucker got my neck and arm," he replied. His gaze

swept over me, checking for nonexistent injuries. "You okay?"

"I'm fine. They didn't attack us."

"Phineas?"

I scanned the lot and nearby streets, but all was quiet. No sign of Phin or the wolves, no sounds of nearby brawls. "He followed the wolves," I said, both pissed that he'd disappeared and grateful that he hadn't let them get away without a tail (no pun intended).

"What did they want?"

I explained the conversation we'd had with Teen Wolf while I helped him unwedge himself from the floor. Three long gashes went from just below his right ear all the way to his collarbone, each nearly as wide as my pinkie, each oozing blood. The lack of gushing was a good sign that the wolf had missed his carotid artery. His left arm looked just as painful—a deep bite circled his forearm, and even below the mixed blood, the skin looked swollen and tender.

"You need to get those looked at," I said as I climbed back out of the Jeep and patted the passenger seat. "Scoot."

"This side's soaked with blood," he said.

"I don't care. You can't drive like that."

"You don't have a license."

"Are we really having this conversation while you're sitting there bleeding?"

He blinked, already a little glassy-eyed. He was pale and breathing through his mouth. Those wounds had to hurt like hell. "Good point."

He slid over. I circled the Jeep and climbed into the driver's side, trying to ignore the wet seat and the stink all around me. The summer heat and humidity were not helping matters, and my stomach curled in on itself. I rustled someone's dirty T-shirt out of the backseat and helped Wyatt wrap that around his arm.

"Guess you got the wolf pretty good," I said once we were on the road and pointed south.

"Right in the stomach, I think. Why?"

"Uh, because his blood's all over the place?"

Wyatt shook his head, then winced. "No, I mean why did they attack me and not you two?"

Good question. "Teen Wolf didn't seem too keen on starting anything today, so I don't know why he'd let one of them bite and run."

"To prove a point?"

"Which is what? We've got bigger teeth than you?"

"Well, that point's definitely taken."

I snorted. More and more cars were joining us as the city's nightlife went to sleep and the rest of the world woke up. Heading out for their morning coffee and donut, oblivious to the trouble heading their way. A whole lot of shit was about to hit the metaphorical fan, and this time I didn't know if we could stop it.

Halfway back to the Watchtower, Wyatt's cell rang. He shifted his hip, and I reached over and retrieved the phone from his back pocket, noting the way his mouth pinched in the corners. He was in pain and trying hard to not show it.

The I.D. read "Marcus." "Stone," I said.

"Did you find Phineas?" he asked without preamble.

"Yeah, right where I thought he'd be."

"Is he with you?"

"No, he's probably flying over the city, tracking down a trio of werewolves."

"He's what?"

I gave Marcus the condensed version, and ended with, "Have Dr. Vansis standing by in the infirmary. Wyatt's injured."

"What happened?"

"One of the wolves tried to take a bite out of him. He's conscious and aware, but he's bleeding a lot."

Wyatt made a face that might have been humorous if I wasn't so worried about him.

"I'll send someone to wake him," Marcus replied.

"We'll be there in less than ten minutes. Let me know if you hear anything from Phin."

"I will."

I tucked the phone into my own pocket and nearly missed my turn onto Lincoln Street. We passed a woman with six dogs of various sizes on leashes practically yanking her down the street while she listened to someone on her earbud. Oblivious.

"Evy?"

The shakiness in Wyatt's voice caught my attention immediately. He was beyond pale, the smudges of blood on his cheeks like berry stains on a white napkin. Perspiration trickled down his temples and cheeks. He stared straight ahead, but he wasn't watching the street.

I touched his shoulder, my wheel hand shaking lightly.

"I'm going to be sick."

Common sense would have had me stop so he could hurl onto the sidewalk. But terror slammed my foot down on the gas and, ignoring the chances of being pulled over by an observant city cop, I sped over the bridge. Wyatt grabbed the dash with both hands, breathing hard through his mouth, eyes shut.

"Be sick if you have to, but I am not stopping," I said, as much to clarify my own racing thoughts as to reassure him. "You need to get to the doctor right now."

"Feels so weird."

"What does?"

"Me. Hot. Uh—" He jerked sideways and leaned over the Jeep door, head out. The sounds of retching were lost to the wind roaring around us. I gripped the wheel with both hands as I navigated through the East Side, south along the Black River to the mall.

A thought hit me with horrifying clarity: Wyatt was

infected with something. Or poisoned, probably by the werewolf's bite. I'd had a minor reaction to my own werewolf bites a month ago, but they had healed quickly. Because I healed quickly. Wyatt didn't.

I'd never heard of a human being having such a violent reaction to a Therian bite, but the Lupa had been extinct for centuries. And they'd come back to us courtesy of Walter Thackery, King of Genetic Meddling.

God only knew what those wolves were carrying.

"We're almost there," I said. "Stay with me, Wyatt."

His only answer was a loud groan.

I zipped across the Capital City Mall parking lot, making tracks for the entrance to the Watchtower at a dangerous speed. I hit the brakes at the last minute as I went through the barrier and nearly clipped a parked car. All thoughts of procedure flew out of my head, and I just kept going. I drove right down the short hall that spilled into the broader mall corridor. It was wide enough for two cars to drive side by side and still have room for a third to pass them.

A handful of familiar faces sprang out of my path. It wasn't very far to the infirmary, and I hit the brakes again and swore I smelled them burning. I didn't even turn off the engine, just shifted into park and tumbled out the driver's-side door.

"Dr. Vansis!" I shouted as I circled to Wyatt's side of the Jeep. "I need help!"

Wyatt was slumped over the passenger door, head lolling. He hadn't passed out, but he wasn't completely conscious, either. His pale skin burned with a fever I could feel without touching him, and sweat had soaked through his shirt.

"What happened?" Dr. Vansis asked. He shouldered me sideways, and if he had been anyone else, I'd have reacted way more violently. The doc was of average height and build, with curly multihued brown hair and a prickly personality, but he wasn't my enemy.

"Werewolf attack," I said. "Maybe fifteen, twenty minutes ago."

Dr. Vansis gaped at me. "You're serious?" My glare stopped any more questions. "All right. Hold his head while I open the door."

A small crowd of gawkers watched us get Wyatt over Vansis's shoulder in a fireman's carry and take him into the infirmary. His actions seemed effortless, but all Therians had a way of surprising me with their hidden strength. He deposited Wyatt on the exam table and turned on a bright overhead light.

"He has gashes on his neck and a big bite on his left arm," I said. The wounds were fairly obvious, but all the extra blood could be confusing. "He got the wolf pretty good before it ran off."

"The Lupa blood could be what's irritating his wounds," Dr. Vansis said.

"Does that happen a lot?"

"To my knowledge, Lupa have been extinct for centuries."

"Then why—?"

"It's a theory, child," he snapped as he examined the wounds on Wyatt's arm. "I once saw a vampire react rather violently when she accidentally drank from a Cania, so there is grounds for it. But humans rarely react to Therian blood, and certainly not this badly."

The infirmary door burst open, depositing Kismet and Marcus into the room. And if Kismet looked half as freaked as I did, I had to be a sight.

"There's something wrong with him," I said.

"Is he going to live?" she asked.

"I don't know," Dr. Vansis replied before I could. "Everyone out. I need to examine him and run some tests."

I took a step toward him. "But—"

"Out!"

Marcus steered me into the corridor, where I promptly fell back against the storefront wall and collapsed onto my ass. My heart hammered against my ribs, and I felt sick. Kismet crouched in front of me and rested her hands on my knees.

"Are you hurt?" she asked.

"No, they didn't come after me. Just Wyatt."

"Why?"

"I don't know. What about Phin?"

"Nothing yet," Marcus said. He was tense, coiled, as though his jaguar form was waiting just below the surface, ready to spring free and pounce.

"Anything else from Felix?"

Kismet shook her head. "No, and I don't think we'll get anything else out of him now."

"Why?"

"I've tried, Tybalt's tried. We even floated your Serenity Serum theory past him with no response. The only person he wants to see is Milo, and Milo refuses to go in that room."

I wanted to pretend I was surprised, or even upset at Milo's unwillingness to face his former Triad partner, but I wasn't. I'd once witnessed a friend in a similar position, and I couldn't imagine the horror of seeing someone you loved going through that.

"You know why he won't do it," she said.

"Yeah, I know."

"Well, I don't," Marcus said.

Milo told me about it the day Felix was infected. In some ways, I'd expected the confession. I wasn't completely oblivious to the people around me. But it wasn't something for me to share with Marcus.

"Why the blue hell is there a Jeep in the corridor?" Astrid's question boomed down the hall. She stalked toward us with long, angry strides; Isleen followed, taking shorter, more precise steps to keep up with the almost-sprinting were-cat.

Kismet stood and shifted closer to Marcus.

"My fault," I said, still sitting. Now that my adrenaline was wearing off, I hadn't yet mustered the energy to get up.

"When Phineas called, he said someone might be injured," Astrid said.

"You spoke to Phin?" Hope bloomed in my chest, and I sat up a little straighter.

"Just a moment ago, yes."

"Did he track the werewolves?"

She gave me a critical eyeballing. "He lost two of them in Mercy's Lot but managed to backtrack and find the injured third. He's holding it in a secure location until Baylor's squad can get there."

An osprey was holding a wounded werewolf captive. Sometimes my life was too strange, even for me.

"What location?" Marcus asked.

"He mentioned the trunk of a parked car."

"They can't interrogate the wolf in a car," I said.

Astrid gave me the look that impatient teachers give their dumbest students. "Once the Lupa is secure, he'll be brought back here for interrogation."

"No way." I mimicked her expression. "Those wolves are working with Walter Thackery. Teen Wolf admitted it to my face, and if Thackery loves anything, it's to keep track of his toys. He tracks his hounds and his hybrids, and he probably tracks the wolves, too." Just because Astrid's people hadn't found a tracking device on the wolf I killed at Boot Camp, didn't mean these guys were clean.

"Evangeline is correct," Isleen said, inclining her head in my direction. "It would be decidedly unwise to bring the Lupa back to the Watchtower."

Something niggled at the back of my mind like a fire alarm in a faraway building.

"Okay, you're right," Astrid said. "I'll have Baylor find someplace in the city to interrogate the wolf. And to be on guard for possible tails to their location. Now, do you want to tell us what happened on your end, Stone?"

"Fuck me." It hit all at once, a wall of ice water that turned my guts inside out. *No, no, no, no. . . .*

"Stone?"

I don't know who said it, because I was on my feet and running. Trying to outrace the panic of having done something so fucking stupid—unable to believe we were all capable of such obvious idiocy. Someone was following me, and I probably looked like a crazy person racing down the corridor in bloody clothes. No one, thankfully, was stupid enough to try to stop me.

Nevada was sitting on top of his desk chatting with Morgan, who was seated in the desk's actual chair. They both gave surprised squawks when I slammed through the jail door.

"I need in there right-fucking-now," I said, pointing at the interrogation room.

Nevada took in my state, then leapt off the desk. "What's going on?"

"Please, just open the door."

Maybe it was me using "please," which rarely happens. Or someone with actual power to order him around came into the jail behind me and silently gave him permission. I don't know, and I didn't care. Nevada punched in the door code, and the lock snicked back.

I gave little consideration to just how terrible Felix looked after his long exposure to the wooden chair and whatever creative interrogation methods Marcus and Wyatt had used. He was about to be very, very dead anyway. He watched me with bleary eyes and a sad half smile, as if he knew exactly why I was there.

I plucked a slim wooden spike off the table behind him, circled around to his front, and drove it as hard as I could into his right thigh. He shrieked. Saliva sputtered from his lips. I pressed the spike down harder until he started to cry.

"You son of a bitch," I growled, getting in his face. "Is he tracking you?"

A flash of clarity stole through his agony, and Felix nodded.

"Thackery is tracking you?"

Another nod.

I swallowed back bile. "What's the plan, Felix? We go after you, bring you back here, and Thackery sends his werewolf army to tear us down in our own head-quarters?"

He lifted his head, clearly astonished by some part of my accusation. His leaky nostrils flared. "You smell like them."

"That's because one of them tried to kill Wyatt to-night, so he returned the favor by slicing its guts open. Now what's the plan?"

"I don't know."

"Really?" I yanked out the spike, then slammed it down into his left thigh.

He jerked forward, snapping at my throat even as he squealed; I leaned just out of reach. "I was there to re-cruit; I wasn't supposed to get caught!"

"Bullshit. What's the fucking plan, Felix?"

"I don't know!"

"Tell me what you know."

"I can't!"

"There are a dozen more spikes on that table, Felix. You know you're going to die today. How many holes do you want before we end this?"

He closed his eyes. Tears feathered his lashes and ran down his blotchy cheeks. Judging by the blood on the floor and the cuts on his exposed skin, he wasn't as upset about the pain as the emotions warring inside him. The little bit of humanity still lingering in his brain as opposed to the instinctive rage of the vampire infection.

"I don't know what he's doing with the werewolves, Evy, I swear," he said. "Just that they're freely loyal to him."

"How many does he have?"

"I don't know. I've only interacted with one."

"When?"

"The night I was infected. He was sent to follow you. He saw the bus crash, then followed me. He took me to Thackery." His voice cracked and his iridescent eyes begged me for mercy—something I wasn't about to give. Not now. Not when he'd walked into our home wearing the equivalent of a police wire.

I believed him, though. So far. "How do you control the bloodlust, Felix? What's Thackery giving you?"

"What's that sound?"

"The voices in your head? Sorry, pal, they're all yours."

"Something else." He shrank into his chair, curling forward like someone with a severe stomach cramp. The oddest look crossed his face, as though he suddenly understood the punch line to a frightening joke. "Goddammit. You should have killed me."

"Give me time. I promised, right?"

"It's too late."

"You're not going anywhere." The look on his face said he thought otherwise, and a cold knot of dread squeezed my heart. "Felix?"

"This is wrong."

"Now that's a fucking understatement," said a familiar voice that got our collective attention. Milo stood just inside the interrogation room, stone-faced, arms pulled so tightly across his chest that they seemed ready to snap. Marcus hovered just behind him.

Felix jerked upright, unable to move far thanks to his bonds, but struggling nonetheless. "You came now?"

Milo took a step backward and hit Marcus's chest. His expression shifted from cold to furious. "I didn't want to come, but Marcus told me you're being tracked. You bastard!"

"It wasn't my idea."

"Of course not. You're the victim, right? Poor crazy Halfie?"

"I was trying to protect you."

"By leading Thackery right to our doorstep?" Milo came forward, stopping next to me. "What the hell do you want from me, Felix?"

"Get out of here."

Milo made a choking sound. "Oh, so now you want me to leave? Fuck you."

"It's not a tracker." Felix's face pinched, and he doubled over again as far as his restraints allowed. "Get the fuck out of here!"

The hair on the back of my neck prickled as Felix's words rang in my head. If he hadn't been given a tracker, then what? Something was very, very wrong. Milo moved toward him. I grabbed Milo's arm and pulled him back. Gave him a hard shove toward the door.

"Marcus, get him out of here," I said.

"Should have never brought me here," Felix said. "So sorry." He looked up, his youthful face twisted in pain. "Run."

"What is Thackery giving you?" I needed this answer, dammit.

"Get out!"

"What is it?"

"Blood."

"What?"

"What's that sound?" someone asked in a terrible mirror of Felix's earlier words, just as a second person yelled, "Stone!"

I was grabbed around the waist and hauled through the interrogation room door. A sharp whine cut through the voices, followed by a high-pitched beep. Felix looked right at me, tears streaking his face, and then he exploded.

Chapter Ten

Wednesday, July 2
The East Side

The handshake agreement establishing a three-way police force among humans, vampires, and Therians became an official arrangement the day after Boot Camp's
destruction and subsequent evacuation. Every Handler,
Hunter, and trainee was given a choice to join or leave.
In the end, we all said yes to joining, and we began as-
similating on Wednesday.

"Seriously? This is your headquarters?"

I blurt it out as Wyatt drives into the parking lot of the
defunct Capital City Mall, through what has to be a
magical barrier of some sort because it tickles the back
of my mind in the place I've come to associate with my
tether to the Break. Kismet and Milo are in the backseat
of the nondescript sedan that's so unlike what I'm used
to seeing Wyatt drive. I don't know what I expected
when he said the Watchtower was on the East Side near
the Black River, but this isn't it.

It isn't so much the fact that, the last time I was here,
I was attacked by well-organized Halfies and saw two
Hunters murdered. It isn't even the fact that this mall,
abandoned fifteen years ago when a new one opened
across town, protects a Sanctuary. I can even kind of
look past the knowledge that Chalice Frost, the woman

whose body I now inhabit, was born here on this very hot spot.

No, the thing that makes my palms sweat is what happened in the Sanctuary when Isleen brought me here the first time. She used a vampire meditation technique to help me remember the days leading up to my death—tortured mercilessly at the hands of the goblin Queen, taken apart bit by bit. It all came back at once in a crushing rush of emotion and pain. Alex had been there to hold me, let me cry it out. My last moments with him before he was infected by the vampire parasite are entwined with this place, as are the last moments of my old life.

Living and working here feels like a cruel joke.

Wyatt drives through the weedy parking lot, aiming for the interior of the U-shaped mall's curve. Any remains of the helicopter that exploded here months ago is gone, cleaned up as though it never happened. Just as Isleen had, Wyatt drives straight through the illusion of a wall.

Inside is a host of other vehicles—cars, sport utilities, pickup trucks, and vans—all parked in the lot once occupied by several hollowed-out restaurants (if memory serves). Walls are knocked down, carpet is ripped up, and lines are painted on the bare cement floors. I must be gaping at the impressive utilization of space because Wyatt grins at me as he parks.

"So far I'm impressed," Kismet says with a hint of awe in her voice. "How do you keep folks from seeing you drive through a wall?"

"The entire perimeter is protected by a barrier spell," Wyatt replies. "Makes it impossible for someone outside it to look straight at the mall, and it kind of urges them to stay away. Think of it like a magical repellent."

"Human bug spray," I say.

He nods.

"And if they somehow cross the barrier?" Kismet asks.

"Then security deals with them," he replies.

I can imagine what that means. Overall the location is perfect. It's in the middle of an older part of town that is mostly abandoned, so traffic is light enough to not cause us many problems. We're also in the middle of a sea of pavement and construction, and I have no doubt the foundation has been reinforced with tar—precautions against bridge trolls, who are part of the earth and known to form in unfinished cement. They also answer to the Fey, and I hate the idea that Smedge, a troll I once considered a friend, is now my enemy.

We tumble out of the car and follow Wyatt on a tour of our new home.

The original tiled corridor is still intact, leading us to an intersection and an old fountain lit by a skylight. The fountain holds a variety of plants and herbs, all new and alive. The entire mall is freshly scrubbed and carries the scents of food, new paint, and cut wood, as well as the distant sounds of construction and voices. The long corridor is clear of kiosks and benches. To the right and all the way down is the old food court. To the left, halfway down and tucked into a service corridor, is the Sanctuary.

"The food court's been modified," Wyatt says, jacking his thumb over his shoulder even as he leads us in the opposite direction. "We combined some of the kitchens, walled off the others, and now have a working cafeteria. The windows are all blacked out, but Kyle's a good artist and he's been painting some murals in his spare time."

A were-dog who paints. What are the odds?

It's probably good that I keep the thought to myself because the muralist in question pops out of a storefront and waves.

"Astrid was just asking if you were here yet," he says, his voice echoing down the corridor.

"Just got here," Wyatt replies. "Does she need something?"

"I don't think so, but I'll let her know you've arrived." He disappears as quickly as he came, back into the storefront.

Wyatt leads us straight for it.

Both stores on either side have been blacked out. The center was probably a trendy clothing store at one time, with a blacked-out glass exterior and an entrance the size of a pair of double doors. We follow Wyatt inside. All three stores have been combined into one huge space. To our left, partitioned by a row of folding screens, is a long conference table and chairs. At least a dozen people—Therian and vampire—move around, doing their work and ignoring us.

"Welcome to Operations," Wyatt says. "The name's pretty self-explanatory."

It is. I can't help being impressed by what they've pulled together in less than a month, and this is only one room.

Kyle appears with Astrid in tow. She gives each of us—me, Kismet, Milo—a careful once-over that's assessing without being violating. To Wyatt she asks, "Where's Mr. Baylor?"

"Coming in with Leah," he replies. "They'll be along in about an hour."

She frowns. I don't think she's happy with the decision to make Adrian Baylor the human representative in the leadership trifecta, but it's a compromise that secured the loyalty of the rest of the Handlers and their Hunters. Kismet didn't want it, and several folks, led by Sharpe, objected to placing Wyatt in charge, given his record of recent behavior. Wyatt seemed annoyed at first but quickly adapted to the idea. Baylor is a good leader, and he knows better than to try to control Wyatt.

"The construction materials you requested will arrive shortly," Astrid says.

"For the maze?" Wyatt asks, a spark of excitement in his voice.

"Yes."

"Maze?" Kismet says.

He turns to her, smiling. "Remember how you helped us design the obstacle course we used at Boot Camp? You gave us all those ideas from your Army training."

"Yeah?"

"We're going to do the same thing in the old Sears building, at the west end of the mall." The delight in his voice is amusing and something I haven't heard in a long time. "Actually, I was hoping you'd take a look at the plans and give me your input."

Kismet's eyebrows arch. "Sure, okay."

He strides to a computer several desks away, then waves her over. She hesitates, then goes, tossing a look over her shoulder that clearly says she didn't think he meant right now. Astrid wanders off. I glance at Milo, and his expression mirrors what my own must be. *Now what?*

We're some of the first humans to be brought inside the Watchtower—I'm not crazy about the name, but it works—and I'm not a hundred percent comfortable wandering around on my own. Yet.

A shadow shifts behind me, and I spin. Marcus stands close by, hands tucked casually in the pockets of his well-fitted jeans. His black hair, usually tied back, is loose and hangs well below his shoulders. He smiles, glinting eyes shifting back and forth between us before settling on Milo. "Would you two be interested in a guided tour?" he asks.

"Yeah, I guess," Milo replies. He's even more tense than I am.

"Definitely," I amend. Marcus and Astrid have a history with Tybalt—whose inclusion in this little unit was part of Kismet's terms of agreement—and I'm insanely curious about it. Tybalt told me once that he chose his name because of its Shakespeare association. Prince of Cats. Knowing that both Marcus and Astrid are Felia is a fascinating clue into the life of a Hunter with whom I've become friends, despite our violent history.

In the main corridor, a quartet of black-clad vampires strides past us, practically marching in step, heading toward the east end of the mall. One gives Marcus a cursory nod; the rest ignore us.

"That was slightly awkward," Milo says.

"As it will continue to be for a while longer," Marcus replies. "Our three peoples aren't natural allies."

"Good point."

"We don't have much at the west end yet," he says, pointing without leading. "Two stores are being used as a gymnasium, as well as a room for physical combat training. We have a good amount of equipment already set up and are expecting more. In time, the department store will be redesigned as an obstacle course, but for now it's simply under construction."

"Segregated gym?" I ask.

His nostrils flare. "No, all are welcome to use it."

"Awesome."

"The Sanctuary is also this way, as you probably know, Miss Stone."

"Good lord, please call me Evy or Stone. Not Miss." It makes me feel like a schoolteacher.

"The vampires keep a guard on the Sanctuary at all times. Not that I suspect you'd have any reason to access it, but I'm informing you nonetheless."

"Appreciated."

"Most of the activity happens on the east end right now." He leads us in that direction. The first entrance on the opposite side of Operations has a fancy keypad next to a heavy, reinforced door. "This is weapons storage. Only a handful of people have the lock code, although I expect you'll both be given it at some point."

Nice to have his vote of confidence.

As we walk, I notice that some of the store windows are papered over. A few are open and in various stages of construction. Marcus doesn't comment on what they'll eventually be used for, and I don't ask. Some tour guide. We near the end of the corridor, where it turns ninety degrees to the right. Straight ahead is the food court, and even from here I can see the rows of tables and booths, neatly ordered and clean, and half a dozen people seated.

"This is the Rec Room," Marcus says, pointing to the left. "Right now it's two rooms, one of which has a television for playing games and the other for movies. We're working on a library for those who prefer quieter methods of relaxation."

"Cool," Milo says, peeking inside.

"Here on the right are the vampire quarters."

I quirk an eyebrow at this.

"Before you ask, they asked for the separate quarters," Marcus says. "Vampires require very little sleep compared to our two peoples, and they prefer much cooler climates when they rest."

"Sounds reasonable," I say.

The vampire quarters seemed to take up two stores, one entrance facing our corridor, the other down the east wing. Marcus goes this way. The remaining stores on both sides are sealed over with a single entrance on either side of the corridor. He points at the side neighboring the food court.

"Quarters for everyone else," he says. "They're divided into walled units that currently house two sets of bunk beds each, and curtains acting as doorways. There isn't much in the way of privacy. It's very dormitory-style."

Milo catches my eye and we're probably thinking the same thing—Boot Camp. The setup for trainees there was very similar to this, living on top of each other knowing you'd probably have to kill your roommate in order to graduate alive. It's also very similar to Juvie, and that makes my insides squirm.

"We're working on more private quarters for those of us with higher ranks, but it's not a priority at the moment," he continues. "There are still quite a few empty rooms, though, so pick one and enjoy it while it lasts.

"Showers and toilets are across the hall there." He tilts his head toward the storefront on the other side, this one carefully covered over to create privacy. "It's been the largest project so far, what with installing all that plumbing and putting down sealed cement. But don't worry, it's not a group shower."

My sense of relief at this news is palpable. "Thank God for that."

Marcus grins. "I can't imagine you have anything to be ashamed of."

"No, just a missing finger and too many visible ribs," I deadpan. My appetite is mostly back, but even on my high-protein, carb-heavy diet, the weight isn't packing back on as quickly as I'd prefer. It's been only five days since my return to the city, but I still feel too damned frail, and I hate it.

The department store capping this end of the wing is blocked off, the door sealed. "What's going in there?" Milo asks.

"So far, nothing," Marcus says. "However, if our efforts succeed and expansion is necessary, we hope it will become residences of a more permanent and comfortable sort."

Interesting. And if he doesn't consider all the alterations to the mall to be permanent, I'd hate to see his definition of the word "temporary." "Just so we don't step on any toes," I say, "are there any restrictions on where we can go? Besides the Sanctuary?"

Marcus shakes his head no. "Although I would knock before entering the vampires' quarters."

"Duly noted."

"Are the training areas open?" Milo asks.

"Certainly," Marcus replies.

Without prompting, he pivots gracefully. I watch him as he walks, noting that every step is both graceful and powerful—the very definition of a large, predatory cat. I don't know which cat, specifically, but I know he's not a house kitty. Jaguar, maybe, given the black hair.

In my ever-expanding knowledge of the Clans and how to identify them, so far only the Felia and Cania have hair that reflects their animal coat. Which is probably not a bad thing. You can't exactly tell a stranger that your child has shockingly white hair because they can shift into a polar bear. Not that the multihued bear hair is easy to explain.

The mall's main corridor is about the length of two football fields, with each wing less than fifty yards long. Not huge by mall standards (maybe a third the size of the new mall), but pretty damned big by headquarters standards. We lucked out getting it—considering the amount of space and the ease of protecting it from enemies—but walking from one end to the other on a regular basis is going to get exhausting.

And I'm already out of shape. I regulate my breathing so I'm not panting by the time we reach the gym. It's impressive, with its array of equipment for cardio, strength training, and general exercise. An entrance to a second room has been cut out of the wall, and beyond it are blue mats. It's a good setup.

Two men I don't recognize, both with pale green eyes and the same multihued brown hair as Leah, are spotting each other on the free weights. They greet Marcus by name.

"Jackson, Shelby," Marcus replies, although I have no idea which is which. Just a sneaking suspicion they're both Ursia. He introduces us.

The man who was spotting takes a step closer, staring at me intently. "Stone," he repeats.

I tense, shifting both feet into a fighting stance. It's instinct, and he notices. Stops heading toward me.

He smiles. "Jackson de Loew. I'm Leah's mate. It's an honor to meet you."

"It is?" I blurt.

"Your reputation among the Clans is colorful, but what you did for Phineas el Chimal is . . . well, legendary, for lack of a better word."

"Phin was my friend." I fall back on a familiar refrain. Praise for doing my job isn't something I take well, and, thankfully, Jackson seems to get the hint.

"All the same, I'm glad to be working with you." He returns to his friend Shelby, who hasn't stopped staring but also hasn't directly acknowledged me or Milo. Guess I haven't impressed everyone.

Milo clears his throat. "The gym's great. With everything that's been going on, I haven't had a good workout in ages."

"You don't consider Sunday to be a good workout?" I ask, caught between amusement and surprise.

He gives me a baleful look. "I was thinking more along the lines of improving mobility and fighting skills, and less battling for my life."

"Good point. The barbells don't usually fight back."

"That removes some of the fun, don't you think?"

Marcus asks. One corner of his mouth quirks up, and I swear there's an amused glint in his eyes. "You spar?"

He isn't asking me, and it takes Milo a moment to realize it. "Boxing? No, not really."

I manage to keep surprise off my face. He knows how to fight as well as I do, but I don't contradict him. Not in front of a cat and two bears.

"Wrestling?" Marcus asks.

"Some."

Some? Learning basic holds, pins, and throws was part of Boot Camp training. We all took the course. I remember all the moves and can re-create them all in my mind, but even if I wasn't in such poor shape, I'd hesitate to try wrestling in this new body before it's properly trained. Especially not wrestling against a were-cat who outweighs me by a good fifty pounds.

"Great." Marcus strips out of his T-shirt without ceremony, showing off a ripped torso and tanned skin. I know my jaw dropped. "Let's go, then." He strides toward the far end of the room and the archway into the matted area. He pauses there and looks back, grinning right at Milo. "Do you have somewhere to be?"

"Uh, no?" Milo says.

I lift a shoulder in a half shrug, offering him no help. His own attempt at reverse psychology didn't get him out of it. He responds by sticking his tongue out at me, then following Marcus. I laugh. Sometimes I forget how young we both still are.

Okay, maybe Milo more than me. He's legitimately twenty years old. I was twenty-two when I died almost three months ago. The body I have now is twenty-seven—a five-year gap physically, but my emotional and mental ages are playing catch-up. Still, I manage to not flip Milo the bird as I trail behind the pair, curious about how this impromptu wrestling match will turn out.

Both men are in jeans, which aren't ideal for wrestling, but I bet that neither is going to strip down to his boxers. Or briefs. Or whatever. Milo follows Marcus's lead and takes off his own T-shirt. He's got a fairly average build, lean, with muscles hinted at beneath his tanned skin without being obvious or bulked up. An odd pattern of faint, pencil-thin scars checkerboard his back and shoulders—a peek into his past and a story I don't know.

Marcus notes them, I think, with a flare of his nostrils, then redirects his attention to the fight. Physically, Milo is no match for Marcus. Strategically . . . well, we're going to find out.

I lean against the wall to watch.

The first round goes as expected—the bigger, stronger Marcus has Milo on his back in less than ten seconds. They reengage. Marcus pins him again, but this time it takes longer. As Milo rolls up off the mat, he flashes me a confident grin.

We've also gained an audience. Shelby and Jackson stand by the wall opposite me, smirking. I bite my lower lip, confident the tables are about to turn.

Round three ratchets up my respect for Milo. Now that he's tested Marcus's strength and maneuvers, Milo adjusts his own movements to compensate. He skillfully rolls and ducks, easily avoiding the larger, slightly slower were-cat bearing down on him. Marcus lunges. Milo twists away. It's an amusing dance that's lasted more than a minute already.

Marcus turns again, and I catch a glimpse of his face. His teeth are bared like any predator, but he's smiling. If I didn't know better, I'd swear he was on the verge of laughter. Milo seems equally amused—enjoying the challenge.

"Come on, Marcus, pin the child," Shelby says.

Milo flips him off without breaking concentration, and I snort laughter. Shelby growls. Milo pulls to his right, and Marcus compensates—perhaps anticipating it as a feint. Only Milo doesn't feint. He keeps going around, twists, and ducks lower. His shoulder hits Marcus's lower abdomen full-force.

In a move as graceful as a ballet dancer's, Milo lifts Marcus up with his shoulder while anchoring him hands to ribs, and executes a perfect flip while falling backward. Both men land on their backs, Milo angled higher up so Marcus's shoulders hit the mat at the same time. It's a beautiful pin.

Milo rolls away, then comes up standing, practically bouncing on the balls of his feet. I half expect him to crow a little over the victory, or at least smirk. He just watches Marcus with a comical wide-eyed innocence as the larger man stands up, making a show of dusting himself off.

Jackson and Shelby are silent.

Marcus crosses well-toned arms over his chest. "You must have made a fortune hustling pool," he says with a grin.

Milo laughs.

After fetching my duffel bag from Wyatt's car, I find one of the living quarters' unoccupied cubicles. Staking a claim is easy enough—all I have to do is unpack. We officially abandoned the apartment on Cottage Place where I spent four years living and working with Jesse and Ash. The place is riddled with memories both wonderful and awful, and I'm torn about leaving it behind. Although I need the fresh start, it's the only place I've ever really considered home.

Packing didn't take long. My meager collection of clothes isn't very useful after losing so much weight. I'll need to go shopping soon. I hate shopping. Personal items consist of a laptop, a photo, and some hygiene

stuff from the bathroom. I've never been one for senti-
mental things, and the fact that it took me five minutes
to pack and half that to unpack is a little . . . sad.

The cubicles are impersonal and simple. Bunk beds
with a trunk at the foot, and next to the head is a pair
of small, two-drawer dressers. Assuming that one item
belongs to each bed, I choose a trunk for myself and
toss my things into it, then plunk my duffel bag onto
the top bunk. I'll figure out the linens later.

I stare at the crumpled blue duffel, a little lost as to
what to do now.

"Evy?" Phin's standing just outside the little room. It's
the first time I've seen him since the group meeting on
Sunday. He's still paler than normal, and I wonder if—
like me—he's been forever changed by his ordeal at
Thackery's hands.

"Hey," I say. "I didn't know you were around."

"I just got here a bit ago. Astrid told me your people
will begin moving in soon."

"Looks that way."

"You know you don't have to live here at the Watchtower. My offer of a room at the condo still stands."

I offer him a grateful smile. "And I really do appreciate the offer, Phin, but I think I'd like to stay here. For a
while I just want to be a little cog in a big wheel without
the fate of the world resting on my own two shoulders."

"Understandable and, I think, well deserved."

"Thank you."

He averts his gaze to the floor. He's avoiding a topic,
and I can guess pretty accurately who it's about.

"Just ask, Phin," I say.

He looks up, eyes meeting mine, curiosity in them.
"Have you and Wyatt spoken at length about the time
you were missing?"

"Not in any great detail, no." I plop down on the lid

of my chosen trunk, predicting this to be a long conversation. "We hit the Cliffs Notes version of events for each of us. Kind of came to the conclusion that we both changed and we need time to figure out who we are before we try to be together."

"Is that really wise?"

"Guess we'll find out."

Phin sits down on the trunk opposite mine, his expression drawn, uncertain. "I'm surprised, I admit."

"Why's that?" I have no energy to be snarky with Phin, so I settle on genuinely curious.

"I've witnessed the depth of your love for each other. That you would both step away, rather than fight for it, surprises me, especially after—" He stops the thought.

Well, I can't have that. "After what?"

"The second day of your abduction, Michael Jenner asked Wyatt if you were his chosen mate. Because you were owed a debt by the Assembly, that debt was extended to your mate."

Nervous butterflies set to work on my stomach. "Wyatt said he was my mate?"

"Jenner made the assumption. Wyatt did not deny it."

"He's too smart to deny it." I'm rationalizing. As much as I love Wyatt, and probably always will, the future scares me. I've always lived one day to the next, not making plans for tomorrow. It's not that I'm scared of commitment, I just don't know how.

Phin nods. "True. By agreeing with Jenner's assumption, he was granted protection by the Assembly, as well as assistance in his search for you." Something in his tone hints at more he isn't saying.

"But?"

"I don't believe Wyatt said it only for those reasons. You are his life, Evangeline. He was . . . broken without you."

I study the scrubbed cement floor between us, the words echoing in my mind. Rufus told me that Wyatt drank a lot during those few weeks, that he was cold to everyone. Wouldn't talk to any of his friends. I know Wyatt's temper, and I've seen his moods range from joy to rage to despair. I've seen him drunk, and I've seen him sober. We've both seen each other at our worst. I knew what my leaving would do to him.

I just never imagined how badly returning would hurt him.

"Broken people heal, Phin," I say. "Unless someone keeps breaking them all over again."

He's silent for a long moment. "You think coming back hurt Wyatt more than accepting your death did?" It's simply asked, without rancor or accusation.

"No, I'm pretty damned positive it hurt more. But I can't change going with Thackery, and I can't change the fact that I was rescued and proved not dead. And I know Wyatt." Something tightens in my throat. "He probably thinks he deserves this. That he's earned all this heartache and pain, because of the things he's done. But he hasn't. He's saved so many lives, and all he can ever focus on are the people he's failed."

Phin coughs. "Sounds like someone else I know."

"Yeah, well, we're a lot alike."

"Indeed."

I wish fixing it was as simple as Phin made it sound. But people don't just change twenty years of bad habits overnight. And I'm still carrying two heavy secrets, keeping them from him. If we're together, it has to be all or nothing. As much as I want Wyatt, I owe him too much to do anything less.

"Wyatt has something to live for now, Phin. He has the Watchtower and building up this new group, and that's what he needs. Everything should go back to what it was six months ago when we just worked together. After we figure out who we are apart, we can start thinking about giving us another try."

"Because it's what he needs," Phin says.

"Yes."

Something flickers in his bright blue eyes. "And what do you need, Evangeline?"

A hug. A kiss from someone who loves me and means it. One night of peace when I don't feel the weight of five hundred thousand lives resting on my shoulders. Respite from fear. So many impossible things, and all outside the realm of Phin's abilities.

I think back to Milo and his wrestling match with Marcus, and I realize there is one thing I can ask Phin for. "I need someone to help me train," I say.

He frowns. "Train?"

"Yes. Even before Thackery, I never managed to get this body into peak physical condition. But it needs to happen, especially now, and I have all the time in the world."

He's quiet for a moment, lost in his own thoughts. I don't have a clue what he's thinking—the things he's weighing. Finally he speaks. "All right. When would you like to begin?"

I don't wear a watch. I have no idea what time it is and don't really care. I flash him a bright smile. "How about right now?"

Chapter Eleven

Friday, July 11

It should be easy, and it isn't. I've done this move hundreds of times in the past. Emphasis on past, I guess, since my sixth attempt at a spinning roundhouse kick ends the same way the first five did—with me flat on my back.

"Fuck!" I slap my palm on the mat to put a little power into the word. My frustration level is topping out. Ten days of training has put a little muscle back on and increased my flexibility, but my coordination is shit. Granted, Chalice Frost didn't seem like the most acrobatic chick before she died, but this is ridiculous. Like riding a bike that won't let me take off the damned training wheels.

Phin looms above me, his face upside down. He's been my dutiful teacher since the day I asked for his help, in between his duties to the Assembly and assisting Astrid in readying our tactical squads.

The squads have started patrolling, getting out and making ourselves known. The Triads have expanded, is the word on the street. We're feeding the existing fear to create a new reputation for the Watch. The challenge has been folding five active Handlers, sixteen Hunters, and a dozen trainees into the ranks of existing vampire and Therian volunteers with as few issues as possible.

Matching up temperaments and skill sets is like a chaotic game of Memory.

Or sudden-death overtime.

"Again?" Phin asks, reminding me of my aching back.

"You're a sadist." I sit up fast, nearly clipping his chin with my forehead. "I used to be able to do this without thinking."

"You used to be an entirely different person." He circles around and offers his hand. A quick jerk and I bounce up to my feet, sore and a little sweaty. "Again?"

"Fine."

The seventh time is not the charm, but it is my lucky number. As Phin yanks me back to my feet once again, his phone beeps from its place on the floor. He retrieves it. Checks the message while I stretch a little.

"I'm needed in the War Room," he says, frowning. The War Room is what we call the conference area in Operations—which means something's up. Something that doesn't include me because Phin grabs his shirt on the way out the door.

Terrific.

I snatch a towel from the stack in the other room and dry off as I amble out of the gym, unsure of my destination. Maybe a shower. But a shower will only relax me, and I'm warmed up, keyed up, and eager to do something, dammit. I haven't been out in the field in what feels like forever. More than almost anything, I hate feeling caged. Although the Watchtower is a far cry from a tiny utility closet in an abandoned train station, it's starting to feel just as claustrophobic in terms of my freedom.

Maybe I can talk someone into doing a little two-man patrol. I need out.

After I change into jeans and a T-shirt, I nearly smash right into Milo at the living quarters entrance. He's in regular clothes rather than his patrol outfit, but he's definitely on his way somewhere.

"Hey, sorry," he says.

"Are you heading into the city?"

He blinks rapidly. "Uh, yes?"

"That wasn't a trick question, Milo."

"Oh, sorry. I'm taking Felix into the city for his appointment with a pain management specialist."

As soon as he speaks, the object of conversation hobbles around the corner and into view. Given the horrific injuries he sustained weeks ago at the claws of a genetically engineered hound, Felix looks good. He's upright and mobile, even if he manages to hide the pain he's in constantly because of nerve damage. He'll probably never go out on patrol again, but Astrid agreed to let him come in as an Operations communications coordinator—which is a fancy way of saying he monitors our phone calls when we're out. It isn't what he's used to, but he's here with Kismet, Milo, and Tybalt. His family.

I envy that through all of the drama and injuries of the last few months, the four of them are still together. My heart aches for Jesse and Ash, and for the closeness I once shared with Wyatt.

"Hey, Evy," Felix says, offering a pained smile. "You gaining weight?"

If I was any other kind of a girl, I'd slug him for such a thing. As it is, the observation is a compliment. "A little, yeah. One of these days I might even be able to do a roundhouse again."

"You always seem to manage anything you put your mind to."

"Mostly." I clear my throat. "Listen, you mind if I tag along with you guys today?"

His eyebrows furrow. "You want to come to my doctor's appointment?"

"Not particularly, no, but I need to get out of here. I

haven't left since I first arrived—Phin hasn't signed off on me being fit for patrolling—and I'm going a little stir-crazy."

"I hear that."

"No one's going to wring my neck for taking you into the city, are they?" Milo asks.

"I doubt it. No one ever said I couldn't leave, I just haven't yet."

The guys exchange a look.

"Come on," Felix says. "We'll get some burgers or something afterward."

Considering the diet of lean protein, complex carbs, and vegetables (weight gain without inducing high cholesterol was apparently the point of such a diet) I've been on since my abduction, the idea of a juicy hamburger with the works and a pile of crispy fries makes my mouth water. It must also affect the look on my face, because Felix laughs.

The walk from the living quarters to the parking area isn't unusually long, but Felix is red-faced and sweating by the time we reach the corridor outside Operations. He accepts silent help from Milo, draping his arm across the slightly shorter man's shoulders and leaning some weight on him. To the former Hunter, the show of weakness must be almost as painful as the nerve damage causing it.

Milo has the keys for Kismet's Explorer, and he helps Felix climb up into the passenger seat. The hair on the back of my neck prickles. I glance over my shoulder.

Marcus is watching from the entrance to the parking area. He nods at me, then turns and walks away. I stare at the vacant spot where he stood just a moment ago, confused.

"Evy?" Milo asks. "You okay?"

I shake myself out of it. "Yeah, fine. Let's get the hell out of here."

* * *

The appointment is at 4:30, which means the schedule is already backed up by about an hour. The fact that the doctor's office is in a wing of St. Eustachius Hospital next to the Emergency Room has me on hyperalert. Two of the staff members here once saw me as a frozen corpse, and I don't need the recognition. Not to mention that, the last time I was here, Felix lied to my face about Wyatt being attacked by a were-cat and then utterly failed at kidnapping me.

Unfortunately, we can't discuss these amusing anecdotes out loud in a waiting room full of normal people here for their own appointments. So we trade magazines and stare at the news program playing on the room's only television. As far as mundane tasks go, it's oddly refreshing.

Felix is more restless than I am, and I don't know him well enough to guess if it's physical pain or hospital memories. Forty-five minutes past his appointment time, he leans a bit toward Milo, who's sitting between us, and whispers, "You know what this feels like? It's the same damned waiting room."

My ears perk, but I don't look up from the article on fall fashion tips I'm trying to pretend I want to read.

"The day you guys brought Lucas in and were waiting for word," Milo replies.

"Yeah."

"The Hunter Kismet was involved with?" I ask. Two heads swivel in my direction, two pairs of eyes wide and curious. "Um, girl talk." Something occurs to me. "Shit, tell me you both knew."

"We knew," Felix says. "We're just surprised she told you."

"If it helps, she told me right before I went off with Thackery, so she probably didn't expect I'd repeat it."

My intention is humor, but the words don't come out that way. They're almost sad. And now that the topic is open, I crave the conversation. "How long did you know about it?"

"Tybalt and I suspected for a while, but the way she acted when Lucas died kind of proved it. We told Milo about it a while after."

Makes sense. "He was a good Hunter?"

"One of the best. Great physical fighter, quick thinker. He never judged you, no matter your past." Felix falls silent, withdrawing the way one does when memory overcomes you, his face shadowed with grief.

"You and Tybalt didn't judge me, either, when I showed up," Milo says.

Felix's entire body seems to flinch, and I suddenly feel like an intruder in a private conversation. "I did," he says. "I was awful to you those first couple of weeks."

"Because your best friend had just dropped dead in front of you from an aneurysm, Felix. I mean, after I came out."

The simple way Milo says it, especially in front of me, is astonishing, and it leaves no doubt as to his meaning—and it's an answer to a question I've been unable to articulate for a while now. Since the hounds attacked the cabin all those weeks ago and I started wondering . . .

I have no idea what my face looks like, but it catches Felix's attention. His raised eyebrow, in turn, gets Milo to look at me. "Dude, not judging," I say to Milo. Then to Felix, "But if you had given him a hard time, I'd have to punch you in the head retroactively."

Felix grins, and it brings a lightness to his pain-pinched face. A nurse arrives and calls him to come with her. Milo helps him stand, then waits until he shuffles off with the nurse before he sits again. Deciphering emotions isn't really my strong suit, but I've had some very recent experience in the realm of unreturned feelings.

"Does he know?" I ask, keeping my voice low.

Milo laces his fingers in his lap and asks, "Know what?"

I resist rolling my eyes. "How you feel, dumbass."

"About what? Felix and Tybalt are brothers to me. I'd do anything for them."

"So not what I meant."

He heaves a put-upon sigh. I'm not letting it go and he knows it. "It doesn't matter, Evy. It's my problem."

"Problem?" The description throws me a bit.

"Yeah. I let myself fall in love with my very straight partner, so it's my problem." He finally turns his head and glares at me. "Can we talk about something else now, please?"

"Okay." I fully intend to change the subject. Instead, I add, "I'm really glad he didn't die."

Milo blinks, then smiles. "Me, too."

After finally leaving the hospital with a pain med prescription for Felix, we settle into a booth at a nearby greasy spoon called McHale's and each order the biggest, greasiest burger on the menu. They come with heaps of fries, pickle spears, and free soda refills. It's nice, pretending to be normal college-age kids for a while—even though we are anything but—and I love every moment of it.

It's after nine o'clock before we unanimously agree it's time for our trio to return to the Watchtower. We settle the bill and tumble into the street, walking slowly out of some unconscious need to make the trip home last as long as possible. The Explorer is parked a block away in a public lot.

We're closer to downtown than to Mercy's Lot, so I'm not actively looking for Dreg activity. It just seems to pop out of nowhere and ruin my night.

Four individuals at a bus stop catch my attention, and

not in a good way. Two guys and two girls, all about our age, and all sporting telltale silver streaks in their hair. They hang off one another like couples in lust, but they're hunting. Watching.

And about to board the bus pulling to a stop in front of the signpost.

"Fucking hell," I say. "Halfies, two o'clock."

Milo and Felix go instantly rigid, one word putting them on high alert. We're only a quick sprint away, and Felix shocks me by taking off first. It's an awkward gait, more limp than run, but Milo and I don't catch him before he's up the bus steps behind the Halfies. We climb on after him and dump change into the meter.

The Halfies have clustered near the back, standing in the crowded rear and hanging on to the ceiling bars. There are no empty seats in front, so we mirror them and stand. I angle so I can watch them without being obvious. A surge of adrenaline has my pulse pounding, my blood flowing.

I didn't come out tonight looking for a fight, but by God, I'll enjoy this.

Halfies aren't like the other nonhumans. They don't get equal consideration. They're uncontrollable abominations, and they're always considered "kill on sight." Or in this particular instance, "kill when not in full view of a busload of people."

Milo has his cell out and is texting someone. Probably Kismet, so she knows what's happening. I catch Felix's eye and mouth "Weapons?" He shakes his head no. Then he mouths, "In the car."

Shit.

The bus rattles along to the next stop. Several people board and disembark, but the Halfies stay put.

Milo puts his phone away. "Kis says Marcus's squad is nearby. He's going to intercept and follow the bus until they exit. She says don't engage unless necessary."

Normally, an order like don't engage will rile me up enough to do just the opposite. Only we're sans weapons of any kind, and the Halfies have at least twenty other people to use as human shields if we get frisky. Human shields they could turn into more Halfies with one little bite.

At the next stop, several people get off. Felix sits in the closest empty seat. The route appears to be taking us into Mercy's Lot.

Milo jumps, then fishes his cell out of his pocket. "They're behind us, following," he whispers as he puts it away again.

Two stops later, we're down to eight civilians, plus the driver. Milo and I take seats across the aisle from each other, Milo just behind Felix. As the driver reaches to pull the door shut, a familiar face slips on board. Marcus doesn't look at any of us as he drops his coins into the meter, then takes a seat near the rear, between us and the Halfies. The odds are a little more even, and Marcus has the added bonus of being Therian and immune to the vampire parasites that turn humans into raving Halfies. Not to mention that, according to Tybalt, Marcus can shift into a huge-ass jaguar.

We're traveling north, into the outskirts of Mercy's Lot, and the stops will likely become fewer and farther between. Getting off with the Halfies is going to look suspicious no matter what we do.

One of them, a stocky boy in a ratty denim jacket, breaks off and shuffles to the front of the bus. The girl he was hanging on steps closer to where Marcus is sitting, her too-red lipstick smeared across her lips like blood. My stomach knots. This isn't going to be good.

Denim Jacket pulls a handgun out of his coat and presses it to the bus driver's temple. I tense, heart hammering. Someone behind me gasps, then shrieks, catching the attention of the other passengers.

"Turn left up here," Denim Jacket says.

The driver, an elderly man who's probably seen it all and then some, merely nods. He won't be playing hero today.

"Anyone who wants a bullet in their fuckin' head," Denim Jacket says to the entire bus, "please try and fuckin' stop me."

Someone begins sobbing rather loudly, but no one speaks up. DJ has the gun; DJ has the power. Too bad he doesn't know who four of his hostages are and what we're trained to do. We just need to get that gun away—

A peal of laughter from the rear of the bus drags my attention behind me. The other Halfie male has a second gun, and he seems far less stable than his buddy. It's bizarre to see the quartet acting as if they've actually planned this.

The idea makes me ill.

I take stock of the eight civilians. All between twenty and thirty years old, give or take. All in relatively good shape, probably decent health. Are the Halfies hunting for food? Or something else entirely?

Old instincts have me turning to ask Wyatt his opinion—only he's not here.

The driver follows directions, taking us off the bus route and into a partially abandoned part of the Lot. We pass a defunct Burger Palace building—I've been here, months ago. Road traffic is thin, foot traffic almost non-existent. If the car with Marcus's team is still following us, they turned their headlights off and are keeping a good distance.

"We should fucking do something," a voice behind me whispers. Male, angry.

I turn around just far enough to give him a deadly glare and mouth "no" with as much emphasis as possible. He's in his late teens, bulked up, probably a high school wrestler who thinks he can be badass against a couple of stoned punks and their girlfriends. And he looks just stupid enough to get us all killed.

Stupid wins—he lurches sideways at DJ's girl. Hoping to get her into a headlock and threaten a man with a gun? I have no idea, and it doesn't matter. Red Lipstick snarls and punches Stupid in the nose before he can rise halfway out of his seat. He drops back down, howling, clutching his bleeding nose.

At the head of the bus, DJ growls. Someone in the middle of the bus sobs.

"Looks like someone thinks he's a hero," DJ says, baring his fangs for the first time. Gasps rise from the other passengers. He levels his gun at Stupid. "I look forward to tasting you."

Stupid grunts behind his hands.

DJ angles his wrist sideways and squeezes the trigger. His gun roars.

Milo cries out.

The bus driver jerks the wheel and hits the gas. I tumble out of my seat and into the aisle. Passengers are screaming, and then the entire bus tilts. Tumbles. I crash into someone, then a seat, a window. Metal shrieks. Maybe me, too, until everything comes to an abrupt, crunching halt.

Someone's beneath me, or maybe they're on top of me; I don't know whether I'm upright or not. My jaw aches. I smell blood, rubber, gasoline—not good smells. The snarl of a large cat precedes a piercing shriek. Someone kicks my leg, and then the world seems to focus again.

The bus is on its door side, its passengers trapped in a dark maze of broken glass and bus seats. People are moving around, panicking. My first thought is for the Halfies and who they're about to bite. My next is for my hands, pressing down on something warm—blood. *Shit.*

Milo's beneath me, clutching his abdomen. His eyes

are open, wide, a little dazed, even in the faint light seeping in from outside the wrecked bus. He looks at me, then past me. His eyes widen.

I twist and bring my right arm up, driving my fist hard into DJ's gut. He grunts and steps back, trips over someone (Felix, I realize), and lands on his ass. I grab a shard of glass and tackle DJ. Slam him flat on his back and drive the glass into his Adam's apple. Blood spurts from his mouth and throat. It splashes my shirt and neck. I press deeper, aware of the glass slicing my palms, cutting halfway through DJ's throat before he quits fighting.

"Evy!"

A body hits me from behind before I can figure out who shouted, and I fall forward into DJ. I shove against the weight on me, praying that my skin stays far away from anyone's bare teeth, and twist. I may have survived an infection a few weeks ago, but I don't want to go through that particular hell ever again, thank you. The screeching female on my back—Red Lipstick, I think—digs her fingernails into my chest.

I drive my head backward and am rewarded with a solid crunch of cartilage. They never protect their damned noses. Passengers are still screaming, trying to climb out the windows that are now our roof. Marcus is in the back of the bus, in jaguar form, battling the other pair of Halfies with swipes of massive paws and loud hisses.

Felix is on his feet, seeming unsure if he should help me, help Marcus, or help Milo. I pull Red Lipstick's nails out of my skin and give her another head butt for good measure. The back of my skull aches and my chest stings, but the human-sized tick isn't sucking my blood.

At least half the civilians are out.

Marcus throws his Halfie male halfway across the bus, knocking down several other freaking-out passengers like a hellish bowling ball down a lane of human pins. The Halfie lands and rolls, coming up next to Stupid, who's helping a woman climb out a window. Halfie lurches at Stupid. Milo grabs the Halfie's leg and yanks.

The Halfie growls and reaches for Milo. Felix tackles the Halfie with a shout, and the pair goes tumbling over a seat and out of sight.

Lacking other weapons, I select another large shard of glass and give Red Lipstick the same tracheotomy I gave her late boyfriend. The thick odor of blood sours my stomach. Gross.

Familiar voices shouting outside—our backup has arrived. Awesome.

Stupid once again tries to be a hero by jumping onto the back of the Halfie who's fighting with Felix. He latches on like a monkey, arms around the Halfie's throat, and the two tumble sideways onto the glass-strewn floor/side of the bus. All I can see of Felix are his legs.

Apparently finished with his Halfie, cat-Marcus lopes over and hisses in Stupid's face. Stupid smartly lets go of his hostage. Marcus clamps bone-crushing jaws down on the Halfie's throat, finger-thick teeth piercing skin. He snaps the Halfie's neck with a jerk of his own.

I stumble over to Milo, who's twisted halfway around trying to get a look at Felix. "Hold still and keep pressure on that," I snap. The sound of my own voice startles me. It was a strangely silent battle, save the shrieks of the civilian passengers.

"Felix," he says.

"I'll check on him, just stay." Adrenaline has me shaking. My heart's pounding hard enough to crack a few ribs. I grab Stupid's arm and yank him down. "Put your hands on that wound and don't you fucking let go, you hear me?"

Stupid nods, and he puts enough pressure down to

make Milo cry out. He's losing blood, but not life-threatening amounts, and I want it to stay that way.

Marcus is making the rounds, sniffing the bodies. I'm positive that whoever's outside is making sure none of the escaped passengers was bitten. I haul ass to my feet and pick my way over to Felix. He's curled on his right side between the seats, arms tucked beneath his chin, eyes shut. His jaw muscles twitch, eyes moving beneath the lids. The pose sends a chill racing down my spine.

"Felix," I say, shaking his ankle. "Felix, are you bitten?"

"Fuck." The single word is as much an answer as a prayer. "Fuck, fuck, fuck . . ."

Bile scorches the back of my throat and I swallow it down, suppressing the rising tide of panic. Not again. I can't watch someone else I care about turn into one of those fucking things. I won't. "Let me see, Felix."

"Evy?" Milo shouts. "Is he okay?"

"Felix, let me see," I say, ignoring Milo.

The eye I can see rolls again, then the lid peels open. I don't remember what color Felix's eyes were, but they shouldn't glimmer with an opalescent sheen. And it cements my greatest fear. My stomach flips and threatens to empty. Tears sting both of my eyes. *Shit.*

I choke. "Goddammit."

"Evy! Is he—?"

Felix snarls and lunges.

Chapter Twelve

Voices drew me out of a nice, quiet place, and I wanted to tell them to shut the hell up, only I couldn't. My mouth felt dry, stuffed with cotton, and getting it moving took way too much effort. I considered going back to sleep for a while and ignoring whatever urgent crisis was likely unfolding around me, but someone squeezed my hand and said my name.

No one ever let me sleep.

I peeled one eye open, then the other, blinking up at Milo's concerned face. He leaned down, staring so intently that I croaked out a "What?"

"Just checking," he said.

"For?"

"You were, uh, drenched, Evy." He blanched, a little green around the edges. This close, I saw the red lines webbing his eyes and their general puffiness. "We had to make sure it didn't infect you."

Drenched in what? I tried to sit up, only to find my wrists restrained. Panic hit like a cold slap, and I lunged, nearly clipping Milo's chin with my head. I was on a cot somewhere, handcuffed to the frame, my clothes soaked, and I had no idea what . . . *Felix. He exploded in our jail.*

"Get these damned things off me," I said.

"Calm down, I've got the key." Milo unlocked my wrists, then scurried back away.

I sat up and swung my legs over the side of the cot. The room tilted. My head spun a little and I gripped it in both hands.

"Sorry, but we had to," he said.

"I know." My back ached, probably from being thrown by the explosion I only vaguely remembered. And I was moderately grateful that I'd been hosed down. I'd never seen a person explode from the inside out and did not want to see the gore left behind in the interrogation room.

We were in one of the infirmary patient rooms, and the sounds of nearby voices hadn't diminished. People were talking, lots of them, but too far away and too many at once to distinguish individuals or actual words.

"Was anyone hurt?" I asked.

"You and Marcus took the brunt of it," Milo said. His voice was cold, emotionless, like he was trying his damnedest to not lose his shit. "Dr. Vansis pulled some shrapnel out of your back, and Marcus took a big chunk in his left ankle."

"Shrapnel?"

"Mostly wood from the chair. Some, uh, bone."

I twisted my arm backward, poking at the source of the ache, and found a taped-down square of gauze. "Marcus is okay?"

"Stitched up and grumpy as ever. He saved your life."

"I'll be sure to thank him. How are you?"

He lifted one shoulder in a half shrug. "I was in the outer office. I wasn't hit."

"Not what I meant."

His expression cracked and a flash of grief and horror made it through. Then he blinked, and a perfect mask of anger settled back into place. "A half-Blood exploded in front of me. Not an image I'll soon forget, but we've got way worse problems now."

"Such as?" Hey, wait a minute— "How's Wyatt?"

Milo frowned. "Sedated, I think. You were out for only about twenty minutes, so I don't think Dr. Vansis knows anything about his condition that you don't already know."

"Condition? What's that mean?"

Dr. Vansis stepped into the cubicle, his customary scowl in place. "It means I still don't understand the reason for Mr. Truman's rather violent reaction to the Lupa blood and/or saliva," he said. "I've made a formal request to the Assembly for information. Hopefully, they'll have something more useful for me than speculation and hearsay."

"So he's still sick?"

"Extremely sick, unlike you." He took a penlight from his lab coat pocket and flashed it in my eyes as he spoke. "He's running a one-hundred-and-four-degree fever, has the shakes, complains of flulike aches all over his body, and both wound sites show signs of serious infection. I have him on IV fluids and a broad-spectrum antibiotic, but I don't know that the antibiotic is helping."

I followed his finger with my eyes, feeling like an idiot but understanding the reason for the little tests. I'd taken yet another blow to the head and, healing ability or not, he was a studious doctor. "All that from werewolf bites," I said, once he seemed satisfied with my condition.

"The bites or the blood, I'm not sure yet," Vansis said. "All of our knowledge of the Lupa is carefully guarded by the Elders. Hopefully, I'll hear from them soon."

"What about the vampires? They're old. Isleen is centuries old. Maybe they know something. . . . What?"

The look Milo and Dr. Vansis exchanged set my teeth on edge.

"All the vampires in the Watchtower are being quarantined in their quarters," Dr. Vansis said.

I couldn't have been more surprised if he'd said they were staging a musical production in the cafeteria. "Why?"

"Because the purpose of detonating that half-Blood you captured wasn't to cause internal structural damage to the facilities, or to necessarily try to kill whoever was standing closest to him at the time."

"So why, then?"

"The half-Blood was used as a delivery system for some sort of pathogen," Dr. Vansis said. "It was aerosolized during the explosion, and many of the vampires have become infected."

"How many were exposed?"

"All of them."

Oh God. The sun rises around 5:45 in the summer, and the majority of our vampires patrol at night. Even the vampires who used that fancy UV-blocking sunscreen preferred nighttime, as it enhanced their vision. They were always back by 5:30. Felix had known that. He'd known exactly when the most vampires would be in the Watchtower because he'd once been part of this, which meant that Thackery would have known the perfect time to blow his little present.

Walter Thackery and his hatred of all vampires strikes again. "Isleen?"

"She's sick, as is Eleri and at least twenty more." At least twenty out of the forty-five or so who worked here on any given day.

No, no, no, no! "Quince?"

"Fine, so far," Milo said. "It's affecting them randomly. So far there's no way to know if they'll all get sick, or if some of them are immune."

"I've taken blood samples from a dozen, both sick and healthy," Dr. Vansis said, "but contagious diseases is not my area of expertise. And seeing as how you're fine, I need to get back to work."

He left without further information. I hauled ass to my feet, and my very wet shoes squished on the floor. Pink water oozed out.

"Have any humans or Therians been affected by this pathogen?" I asked.

"Not so far," Milo replied.

"What's it doing to the vampires?"

"Hypersensitivity to light and sound, shooting pains in the extremities, and they bruise if you touch them too hard."

Sounded like the vampire version of a migraine—except for the bruising thing. "And these are just the early symptoms?"

"Yeah. Like I said, it's only been about twenty minutes, but the first ones infected got sick fast."

"If they aren't all sick, is putting them in one confined space a good idea?"

Milo shrugged. "It was Isleen's decision. She called her Family's royal Father and he agreed with her. I guess they don't want to risk exposing any vampires outside the Watchtower until they know what this is."

The choice was understandable, from the vampire's point of view. We didn't know what was affecting them, what else it would do, or how far it would spread uncontained. Still . . . "Are we allowed to leave, or are we confined, too?"

"I really don't know, Evy." A flash of distress creased his forehead, and he looked lost. Young. "I mean, I just saw Felix blow up and I'm really not sure . . . I don't . . ."

"I'm sorry." I took a step toward him, then stopped when he flinched away. "It's not easy to reconcile the thing you saw die with the person you knew."

"Yeah. He seemed surprised."

"That he'd been rigged to blow?"

"Yeah."

"I think he was. He said something about his tracker not being a tracker. And I don't think he expected to be caught last night."

"Thackery sure did. He had to know we'd be at the rave."

"Well, Thackery likes to have backup plans in place." Hell, he could have the Lupa set to explode somehow, too, and the thought made me doubly glad we hadn't brought our prisoner back to the Watchtower.

Milo ran a hand through his short hair. "How do you not know someone's planted a bomb on you? Or in you?"

I had no answer.

"I just . . ." Milo sighed. "I can't believe so much has gone so wrong so fast."

No kidding. In just the last six hours, we'd captured Felix, had half a dozen Therians kidnapped, Wyatt was attacked by a werewolf, Felix exploded, and now the vampires were getting sick. Somehow everything connected back to Thackery, but I hadn't yet drawn all the lines between the crazy dots.

"Did we save any samples of Felix's blood?" I asked.

"I think so. Why?"

"Because something besides willpower was helping Felix, and we might find a hint in his blood."

Determined to do something, I circled past Milo and stepped into the short hall. My room was at the end of the row of four, with all the noise activity happening farther down in the main infirmary area. The next door down was half-shut, and Marcus was arguing with someone about being allowed to use a cane. I made a mental note to thank him later.

The third room was empty. Wyatt was in the fourth. The conversation just a few yards away had my attention, but I went into Wyatt's room anyway. He looked awful, like someone fighting a losing battle with a deadly disease—all fevered, blotchy skin and labored breathing. The bandages on his neck and arm were stained red and yellow, hinting at the infection raging below the surface.

Frail came to mind, and I despised using that word to describe Wyatt Truman. Once again, the people I cared about were at the mercy of Walter-fucking-Thackery and his diseased whims.

I stepped toward the bed. Froze. I wanted to find a chair and sit next to Wyatt, hold his hand until he woke up. Be there so he wasn't alone if he died from whatever ravaged his body. I needed to be there for him, like he'd been there for me countless times in the very recent past.

Only I couldn't. There was too much to do, and if I could get to Thackery, maybe I could beat an antidote out of him. As much as my heart wanted me to stay with Wyatt, logic told me I'd help him best by being out in the city. Doing something.

I brushed his cheek with my knuckles, noting how the damp skin radiated heat. The last time I'd seen him in a bed like this, he'd just shielded me from another exploding Halfie and taken a piece of shrapnel in the back for it. The perfect alignment of it made me smile in spite of the situation.

"You keep fighting, hear me?" I said. "Fight for me."

He slept on.

Milo trailed me into the main part of the infirmary, where I nearly walked into Astrid.

She gave me a quick, assessing glance. "Nothing keeps you down long, does it?"

"I'm contrary. What can I say?"

"Did Milo bring you up to speed?"

"Yes. Have we heard from Phin?"

"They're having trouble questioning the werewolf. It's got some sort of tracer. They've switched locations twice and are still being trailed."

"By?"

"The other wolves. They seem to want their brother back. If this continues, Phineas may have no choice but to kill the werewolf and return."

"Can't they trap the pursuing wolves?" As soon as I asked the question, I saw its logical fallacy. "Guess it wouldn't matter, since Thackery could just trace them, too."

"Correct." Her attention shifted to something behind me. "What are you doing up?"

Marcus shuffled down the hall using Kyle for a crutch. His left foot and ankle were wrapped in gauze and one of those walking boot things, but if the pain bothered him he gave no sign of it. "Walking," he said. "Okay, limping, but you need me on this."

Astrid glared. "Fine. But if you pull stitches, you're answering to Dr. Vansis."

"Noted."

"Do we know anything new?" I asked, impatience growing.

"No," Astrid replied.

"Is everyone quarantined here, or just the vampires?"

"Everyone," Dr. Vansis said from across the room, where he was hunched over a microscope. "Until I'm certain it isn't communicable via Therian or human, no one leaves the premises."

Not the answer I wanted to hear. "Who's out in the field?"

"Phineas. Baylor is out with his team. Jackson took Leah's squad out looking for her several hours ago."

"That's not many."

"It's what we have." Astrid's phone rang. She checked the display. "What?" Her eyebrows shot up. "Okay, send it to the infirmary computer."

"Send what?" Marcus asked.

Astrid plunked down in the desk chair and tapped

away at the keyboard. "Incoming video conference call with Elder Macario Rojay of Cania and Elder Marcellus Dane of Felia."

Dane? Milo and I turned to stare at Marcus, likely wearing the same curious expression. I knew the Felia were something of an anomaly, because they had both a Pride Alpha and a Clan Elder. The former was a position of authority that had been in place for centuries before the Assembly formed; the latter was their voice on the Assembly. I'd just never connected the Felia Elder to Marcus or Astrid before today.

"What?" Marcus snapped. "The Elder is our grandfather."

From what little I knew of Assembly politics, the majority of Elder positions were inherited from parent to child. Marcus and Astrid were already at the half points of their lives and had no mates or children. Judging by the steely glare coming my way, it was a touchy subject. One I wasn't about to broach with either of them.

I'm not a huge fan of computers, but the fact that Astrid could bring up two different screens with two different men's faces impressed me. Even more so that we could all apparently talk to one another via a little camera and microphone already embedded in the infirmary's laptop.

Elder Rojay was the younger of the pair, with a ruddy complexion and wild brown hair. Even across the desk, I could see that his eyes were the same striking brown as Kyle's—as dark as a mug of black coffee. He had a large mug of something steamy on the desk in front of him, and just visible on the corner of the screen was a silver flask. Elder Dane, on the other hand, had more wrinkles and folds than a shar-pei dog. His hair was white, and his demeanor sullen, but life sparkled in those sharp copper eyes that all of his people possessed. Identical eye color was a consistent characteristic among many of the

Clans. At least, it was in the Clans I'd met so far, which was only half of them.

Dr. Vansis circled to stand behind Astrid. Marcus and I hung to the side, Milo behind us.

"Who is witness to this call?" Elder Dane asked.

"Astrid and Marcus Dane of Felia," she replied. "Reid Vansis of Ursia. Humans Evangeline Stone and Milo Gant."

"Stone may stay. The other human must leave."

Milo rolled his eyes—*politics,* he seemed to say—and left the infirmary. I considered protesting on the grounds that I'd probably just tell him everything anyway, but I held my tongue. Back-talking an Elder was a good way to get on their bad side, and I had enough enemies.

"Where is Phineas el Chimal?" Elder Rojay asked.

"He is in the city, completing a task for us," Astrid said. "He will be briefed on our conversation as soon as possible."

"We have no time for formalities, Elders," Dr. Vansis said. "Have you approved my request for further information on the Lupa?"

"We have," Elder Rojay said. "We realize that with recent events, what we know will soon become common knowledge amongst our people—something we have tried to prevent for a variety of reasons. All of our compiled medical data, sparse though it is, is being emailed to you now."

"Good."

"Did the Coni hunt and kill off the Lupa?" I asked. The question earned me an elbow in the ribs from Marcus.

"Yes," Elder Dane replied. "Humans were spreading rapidly across the globe, settling in the wildernesses that had once been our sanctuaries. The Lupa were out of control, attacking humans and creating fear throughout Europe. There were cries of witchcraft. Innocents were accused and murdered. Our ancestors decided that integration with humans was the safest course for the future, which meant concealing our true natures."

"The Lupa disagreed," Elder Rojay said when Dane faltered. "A pack destroyed a village in Tuscany out of spite for our decision. As protectors of our kind, the Coni were tasked with hunting and executing the Lupa."

I recalled the open hostility between Phineas and Teen Wolf, and now understood it more than ever.

"We had thought they succeeded," Rojay continued, "but it appears we were wrong."

"Or simply deceived," Astrid said. "The Fey are adept at that."

"Yes, we have heard the admission that the Fey are responsible for the survival of the Lupa. It's their motivation that baffles us."

"The motivation of the Fey is the least of my worries right now," Dr. Vansis said. "Is Lupa blood poisonous to humans?"

"Their saliva can be quite toxic if it enters the blood through a bite or other wound," Dane said.

My heart pounded harder, even as my stomach soured. This wasn't what I wanted to hear.

"Historically, bites caused the human to go quite mad. It affects them not unlike rabies would, without the period of dormancy. The toxin causes neural inflammation, and in those early days before proper virology studies, humans didn't understand why this happened."

"The bites never caused a transformation among the infected humans?" Dr. Vansis asked.

"Of course not." Dane's tone told us exactly how daft he thought that question was. "Such a notion is pure fiction. A human cannot become Therian any more than a vampire can become a goblin."

Wyatt isn't just any human. The thought did little to comfort me.

Dane continued. "The Lupa bites are not mystical. They cause a violent fever, madness, and eventually death."

"There's no cure?" I blurted out.

Elder Dane shook his head. "There has never been a need for one. Those early infected humans were killed by their own. Your infected human is the first in centuries."

My infected human. It sounded so cold when put like that, but Elder Dane didn't know Wyatt. He had no stake in Wyatt's survival. His only major loyalties were to the Pride and the Assembly. But Wyatt was strong. He was Gifted, dammit. He could beat this.

"Is there anything else about the Lupa that you can tell us?" Astrid asked.

"They are an old race, second only to the Coni, and strong."

"And bi-shifters," I said, thinking back to my Boot Camp battle with Wolf Boy in his half-wolf form. He'd been one scary son of a bitch.

Both Elders glanced at separate corners of their screens, probably where each saw the other, and shared a look I couldn't decipher. They had to know I'd been told about the bi-shifters in general; I just didn't know which Clans had the ability. Only my own guesses, based on an old clue from Michael Jenner.

"Yes, they are also bi-shifters," Elder Dane said.

Fabulous.

"The medical information should have arrived," Elder Rojay said. "Best of luck." He signed off.

The monitor expanded the angry visage of Elder Dane. "Astrid," he said.

She stiffened. "Yes, sir."

"You have three very serious problems, and as the chief security liaison to the Assembly, need I remind you of your priority?"

"No, Elder Dane, you needn't do that."

Dane's gaze flickered up and past me to Marcus. "Do

not disappoint." The three words fell like anvils, and then the screen went blue.

Marcus growled, deep and low.

Dr. Vansis snatched up the laptop.

"What's your priority, exactly?" I asked Astrid.

"Protecting the Clans," she said in a flat tone. "Which means my first priority is finding and destroying the Lupa, and then finding our missing people."

I bristled, hands balling into fists. "So Wyatt and the sick vampires come in a distant third?"

"Yes."

"You do realize that all of these things are connected, right?"

She stood up, my height, but somehow impossibly taller. Fury flashed in her eyes, and her true form prowled just beneath the surface. I'd seen Astrid shift several times in the last month, but her leopard was nowhere near as intimidating as the woman. "Yes, I realize all these things are connected, and I also realize that you aren't used to taking orders and following the commands of your superiors, so let me make something clear. Isleen is sick. Baylor is in the field. Right now, I am in charge of the Watchtower, and if you wish to continue working with us, you will follow my fucking orders."

Hot damn, I'd never heard her cuss before. The cold delivery of her mini-rant didn't cow me, but it did make one thing perfectly clear—she wasn't happy about the ordering of her priorities. Good. It meant she cared about more than just her Clans.

"Understood," I said.

She blinked hard, as though surprised by my sudden acquiescence. "Good."

"I need permission to leave the Watchtower."

"Stone, we still don't know—"

"I know what we don't know, Astrid." I was toeing the line with her, but had the faintest outline of a plan forming in my head. I just couldn't do anything about it stuck here. "We don't know a hell of a lot, including what this disease will eventually do to the vampires here, or if Wyatt's going to die from that werewolf bite. But Thackery does know, and I can at least get us a few more werewolves."

She gave me a dubious frown. "How?"

"I need to know Phin's current location, and I need two tranq guns with the strongest local anesthetic we have."

"For?"

"I used to be a Hunter, right?" I smiled. "I'm going hunting."

Chapter Thirteen

Ten minutes later, I met Baylor's van in the parking lot of a discount grocery store in upper downtown. I climbed in, armed with my requested guns and a cell phone set to speed-dial Astrid. Baylor wore the same concerned, pinched expression I'd seen on everyone in the last few hours.

"Squad's in position," he said in lieu of a greeting.

"Good," I said. "Phin?"

"Construction site across the street, just like you said."

"What's our lead time?"

"Ten minutes, max."

Cool. I hated waiting. My plan was simple—bait and shoot. The wounded werewolf had died a few minutes ago from blood loss—which may or may not have been helped along, but I wasn't going to question a good thing—so the body had been dumped at the construction site. Phin was watching downwind in osprey form, and the rest of Baylor's team had taken surveillance positions nearby. As soon as the other werewolves tracked their dead buddy, I'd get a signal and teleport in with my tranq guns ready to blast the bastards. We'd have twenty, maybe thirty minutes to interrogate them before anyone tracking realized they hadn't moved locations in a while.

A very simple plan.

With so many chances to go terribly wrong.

Less than three minutes of tense silence passed before Baylor's phone beeped. He checked the message. "They're coming up the street, about a hundred yards to the north, human form."

Even better, if they were tracking as teenagers. "Okay, good, see you in a few." I reached for the door handle.

"Watch your back, Stone."

I winked, then bounded out of the van. The guns were tucked in the waist of my jeans, hidden by a loose T-shirt I'd changed into after a quick shower; no sense in coming to an ambush smelling like Halfie blood. The wound on my back had been rebandaged, and the itch-ache of it healing kept me company as I jogged across the street south of the construction site. It was still early, the city not fully awake. Cars zipped past, but the foot traffic was minimal—good for our purposes.

A tall construction wall created a fairly solid barrier between the sidewalk and the stalled project inside. I'd hunted Halfies here a few times and knew the lay of the land pretty well. Financing on a hotel had fallen through nearly two years ago, and all work on the site stopped. It had yet to restart.

I was near the empty and rusting trailer housing the site office. The frame of the hotel was in place, creating an iron maze with only the barest sense of structure. Tarps had been draped over large sections to protect equipment from the weather. Phin should have put the dead werewolf in the center of one of these tarps. The logic: open placement screamed bait, but covering him theoretically limited our ability to ambush the other werewolves from a distance. That's where my teleporting ability would come into play.

I could appear out of nowhere, far enough to prevent them from smelling me first, and shoot them before they could react to my presence. Theoretically. Everything hinged on my ability to not teleport into one of them or, worse, into an unexpected support beam.

The fence had half a dozen different weak spots, and with the werewolves approaching from the north, they'd stumble across at least three of those before they got close to my position. So I waited. Waited for a very simple signal: Phin landing on the roof of Baylor's van.

I leaned casually against a telephone pole, pretending to bite my nails, glancing around as if waiting for someone, all the while facing the van. Minutes ticked by. My anxiety grew exponentially, sending a gaggle of butterflies loose in my guts. This had to work. I didn't have another plan, couldn't think of another way to learn if there was an antidote for wolf bites.

A shadow drifted across the sidewalk, and then a bird that had no business living in a city perched gracefully on top of our van. I swallowed hard, mouth dry, and pulled my guns. Checked for potential witnesses and saw none.

Here goes nothing.

I tapped into the Break—a little easier each time I did it, with loneliness, my emotional trigger, so close to the surface at all times, despite living with more than a hundred and fifty other people—and the Break snap-crackled around me. Buzzed on my skin like static. It filled me, and I fell into it, focusing on my intended destination in the middle of the construction site. The Break pulled me apart, and the faintest ache poked me between the eyes.

The journey was quick, and I pulled out precisely where I intended to land, materializing directly behind a pair of slim, pale-skinned bodies wearing cargo shorts too large for their frames. They were crouched over the body of their dead brother, growling low. I ignored my sharp headache, raised my hands, and fired. Red feathered darts hit both of them right between the shoulder blades. They stood and spun in perfect unison, snarling loudly, teeth bared.

I scurried backward, giving them room to falter a few steps as the anesthetic took hold and froze their basic motor functions. Legs dragged, arms flopped, and both of them—Teen Wolf, and his companion, whom I dubbed Freckles because he had a lot of them—collapsed face-first into dirt.

"Hot damn, it worked," I said.

Baylor's squad was an eclectic bunch who regularly worked daytime detail, so they didn't have a vampire assigned. Carly Hall had been one of Baylor's Triad Hunters, and she looked a bit like I did once upon a time—short, thin, blonde, and a firecracker of fight hiding beneath a demure exterior. Not that I'd ever looked, acted, or pretended to be demure . . .

The other human was Paul Ryan. I disliked him for personal reasons, but respected his ability to kill things efficiently now that he'd grown up a little. Baylor's other members were Autumn, a female Vulpi/Kitsune who shifted into a Bengal fox, and Sandburg, a gray-eyed Musti who was the only Therian I'd ever met who shifted into a ferret.

I saw it once, and he promptly bit Carly for cooing at him.

Phineas rounded out the group, but he flew in only long enough to make sure things were progressing according to plan. His simple presence put the Lupa into a rage, so he volunteered to keep watch and promptly flew back out of the construction site. Once the two Lupa were put into seated, upright positions and chained to individual iron pylons, Baylor handed me a wooden box with a few special implements.

"Is this the reckoning you were talking about earlier?" I asked Teen Wolf.

He snarled, head tilted slightly to the side. The anesthetic had the awesome effect of numbing his extremities while allowing him to remain conscious, but it also made holding his head up difficult. Paul was on standby with two more rounds of the stuff. Therians heal quickly, and we didn't want the numbness to wear off before we were through. Sometimes the knowledge of grave injury is a more effective weapon than the actual pain.

I opened the box and removed a pair of wire cutters. The blades were sharp, fashioned from silver, and able to cut through solid objects up to two inches thick. I handed them to Carly, who circled around behind Teen Wolf. He tried to track her movements and failed.

"Now," I said as I crouched at eye level with Teen Wolf, "I could lie and tell you that I'll let you live if you cooperate, but we both know I have orders from the Assembly to kill you."

His expression remained the same—cold fury.

"The only thing I can offer you is a much faster death than your friend over there. Bleeding to death from a belly wound over the course of an hour is a nasty way to go, don't you think?"

"He was my brother," Teen Wolf snarled, the words slightly garbled through his half-numb lips.

"Sucks for you. Are you going to talk?"

Silence was a good answer, given the question.

"Okay, then," I said.

Teen Wolf frowned, then blinked rapidly. He certainly felt something, he just didn't know what, with most of his nerves numbed by the anesthetic. But he'd find out in a moment.

Carly stepped back around to his front and dropped something into the dirt by his feet. Teen Wolf stared at the blood-covered pink object until it dawned on him what it was. His eyes widened; his nostrils flared.

"That was your index finger," I said, careful to keep my tone even and commanding. "The next thing she cuts off is your thumb." This sort of bargaining was something I hadn't done in a long time, and the sight of a severed finger made my skin crawl. I just couldn't show my distaste to the Lupa. *Would not.*

Baylor stepped up behind me, muscled arms folded over his chest. "Why did your brother attack one of our humans tonight?" he asked.

"Fuck off," Teen Wolf said.

I clucked my tongue. Carly slipped behind the pylon. Sweat broke out across Teen Wolf's forehead. I heard the distinct snick-crunch of the shears doing their job, and my insides went a little wobbly. God, when had I lost the stomach for this? I used to revel in it.

Moments later his thumb joined his index finger in the dirt.

Freckles whined. Teen Wolf snarled at him.

"Why did you attack us last night?" I asked, toeing his thumb with my shoe. Ugh.

"To send a message," Freckles said. It earned him a second, louder snarl from his buddy.

I stood and turned, giving Freckles my full attention. He was the same age as Teen Wolf, similar coloring, with a sea of freckles on his face, chest, and arms. He looked as dangerous as the science nerd who trips over his own too-large sneakers. "Looks like we're cutting pieces off the wrong wolf here," I said. "You have something to say?"

Freckles swallowed, his Adam's apple bobbing. He was sweating, drooling, and might have even peed on himself. Not the bravest wolf in the pack, that was for sure.

"I'll kill you," Teen Wolf said.

"We're dead no matter what," Freckles snapped back. "They win this round, brother."

"Why did your brother attack?" I asked.

"To send a message of fear. To remind humans what we can do to them."

"The infection, you mean?"

"Yes."

"Why didn't you bite me or Phineas?" Freckles frowned, puzzled. "The Coni."

"We were ordered to harm neither of you. The other human had no such protection."

"Ordered by who?"

Teen Wolf snarled again, a warning if I ever heard one. It made me more desperate to hear the answer. Only Freckles hesitated.

"Carly?" I said. "You wanna jog his memory?"

She came around the support beam, bloody shears clutched in one hand. Unlike me, she seemed to be truly enjoying herself. I wanted to look at the others, see the faces of Paul, Autumn, and Sandburg, and judge their reaction to the gory scene playing out in front of them. Looking away, though, might display weakness to the Lupa, and I couldn't risk it. I barely dominated the conversation as it was.

"Our master," Freckles replied meekly.

I heaved a put-upon sigh. "Look, we can take you apart a little bit at a time, or you can just be fucking straight with me."

"Master Thackery."

I fully expected his answer, but it still stung a little. "Who else?"

Freckles made a bizarre face—like he'd tried to shake his head and forgot he couldn't move it. "I don't understand."

"You started working for Thackery only recently—"

"No, my entire life has been in his service."

Yikes. His young age put him at maybe three and a half years—for a Therian. Which meant it was likely the Lupa were given to Thackery as babies to be raised as his own personal rabid pack dogs.

"Who put you into Thackery's service?" Baylor asked.

"I don't know," Freckles replied. Carly stepped behind his support beam. Freckles turned a terrible shade of red and yelped. "I don't know, I swear! We weren't told!"

"How many more of you are in service to Thackery?"

"Don't tell them," Teen Wolf said. "Don't tell them anything else, you coward."

"I don't want to die!" Fat tears rolled down Freckles's cheeks, and I was torn between believing his fear and suspecting it was all an act.

I squatted in front of him, elbows on knees, hands dangling loose in front of me. I tilted my head until he met my gaze, his silver eyes glimmering. "We all die at some point, kid. There's no stopping it, not for any of us. The only thing you can do right now, in this moment, is change how you face death. You can opt for fast and painless, or"—I jacked my thumb at Teen Wolf—"piece by bloody, painful piece."

Freckles sobbed in earnest now, unable to wipe away tears or snot. His misery was palpable. He was just a boy, raised by a madman to do his bidding, facing an impossible choice—a boy with a vicious monster lurking deep inside of him.

His monster manifests itself as a wolf. What's your excuse, Evy?

I mentally batted away the question. I could second-guess and self-analyze my own internal demons at a later date.

"I don't want to die," Freckles whispered between choking sobs.

"Tough shit," Baylor said, taking over the role of the

heavy. "How many fingers do you want attached when you do?"

"Three."

"You—what?"

"Three others," Freckles said.

"Bastard!" Teen Wolf lunged against his chains. Paul popped him with another tranq dart to keep him docile.

Freckles whined at the sight of it.

"Okay, now we're getting somewhere," I said. "Three others serve Thackery. How many Lupa are in or around the city?"

"I don't know," Freckles said.

I sighed. "Didn't we go through this once?"

"I don't, I swear. We serve; we don't ask questions."

"Two weeks ago, one of you was following me around the city. You found a human male recently infected by a half-Blood and took him to your Master."

"Yes."

"Who found him?"

"Not us. Our brother Mark."

"Mark is one of the three still free?" I asked.

"Yes," Freckles said.

"Why?"

"Ask Mark."

Oh, I intended to, as soon as I found him. "Do you know anything else?"

He looked at me with weepy eyes, a sad smile tugging the corners of his mouth. "I know I'm about to die."

"Did you know that your saliva can cause a serious infection in human beings?"

"Yes."

"Do you know if there's a cure?"

"No."

"No what?"

"I don't know."

Well dammit it all anyway. Not that I was surprised. It

wasn't information that Thackery was likely to share with teenage werewolves who lived to do his dirty work. "Okay, then, kiddo, here's the million dollar question. Where is Thackery?"

His eyes went wide. "You'll kill my other brothers."

I could have bullshitted him just to get the answer, but something kept me from doing that. "If we catch them, yes, we'll kill them. You're our enemies."

"No!"

"No, you won't tell us where Thackery is?"

He clenched his jaw in a show of mock bravery. I didn't even have to signal Carly. She disappeared behind the beam. Freckles's eyes bulged and his left shoulder jerked. The easy movement was Paul's signal to send a second tranq into the Lupa's chest. Moments later, a finger landed in the dirt.

Freckles choked. I barely managed to stay still while my insides shook.

"Where's Thackery?" Baylor asked.

After the fourth finger, it became obvious that Freckles wasn't going to budge on this one. I stepped away, curiously close to losing my . . . well, whatever I'd eaten last. Might have been lunch. We were running out of time. I gazed up at the morning sky, and a shadow swooped toward us.

Phineas shifted midair, choosing to remain in his bi-shift form. He surveyed the captured wolves with cold disinterest, then held his hand out to Baylor. Baylor gave him the ancient, decorative knife I'd last seen in the empty lot. Phin clasped it in his hand, approached Freckles, and gazed down at him.

"Lupa," Phineas said, "you have been judged by the Therian people, and their sentence is death. What say you?"

Freckles tried to look up. The heavy doses of anesthetic prevented it, and he managed a sideways tilt. Tears, drool, and sweat coated his cheeks and chin—the very picture of misery. I swallowed hard against the tide rising in my stomach and tried to not feel sorry for him.

"Our master will avenge us," he gasped.

"Unlikely," Phin said. "You and your brothers are his pawns, nothing more, and you are easily replaceable."

Freckles muttered something that might have been "fuck you." In a swift movement that I almost missed, Phin drove the twin blades of his knife into Freckles's chest and twisted. Blood gushed over the gleaming gold. Freckles slumped against his bonds. It was a fast death, and yet I still wanted to cry.

Teen Wolf howled. I didn't watch the second execution, or listen to his response to Phin's question. I walked away, disgusted with the entire scene, and determined to not let the others see my weakness.

Sounds of the city seemed so far away, hiding behind the tall walls around the construction site. I leaned against a support beam and listened to rumbling engines, car horns, someone's blasting radio, the deeper roar of a bus trundling past.

"You're upset," Phineas said. He circled the support beam, hands clasped demurely in front of him, wings still out. A fierce anger hung around him. His eyes sparkled with life, and his cheeks were flushed. He'd enjoyed killing the Lupa, and he wasn't hiding the fact.

"I'm fine," I said.

"Liar."

"They were just kids, Phin."

"Yes, but they were also our enemies."

"Logically, I know that. And I also know that Wyatt might die because of them, but . . ." I didn't have the right words to express how I felt. I wasn't even sure how I felt to begin with, only that this entire exercise had wrung me out. Left me sick of the bloodshed and hate and tangled web of lies I'd lived in for too long.

"But you feel they are innocent victims because of Thackery's manipulations," he finished for me.

I blinked. He'd just articulated it perfectly, damn him. "Yeah, I think so. I know what it's like to have your strings pulled by other people."

"My orders are to kill the Lupa, Evy."

"I know, and I won't ask you to go against the Assembly's wishes."

"But?"

"No buts." Yet. Not until I figured out my own thoughts on this and could live with the decisions I made.

"Guys?" Carly said. "We gotta go."

Phin held out the ceremonial knife, thankfully cleaned of blood. I took it from him.

"I'll stay here and monitor the scene," he said. "If anyone shows up looking for the bodies, I will contact you."

"Okay," I said. "Be safe."

"You as well."

We exited through different parts of the construction site and assembled in the van a few minutes later. I took shotgun without asking; the rest of Baylor's squad tumbled into the back.

"What now, boss?" Paul asked.

"We have more information than before," Baylor said, "but we still don't know where to look for Thackery or the missing Therians. Who's got a source that might be useful?"

I zoned out as the others debated the few informants they had among them. My two biggest sources of information were no longer available. Max, a gargoyle I'd trusted until he turned his back on me, had left the city several months ago with his coven. Smedge was a bridge troll I hadn't seen since the second day of my resurrection. He was an Earth Guardian for the Fey, and I wasn't likely to meet him again unless it was as enemies.

In some ways, I missed talking to his big, cement head and the sound of his wind-through-reeds voice. He was part of the earth, moved through it like a fish through water, and had given me a lot of good information over the years.

"Stone?"

I looked at Baylor. "What?"

"Thoughts?"

I almost said no, all of my informants were out of town. And then it came to me, so obvious I almost laughed. "Do you know which factory the gremlins were moved to last month?"

"Yeah, why?"

"You want information? Where's the nearest bakery?"

Chapter Fourteen

8:15 A.M.

The city's entire population of gremlins used to inhabit a defunct potato chip factory on the outskirts of Mercy's Lot, surrounded by other factories both functioning and abandoned. For several square city blocks, you could travel through a veritable boneyard of the industrial age. We even had an old ironworks-turned-fancy restaurant on the Black River, where iron and steel were once shipped south during a very different time period.

Almost two months ago, Gina Kismet had convinced the gremlins to move to a new factory, and then promptly tried to blow me up in the old one. I survived (barely), and the gremlins had brand-new digs near the docks to nest in and fill up with vats of their alcohol-like piss. Why they saved it, instead of just peeing on the ground, was way beyond me. The new factory was larger than the old one—longer and narrower, about four stories with lots of papered-over windows, and a tall chain-link fence surrounding it, complete with razor wire on top.

Baylor parked alongside the fence, on the factory's river side, near what had once been a gate and guard hut. He climbed out and walked into the hut. With his van door still open, I could hear him say "Ballengee be blessed" to someone. It was a familiar greeting.

The gate buzzed, then hummed with electricity. It

rolled sideways along a track I hadn't noticed, giving us entrance.

"I'll be damned," I said. It seemed the gremlins had learned to use technology to their advantage rather than simply destroying it in service of chaos.

We drove across a narrow strip of parking lot. A garage door opened in the side of the factory, and Baylor took us right inside the building. The interior was dim, lit only by the natural light filtered through the covered windows. The majority of the open factory stretched out to our right, blocked by a wall of . . . well, stuff. Boxes and metal siding and old tables all stuck together like the world's most bizarre honeycomb.

"Everyone but Evy stay inside the van," Baylor said.

I got out first, and was struck by the familiar and nauseatingly gross odor of gremlin piss. It smelled like too-sweet liquor left to warm in the sun—or in the baking factory, in this case. Maybe gremlins liked heat, I don't know, but summertime and the lack of working air-conditioning combined to make sweat break out across my face and neck.

The noise came last. Thousands of scurrying feet and raspy, high-pitched voices speaking a foreign language of their own design. It was raucous, and it echoed in the cavern that was their new home. I wanted out—now!—but held my ground.

Baylor and I unloaded six boxes from the back of the van—four cheesecakes and two boxes of jelly-filled donuts. Gremlins lived on an entirely sugar-based diet, and providing sweets was the best way to curry a favor. We placed the boxes in a row near the three-foot hole that tunneled through the city-dump wall. It had to be their front door. There was no other way past the barrier.

Long, hot minutes passed. Sweat trickled down my back, and I longed for the air-conditioned comfort of the van. Finally, a gremlin emerged from the hole. Twenty inches or so tall, the creature had long, spindly arms, knobby knees, and wrinkled yellowish skin. Green fur tufted from its long, rabbitlike ears and covered its round head. Its red eyes moved from the food, to us, to the van, then back to the food. This gremlin wasn't as old as the first one I'd met, but that gremlin was long dead. Their life spans were about eight days.

"New," it said to Baylor.

"Yes, we have not met. But your people have met my companion."

It eyeballed me, then pointed one clawed hand at the bakery boxes. "For what?"

"Payment for a favor," I said.

"Ask."

"I need information on a human male named Walter Thackery. He consorts with half-Bloods, humans who have been bitten by vampires. He also consorts with men who shift into wolves. Lupa."

The gremlin nodded.

"We have to find Thackery. He's hurting people, and he's our enemy. If any of your people have heard talk, or seen these creatures congregating anywhere in the city, will you tell me?"

"Yes, will tell." It licked drool from its wide lips, displaying two rows of tiny, pointed teeth. "Eat. Learn. Tell."

Okay, this was promising. The gremlins were small, gross, and decidedly inhuman, but their intel was always accurate. Deception wasn't something they understood. They needed food; they traded favors for food. Sweet and simple. "When shall I return for this information?"

"Meet. Old home. Three hours."

"All right. Thank you."

It made a noise in its throat. Half a dozen gremlins swarmed from the hole, grabbed the boxes of treats, and disappeared just as quickly as they had come. The gremlin who greeted us waited until the last one was gone, then followed it inside. Summary dismissal.

"Do you trust them to do what they say?" Paul asked once we were outside the factory gates and had explained the plan to him.

I twisted around in my seat and leveled him with a glare. "The gremlins have never betrayed me."

He made a sour face.

The phone I forgot I had on me buzzed in my back pocket. Damn thing was small. I pulled it out, not surprised to see Kismet's name on the I.D. My heart skipped a beat anyway. "Stone."

"What's your status?" she asked.

"Leaving the factory. If the gremlins know anything, they'll tell us in three hours. Anything new on your end?"

"So far no new illnesses among the vampires. We're talking to them, trying to find a common connection between the ones who are sick and the ones who aren't."

I repeated that for the group in the van. "Nothing on the missing Therians?"

"Not yet, no. Speaking of, Astrid chewed me out for letting you off the premises during an unofficial quarantine."

Oops. "What did you say to her?"

"I threw the word 'unofficial' back in her face and said, 'Thanks to Evy there are two fewer werewolves in the world.' It shut her up."

Laughter bubbled up inside, but I kept it down. A well-oiled machine we were not.

"Then she made the quarantine official," Kismet said. "Everyone who's in the field now is all we have until she, Dr. Vansis, and the vampire Fathers are convinced the infection won't spread."

"Terrific."

I repeated that, too, to a chorus of soft groans from the other passengers. Backup, weapons, technology—so many things now completely inaccessible to us. That sucked big-time.

"How's Wyatt?" I asked. Her silence sent tremors through my stomach. "Gina?"

"He got worse fast, Evy. His temperature shot up two degrees, and his blood pressure spiked. Dr. Vansis induced a coma a few minutes ago."

A dull roar filled my ears. I pressed my forehead against the cool glass of the passenger window and closed my eyes. Nothing felt real. "Why?" was all I could manage to squeak out.

Kismet's own voice was tight when she replied. "The Assembly's information was pretty useless. No one did viral analysis five hundred years ago, but his symptoms match what's been noted. Dr. Vansis explained it with bigger words—"

"Use your own words."

"He said before that the virus seems to work similarly to the rabies virus. He did some research and there have been successful rabies treatments using induced coma and various drugs, but since this isn't actually rabies, it's just a shot in the dark. But he hopes that the coma will at least reduce, um, brain damage—"

I flinched and bit hard on my tongue to stop a spew of angry cussing.

"—from the fever."

"What are his chances?" I asked after a moment of silence.

"Not great. And if he does survive, the chances of him being the same person are . . ."

"Not great."

"Yeah. I'm so sorry, Evy. I wish I had better news."

"Me, too."

I fought the instinct to demand Baylor drive me back

to the Watchtower so I could be with Wyatt. Be there to do what, though? Watch him sleep? Hold his hand while he was unconscious, as he'd done for me so many times in the recent past? Yes, definitely. The part of me that still loved Wyatt—had never really stopped loving him—insisted I be with him. He'd been there when I died. I'd been there when he died, and if he died again today, there was no gnome healing crystal to bring him back to me.

Logic tied me in knots. The Watchtower was on lockdown. The gremlins would have information for me in three hours. If I went back, I might not be able to leave, and that was not acceptable. Not with so many other lives depending on us finding Walter Thackery and his Merry Band of Werewolves. Duty above self.

Fuck!

Someone in the van made a noise. Guess I'd said that out loud.

"You can't do anything here," Kismet said. She might as well have read my mind. I didn't know all the details of her nine-year friendship with Wyatt. Just that they were close, and this had to be hurting her, too. I hated sharing my misery with others, and at the same time I was glad she was there.

"I know."

"He won't be alone. I promise."

"Thanks."

"I don't—hold on a sec." I concentrated on the muffled voices on her end so I didn't have to think about the way my life was slowly spiraling down, down to its very lowest point. First Aurora and Ava, now Wyatt. There wasn't—

"Stone?"

"Still here," I said.

"We got a call from James Reilly. He has some information to pass along to you guys, if you can meet him."

Reilly. His was a name I hadn't consciously thought about in weeks. He was a private investigator who showed up in the city a few days after my resurrection, asking questions about Chalice Frost and Alex Forrester. He ended up having an agenda (seriously, does anyone not?) and knew more about vampires than any outsider had a right to.

I'd pressed the issue with Kismet once, and she'd given me the bullet points. Decorated West Coast police detective who stumbled onto a crime scene involving two half-Bloods and the full-Blood vampire who executed them. The case disappeared, along with all the files, but Reilly never forgot what he saw. His obsession with vampires grew, and after a nasty divorce he quit the force, got his PI license, then hit the road.

Reilly had definitely made an impression on the Triads when he showed up in the city. He was detained none too politely, questioned, and then put on our payroll. With the brass dead and our insight into the Police Department cut off, having a PI with his own connections had proved valuable. His specific connections had become "need to know" as well, so I didn't press the subject. I knew the value of protecting your sources, and as long as Reilly handed us good information, I'd play nice. I just couldn't help wondering if his motives for assisting us were really as selfless as they sounded, or if he had hidden reasons.

Then again, I'm used to seeing conspiracies and deceit around every corner, so it was just as likely that I was being paranoid.

"When and where does Reilly want to meet?" I asked.

"Nine o'clock, Sally's Coffee Shop on Church Street."

"I know it." I checked the clock on the dash. We had about twenty minutes. Plenty of time from our current location. "We'll be there."

"I'll let him know."

"If anything develops—"

"I'll call you."

"Thanks, Gina." I put the phone away and filled Baylor in on our new meeting, realizing for the first time that he'd pulled over in the lot of a mini-mart.

"Well, that's something," he said. "I've got a thought, too. Autumn, how good is your sense of smell?"

"Better than yours," she replied with a toss of her auburn hair. "What would you like me to ferret out?"

Sandburg grunted.

"Think you can pick up the werewolves' scent from the old Sunset Terrace lot and track it to wherever they went afterward?"

"I believe so. I got a good whiff of the bastards back at the construction site. I'll have to track in my true form."

"Not a problem. We'll drop you off. Take Sandburg and Carly to watch your back. Paul, Stone, and I are going to meet with James Reilly."

Sally's Coffee Shop was a familiar, somewhat popular place for the Hunters who used to patrol in Mercy's Lot. One of the few greasy spoons brave enough to stay open twenty-four hours a day, seven days a week, it was a good place to hit for a cheap plate of food and decent coffee. The patrons minded their own business, and the waitresses did the same.

Reilly was already waiting in a back booth, leisurely eating a plate of syrup-laden pancakes. He looked like someone's underpaid, overworked office manager in a rumpled suit and tie. He had flyaway curly hair and a simple, guileless charm that made me want to like him. He quirked an eyebrow at our numbers, then slid over to make room.

I sat next to him, more for my own amusement than

anything else. He'd been shocked as hell to learn my story, and the expression on his face was about the only enjoyable thing in my day so far. Baylor and Paul slid in across from us, and a waitress promptly appeared with mugs of coffee.

"You folks need menus?" she asked.

"They'll have the pancakes," Reilly said. "The pancakes are excellent here."

"That sounds fine," Baylor said.

The waitress nodded, then wandered off. I dumped sugar into my mug of coffee, unsure if I'd be able to do more than stare at my pancakes. I was hungry, but my stomach was tied up in so many worried knots that getting food into it would be an exercise in nausea control.

"When it rains, it downpours, wouldn't you agree?" Reilly asked.

"I'd say that's an understatement."

Reilly nodded, then pushed his half-finished plate aside. He produced a manila folder from the booth seat and handed it over the table to Baylor. "I've been chatting up a young lady in Animal Control about recent sightings of wild animals in the city. Wolves, in particular, and we may have a pattern."

Baylor withdrew a map of the city—easy enough to identify, even upside down, because of the way the Anjean and Black rivers intersected in the center to create one south-flowing river. A cluster of highlighter marks singled out one particular neighborhood, and it wasn't Mercy's Lot, which was traditionally where the majority of paranormal shit went down.

"Uptown?" Paul said. His face scrunched up. "Seriously?"

Reilly nodded. "It's possible that wolf sightings in other areas were simply not reported, since odd occurrences are not abnormal in certain neighborhoods. But there have been sixteen separate reports of large, nondomestic dogs resembling wolves roaming wild through Uptown in the last three months. Forty-six over the last two years."

Uptown was the upscale business district of the city, home to a modern art museum, the Fourth Street Library, several large banks, expensive condos, office buildings, medical centers, restaurants that served food portions the size of silver dollars, and our state university satellite campus.

The same fucking campus where Walter Thackery taught until five years ago, when his wife was turned into a Halfie and he began his long trek toward crazy.

"Are you shitting me?" I said.

Baylor scrutinized the map. "The university?"

"He's hiding them in plain sight. He probably assumed we'd never think him dumb enough to go back to his old stomping grounds."

"He was obviously right," Reilly said.

"So the other Lupa are living somewhere on or around the campus?" Baylor asked.

"That's certainly one interpretation."

"How else would you interpret it?"

"He could want you on that side of town when he does something elsewhere."

"No." I shook my head, positive this wasn't just some long con on Thackery's part. "These sightings took place over the last two years, long before everything started coming undone. He's damned smart, but even he couldn't have thought two years ahead."

"You think the wolves are there," Baylor said.

"I think they live somewhere in the direct vicinity of the university, yes. Doesn't mean that's where Thackery is, though."

"Because that would be too easy," Paul deadpanned.

The waitress returned and plopped down three plates of pancakes, each topped with a mound of melting butter and whipped cream on the side. I stared at mine, debating the intelligence of testing a bite or two. Baylor reached for one of the syrup pitchers and poured blue goo all over his.

"They look like kids, not old enough for college so they can't be living in the dorms." I punctuated the thought by ripping a piece of butter-free pancake off the mound. "What else is close by?"

Paul took the map and squinted at the streets of Uptown. "Couple of condominiums, a neighborhood of historic homes, and two apartment complexes are all within a few blocks."

"Apartments and condos offer less security, more visibility. The historic neighborhood is a good place to start. Trees, backyards, things like that." I popped the piece of fried batter into my mouth. It was moderately sweet, done as well as a pancake could be, and went down easily. Not bad.

"I thought you might say that." Reilly tapped the pages remaining in the manila folder. "I did some digging on your behalf. Two of the homes are registered landmarks, one is a highly regarded bed and breakfast, and eighteen of them haven't changed family hands in decades. Twelve are possibilities."

I grabbed the pages and shuffled through the lists of addresses. Some had photos, printed in black and white, and all had been on the market in the last six years. "I don't suppose we could be lucky enough that Thackery took out a mortgage in his own name."

"Unfortunately not. No leases, either."

"This is a good head start, though. Thank you."

Reilly smiled over the rim of his coffee mug. "You're welcome, Ms. Stone."

Chapter Fifteen

Twelve houses didn't seem like a lot to investigate at first. After twenty minutes sitting in the van listening to Autumn and Sandburg pretending to be a lost couple looking for grandma's house, I was ready to climb out of my skin. Even Baylor, normally the picture of burly calm, seemed agitated by the slow going and lack of results.

We'd picked up Sandburg, Autumn, and Carly after they followed the Lupa scent trail from the vacant lot to eight blocks away where it ended in a public parking lot with no video surveillance. A dead end, and Phin still hadn't seen movement on the construction site. So we had Autumn and Sandburg and their heightened senses of smell walking around the historic residential district of Uptown, which they both declared carried the faint odors of Lupa and money.

The money I could agree with. The stained glass windows in some of those homes probably cost more than I'd have made in six months with the Triads (which wasn't a lot to begin with, but still . . .).

"House number seven," Autumn said, obviously bored even over the earbud she wore. "You do the talking this time."

Sandburg muttered something unintelligible. The van was parked a block away under a majestic old oak tree, idling quietly while they did their thing. Our next stop was several blocks farther, if this house didn't turn up anything useful. We had about forty-five minutes until I had to leave to meet the gremlin across town.

I shifted in the hard bucket seat. Two squirrels darted into the street, ran in circles, and then dashed up a nearby tree.

A doorbell gonged faintly. Hinges squealed.

"Hi, I'm so sorry to bother you this early," Sandburg said, affecting a perfect (and hilarious) southern accent. "Um, my girlfriend and I were looking for 756 Cherryvale Lane. An old roommate of mine is getting married, but I don't think you're him."

"Oh, no, dear," replied someone who could only be an elderly woman. "This is 756 Cherryvale Court. I don't know where Cherryvale Lane is."

"Well, drat."

"Should have known, honey," Autumn piped in, playing along with the accent. "You told me Walter had a bunch of younger brothers, and my goodness, your house is beautiful. I can't imagine a bunch of teenage boys tearing around in there."

"No, no, we haven't had boys in this house for many years," the old lady said. "Our grandchildren live with their parents in Europe. We don't get to see them but once every few years."

Autumn cooed sympathy. "That's terrible."

"Yes, but my James and I get along just fine. We have some neighborhood boys who tend the yard and fix what needs fixing."

I sat up a little straighter, my full attention on the cell phone spilling out the conversation. Even Paul and Carly shifted forward between the seats.

"That's wonderful," Autumn said. "It's so nice when children help out their neighbors."

"Oh, no, deary, they are young men, the lot of them.

Should be in high school, but one told me they're taught at home. Good boys, very polite."

"It's good they live close by."

"Yes, somewhere close. I never did get their street, but one of them always seems to know when we need help. Good boys, especially that Danny. He's the oldest of the bunch."

Danny. I thought of Wolf Boy, the one who'd been working so closely with Thackery last month. The one I'd killed at Boot Camp. Logic suggested he was the oldest, to have been Thackery's right hand.

"Well, thank you so much for your time, ma'am," Sandburg said. "We're sorry to have bothered you so early."

"Posh, I was awake. Can't sleep past the sun at my age. You two kids be safe, you hear? Some strange things happening in this city lately."

I snickered.

"Take care," Autumn said.

The door creaked shut. Several long moments passed, punctuated by the faint sounds of breathing.

"Well, that was actually useful," Sandburg said. "Teenage boys who are all homeschooled, and live close by."

"Thanks for the recap," Baylor said. "What about scent?"

"Nothing fresh that we can follow. And 'nearby' could be this street or several streets in any direction."

"There was no way to acquire further information without arousing her suspicion, I think," Autumn said. "More direct questions would have seemed strange."

"No, you did good," Baylor replied.

"That's sweet, boss."

He rolled his eyes. "Keep going with the list while I text an update to Astrid. Maybe change the story this time—"

"Yeah, yeah, we're looking for a neighbor who a friend said does good yard work, I got it."

I liked Autumn. She thought fast and improvised well.

"Which one's next?" Sandburg asked.

"787 Cherryvale," I said. "Next block over."

"Awesome. Let's—do you smell that?"

Baylor fumbled his phone.

"It's coming from over there," Autumn said, to the sound of loud footsteps.

"Do not engage," Baylor said.

"Look out!"

The phone line exploded with snarls, grunts, and shouts. Baylor yanked the gearshift down and slammed his foot on the gas. A car honked as he cut it off. I gripped the dash with both hands, adrenaline kicking my heartbeat up a notch. Phin's knife was tucked carefully between my thigh and the seat, and as soon as Baylor slammed to a halt I grabbed it and bolted out of the van.

A waist-high, untrimmed hedge bordered the property of a house that had once been expensive but now simply looked tired. The eaves were cracked, the paint was peeling, the front walk stones were uneven and broken. It was one of the few unmaintained homes I'd seen in the neighborhood, and its wild lawn was the sight of a stand-off. Autumn was on the ground, both hands clutching her bleeding throat, gasping for breath. A black wolf the size of a small horse had Sandburg by the back of the neck, teeth sunk in deep enough to draw blood. A flex of his jaw, and the Lupa would break Sandburg's spine.

The Lupa snarled, and I stumbled to a halt halfway between them and Autumn. I felt, more than saw, Baylor, Paul, and Carly draw up behind me. For one brief, irrational moment, I had visions of Autumn and Sandburg in the infirmary, as sick and feverish as Wyatt. But then I remembered that they weren't human—they were Therian, just like the Lupa. The infection wouldn't affect them.

"You boys are just a bucket of trouble, aren't you?" I said. Insects buzzed around us, a soft accompaniment to Autumn's ragged breathing. "Danny says hello."

He snarled again, louder. Sandburg's eyes bulged, and his fingers dug into the grass. A loud whistle cut the quiet, bouncing off the homes around us, making the origin of the sound impossible to detect. The black Lupa dropped Sandburg and sprinted toward the back of the yard.

I gave chase, trusting the others to stay behind and tend to our wounded. Blackie charged through the tall grass of the front yard, past the aging house, and into the even taller grass of the backyard. I ran as fast as I could, little bursts of energy keeping me from feeling the instant burn in my legs. Someone was behind me, and I didn't waste time or strength by looking over my shoulder.

Blackie sailed over the rear hedge and into another yard. I'd never run hurdles, but I didn't stop or slow down. Just pushed off and hoped I didn't break a bone on the landing. My foot caught the edge of the hedge, and I tumbled to the grass. Came up in a roll, left arm and ribs sore from the fall, and kept going. Miraculously, I hadn't cut myself with the knife. A shout from behind told me that my companion hadn't fared much better than I had.

Blackie veered left, crossing the new backyard at a diagonal. I kept my focus on him, so I missed who screamed and didn't much care. I was chasing a full-grown werewolf through an historic neighborhood in broad daylight, with an ancient Coni weapon in my hand. Explaining it away to civilians was not on my To Do list. I just didn't want to lose the damned Lupa.

And he was quickly putting distance between us.

A fence loomed ahead of him, this one solid wood and at least five feet high. I could scramble over, but I'd lose precious seconds doing so. Blackie galloped full-steam at the fence.

Shit, shit, shit . . .

He shifted hard right at the last moment and took off toward the front yard. I skidded a little, but had a wider angle to turn. My lungs burned, and my legs felt like jelly from the hard run. Up ahead in the street was an idling work van, plain white, its side door open. A pale face peered out from the dark square. Waiting.

Fuck no!

If Blackie got into the van, we'd lose them again. I pushed harder, desperate.

The Lupa in the back of the van shoved a large black-wrapped bundle onto the sidewalk—a bundle the size of a person. Blackie leapt over the bundle and into the van, which tore away from the curb before he was fully inside. Rubber squealed and exhaust plumed.

"Get the plate number!" I screamed as loudly as I could, given my severe lack of oxygen.

Paul raced past me. I fell to my hands and knees near the bundle, panting and sucking air into my starved lungs. Sweat dripped into my eyes and down my back, and I was mildly grateful I'd managed only a few bites of dry pancake at breakfast, or I'd probably be chucking it back up right about now.

The black sheet was bound with bungee cords. No damp spots indicated blood or wounds. Absolutely no movement—whoever was inside wasn't breathing.

Still trying to control my own erratic lung functions, I chose the end of the bundle that looked most like a head and unsnapped the first bungee. Unwound it far enough to begin pulling back the sheet. Wide, empty eyes stared up at me from a too-pale, too-familiar face. I choked.

Something was tucked into his mouth. I pulled it out with trembling fingers and unfolded a handwritten note.

FOR MY BOYS. AN EYE FOR AN EYE.

Rage coursed through me stronger and more bitter than any adrenaline rush. Tears stung my eyes and closed my throat.

"Stone?" Paul came up behind me, breathing hard. "Holy shit, is that—?"

"Yeah."

"Is he dead?"

I nodded, numbly reaching for my phone. Fumbled it twice before I managed to speed dial. Didn't even know who until someone picked up.

"Kismet." When I didn't speak right away, she asked, "Stone? You there?"

"We need a car on, uh . . ." I had no idea where we were.

"840 Palmer Drive," Paul said.

"On the eight-hundred block of Palmer Drive, Uptown."

"What happened?" Kismet asked.

"Thackery sent us a message. Michael Jenner is dead."

Sitting on a well-manicured lawn behind a trio of ornamentally cut trees with the dead body of a friend baking in the summer sun served as the perfect reminder of why I resented my afterlife. Jenner was a tall guy. Paul and I were not. Between the two of us, we had barely managed to drag the black-wrapped bundle off the sidewalk and into the yard next door.

We didn't speak. After my initial call to Kismet, I turned the phone on vibrate and ignored it. Help was on the way. All that was left to do was wait and grieve.

The first car nearly overshot our position. Paul stood up and waved, and the car came to a brake-burning halt. All four doors opened simultaneously. Astrid, Marcus, Tybalt, and Kyle climbed out. Marcus still wore the walking cast, but he showed no sign of a limp from his wound. A thundercloud of fury hung over him, shared equally by Astrid and Kyle. Jenner had been one of theirs.

"What about the lockdown?" I asked dumbly, curious

as to their appearance. I'd expected the Assembly to send someone outside the Watchtower to collect Jenner.

"Baylor and I overrode the decision," Astrid said. "The Assembly is convening an emergency session in half an hour to discuss what's to be done."

Marcus crouched next to Jenner's head and lifted the drape. He winced, then frowned.

"What's to be done?" I parroted, confused now.

Astrid glared. "Yes, done. Kidnapping Clan members was bad enough, but the cold-blooded murder of the Assembly's Speaker may be considered an act of war. If that determination is made, retribution will be required."

Just like with the Sunset Terrace slaughter. For the deaths of his people, Phineas had asked the Assembly for the execution of former Handler Rufus St. James, who'd led the devastating raid. Only some complicated maneuvering had saved Rufus's life all those months ago.

"Retribution from Thackery?" I said. "Get in line."

"I don't think you understand, Stone. Thackery may be acting alone, but he also acts in the supposed best interest of preserving his race. The human race. Murdering Michael Jenner was more than just a personal act of war against Therians. It was a human act against Therians."

My heart thudded. I glanced at Tybalt, who looked as miserable as I felt. "So you're saying that Walter Thackery might have just declared war for all humans against Therians?"

"According to our ancient traditions, yes." Astrid looked less happy about it than Tybalt. "And if the Equi Elder demands immediate recompense, we must follow the wishes of the Assembly."

"What does that mean, exactly?" Tybalt asked.

"It means revenge," Marcus said. He stood, letting the black sheet fall back over Jenner's face. "It means Elder Dannu can make any request he likes, and if the

Assembly casts a majority vote, his people are obligated to carry it out and we cannot interfere."

A chill danced up my spine. "So if the Assembly votes to let the Equi execute ten humans in retaliation for Jenner's death?" I asked.

"Then ten humans will die by Equi hands."

"Fuck."

"Have you examined the body thoroughly?"

"No."

"Judging by the skin tone and lack of settling, I'm guessing he died of massive blood loss."

The Halfies. Shit. "Did you see—?"

"There were no visible bite marks, but Dr. Vansis will have to examine him to be certain."

"So Thackery's pissed we killed a couple of his werewolves," Tybalt said, "and he feeds the most valuable of his kidnapped Therians to his Halfies. That's our working theory?"

There were so many things wrong with that scenario, I didn't know where to start. It was as ludicrous as it was perfectly logical. We'd fucked with Thackery's plan, and now he was fucking with us.

"That's the theory," Astrid said. "And it makes sense, given what we know of Walter Thackery. Such an act of aggression may, depending on what the Assembly decides, break the fragile alliance we have created between humans and Therians."

"And with the vampires busy trying to fight this new illness," Marcus said, "our Watch is effectively divided."

"Not yet it isn't," I said with a sharp shake of my head. "How long does it usually take the Assembly to make a decision on something like this?"

"It depends on the situation and how the Elders are likely to view it. The Equi are greatly respected, and Elder Dannu's words will hold great power among the others. Eight votes are a majority."

"So are we talking days? Hours?"

"Given the fact that other Clan members disappeared at the same time as Jenner, hours is optimistic."

Damn. "We aren't sure yet how Jenner died. The Assembly still has to rule on the Equi's request, and we don't even know what that will be, right?"

"Correct."

"We also know the Lupa live around here somewhere, and considering what just happened, they're probably not coming back. But if we get some noses out here, maybe we can find the house and some sort of lead."

Kyle, who'd been completely silent until that moment, spoke up. "I'll volunteer for that. My true form is a dingo. On first glance, most humans assume I'm some mixed mutt."

Dingoes were beautiful animals, and I'd seen Kyle's true form once. Thick golden fur with a dusting of white on the paws and chest, and an intelligent face. He did look a bit like a mix between a golden retriever and an Akita.

"Good," Astrid said. "Check in every fifteen minutes."

"Will do." Kyle didn't waste a beat. He started to strip.

"Marcus and I can assist on foot. I don't think a pair of big cats will go unnoticed on these streets."

I grunted. "What about—?"

Before I could voice my question, a utility van pulled up behind Astrid's car. Two Therians I knew by sight, if not by name, got out.

"They'll take Jenner back to the Watchtower," Astrid said.

"I need to get across town to meet with the gremlins soon," I said.

"Take the car. And them." She pointed individually at Paul and Tybalt.

"Fine."

Kyle trotted into the middle of the group and shook

himself, his golden coat gleaming in the morning sun, and then snorted. His way of saying he was ready to go. Astrid conferred with the newest pair of Therians. Afterward, she tossed me a set of car keys.

"Be careful," she said.

"You, too," I replied. "And I'm sorry about Jenner. He was a good man."

She gave me a long, assessing look. "Yes, he was."

Kyle whined softly. At first, I thought it was impatience— a theory laid to rest as soon as I looked at him, facing north, nose in the air. He sniffed with purpose, then turned his head and whined at Astrid, seeming to ask *Do you smell that?* I didn't.

"Something's burning," Marcus said.

Oh hell.

Chapter Sixteen

11:10 A.M.

With my deadline looming to meet the gremlin, I got an update on the fire about fifteen minutes later via a phone call from Marcus. Tybalt was driving, and doing an impressive job in rush hour traffic with his prosthetic hand. I put the phone on speaker so I didn't have to repeat the conversation.

"House was one block up, two over from that old lady you talked to earlier," Marcus reported. The faint sounds of raised voices and sirens still hummed over the line. "The fire was going so hot and hard, it nearly took out a neighbor's house. All the fire department can do is control its burn."

"Do we have any information on who owns it?" I asked.

"Yes, and it wasn't on your list. You'll never guess, so I won't even ask you to try."

Thank God for small favors. I wasn't in the mood for guessing games; I doubted anyone else was, either.

"Winston Zeigler," he said.

The name seemed familiar, yet I couldn't place it. Paul saved me from looking like an idiot by asking, "Who's that?"

"Former head of the biology department at the university."

Of course he was. "Don't tell me," I said. "He was there at the same time as Thackery."

"Bingo."

"How the hell did Reilly miss that connection?"

"He didn't. Zeigler's name wasn't on the deed. It was his late wife's family home and under her maiden name, so unless Reilly dug extra deep on all the homes, he wouldn't have found it."

Good. It saved me having to rip him a new one for the oversight. "How'd you find it?"

Marcus made a huffing sound that might have been laughter. "Reilly's a PI, but he's only been in the city a few months. My sources are still better."

"So Winston Zeigler is our only lead?" Tybalt asked.

"At the moment, yes, but it isn't a great one."

"How's that?"

"Astrid already called the university. Mr. Zeigler quit his position—"

"Three and a half years ago?" I said.

"Yes. He was diagnosed with a rare kind of cancer, and even with treatment he was given just a few years to live. He told colleagues he inherited a bit of money from a recently deceased relative"—

"I just bet."

—"and wanted to travel the world before he died."

"So Zeigler is living out his last days on a cruise ship somewhere, while an old pal uses his house to raise werewolves."

"It seems so."

"Which means Zeigler is a dead end?"

"Not entirely. Someone was likely put in charge of maintaining the home while Zeigler's out of the country. Astrid and I are going to pay a visit to the family lawyer and see what they have to say."

It was something—way better than the big fat nothing

we'd had just a few minutes ago. "Hey," I said, "any news on Autumn and Sandburg?"

The pause made my heart sink. "Sandburg will be fine. Autumn's hanging on. Dr. Vansis has done all he can."

"They're not infected?"

"By the Lupa? No. Their bite has never been known to affect other Therians."

I expelled a deep breath, glad for that bit of clarification. "Okay, thanks."

We arrived at the old factory site a few minutes later. Police tape hung in tattered shreds across the main parking lot. The rubble was mostly gone. Only a blackened steel skeleton remained. Tybalt parked a few yards from the side entrance and idled there. He glanced at me, one eyebrow arched high.

I mirrored his expression, remembering the last time we'd both been at this particular location and the explosion that had decimated the structure.

"Okay," Paul said from the back, "what did I miss?"

"Nothing," we said in stereo.

"Wait here," I added.

The air reeked of char and oil. I navigated an archipelago of water-filled potholes, reasonably sure I wasn't being watched. Hunters often gain an overdeveloped sense of paranoia, and mine was quiet. Thackery had been one step ahead of us all night long. Maybe luck was on our side this time.

Reasonably sure that the two steel pillars I stood near had once been the side entrance, I turned in a slow circle. The lot was quiet, with no immediate sign of the gremlin that I was here to meet.

So I was mildly startled when it emerged from the other side of a support beam clutching some folded paper in its hand. It crawled on all fours, body slunk low to the ground. Gremlins didn't much like daylight, and it probably felt exposed coming out like this. I allowed it to approach me.

It dropped the folded paper at my feet, then inched backward until it found a shadow to melt into. I snatched the paper. Unfolded a drawing of a squiggly Y with a couple of dots here and there. No, not a Y . . . the rivers. Three red dots littered the area that was probably Mercy's Lot. A single black dot was very, very close to our current position.

I turned the drawing around. "Explain?"

The gremlin pointed a gnarled, clawed finger at the paper. "Red. Many infected. Black. Animal men."

"Animal men?" *What the holy hell did—?*

"Prisoners."

My heart slammed against my chest. "Shape-shifters? Therians? There are Therian prisoners at the black dot?"

It took a moment to process my words. "Yes."

"Are there infected at the black dot, too?"

"Yes."

"It's somewhere along the Black River, right? The docks?"

"Yes. Sit on water."

Gremlins were completely literal creatures. I dug through my own vocabulary to figure out what it meant. "It floats? The place where the captured Therians are? It floats on the river?"

It blinked at me. I took that as a yes, which likely meant a boat. Some of the still active docks had cargo ships coming and going. A few rusted, abandoned ships were docked here and there, slowly becoming part of the waterfront's permanent landscape—those were very likely locations to stash dozens of Halfies.

Wind in the walls. Token's rough, garbled voice repeated the description of the place he'd been imprisoned. I hadn't consciously thought of the missing goblin/human hybrid in weeks. He'd tried to kill me, then tried to help me, only to disappear with no reported sightings these last two months. If our initial plan had worked as expected, he might have led us to this location ages ago. If only.

"Thank you," I said. "This is more than worth the price I paid for it."

It nodded, then turned and slunk away. I gazed at the map, hand trembling slightly. It was the break we needed. My desperation to find the kidnapped Therians before any more were killed threatened to overtake my good sense. I wanted to charge down to the docks, procedure be damned, and start hurting things. And I'd succeed only in getting myself killed. Or kidnapped. Probably the latter, then the former.

Dammit.

I jogged back to the waiting car; Tybalt looked ready to climb out of his skin. As I slid back into the passenger seat, his expression switched from pensive to curious.

"Good news?" he asked.

"Great news."

By the time Tybalt and I returned to the Watchtower twenty minutes later, two things had happened. Astrid called demanding a noon meeting in the War Room of all available squad leaders. My gremlin information got me an invite, but she didn't offer any hint of what she'd learned from Zeigler's lawyer. And I found out that the Assembly of Clan Elders was officially in their emergency session discussing what was to be done about Michael Jenner's murder.

I handed the map over to Tybalt for delivery to Operations. Smarter people than me could go over the Black River waterfront and decide the best places to start looking for a target. The only thing I could think was to call the place where the Therians were being held, and Thackery's possible headquarters. My curiosity as to the condition of Isleen and her fellow vampires took far second place to my need to see Wyatt, so I ignored the questions being thrown at me from various sources and beelined for the infirmary.

Dr. Vansis was in Wyatt's room, making notes on a chart, his body blocking my immediate view. He glanced up, eyebrows arching in surprise. "Ms. Stone," he said.

"Hi." I also noted with rising annoyance that we were the only ones in the room. "Where's Gina?"

"Restroom. She'll be back shortly."

I stepped around the bed, really taking in Wyatt's appearance for the first time. His skin was blotchy with fever—deathly pale in some places, marred by spots of red and pink on his face and chest. He'd been intubated, and the various tubes and wires were awful reminders that Vansis had induced a coma to try to save him. He was so still. Even asleep, Wyatt had always seemed vibrant and alive. Now he looked much like he had three months ago, dead in my arms in the mountains north of the city.

"I'm doing what I can," Vansis said, "but next to nothing is known about how the Lupa virus interacts with human physiology. No one has seen its effects in centuries."

Wyatt's hand was cool in mine. I held it tight between my palms, hoping to warm it just a little. "What do you know about rabies, Dr. Vansis?"

"It's treatable, if caught early. However, this virus is acting more like rabies that has gone undetected and traveled to the brain. Once it reaches that stage, cranial inflammation begins, and it's often fatal."

Vansis turned, as if to leave, then paused in the doorway. "I know it's little consolation now, Ms. Stone, but the Lupa are alive and well, and anything we learn from Mr. Truman's illness may help us treat the next human they infect. If we're lucky, his is the only life we'll lose to them."

His is the only life we'll lose. Pragmatically, it was a nice thing to hear. In reality, the idea of losing him to the Lupa's bite broke my heart into sharp, frozen pieces. I didn't want to be pragmatic, or to look at the bigger picture. It was Wyatt, goddammit, and I wanted him alive.

Vansis left, and I perched on the narrow space between Wyatt's arm and the edge of the bed. "Hey," I said. "We've got good news. We might even have Aurora, Joseph, and Ava home by dinner. I want you there when we bring them home." Wanted him there so badly that my chest ached with the need.

Or was that with unshed tears?

"I'm an idiot. Did you know that?" I could almost see him nodding at me, agreeing with a teasing smile. "Of course you do, but I'm going to share this little epiphany with you anyway. Most of my life, I thought love was just something people did in movies. That in real life, people hurt each other and left and you just picked up the pieces for the next person who came along to hurt you. I mean, let's face it. My role models have sucked.

"I never wanted to fall in love. Not before I died, and not after, but I guess we don't get to decide who we love. Whoever I am—this person I became the night you died and this body switch was made permanent—this person loves you. I love you. I haven't said it much, but I like to think you believed me when I did."

My throat closed; hot tears stung my eyes. "I didn't want to love you, but I do anyway. And I think I finally grew up and realized a few things. I realized being in love doesn't exempt you from hurting each other, but when you do, you don't give up. You fix it. With Thackery . . . I was a coward, and I didn't want you to see that side of me. I didn't want to admit I'd been so weak. That

I was weak with Felix. Pushing you away was easier than talking about it, and I'm so sorry for that."

Warm wetness splashed my hand. I allowed the tears to fall, not caring anymore who saw me cry. "We flirt with death every single day. It's always around the corner, Wyatt, waiting to take one of us away. And I can't keep allowing death to control my life. Not anymore. Loving doesn't make me weak, Wyatt, I know that now."

Images of him, of Alex and Phin and Aurora and Ava, even of Jesse and Ash—they telegraphed through my memory, reminding me of people I cared about. Loved. Some I'd lost. Others I was still battling against all odds to protect.

"Loving makes me stronger." I laughed, choked, and wiped my nose on my arm. "That sounds like a fucking greeting card, I know. But it gives me something more powerful to fight for than just honor and nameless, faceless innocents. There's real power in loving someone, and I know it now." I leaned down and pressed my forehead to his, aware of the heat of his skin, the machine that drew his breath, the monitor that ticked off the beats of his heart. "I just hope I didn't learn it too late."

I sat like that awhile, pretending he felt my presence and could feed off my strength. Sat until my back hurt and my neck ached, and I simply had to sit up again and stretch. He hadn't moved; I hadn't really expected him to.

"I have a meeting," I said. "A meeting that will hopefully lead to a plan that includes reconnaissance, invasion, extraction, and lots of enemy decimation."

"That was kind of poetic," Milo said.

His voice startled me right off the bed. I barely had my balance back before snapping, "Make some noise or something next time."

He leaned in the doorframe, hands in his pockets, wan and fairly simmering with untapped energy—rage, grief, frustration. He wanted to be out in the field, part of the solution, instead of left behind due to his recent gunshot wound.

"Everyone's buzzing about your information and wondering where you got it," he said.

I blinked. I hadn't asked Tybalt, Astrid, or anyone else in Baylor's squad to keep my informants a secret. They'd just done it. In the Triads, we'd often operated on a version of "don't ask, don't tell" when it came to acquiring information. The more people who knew about your informants, the less likely you were to get good info when you asked them. Nice to see that the policy was still alive and well.

"Doesn't matter where as long as it's accurate," I said.

"I know, but the Therians aren't used to working like that. I did float the idea that you probably got the info from the gremlins."

"You what?"

He lifted one shoulder in a half shrug. "Shelby didn't believe me. The Felia he was with thought it was a ridiculous idea, that the gremlins are nasty little creatures who don't help anyone except themselves."

I very nearly laughed. Apparently, humans weren't the only ones with hidden prejudices against other races. Recalling Phin's violent reaction to the odor of vats of gremlin urine, I imagined that Therians and gremlins didn't mix it up very often.

"That *is* where you went, right?"

"Yeah," I said. "With Tybalt, no less."

"How was that?"

"Nostalgic."

"Things have a funny habit of blowing up when you're nearby."

A sharp retort died on my tongue. He was right. Rufus's first apartment, the potato chip factory, the half-Blood in the hospital parking garage, Felix . . . "They do, don't they?" I said. "I'm sorry you had to see that happen to Felix."

Milo frowned. "Felix died two—"

"I know, he died two weeks ago. But that doesn't make seeing his shell explode any easier, right?" It certainly hadn't made shooting Alex Forrester in the back of the head any easier for me. The Halfie I'd killed wore the face of a man I'd once cared about; the Halfie who'd blown up in our jail wore the face of a man Milo had once cared about. Loved.

"No, it doesn't," Milo said. "At least he's at peace now."

"You're not."

"No, I'm not. Not even close." He clenched his jaw, seemed on the verge of adding to his statement. Then he swallowed hard. "I, ah, Gina asked me to stay here during the meeting."

I didn't know what time it was, but probably damned close to noon. "Thanks for sitting with him."

"Nothing better to do."

"Even so."

He nodded. A heavy weariness settled over him and he seemed the oldest twenty-year-old I'd ever met. I gave Wyatt's hand another strong squeeze, and then left.

The War Room was packed with more than just squad leaders—every human ex-Handler, a handful of ex-Hunters, and quite a few of the higher-ranked Therian squad members were there, alongside their squad leaders. The only noticeable absences were the vampires stuck in quarantine.

An unexpected face stood out from a cluster of ex-Handlers near the far wall, and not just because he was sitting while the others were standing. Rufus St. James had been invited more than once to join us as part of the Operations staff. His experience as a Handler was invaluable, and he had a terrific tactical mind. His old

Triad had rivaled my own in effectiveness, until they were all killed and he was shot by Halfies, effectively crippling him.

I guess an epic crisis really does bring people together, because Rufus was in Operations, chatting quietly with Nevada, Sharpe, and Tybalt.

He watched my approach with a steady gaze, studying the telltale signs of my minor breakdown. "How is he?" he asked.

"Dying," I said, in no mood to sugarcoat what my mind told me to be true. Unless Thackery had a cure hiding up his sleeve. I just had to find the bastard first.

Rufus gave a slow nod and blink. "With everything happening, I thought I might be of some use here."

"We've been saying that for weeks, buddy," Nevada said.

"All right, people," Astrid said, voice booming around the crowded room, "let's do this." She stood near the head of the long conference table, whiteboards behind her covered in scrawled writing. A laptop was open, and a projector light shone against the only clear section of the board. Baylor and Phineas flanked her on either side, with Gina and Marcus nearby. Heads turned and all other conversation in the room ceased.

Astrid looked as agitated as I'd ever seen her. Her long black hair was in a hasty, messy braid, her clothes were wrinkled and dirty, and a soot streak still lingered on her neck. The shadow of her true self seemed to pace just beneath the surface, tail twitching, eager to hunt and punish.

"I doubt anyone hasn't heard the news by now," she continued, "but just in case you've had your head in the sand these last twelve hours, here's a recap. First, a half-Blood was captured tonight, brought back for questioning, and a few hours ago he blew up from the inside out. The purpose of this was to infect our vampire comrades with an unknown agent that is negatively affecting a good percentage of them, so they are all in quarantine until further notice.

"Second, seven Therians were kidnapped from their homes, and it is confirmed that the wanted human Walter Thackery and several Lupa are involved. At least three more Lupa are currently at large in the city, and it's possible there are more." She paused, wetting her lips. "We have a working theory on how they've remained concealed from us for so long."

They did find something out from the lawyer, and it wasn't good. That much was evident in Astrid's expression, and in the way Marcus stood a little straighter.

"Third," she said, "is the threat these Lupa present to humans. No other Therian's bite has proved harmful to humans in the past, but the Lupa is the exception, and its bite is still harmful now. One of ours is fighting for his life against this Lupa virus, so my warning to the humans here is this: do not let them bite you. As of now, there is no cure.

"Fourth, we know where to start looking for Thackery, the missing Therians, and all the half-Bloods we've been hunting these last two weeks."

A murmur ran through the room. Apparently, this tidbit hadn't yet made the rounds.

Baylor stepped forward, and attention shifted to him. "Reliable intel places our target along the Black River waterfront, roughly between West Chestnut Street and Cottage Place." He touched the laptop's keyboard, and a satellite image of that section of the river appeared. "Our research has narrowed that field down to three possible locations. First is the old Waylander Shipping Company building."

He clicked again, and a photo of that particular site blinked onto the wall. It was a four-story white-walled cement block building, at least a hundred yards long and no telling how wide. It butted right up to the river, its visible wall dropping straight to the water below. A few remnants of the old pier remained. I mentally checked it off my list. Too stable; none of the rocking motion that Token had mentioned.

"Waylander's size and location make it our most likely target," Baylor continued. "It has a large parking lot around it, and no neighboring buildings currently in use. Second possibility, just north of Waylander's, is Snyder's Marina." I perked up as he switched images. I knew that area, had hunted there a few times my first year in the Triads.

The Marina had been carved out of a natural curve in the river. It had eight piers, six slips each, and a boathouse anchoring it onshore. According to people who knew and cared about local history, it had been a busy place for locals who wanted to go out on the river to fish or simply putter around in their shiny new boats. Until about forty years ago, when pollution kept fish away from this length of the Black River and the Marina closed.

The current satellite image showed a boat boneyard—speedboats, small yachts, some pontoon boats, even a few fishing boats. Nothing seemed singularly large enough to house dozens of Halfies and a couple of kidnapped Therians.

"South of Waylander's is the third possible target, the old Black River Ferry port."

As soon as the photo appeared, a mental lightbulb went off in my mind. Until the Wharton Street Bridge was completed some sixty-odd years ago, the only way to cross the Black River from the north was via the ferry system. Three boats were in operation at its peak—two passenger and one freight. Each boat had three levels, excluding the upper deck and lower engine deck. The pier-level deck on the passenger boats held up to forty vehicles and up to five hundred foot passengers, all interior except for the aft and stern balconies. The freight ferry ran for about a decade after the passenger lines shut down, but now all three boats were permanently anchored at the old port. Someone tried briefly to turn the port into a museum, but the project quickly fizzled. One boat had been refurbished into a seafood restaurant for a couple of years, but nothing ever stuck because it was in the middle of a mostly abandoned industrial portion of the city that just didn't draw the traffic needed to sustain any real business.

It was absolutely perfect.

"Daytime isn't ideal for recon, but we're on a bit of a time crunch," Astrid said. "We'll get as close as we can with surveillance equipment on land, but meanwhile I have some volunteers from the Pinnia Clan reconning by river."

I glanced around the room, and sure enough most of the human faces wore the same question mark mine had to display. Baylor coughed softly.

Astrid puckered her lips, not thrilled with letting another bit of information slip out. "Their true forms are seals. They should be able to move undetected."

Were-seals. Okeydokey. One more of the fourteen Clans whose name I finally knew. For as much as the Assembly preached cooperation, they still liked to keep some things to themselves.

"I want four teams prepped and ready to go in thirty minutes," she continued. "Three are tactical advance teams, one outfitted and briefed for each specific target. The fourth team is backup for whoever strikes gold. Marcus will remain and run Operations here. Myself, Phineas, and Baylor will lead the three advance teams. Kismet will lead the backup team.

"Volunteers?"

Except for Rufus, everyone in the room had a hand up.

A small niggle of pride warmed my chest to see humans and Therians coming together over this crisis—not something I ever expected to see just a few weeks ago.

Astrid's mouth twitched. "Good. I'll have team assignments in five minutes."

I met Phin's gaze from across the room, those bright blue eyes staring holes in my head. He mouthed the word "ferry."

I nodded.

Time to get his family back.

The crowd broke up, most of them wandering out of Operations to wait in the hall. I cornered Baylor after the majority of them had left. "What did you get from the family lawyer?" I asked.

His intense frown soured even more. "Nothing Astrid wanted to share with everyone quite yet."

"My lips are sealed."

"Zeigler's estate was managed by Johnson and Crown, one of the oldest established law firms in the city. Only two partners, but they handle a lot of the wealthiest families, and their associates are hand-picked, usually with connections. Including the junior associate assigned upkeep on Zeigler's house, who went over once a week to water the houseplants, monitor lawn care, and collect the mail. And apparently knew that seven teenage werewolves were living there, because that would be damned hard to miss."

Wow. "Who is this guy?"

"Her name is Edwina Fair."

"Seriously?" It was the most ridiculous name I'd ever heard. Okay, maybe not ever, but it definitely ranked.

"Yeah."

It wasn't the reason why Baylor looked like he'd just sucked on a lemon, though. "And?"

He glanced at the few people lingering in the room,

then plucked a folder off the conference table. Took out a glossy photo. "Meet Edwina Fair." Handed it to me.

The first thing I saw was the sparkling blue eyes. Past the eyes, thick spirals of sunset red hair. A beautiful, toothy smile. A chill danced down my spine; gooseflesh crawled across the backs of my legs and shoulders. I knew this woman. I'd spoken to her several times, always in the guise of another.

Edwina Fair was the human avatar of Amalie, Queen of the sprites and leader of the Fey Council. She'd given refuge to me and Wyatt once. She'd opened her home to us, told us secrets about First Break and the doorway her people protected. She helped create the Triads ten years ago. She gave werewolves to Walter Thackery.

She was once our ally, and now we had indisputable proof that she'd been working against us the whole fucking time.

Our team was ready to go in twenty minutes. Destination: Black River Ferry port. Phineas, myself, Tybalt, Kyle, Shelby, and Paul Ryan on the assault team. I wasn't sure how I felt about working with Paul again, but he'd been an asset earlier in the day when we found Jenner's body. He was, despite my best efforts, growing on me. I tried to get Jackson into our group so he'd be there to fight for his mate, but Astrid overruled the request. I guess she didn't want everyone who was personally involved on the same team.

I'd been hunting at the ferry port twice in my career, Tybalt three times. All had been tips about goblin activity, rather than Halfies, and it occurred to me on the drive to the river that overall goblin activity had been negligible lately. We'd seen very little from them since the battle at Olsmill almost three months ago. I didn't want to look a gift horse in the mouth, but it worried me a little. Goblins were not subtle creatures.

Each of us humans was loaded down with more weapons than I was used to carrying into a single fight. Two guns each, one primary and one backup. Four clips of bullets: two regular and two of a new variety tipped with an infusion of garlic and onion oil. The latter wouldn't bother the Lupa much, but they'd be painful as hell on the Halfies—like shooting them up with poison. Our access to anticoagulant rounds was diminished after the destruction of the lab at Boot Camp. The oil-tips were our first collaboration with the vampires on an effective weapon against their kind.

The fact that Isleen suggested the bullet never failed to astonish me all over again.

We also had a variety of other weapons, depending on our comfort levels. Tybalt had a scary blade attachment on his prosthetic hand. I had three serrated hunting knives strapped to various parts of my body, as well as a pair of silver chopsticks in my ponytail. Paul favored brass knuckles and an aluminum baseball bat. He had apparently developed a fondness for whacking his victims with solid objects.

Kyle and Shelby had only a single gun each, which they'd likely pass off to one of us when they shifted into their true forms. I'd never seen Shelby shift, and knowing he was a polar bear made me a little eager to witness the Halfies' reactions when they first saw him.

Phin, of course, had his Coni blade loosely belted to his waist.

We had a handful of photos to study, as well as Historical Society literature that came with a handy map of the port. The Terminal Station has a chain-link fence built around it to prevent vandalism (in theory), but no security measures were in place around the weed-strewn parking lot. A single cement and steel dock jutted out from shore, directly in front of the Terminal Station, its aluminum roof with the same faded blue paint as the ferries themselves. All three were anchored in a row—one south of the dock, and two north.

Astrid's orders to all assault teams were to get into position no closer than one block from our target, create a tentative plan of attack, and then wait. As soon as Marcus got word from the Pinnia scouts, he'd pass along anything of relevance and we'd go from there. Thackery could be at only one of the three potential targets, and we needed to be ready to move on all of them. Even though I'd wager my handy healing powers on him being at the ferry terminal.

Kyle was driving our SUV through the city. Paul rode shotgun, and Phin and I took over the middle two seats, with Tybalt and Shelby in the rear. Mercy's Lot gave way to the industrial section that lined the east bank of the Black River. Cheap apartment buildings gave way to businesses and storage facilities. A block from our destination, Kyle found an alley between two crumbling brick structures, one of which had once been a fire company station, and parked.

"The ferries are almost completely enclosed except for the lower car deck," I said. "Seal the windows on the upper levels and he'd have a lot of space to work with."

"Agreed," Phin said.

"Could he be on more than one ferry?" Tybalt asked.

"Unless he found a way to travel between them underwater, I'm doubtful. The Terminal is abandoned, but still within sight of a street and intersection."

"What about this sheltered area?" I said, pointing at the covered pier between the ferry on the south and the two on the north. "If he's in the boats on either side, he could use that awning as cover to move between them. Plus they have the most direct access to land."

Phin nodded. "So they are our most likely targets."

Paul shifted around in the front passenger seat. "You two are really convinced that Thackery's got the Halfies here, aren't you?"

"Yes," Phin and I said in stereo.

"This isn't you letting personal bullshit affect your judgment?"

Phin deferred that one to me, and I just shrugged one shoulder. "Maybe, but I learned a long time ago to trust my instincts on stuff like this."

"Baylor thinks they're at Waylander."

"And it could be, if one of Thackery's little science projects hadn't told me he felt movement like water where he was held," I said.

Paul frowned. "You didn't share that?"

"Then we wouldn't have been the first ones here."

He opened his mouth as if about to object, then snapped it shut. His lips twitched into a half smile. "So if they're on two boats, how do we go in?"

I glanced at Phin, sure that he was thinking the same thing as I was—we both wanted to hit the boat with the Therians first. As soon as Thackery realized he was being breached, he was likely to kill them all. The man had taken a nosedive off the crazy board weeks ago, and I wouldn't put anything past him now.

"I can get onboard in my true form," Phin said. "I'm small enough. Once I know which boat is holding my people, we'll be better able to formulate a plan."

"Thackery's going to have scouts watching land and air," I said. "And he'll make sure they know what an osprey looks like."

He gave me a slow, deliberate blink, then reached over the backseat for a duffel bag. Rummaged around inside until he produced a can of black spray paint. "They may not notice me if I don't look like an osprey."

Tybalt chuckled. "That's fucking genius."

"Spray paint?" I took the can from Phin like I'd never seen one before. "You want me to spray-paint you?"

"Yes," Phin said.

"Black?"

"Yes."

"Okeydokey." A bizarre thought occurred to me. "If I spray-paint your feathers, will you still be painted when you shift back?"

He started to answer, then paused with his mouth open. Blinked. "I have no idea. But if it gets me on-board, I don't care."

"Good enough."

"So we aren't waiting for information from the Pinnia?" Tybalt asked.

"Why bother?" Kyle said, adding to the conversation for the first time. His lover was out there somewhere; I couldn't imagine what was going through his mind as he turned his intense gaze on Phin. "I trust your instincts."

"I'm in," Paul said.

"Okay, then," I said. "Phin gets onboard, figures out where to find the Therians, comes back to tell us, and we go from there."

"If we confirm this target before Astrid hears from the Pinnia scouts," Phin said, "we'll inform the other teams before we move in."

"Right." We'd need all the muscle we could get, depending on— "And try to get a rough estimate of how many Halfies we're looking at."

"Of course."

"Then let's do this."

Chapter Seventeen

The fact that Phin reeked of fresh paint didn't strike me as a concern until he was in the air and on his way toward the ferry terminal. Feathers glistening black, he was the only hooked-beak raven in existence, and I couldn't rid myself of the ridiculous image of his human form with black paint streaks all over it. If nothing else, it was something to occupy myself with while we waited for him to return. Or for Astrid to officially declare a target.

Either one, as long as something happened soon.

Kyle twisted around in the front seat to face rear, his expression pinched. Someone he loved was out there, hoping for rescue, and I waited patiently for his accusations—that Lynn was targeted because of Kyle's connection to me, and this was all my fault. Standard fare, really. Anyone in my orbit was fair game for inclusion in the violent insanity of my afterlife.

"You do your mate proud," Kyle said. For a moment, I thought he was talking to someone else in the car, maybe Shelby. But no, he was staring right at me with those sad, coffee-colored eyes. I'd forgotten that in the eyes of the Therians, Wyatt was my mate. He'd declared it so during my disappearance/kidnapping, in order to secure the assistance of the Assembly. Although we weren't technically together (if we ever were) anymore, the declaration stuck. Therians didn't divorce. Mates were chosen for life.

Maybe if we humans chose for life, we'd pick more carefully the first time around.

"How's that?" I asked.

"You're here, continuing to assist in the rescue of others while he lays dying of a disease wrought by one of ours."

"You're wrong." Kyle blinked, surprised by my snapped response, so I hurried to clarify. "The Lupa are not one of yours, Kyle. They're nothing like the Therians I've met since coming to the Watchtower."

He tilted his head, a gesture of understanding.

"Besides," I added, "Wyatt would want me here."

Phin's cell phone rang. Crap. I yanked it out of his discarded jeans—Astrid—and set it to speaker.

"Yeah?" I said by way of greeting.

"Why the blue hell did one of my Pinnia scouts tell me that a crow about the size of the average osprey just flew onto one of those ferries?" Astrid asked without preamble. Oh yeah, she was pissed.

"I have no idea why the Pinnia scout would tell you that," I replied. Not exactly denying it, just not confirming it.

Astrid huffed. "Regardless, they confirmed your target. Two boats, one on each side of the loading pier. Backup ETA is five minutes. If your crow returns before we get there—"

"We're going in from the pier. Tell Baylor's team to come down the loading driveway from the north, and Kismet's to come up the parking lot side from the south. Everyone else, straight into the pier."

A pause, then, "Okay. I'll signal when we're in position. We go in hard and fast."

"We'll tell you which boat we're hitting first as soon as the crow gets back."

"Good enough."

After I hung up, I gave the others a wry smile. "That went better than I expected."

Our "crow" returned before two more minutes had passed and, sure enough, Phin shifted back with black streaks running across his torso, arms, and legs. One smudge went straight across his forehead like a painted-on bandanna. "North boat," he said.

"Did you see them?" Kyle asked as we piled out of the SUV.

"No. They're likely being kept in interior rooms, and I couldn't get in without being spotted. Michael Jenner's scent lingered on the pier and deck of the northern boat. He was there within the last few hours. No scent carried to the southern boat."

"Fabulous," I said. I texted the information to Astrid and reported my conversation with her to Phin at the same time.

Shelby stripped off his T-shirt and sneakers, leaving on only a pair of loose workout shorts. "I'll shift once we're onboard," he said. "Should scare the beejeebus out of some of those damned half-Bloods, coming face-to-face with a five-hundred-pound polar bear."

"No doubt." I glanced around for Kyle; he'd already shifted into his dingo form and seemed eager for the hunt. Eager to find and rescue his love.

Phin put his jeans back on, then adjusted the strap holding his Coni blade close to his hip. Blue eyes blazing, he looked at each of us in turn. "Let's go hunting," he said.

Street traffic was moderate for midmorning—mostly delivery trucks and the occasional lost motorist. We stuck to the alley we were in, and it led us due west. Past the next block, we crossed a one-way street and came out close to the boarded-up Terminal building. In the shadows of its cracked-glass walls and faded aluminum roof, Phin bi-shifted, allowing his majestic, powerful wings to appear. Streaked in black paint and as menacing as I'd ever seen him, Phin no longer looked the part of the angel I'd once mistaken him to be. He looked like a demon about to unleash his wrath upon unsuspecting victims.

His phone chirped; he checked it. "Other teams in position," he whispered. "It's now or never."

My pulse sped up, as did my breathing. Adrenaline coursed through me. My toes tingled, and I pulled one of my guns, testing its unfamiliar weight. Hard and fast, just like I liked it. I pulled at threads of loneliness, fueled by my need to have Wyatt battling by my side today, and my tap to the Break sparked. I kept that spark close, tickling the front of my mind, just in case I needed it.

"Time to have some fun," Tybalt said.

Boarding the north ferry was something of a blur, spurred by adrenaline and fraught with the lingering fear that, by doing this, we were ensuring the deaths of those we'd come to save. Shelby had shifted, and he used his furry white bulk to break down the passenger loading doors. The ferry was anchored so close to the pier that a ramp wasn't necessary. Just a quick jump across a slice of stagnant water, and we were onboard.

Onboard and in a stairwell of sorts. Most of the glass partitions were shattered, only metal frames remaining. Straight ahead was an empty area where the loaded cars parked. To our right and left, metal staircases led to the upper passenger decks and observation areas. Nothing stirred in the car lot, so up we went. Phin, me, and Kyle-the-dingo to the left; Tybalt, Paul, and Shelby-the-polar-bear to the right.

Our entrance must have both alerted and confused the Halfies we found on the next deck. I barely caught a glimpse of dormitory-style futons and cheap furniture behind the bodies of the Halfies swarming toward us from all directions. Young, in shape, and clear-thinking due to whatever it was Thackery was feeding them, they attacked with a precision and coordination I didn't expect.

Phin launched himself at the crowd with a cry and a gust of wind from his wings. Kyle snarled and pounced on the nearest bare throat.

I aimed away from them and began firing. I'd never be a perfect marksman, but human torsos made nice big targets. Three half-Bloods went down right away, screeching and clawing at their chests. Bullets hurt no matter who you were; bullets laced with something your kind was violently allergic to hurt like fucking hell.

I fired again, and a fourth went down. The crush of bodies increased. A hand crashed down on my wrist, and I lost the gun. Air exploded from my lungs—I felt the ache in my back a split-second later. My knees buckled. Instead of fighting it and losing my balance, I instinctively dropped to a crouch—well timed, as the air of a missed punch whizzed past my head. Using my right hand for support, I plucked a blade from my ankle with my left hand, then shot that foot out backward. Connected with something hard and made someone scream.

The roar of a bear vibrated the floor, as did the thundering of additional footsteps in the metal stairwell nearby. Backup or more Halfies—we'd soon see.

I sliced upward with my left hand. Blade met skin, and warm blood splashed my arm. I contemplated my backup gun just as a symphony of shots popped off nearby. Too many to be my lost weapon. Backup was here.

A Halfie about my age, long blond hair done up in dozens of small braids, slammed into me sideways. We hit the deck in a tangle of arms and legs. Fangs snapped at my throat. Her breath smelled like old pennies. I worked one leg up between us and leveraged her away, rolled us somehow, and came up on top. I drove my knee down into her stomach. She hissed and kept an iron grip on my left wrist, the blade angled away.

A hand tangled in my hair and yanked so hard that I saw stars. I lost my hold on the girl and was pulled, via hair, to my feet. I couldn't stop the scream of shock and pain. Strong arms looped around my waist and held me tight to a strong chest.

Shit.

The crush of Halfies near the stairwell left a semi-open area that looked like a poor college campus's version of a rec room. I pulled on my tap to the Break and let its power tingle through my body. Focused on that open space and shattered. Heard the Halfie cry out in surprise.

The brief, headache-inducing teleport put us away from the main fight, next to a stained futon. The shock of it loosened the Halfie's arms. I broke free, and spun and sliced his throat in one quick motion. He flopped onto the futon.

I paused a moment to catch my breath. The air reeked of something both familiar and foreign—and ultimately nauseating when I realized it was the smell of sex. I guess the Halfies, being of a certain virile age, needed something to entertain themselves.

This entire deck seemed to be a hangout for the Halfie horde, which meant Thackery was either on the deck above, or he was hiding below in the engine room. And up seemed less likely than down.

Additional familiar faces had entered the fray, and bleeding bodies were piling up. Tybalt moved through the fight like a dancer, his prosthetic blade slicing throats and torsos and limbs, carving a path for more of our fighters to join in. On the other end of the deck, Paul fought like a whirling dervish, cracking skulls and break-

ing bones with each resounding contact with his aluminum bat.

Phin broke away from the battle, arms streaked with
red, eyes blazing with battle lust. He had a particularly
wriggly Halfie by the throat and was dragging him along
like a piece of luggage. Phin threw the Halfie hard
against a metal bulkhead, and I swore I heard bones
crack. Maybe twenty years old, the Halfie slumped to
the floor, whimpering. Phin stepped on the kid's ankle,
and this time I did hear a bone crack. The half-Blood
screamed.

"Where are the Therians being held?" Phin asked.
The intensity of his appearance aside, by his tone he
could have been asking for directions to Uptown.

"Down below," the kid replied, sobbing openly. His
small fangs had torn through his lower lip, and blood
streaked his chin.

"Thank you." Phin reached down and snapped his
neck cleanly. The body slumped to the ground.

The heart of the continuing battle was centered around
the stairwell—the only visible access to the lower decks.
Phin could fly through easily, but I'd have to fight my
way past and that would take time. "The parking area is
below us, right?" I asked.

"Yes."

"Empty, open, no obstacles that you saw?"

He seemed to understand where I was going with this.
"None that I recall. Can you?"

"We'll see."

"I'll meet you down there."

Phin rose up in a gust of air, his wings beating hard in
the enclosed area. He soared close to the ceiling, slicing
a few Halfie throats as he went. I pulled on my tap again,
opening up to even more power. Everything snapped
and crackled as I teleported through the floor of an old
ferryboat and materialized on the deck below. A dagger

of pain poked me between the eyes, and I stumbled. The din and crash of fighting continued overhead, as well as outside and across the dock, echoing through the cavern of the parking deck.

"This way," Phin said.

I spun toward his voice. He stood across the parking area from the stairwell, about ten yards from me. I jogged over and didn't see the door until I was almost on top of it. Probably designed to fade into the walls and not be noticed by passengers, the metal door had NO ADMITTANCE printed in small block letters. Just below it, hand-painted, was a late-addition caveat, probably put there by Thackery: Without Permission, Under Penalty of Execution.

Dude ran a tight ship. So to speak.

"Bingo," I said. The only thing I didn't see was a handle of any sort. "So what do we do? Say Open Sesame?"

"An explosive of some sort would be useful," Phin said.

"I left my C4 in my other pants."

He huffed. Took a step back and slammed his foot down on the spot a doorknob would normally be found. The reverberation shook the wall and echoed behind. Phin stumbled back, eyebrows furrowed, lips tight.

"Sounds hollow just behind it," I said. "Pray it stays that way for the next twenty seconds, or this is really going to hurt."

"Evy?"

I closed my eyes and imagined an empty stairwell landing just behind the metal door. Fell into the Break and let it shatter me. The knife between my eyes stabbed a little deeper, burned a little hotter, and I moved through the door. Sensed the open space around me, and pulled back out. A wave of vertigo nearly bowled me over. Three teleports in less than five minutes. My body felt like jelly, my head like a zit about to pop.

It was also pitch black, so regaining my equilibrium took a moment. A fist pounding on the other side of the door helped orient my sense of direction. I felt along the rectangle of cool metal until I found a solid bar. Pushed down and out, and the door swung open.

The flash of light illuminated a steel stairwell that went both up and down—probably staff stairs to get from the upper deck to the engine rooms. Phin slipped inside with me, and we descended. I kept my hand firmly on the slick, grimy rail as the door swung shut and cast us both into blackness.

At the bottom, I traded my knife for my second gun, unsure what we'd find behind Door Number Two. My heart hammered against my ribs, and my mouth was dry.

"I smell them," Phin said, his voice barely a whisper of sound. "Stay behind me."

I considered objecting, but this was Phin's family. His heritage as a Coni. He slipped around me. Metal squealed. Light splashed through the door, along with the most bizarre odor combination of antiseptic and scorched hair. We were at one end of a long, low-ceilinged corridor of gray metal. Exposed lightbulbs ran along the ceiling, spaced every five feet or so, giving the gray metal a sickly yellowish glow. I expected warm, dank air, something like a basement, and instead got a waft of coolness around my ankles.

Wings tucked close to his back, Phin crept silently forward. I allowed the door to close as quietly as I could, but it really didn't matter. Thackery had to know we were here.

A few paces from the stairwell, we found a long row of Plexiglas windows inserted where walls had probably once stood. Behind them, our Holy Grail. Individual cells, each roughly the size of a modest bathroom, composed of stark metal walls and floors, with a plastic bucket and nothing else. And in each cell, a naked, prostrate body.

Phin pressed his palm flat against the Plexiglas window of the first cell, shoulders tense. "Joseph," he said.

The wrinkled, ancient Coni lay facing us, one bony arm stretched out toward the Plexiglas window. His thin chest rose and fell, and a small puddle of drool had formed on the floor by his open mouth. A bloodstained white bandage was taped to his temple—the source of the blood we'd found at the country house, I'd bet. The sight constricted my chest and settled a ball of hot anger deep in my guts.

The cell wall had a rectangular line that framed the window much like a door, but there was no handle or indication of how the damned thing opened. While Phin continued inspecting the cells I smashed the butt of my gun against the Plexiglas, and the impact shook my wrist without making a dent.

"Leah de Loew, Lynn Neil, Dawn Jenner," Phin said as he spotted each person.

With every name, the heavy weight on my heart lifted just a little. I followed him down the line, glancing at each person, horrified to find each one as naked and unconscious as Joseph. God, what had Thackery been doing to them?

Phin stopped at the last cell and stared. Aurora and Ava had to be in that one. His silence ratcheted up my pulse. I stepped to his side and glanced in, braced to see a helpless child asleep on the floor.

All I saw was an empty cell. Two more windows stretched past us. I checked each one; neither was occupied. "Goddammit!" I said.

A metallic bang echoed from the far end of the corridor. I didn't wait; I just ran. Past other doors that led to unused engines and storage rooms, past newer-looking doors that probably hid whatever horrors Thackery had been conducting down here these last few months. Or maybe years. The lit bulbs thinned out to every third or fourth, and the air took on a slightly danker feel. We were moving out of the used portion of this deck, toward the bow of the ferry, which meant—

"He has a way out," Phin said, keeping pace behind me.

A lot of snarky retorts—*no shit, ya think?*—died before they made it past my lips. I wasn't angry at Phin. I was angry that Aurora and Ava were still missing, and that Thackery had a head start on us. Assuming he was on board in the first place.

The corridor ended at a T junction. To the right was a hatch marked Buoyancy Tank, and to the left another heavy door. Probably a stairwell. I had only a vague idea that a buoyancy tank wouldn't make a good escape route, but the stairwell should take us back up to the sundeck and navigation. If Thackery was getting off the boat, it was from above.

We thundered up the stairs, once again in pitch dark. Light sprinkled down briefly from two decks above, and an upper door banged shut. The narrow, twisty stairwell made it impossible for Phin to fly straight up, and I didn't have the concentration to attempt another teleport—not with zero idea of what to expect on the sundeck.

I burst out into bright sunlight, heedless of how stupid a move it was. We faced west, over the river, nearly at the bow of the ferry. Behind us was a slightly elevated platform and the wheel room. The deck was warped with age and covered in piles of dried bird shit.

Movement to the north caught my attention.

Walter Thackery stood on the sundeck of the next ferry, drawing the last corner of a plank of wood over to his side. Tall, lean, and movie-star handsome, he looked a bit like a wannabe spy preparing a hasty getaway. To bad he wasn't the hero in this little adventure. A go ten feet of water and a three-story drop separated him from me. But not from Phin.

Phin snarled. Thackery raised his right hand. We both dove to the nasty deck as Thackery fired. The shot pinged off the metal door. I lurched to my knees and returned fire. Thackery ducked and shot back. White fire grazed my shoulder. I didn't stop, just peppered the deck all around him.

Taking advantage of my distraction, Phin dropped his Coni blade and his pants, shifted into a smaller target, and flew across to the next boat. Hovered. I stopped shooting, having run out of bullets. He shifted in midair as he dropped right down on top of Thackery with a rage-fueled battle cry.

"Stone!"

I didn't stop to identify the person calling my name. A fourth teleport so soon after the others was going to hurt like hell, but I grabbed the blade and did it anyway. My tether to the Break was wide open, sharp and agonizing. My wounded shoulder shrieked in agony as I fell apart and came back together on the deck of the other ferry. Everything tilted and spun, and I crashed to my knees.

The skin-on-skin sounds of two men wrestling kept me from pitching into a serious faint. I inhaled several deep breaths, and exhaled hard through my mouth. Sometimes the physical price of magic sucked.

"Where are they?" Phin snarled.

I blinked the pair into focus. Thackery was on his stomach, both arms twisted behind his back and up so high that I half expected one to pop out of its socket. Phin straddled Thackery's waist and held his wrists tight be-ween his shoulder blades, Phin's own weight keeping n facedown on a rough bed of sun-baked bird black-streaked wings stood up high, arched, s angry as the rest of the warrior.

"Stone!"

Tybalt's voice. He and Paul stood on the other ferry, watching us with weapons drawn, clothes speckled with blood.

"They're on the bottom level, near the engines," I said.

Paul nodded, then turned and bolted.

"Where are they?" Phin asked again, pulling harder on Thackery's wrists.

Thackery grunted.

The skin on the back of my neck prickled. The last time I'd been this close to Thackery, I was strapped to a table having my left pinkie hacked off in the name of science. I held out my hand, a sight both familiar and foreign—four digits instead of five, a healed bump instead of a joint. Bastard did that to me.

I inched closer and extended the Coni blade toward Thackery's face. His eyes latched on and followed the twin blades, nearly crossing as I pressed one sharp tip against his cheekbone. "You owe me a finger," I said.

Utter fury blinked across his face. "The vampires you protect owe me a wife and son," he replied.

"One vampire killed your wife, not the entire race. Not the people you infected today."

"They aren't human."

"Neither am I," Phin said. "But which one of us is a cold-blooded killer?"

"By my own hands, I've never murdered a human."

I pressed the blade until a bead of red formed on the ridge of his cheekbone. "They don't have to be human for it to be murder."

"What of the human Rhys Willemy?" Phin asked.

Thackery grunted. "His death was at the hands of my protégé. I merely assisted in carrying out his vision."

"An accomplice to murder still makes you guilty."

"In your book."

"And your supposed friend Bastian Spence?"

Something dark flickered across Thackery's face. "What of him?"

"You set your hybrids and hounds loose at Boot Camp. He was still on-site. Do you feel no responsibility for his death?"

Clearly that wasn't the answer Thackery was expecting, and the barest hint of grief peeked through his cold façade. "I told him to leave."

Thackery was officially insane. Six years spent plotting his revenge against vampires had warped his idea of right and wrong, cause and effect. He didn't even see the world in terms of black-and-white. It was simply his way and our way—and according to his way, his hands were clean of all the deaths he'd left in his wake, including a man he'd once considered a friend.

"Bastian saved my life," I said, feeling no pride in it.

"I bet that makes you all kinds of happy."

He glared.

"Just like it probably makes you happy to hear that I stabbed your protégé through the throat not long after," I said.

Fury flashed in his eyes. Oh, he didn't like jabs at his precious werewolves? Too fucking bad.

"We killed three more of your precious protégés earlier today, too," I added. "And let me guess. You didn't murder Michael Jenner, either?"

"Of course not. Why waste the blood?"

Phin pressed his weight down hard. Thackery groaned.

"What about all the half-Bloods you've made?" I asked. "You were an accomplice to their deaths the minute they were infected."

"The lesser of two evils, child."

"What the fuck does that mean?"

"It means you're too young and ignorant to truly understand the scope of my vision. But you will see part of it come to fruition."

Ignorant my ass. "Not if you're in custody, pal."

"The wheels are in motion. Capturing me now doesn't stop what is to come."

Oh joy.

"The Coni female and her child were not with the others belowdecks," Phin said. "Where are they?"

"Alive, for now," he replied.

"Where?"

"Come now, shape-shifter, I never put all my leverage in one place. By the way, you might want to tell your cohorts to begin abandoning ship."

"Why is that?"

A distant rumble of thunder caught my attention. I glanced at the sky and saw only cloudless blue. Then a groan of metal joined the thunder. Across the slice of water, on the opposite ferry, Tybalt braced himself on the deck rail with his right hand and was gazing at his feet. He looked up, puzzled. Then concerned.

"Because it's about to sink," Thackery said.

Chapter Eighteen

Letting Thackery out of my sight, even in the capable hands of Phineas in full-on protector mode, took a little effort. I trusted Phin to keep a handle on him, but I didn't trust Thackery. He was slippery, and we could not allow him to get away again.

But knowing that others needed me more had me back on the lowest level of the ferry, searching frantically for a way to open those damned Plexiglas cells. Cold water already swam around our ankles, as whatever backup plan Thackery had rigged allowed the river inside the slowly sinking ferry. It wasn't deep enough to sink completely, just enough to submerge this entire level—and probably the parking level, too. We had to get the Therians out.

They were still unconscious, although Leah showed signs of waking. Water oozed up through cracks in the floor's metal plates at a slower rate than in the corridor. At least an inch deep already, the water would either snap everyone awake or quickly drown them.

Baylor, Paul, and bear-Shelby prowled the corridor, looking for a control panel. Shelby even tried throwing his weight against the doors, with no results. We couldn't risk shooting at the Plexi, for fear of a ricochet killing someone, and I had no doubt it was bulletproof anyway.

Thackery built the thing to contain Therians able to shift into bears and large cats.

Others were farther down the corridor inspecting the laboratories, gathering anything they could save. I left them to it, intent on those cells and the lives trapped behind their slick, impenetrable walls.

Impenetrable to everything but me. I pressed my palm against the cool Plexiglas of Joseph's cell. Goddamn, this was going to hurt a lot.

"Stone?" Baylor asked, coming up next to me. "What are you thinking?"

I looked up at him, forcing a smile. "I'm thinking I'll be lucky if my brain doesn't start leaking out of my ears by the time I'm done down here."

"Huh?"

"I can get them out."

It took him a moment to catch on. He hadn't seen me teleport others with me, but I'm sure he'd heard stories. I'd already teleported too many times today. My head ached continuously, and the pain would only increase. Using the magic of the Break often used humans right back. Our bodies were not physically capable of handling the full force of its power. I'd gotten nosebleeds and migraines from it before.

This was going to be a doozy. If it didn't kill me.

Slowly, Baylor nodded. "We'll keep looking for a release mechanism."

"You do that."

I closed my eyes and took a breath, trying to calm my unraveling nerves. The Break snapped and crackled close by, eager to be used and yet still playing the bashful virgin. I pulled it in and it danced away. I tugged harder, drawing on everything in my arsenal to power it with loneliness—Wyatt drifting away from me, Alex dying, my Triad life gone and taking all my security and acceptance.

I slipped in and through the wall. White lightning struck between my eyes. I materialized in front of Joseph, and before I had time to reconsider, I crouched, looped my arms around his narrow, bony chest, and fell into the Break again. We reappeared in a tangled heap in eight inches of water that stank of river rot. My chest ached and my head throbbed. I let strong arms take Joseph away.

Baylor helped me sit upright. "You gonna make three more?"

A canine bark startled me. Kyle bounded through the water, shifting from dingo to human even as he ran. He skidded to a hard stop in front of Lynn's cell. Someone else's blood covered his hands, chest, and face, and through the gore, love and need shone through.

"Yeah," I said, "I can."

Tremors rocked the ferry. A blast of cold water ran in from somewhere down the corridor. Voices bounced and echoed on the low metal walls, only adding to the confusion, panic, and awful noise. The water level in the corridor rose to knee height quickly; in the cells, it was dangerously close to the mouths of those still unconscious.

I got Lynn next, then Dawn. They were civilians, so they got to go first. I was moving on automatic, exhausted, nauseated. My head hurt so badly I could barely see past the red haze over my vision. Teleporting while so disoriented was stupidly dangerous, but I had no choice. No mechanism had been found to open the cells, and the Therians had to come out.

Without my healing ability, I'd have surely passed out. Or simply keeled over dead from the shock of it all. As it was, I'm pretty sure Baylor carried me over to the last cell and put me down as close to the wall as possible. The water was up to my chest while sitting, and the cold shock of it cleared my mind just enough to concentrate.

Had to get Leah, and then I was done. Could rest for a bit. Maybe pass out for a few hours. That sounded nice.

Leah first, then pass out.

"Yeah, you can pass out soon," Baylor said.

Okay, so I hadn't just thought that last part.

He squeezed my shoulder. "I think your brain-to-mouth censor is fried."

Fuck it all. I looked into the cell and picked my spot. Felt for my tap. It danced out of reach, the power teasing me, there and yet impossibly far away. God, I wanted Wyatt. He'd help me. Between the two of us, we'd summoned half a Jeep into a log cabin. Together we could get Leah out of that damned cell before we all drowned in the river.

But Wyatt wasn't there. He might never be by my side again. My throat closed and my nose stung. I coughed—it might have been a sob. The Break sparked. My tap hit me like a sucker punch, and I was moving. Flying apart. Coming back together. Less water, metal floor. I reached out blindly, flailing for a body. Touched skin. Grabbed hold.

Back in, to the other side. Agony turned me inside out. Freezing water pushed me down, under. I choked on it.

I didn't want to drown, but I really, really wanted to sleep.

The gentle lull of movement greeted me as I woke. I was on my back, resting on something moderately soft, with the hum of an engine close by. Cymbals still crashed behind my eyes. I was wet, chilled despite the presence of what felt like a blanket.

I grunted something I intended to be "where am I?" and came out a garbled mess of muttering.

"Evy?"

Male voice. I huffed some semblance of response.

"We're on our way back to Watchtower. Just rest, okay?"

Tybalt. Sounded like him. I tried words again and managed, "Therians?"

"They're fine, all coming around. Turns out Thackery rigged up an electrified floor to keep them docile. Used it to knock them all out just as we got there."

The very image of him electroshocking Aurora and Ava made my blood boil. I tried to sit up, and only managed to make my head spin and my entire body spasm. "Fuuuuuuuuuck," I groaned.

"Then keep still."

"Why?"

"Because sitting up is obviously painful."

I almost smiled at his error. "No, why them? What did Thackery do?"

His silence only compounded my unease. I peeked through one eyelid. He was crouched on the floor between the seats of an SUV. I could see Astrid watching us from the front passenger seat, wrapped in loose sweats, her face stony. I didn't know who was driving; I couldn't see.

"Leah told us that Thackery was draining their blood a few pints at a time," Tybalt said. "Because of their accelerated healing, they replenished faster than a human would. He'd use the floor to knock them out, then go in. She said she woke up weak, groggy, and with a cotton ball taped to the interior of her elbow. She put two and two together."

I squeezed my eyes shut. It was a horrible déjà vu to what Thackery had done to me—drained me to the point of physical death, let me heal, then took more blood. What the fuck was he doing with Therian blood?

"He'll be telling us shortly," Astrid said.

I guess the censor button was still broken.

"The what?"

I ignored her and drifted for a while, letting my bruised and mangled brain repair itself. Didn't wake again until movement ceased and a hand squeezed my arm.

"Evy?" Tybalt said. "We're back. Can you walk?"

I wasn't even sure I could sit up. "Think so."

By some miracle, I managed to conquer sitting upright. Any other day, I might have been embarrassed into doing it on my own and risk falling on my face. Today I gratefully accepted Tybalt's help. I leaned on him as we climbed out of the SUV, careful of his arm's blade attachment, and I may have actually clung a little while we walked out of the parking lot and into the main Watchtower hall.

People were everywhere, chatting in clusters. I spotted Paul and Shelby among them, still bloodstained, but as eager as the rest of us to see this thing finished. The crowd knew we had Thackery. They knew we'd found the missing Therians. Well, most of them.

"Ava?" I whispered.

"Nothing yet," Tybalt replied.

"Where's Thackery?"

"Being secured in one of the empty stores, since the jail is still wrecked. They'll interrogate him soon."

"Goodie. I want in."

"You can barely walk."

"Don't need to walk to watch."

"Point taken. You want to change first?"

I took stock. My clothes were damp, but not horribly wet. The chafing I could live with. The front of my shirt was stained with blood—my own and others, I'm sure. I kind of smelled. "No," I said. If I offended anyone, they could suck it.

Tybalt aimed us toward Operations, which didn't seem right. "You said he was in a store."

"Yeah, he is, but you aren't participating in the interrogation. Astrid's orders."

"Seriously?"

"Yes. You could have killed yourself teleporting everyone today, Evy. Relax for ten minutes."

"Aurora and Ava are still missing, Tybalt."

"I know that. But you can't help them if you end up in some sort of magic-overload coma."

Coma. Wyatt. Shit, I should go see him. But I needed answers, too. Needed to find Aurora and Ava, and to make sure they were safe. I was Ava's godmother, her *Aluli,* and I had to save her. Period.

Tybalt steered us through Operations and into the War Room. Some of the seats were already occupied. I ignored exact faces in favor of what was being projected onto one of the whiteboards—Walter Thackery, bound to a chair, in the middle of an empty store.

"Oh good," I said as Tybalt put me into a chair. "Pay-per-view." Further proving my edit button was broken, I said, "He's not going to blow up, is he?"

Someone at the table snickered.

"He was checked out thoroughly before we brought him inside," Tybalt replied. "No detectable explosives or tracing devices."

"Detectable." We hadn't detected anything on Felix. Then again, we hadn't been smart enough to check properly that time—a mistake I bet no one was eager to repeat. "Awesome."

"It is what it is."

"Evy?" Rufus asked. His voice startled me into swiveling my chair around too fast. My ankle slammed into the footrest of his wheelchair and sent a shock up my leg.

I hissed through my teeth.

"You look lousy," he said.

"Well, good, because I feel pretty damn lousy," I replied.

My tone slid right past him. "We watched everything from here. I'm amazed you were able to use your Gift so many times in such a short span."

"Ditto. I think I lost a few million brain cells in the process, though." We hadn't really spoken in almost a month. Since the morning Boot Camp was attacked, and Rufus told me he'd been there eleven years ago when Wyatt's family was slaughtered by vampire bounty hunters. Rufus admitted to being one of those bounty hunters, young, the apprentice of the man who'd decided that innocent victims shouldn't be allowed to live to repeat what they'd seen.

He still hadn't told Wyatt. Now he might never get the chance.

"Have you been to see him?" I asked.

Rufus shook his head, hazel gaze casting downward. "No," he said, lowering his voice. "There's no point. You can't confess your sins to a man who can't hear you."

"Might make you feel better."

"I don't deserve to have my conscience assuaged by a deathbed confession, Evy."

Before I could give him a verbal smack-down for several different parts of that statement, someone closer to the head of the table said "Showtime" pretty damned loud. A hush fell over the group, which had doubled in size in mere minutes. Someone even dimmed the lights.

On-screen, we had a wide, slightly downward angle of Thackery. Three figures entered the frame, easily identifiable from the backs of their heads: Phin, Astrid, and Baylor. Phin was still streaked in black paint, his majestic wings out, Coni blade in one hand. He flanked Astrid on her left; Baylor was on her right. As an interrogation squad, they were an impressive trio.

Thackery remained stone-faced.

"He won't talk," I said. My voice was loud in the hushed room.

"They dosed him with Sodium Pentothal," Tybalt said.

Truth serum meant little to someone with a strong enough mind, and Thackery had that in spades. I guessed we'd see how it worked itself out.

"Walter Thackery," Astrid said, her Command voice sharp and furious, "you are wanted by the Assembly of Clan Elders for the kidnapping of seven Therians, as well as the murder of Michael Jenner. You are also wanted for the kidnapping and torture of Phineas el Chimal.

"You are additionally wanted for innumerable crimes against humankind, including the murder of Rhys Willemy, the deaths of thirty-one humans one month ago at the facility known as Boot Camp, and the infection of dozens of humans with the vampire parasite. You are wanted by the vampire Families for the foreign illness plaguing their membership. How do you answer?"

Thackery looked right at her. And yawned.

A few people in the War Room hissed. Someone growled.

"You are very cavalier with your life," Astrid said.

"No matter what I say to your charges," Thackery replied, "you will sentence me to death. I prefer to not answer."

"This is no human court. There is no right to not incriminate yourself, nor is there a right to a speedy trial. You are guilty of these crimes, whether by your own word or by mine. The question you must answer is how quickly you wish to die."

"I wish to go free."

Laughter rippled through the room. I didn't laugh, because I knew Thackery was dead serious. He still had two people very dear to me, and three Lupa were loose in the city. He hadn't played his last card yet.

"What makes you think that'll happen?" Baylor asked.

Thackery turned his head, aiming his quiet smile at Phineas. "The child is adorable."

I started to stand, my only thought to wrap my hands around Thackery's neck, and was pulled back into my chair. I wasn't even in the same room with him. My heart pounded in my ears. My face flushed with fury.

Phin's only sign of emotion was the slight arching of his wings. He had one of the most impressive poker faces I'd ever seen, and it was on in full force right now, even though his emotions had to be churning like a cyclone. "Where are they?" Phin asked, each word a bullet of hate.

Thackery blinked slowly, likely forcing away the effects of the Sodium Pentothal. I'd felt its effects before; it wasn't easy to fight. "They're safe. They're with my boys."

Shitfuckhell.

"The Lupa."

"Yes. Always have a contingency plan."

"Let me guess," Astrid said. "You in exchange for them?"

"Not quite. Myself in exchange for the child."

"And her mother?"

He pressed his lips together, thoughtful. "I believe the mother's life is a fair trade for all of the Halflings you slaughtered today."

Phin's knife hand jerked. Even through the camera's lens, his control was obviously slipping. My own hands were fisted in my lap, fingers numb, my entire body vibrating with hate for the man in that room.

"Those Halflings, as you call them, were dead the moment you allowed them to be infected," Baylor said.

Thackery clucked his tongue. "You forget your old Hunter friend. They were not like the half-Bloods who roam the streets and mindlessly infect and kill. My Halflings were controlled. I found a way."

How do you control the bloodlust, Felix? What's Thackery giving you?

"You call emotional blackmail control?" Baylor asked.

"Felix was a special case. He had unique insight that I found valuable. As for the rest, if they didn't wish to earn the right to their stability by joining us . . . well, they were dealt with."

"They were executed."

"I couldn't allow them free to mindlessly infect others. I need them to stay close, controlled, until I can cure them."

Goddamn, the nutjob still thought he could cure the vampire parasite. Thackery had moved beyond obsession to absolute fanaticism—a perfect belief in his own superior intelligence.

"And you offered this nonexistent cure to Felix, just in case blackmail wasn't enough," Baylor said.

"Of course. He hated what he was. The dream of one day being free and returning to his loved ones was the perfect incentive."

Next to me, Tybalt let out an impressive string of expletives.

"I gave all of them a purpose," Thackery said. "A mission. Direction, which are things our young people sorely lack."

"You really think you're the hero here?" Baylor asked. "You changed their basic nature without their consent. Making someone sick and then offering them treatment doesn't negate the original crime. It only proves intent and ill will."

"Call it what you like," Thackery replied. "But the vampires you're so eager to help started this plague. I did what I had to do in order to further a cure for our people and to put an end to theirs. My Halflings proved that there can be life after infection. They don't all have to die because of what those vampires have done to us."

"The vampires you infected today did not kill your wife and son."

Thackery flinched and, for a moment, he looked sad. Wore the appearance of the broken man he was inside. Then he blinked hard and the weakness was gone. "Have you ever lost someone you care about to the parasite?" he asked.

Baylor nodded. "Two Hunters. I put them down myself."

Ouch.

"And the half-Bloods who infected them?"

"Killed one on the spot. One got away."

"Do you ever think of the one that got away?"

"I like to think that some other Triad hunted him one night and killed his ass dead."

"But you don't know."

"It's the past, Thackery. I don't live there. My life's in the present."

That irritating, thoughtful face came back out. "You think I'm living in the past, then," Thackery said.

"Hell yes."

"You may well be right, but my actions today are to preserve the future for our kind. There is nothing, save the ruling hand of a few, to prevent the Dregs you used to hunt from taking this world from us. One bite from a vampire, and it's over. And the shape-shifters? An army of animals capable of higher thought?"

Baylor snorted loudly and threw his arms wide. "And what the hell do you think we're doing here, jackass? We're working together for all of our peoples, so we don't have to fight or fear one another."

Astrid touched his elbow, and he backed up a few steps. I hadn't even noticed how close Baylor had gotten. He was as angry as the rest of us, with more direct ability to take his frustration out on Thackery. And as much as I wanted ten minutes alone in a room with the bastard, we needed him to keep talking.

"You're a fool, Thackery," Astrid said. "You profess to protect the longevity of the human race, and yet you are a puppet to those who seek your destruction. You're just too blinded by grief and vengeance to see it."

He frowned, seeming genuinely offended by that. "And whose puppet am I, pray tell?"

Don't tell him, don't tell him, don't tell—

"What's this cure you supposedly discovered for your Halflings?" she asked, switching topics perfectly.

"Good," I whispered. No sense in showing Thackery our last card, either. If he didn't realize the breadth of Amalie's deceptions, we gained nothing by enlightening him.

"Whose puppet am I?" he asked again. The idea distressed him. He liked being in control, the man in charge. Seeing him squirm for a damned change made me all warm inside.

"What's the cure?"

"Whose puppet?"

"The cure?"

They glared at each other. Phineas stepped forward. He reached into his jeans pocket and withdrew a bundled handkerchief. Shook it out. Little pinkish sausages tumbled to the floor by Thackery's feet. No, not sausages. Fingers.

"These belonged to your werewolves," Phin said. "To the two I killed this morning. They chose not to cooperate with questioning. How many of yours would you like added to the collection?"

Thackery gazed at the fingers, and when he looked up, his face was blank. "I'll tell you nothing else."

Phin twirled his antique blade as he took a few steps closer to Thackery. "Do you believe I'm bluffing?"

"No."

"Excellent. You tortured me. You tortured a woman I care about. You kidnapped my family. Cutting off a finger is only a small portion of the pain I wish to heap upon you, Walter Thackery."

In that moment, I hated my distance from Phineas. I'd seen him enraged, but I had never before seen this quiet menace he exuded in both posture and words. It frightened me. I half expected him to reach out and rip Thackery's head clean off his neck and laugh while doing so. Phineas had lost his wife. He'd lost his entire Clan except for three members. We'd recovered one. Two were still missing.

He had very little left to lose.

I was up and out of my chair before I made the conscious decision to leave. Tybalt shouted my name, but I ignored him. Ignored the words still being traded on the projector. Dodged past bodies trying to get inside Operations and listen, and finally burst into the corridor.

My entire body was rubbery, used up, not quite up to the task of figuring out which room Thackery was being held in. Thankfully, a small crowd stood outside a storefront about a quarter of the way down the northern corridor, toward the gym. Nevada stepped away from the quartet of—I assumed—guards once he realized my intended destination.

"Stone, you can't—" he started.

"Are you kidding me?" I said with more oomph to my tone than I felt. I gave him a solid glare. "You can let me in, or I'll just teleport through the wall anyway."

The bluff worked. He let me in through a papered-over hinged door. I kind of expected something like in the movies, where the whole room is dark except for a circle of light hanging right over the suspect. Instead, the store was mostly empty, save a few metal clothing racks, and brightly lit. The video camera was mounted on a tripod, which was balanced on a table to give it height.

Past that was my target.

Thackery saw me first, and whatever rebuttal he was about to deliver died on his lips. His eyebrows arched, which got the attention of everyone else. Astrid tossed me a poisonous glare. I ignored her.

"Ms. Stone," Thackery said. "I had hoped to speak with you again."

"Oh yeah?" I said, circling to stand closer to Phin, hands planted on my hips. "I'd hoped to see you dead and bleeding by now, but we don't always get what we want."

"A lesson well learned?"

"As if I had a choice. You know, you have a bad habit of killing people I care about."

"I have never killed—"

"Blah, blah, blah. You can twist words any way you want, Thackery, it doesn't change your actions. Tie a pretty bow around a jar of horse shit, but it's still horse shit inside."

He snickered. "That's colorful. Then again, you always were."

"You don't know me."

"I've seen you bleeding and screaming, child. I think I know you very well."

Behind me, Phin shifted. I held out my left hand, a stop gesture. My insides were quaking with anger and loathing for the man in front of me, but I would not allow the man behind me to do something he might (intellectually, at least) regret later. If one of us lost it and killed Thackery, both Ava and Aurora would pay the price. That couldn't happen.

"You know," I said, "you always seemed like a man who honored his promises. First you promised Felix a cure, but then you blew him to pieces."

"I promised to free him, and I did. Just not in the way he expected."

Oh, how I loathed that smug bastard. "What about me?"

"I've promised you nothing."

"You're wrong."

"Am I?"

"Oh yeah." I took one step closer. "You remember that day in the tractor-trailer, when you told me what you were going to do to me? You outlined your thoughts on my ability to heal?"

"I remember," he said cautiously.

"We made a deal that day. I promised to cooperate, to answer your questions, and to not fight you or your experiments. Remember?"

His expression went slack. "Yes."

"Do you remember what you promised in return?"

"Yes."

"Did you fulfill your end of our bargain?"

Trapped like the rat he was, and he knew it. Pride was one of the human male's greatest flaws, and I was playing his ego like a piano prodigy. "No. The opportunity was removed when my lab was destroyed by the gargoyles."

A fortuitous turn of events for me, as it turned out. The gargoyles saved my life that day by preventing Thackery from taking it. "Regardless, you welched on our deal. You owe me."

Those dark, haunted eyes simmered with annoyance. I ignored the three people in the room with us, keeping my attention wholly on my target. He was so close to cracking, to giving me at least one of the answers I desperately needed.

"What do you want?" Thackery asked.

Score one for our team.

"Three questions," I said.

"One."

"Three."

"Two."

"Two questions, then."

Phin touched my arm. I turned my head and met his gaze, his blue eyes cold as ice. A thousand different emotions churned in them, asking a thousand different questions. As much as I wanted to ask Thackery where Ava and Aurora were, he'd find a way to truthfully dodge the location. And I had no doubt that Thackery wanted the Lupa to stay on the move. I could ask and get "in a van driving through the hillside" just as easily as a street address.

I had to be more direct, less obtuse. I just hoped Phin would understand. No one had any intention of trading Thackery for Ava only.

"All right," I said, mentally reviewing the wording of my first question. "You say you found a cure for the insanity wrought in half-Bloods by the vampire parasite. What are the ingredients of this cure?"

Thackery fidgeted in his chair, distressed at having to divulge the secret of one of his precious projects. Not that I gave a shit about his distress. I had a suspicion—had ever since I found out he'd been drawing blood from the Therians—but I needed to know from his own lips.

"Therian blood," he replied.

Hell.

"He lies," Astrid said. "Half-Bloods have fed off our people before."

"It isn't ingested," Thackery said, affronted by being called a liar. "Fifty milliliters given intravenously every twenty-four hours. I've been studying this for months, at first using the Lupa to collect samples. Ingested, the blood does nothing. The correct dosage administered directly into the bloodstream, though . . . the change is almost instantaneous."

He was drugging his Halfies with Therian blood. He'd kidnapped Therians involved with the Watchtower and used their blood to drug his Merry Band of Halflings. He'd taken the blood of a child. And he'd initially used the blood of the Lupa pups he'd been given. Three of which were still loose in the city, with half a million potential human bite victims at their mercy.

"Fact," I said. "You, a human male, were given charge of at least seven Lupa children whose saliva is highly infectious to you."

His eyes narrowed.

"Question," I continued. "How is human infection by a Lupa bite cured?"

For such a brief moment that I might have imagined it, Thackery seemed sad. My insides quaked. It was my answer; he didn't have to say it.

"There is no cure that I am aware of, Ms. Stone," he replied anyway. "I was only lucky to have never been bitten by my boys."

I closed my eyes, held my breath, fighting off a wave of despair. Although I trusted Dr. Vansis to do everything he could to save Wyatt, part of me had always hoped for a miracle serum from among Thackery's dozens of illicit experiments. Anything to stop the raging fever and give Wyatt back to me. To prevent a potential disaster scenario if the Lupa trio decided to get snacky on the general population.

"Rumor is your lover is infected," Thackery said. "It's heartbreaking, isn't it?"

The impact of my fist against his jaw vibrated up my arm and shoulder. His head snapped sideways and stayed there. "Don't you compare our losses, you son of a bitch. I wasn't responsible for your wife's infection, but you are wholly responsible for Wyatt's."

Thackery flexed his jaw as he turned his head again to look at me. "Perhaps. But with all the other charges you're leveling at me, one more death is of no consequence."

I saw red at that, and Phineas, bless him, grabbed me

by the waist before I could inflict any permanent physical damage on Thackery's person. I let Phin spin me around and hold me tight against his chest. His heart jackhammered against mine, faster than its usual accelerated rate. My own pulse was threatening to put me into cardiac arrest.

No consequence. No fucking consequence, motherfucker!

"The Lupa have their instructions," Thackery said. "If I don't meet them at a predetermined location at seven o'clock this evening, they will kill mother and child."

Chapter Nineteen

After this morning's round of Question the Werewolves, my tolerance for torture was completely topped out. Marcus took Phin's place on the interrogation squad, and we left before they settled in to pry more answers out of Thackery. He'd hold out, I had no doubt, and it would likely get messy. And as much as I despised Thackery, I just didn't want to see anyone else suffering today.

Or ever, really, if I had my druthers, but my line of work pretty much ruled that out. Violence was part of my job, part of my life, and not something I could escape. Not until I was dead.

We crossed paths with Dr. Vansis just outside the store. He had a laptop balanced on one arm and a sour look on his face. As soon as he spotted me, he shook his head. "Nothing new for you on Truman, I'm sorry," he said. "Is Astrid inside?"

"Interrogating the prisoner," Phin replied. "What's that?"

"Some of the research they found on the ferry. It's all coded, and without the key it's going to take hours to crack. By someone else, mind you. I'm no computer expert."

"Rufus is good with computers," I said. "So's Oliver Powell."

"Thank you. I'll look for them."

"Rufus was in the War Room last I saw him."

Dr. Vansis nodded, then moved along toward Operations. Long, clipped strides. I probably should have told him there was no cure for Wyatt, but he already knew that. He had to know that by now.

The infirmary was across the hall and down several dozen yards. I gazed at the doors, aching to walk there and sit with Wyatt for a while. I also ached to just find a bed somewhere and sleep until this was over. All over, and I didn't have to fight anymore. Didn't have to do any of this shit anymore.

My feet moved of their own volition, carrying me in the opposite direction of the infirmary. Phin shadowed me as I walked. I wasn't even sure of my destination or intentions, until I was standing in front of the entrance to the vampires' quarters. The doors were closed, sealed, and guarded by a pair of lionesses.

I had friends in there. Sort of. Isleen had assisted me several times, even saved my life once by pulling me out of a garbage Dumpster. She was sick. We still didn't know why, and I hadn't spoken to her in hours.

"Are we able to communicate with them?" I asked.

"Yes," Phin replied. He leaned around one of the lounging cats and plucked a walkie off the floor. "The channel is set."

I turned the volume up a few notches, then pressed the Talk button. "Isleen? It's Stone, are you there?" A few seconds of static passed. I repeated my message.

More static, and then, "I am here."

Her voice was . . . wrong. Shaky, broken, nothing like the calm lilt of a stolid, self-assured vampire princess. She was daughter to one of the ruling Fathers, and she was an amazing warrior. I'd seen her in battle, cutting through her enemies like fire through straw. Beautiful.

Now sick. Weak.

I no longer knew what to say. "We captured Thackery."

"We were told."

"He was using Therian blood to stabilize his Halfies. Injecting it, instead of feeding it to them."

A brief pause. "Intriguing. Our illness?"

It shamed me that I hadn't even considered that as one of my two questions. "He isn't saying much. Astrid's leading the interrogation. As soon as they learn anything, I'm sure they'll tell you."

"Of course."

"How are you?" Stupid question to ask, really, but it slipped out.

"Our symptoms have progressed. My skin is dry, cracking. Bleeding."

A shiver tore down my spine, and I squeezed the walkie a little too tight. "How long have you been like that?"

"Perhaps thirty minutes. It does lend itself to a theory."

"Theory?" I glanced at Phin, who looked both puzzled and hopeful. Therians and vampires were not natural allies. However, they had developed a mutual respect in recent months, and for some it extended to friendship.

"I have been asking questions." She grunted, a pained sound that raised my hackles. "I may have found a commonality among we who are ill."

"What is it?"

"Sunscreen."

"Sunscreen?"

"Yes, the UV sunscreen."

Right—the sunscreen developed for the vampires several years ago that allowed them to walk freely in the sunshine. The initial application was quite painful, and few vampires outside the Family warriors volunteered to use it. It made a horrible kind of sense.

"Isleen, are all of the warriors sick?"

"Yes. As well as a courier. She used the sunscreen."

"Have you told your father?"

"Not yet."

"Did Thackery give it to the Families?"

"I do not believe so. The Family Fathers did not recognize his photograph. A human mage sold it to us."

"Do you know his name?" Please, please remember his name. It would give us a small lead, something to look into. Anything except sitting around, watching people I care about die.

"Matthew Goodson."

"Anything else? Description? Cell phone number."

She made an odd sound. If I hadn't known better, I'd have sworn it was laughter. "The woman who made the purchase died in battle at Olsmill. The mystery of Matthew Goodson's appearance died with her."

Terrific.

"Thank you, Isleen."

"We will, in all likelihood, die of this affliction. I feel my body shutting down. Growing weak. Changing."

My eyes stung, and I blinked hard. "I hope you're wrong."

"As do I. If I am not, so be it. I have lived a full life. And I am honored to have called you an ally, Evangeline Stone."

"Me, too." I cleared my throat. "I'm, uh, sorry I punched you that time."

"Forgiven."

Static filled the airwaves. I tapped the antenna of my walkie against my forehead, upset and unsure what else to say. We'd said it all, really. I'd failed her by bringing Felix into our sanctuary, and now my vampire friends and allies were paying the price with their lives.

"Stone?" It wasn't Isleen's voice, and it took me a moment to recognize—

"Quince?" I said. "Are you sick?"

"No, I never used the sunscreen. I remain unafflicted. One of only twenty now."

Shitfuckdamnhell.

"I wish to assist, as do the others," Quince continued, "but the Fathers will not lift the quarantine."

"I'm sorry." I eyed the pair of lionesses, who tracked me with watchful copper stares. "I wish there was something more I could do."

"Find Matthew Goodson. It will be a start."

"Yeah. Is Isleen—?"

"Resting."

"Right. Keep an eye on them all."

"Of course."

"Thank you, Quince."

He didn't reply immediately. "Avenge us."

I glanced at Phin, who nodded sagely. "Working on it."

We stowed the walkie where it came from. My strength was returning in small increments, leaving an unusual and raging hunger in its place. Maybe a quick stop at the cafeteria for something starchy before we fell headfirst into researching Matthew Goo—

"Evy!"

Good grief, what now?

Milo ran down the corridor toward us like his ass was on fire, eyes wide and mouth open. My heart plummeted to the floor. I started backing up, instinctively seeking refuge from what I knew would be horrible news. News I didn't want to hear, an announcement I couldn't know. I backed up right into Phin's chest. His hands gently grasped my elbows and held me steady—trapped me there, too, the bastard.

As Milo closed in, I realized the expression I'd originally taken for panic was actually surprise. Seasoned with just a little bit of . . . excitement?

"What?" I asked when he was close enough so I didn't have to scream it.

He skidded to an awkward stop a few yards away and

flapped his hand at me, beckoning. "Come on," he said. "Wyatt's awake, Evy. Come—"

I tore out of Phin's arms and past Milo before he punctuated his own sentence with "—on."

I think he was still shouting at me, this time to "wait a minute!" as I burst into the infirmary. No one was in the outer office. I took one stride toward the recovery rooms and stopped dead at the furious snarl that echoed from that direction. Only an angry, cornered animal could have made that sound. Something in my chest tightened unbearably.

"Stop a sec," Milo said, panting as he drew up next to me.

"He was in a coma," Phin said. "Did Dr. Vansis bring him out?"

"No, the machines just started going crazy. He woke up on his own and began yanking out the tubes."

Christ.

"Evy, he's different," Milo said.

No, no, no, no . . .

My feet carried me forward. Kismet blocked the door to Wyatt's room, hands braced on either side of the frame. Her profile was pale, jaw set. I touched her shoulder. She turned her head and her horrified expression crushed any lingering hope I'd had.

I don't want to see this. Can't know this. Oh God, please.

She moved out of the doorway, and I stepped into it, greeted by another growl. Low, warning. The bed was empty, blood-dotted sheets rumpled and tangled with abandoned wires and tubes. Wyatt was huddled in the corner, the linen gown he'd been dressed in twisted around his waist. The bandages on his neck and arm were torn, exposing the injured flesh below. Face covered by his hands, he rocked gently back and forth.

He was growling.

"Wyatt?" I said.

The growling stopped, and his entire body tensed. Ceased rocking.

I swallowed, mouth too damned dry. "Wyatt, it's Evy."

He raised his head, hands slipping down his face to cover his mouth. His eyes, once as black as coal, now twinkled a deep silver. No recognition there, just fear. And pain.

And something else I'd seen directed at me from him only one other time in my life—betrayal.

My heart fell to pieces.

Chapter Twenty

Friday, July 11
Watchtower

"What do you mean he got away?"

This is the fourth time someone's asked me that question since we returned to the Watchtower, and this time it's Isleen's turn. She towers over me like a skyscraper, all white hair and tall, thin frame. I don't even bother straining my neck to look up from my spot on the floor outside the infirmary, where I parked myself half an hour ago to wait for news on Milo.

So far everyone's gotten the bulk of the story from Marcus, but they inevitably come to me when they find out Felix is now infected. Astrid came first, then Phineas, then Baylor. They want to know how. They also want to know why he got off the bus alive and is at large in the city. The former question I can answer; the latter question I can't. Not really.

"He surprised me and he got away." It's my canned response, and it's really the only one I have.

My healing palms itch like hell. I rub their bandaged surfaces over my jeans-clad knees, at once furious and desolate. One more name to add to the list of people I've failed.

The noise level in the corridor is pretty high. Humans, Therians, and vampires alike are trolling the hall, gossiping about the bus accident, the human Hunter who was turned, and hoping for more details than I'm laying out. I want to find a quiet corner somewhere and hide for a while, but I won't leave until I know Milo will be okay. It seems the very least I owe him now, and my heart aches for what he's lost.

Isleen seems to accept my explanation more readily than anyone else. "Then I am sorry for your loss, Evangeline."

"Thanks."

The conversation quiets just enough to catch my attention. Bystanders part, creating a kind of path for two sprinting figures. Gina Kismet doesn't pause to look at me. She slams through the door and disappears inside the infirmary. As the door swings shut, her companion stops. I don't have to look up to know it's Wyatt.

He crouches in front of me and covers my hands with his, squeezing tight. I hazard a glance at his face; his expression nearly undoes my composure. Sympathy and regret are all I see. Not a trace of blame or anger. I'd almost rather he be mad at me for fucking up. He doesn't say anything. Just holds my hands.

My throat tightens. God help me, I will not cry in front of all these people.

"Come with me," he whispers.

I let him pull me to my feet. Let him hold my hand as he leads me away from the crowd. I stare at the back of his neck and struggle to retain my tenuous grip on the last threads of my restraint. He stops at a door, enters a code, and a lock springs free. Inside.

He shuts the door, and I blink at the glare of light. The weapons locker. I was given a tour of it last week—a chance to geek out over the vast array of guns, knives, swords, and explosive devices assembled by our combined forces. It's arranged not unlike a store, separated by types of weapons, stacked on shelves and some displayed openly. The biting scents of gun oil and leather tickle my nose.

"Are we going out?" I ask, confused.

"Not for a while," he replies, circling to stand in front of me. He reaches out, then freezes. "You looked like you needed some privacy."

Amusement quirks my mouth. "So you thought immediately of the weapons locker?"

"Well, you and weapons are fairly synonymous in my mind."

If anyone but Wyatt said that to my face, I might be offended, but I can hear the affection in his words. "Thank you."

He reaches for me again, and I tilt my head to show him it's okay. His palm cups my cheek, thumb brushing the corner of my lips. Heat blooms in my chest. I've missed his touch, missed this intimacy I've had only with Wyatt. We've seen each other only in passing these last ten days. Given each other the space we both needed.

I miss *him*.

"Don't blame yourself for what happened to Felix," he says, shattering the magical quiet.

I snort rather rudely and step back, out of arm's reach. "Yeah, right."

"It isn't like what happened to Alex."

My hand rises, reaching for the cross necklace. Too late, I remember I'm not wearing it. Haven't very often since coming to the Watchtower. The silver is poisonous to Therians, and wearing it around them is rude, even if it's a personal keepsake. It's wrapped in a scrap of silk and tucked safely inside my trunk.

"It's exactly like what happened to Alex," I say. Those warm feelings disappear, trampled by equal parts guilt and anger.

Wyatt shakes his head, jaw set, determined. "No. Felix was a Hunter."

"Was, Wyatt. Was. He hasn't been on patrol since he was hurt. He hasn't been training. You saw what that hound did to him." My chest hurts at the memory of those few hours in the cabin, as he lay suffering on an old mattress while Thackery's hounds kept us trapped inside.

"He survived, Evy."

"To become what? He couldn't walk from the car to the waiting room without sweating through his shirt. He was in pain all the fucking time. He was no more capable of fighting that Halfie than Alex would have been, but he did it anyway because it's what he was fucking trained to do!"

I'm screaming, and I hate it. I'm not angry at Wyatt. I'm furious at myself for failing another person. You'd think with all my recent experience at it, I'd be immune. Far from it—every new failure compounds the hurt, increases my shame. Makes me wonder why the hell Fate keeps seeing fit to let me live while better people die.

"If you'd been Felix," Wyatt asks, "would you have done anything different?"

The question works as well as a slap across the face. Goddamn him for knowing me so well. I shake my head no and turn away, examining a tray of immaculately shined blades without really seeing them. My eyes burn. The tray blurs.

Hands slide over my shoulders and gently squeeze. "When I heard you were involved in the crash and that one of ours had been infected, I panicked." His voice is strained, the fear impossible to mistake. "I know you've been training with Phin, but you're also still recovering, and for a few minutes . . ."

I blink, and a hot tear slides down my cheek. "You thought you'd lost me again. Once and for all."

"Yeah." The single word is broken, full of regret and sorrow.

"Guess it's a good thing we broke up, huh?"

"No, Evy." He tugs until I turn around, and I'm crushed beneath the emotion in his eyes. And confused. "No, I was furious with myself. I thought I'd wasted the last two weeks we could have had together, and I knew I'd always regret that."

My head is too light, and I grab his forearms to stay firmly upright. He grips my elbows, holding tight. "What are you saying, Wyatt?"

"That no matter how much I've changed, one thing hasn't and it's that I still love you."

I thought hearing those words would make me giddy with joy. Make me say them back, reassure Wyatt that I still love him. And I do. But all I feel is sad. Sad for him. Sad for Milo. Sad for the two huge secrets I'm still keeping from Wyatt and can't bring myself to tell. Not just the secret of his past that I'm keeping for Rufus, but the secret of my time with Walter Thackery. The thing I asked him to do.

The fact that I embraced my inner Chalice and I gave up.

"I still love you, too, Wyatt, but that was never the problem," I hear myself saying. "It's everything else."

He doesn't patronize either of us by asking what else. He simply nods, thoughtful. "The odds are against us ever being happy, I know. So that means we don't even try?"

"Relationships are hard, and they require trust, right? Both people have to trust each other."

"You don't trust me." It isn't posed as a question, and I want to shake him for it.

"No, you can't trust me."

He frowns, releases my arms, and steps backward several paces. The distance might as well be a mile. "What do you mean?"

I feel as though I'm standing on a cliff and the stones beneath my feet are crumbling. "That there are still some things I can't tell you, and they're not little things, and I know that by keeping them from you I'm being dishonest. And you deserve better than that, Wyatt."

"I don't give a fuck anymore what I deserve, Evy. I want you."

"Are you sure?"

His face is a perfect illustration of *what the fuck do you mean, am I sure?*

"You don't know me anymore, not even these last two months. The girl you fell in love with died. The goblins made sure she died in the worst possible way. I'm not her. I haven't been her for a long time."

"I know who you are." His voice is firm, his expression stormy.

"*I* don't even know who I am. How can you?"

"Because the parts that matter are still there, Evy. Your loyalty, your pride, your drive and willingness to fight for what you think is right. Your ability to out-cuss anyone I know."

He isn't getting this. "I let him go," I say.

Wyatt's eyebrow furrow. "Let who go?"

Shit. It isn't what I intended when I opened my mouth, but there it is. In for a penny . . . "I let Felix go."

"When?"

When? Seriously? "Today, Wyatt. I let him go today, in the fucking bus."

Wyatt freezes completely, so still for so long that I'm sure he's been replaced by a photograph. Then he shakes his head. "What do you mean?"

"I saw his eyes. I saw the color change. I knew he'd been infected and I knew what I needed to do." My stomach is in knots over the split-second decision that I'm not even sure I consciously made. "Marcus was already outside. It was just me, Milo, and that asshole who got Milo shot. I didn't . . . shit."

Why is this so hard? I've owned up to my mistakes

before, admitted them out loud to Wyatt. What about this hurts so much? That I don't think of it as a mistake?

"What did he do, Evy?" Wyatt asks.

"He knocked me down, and he had the advantage. I was so shocked I couldn't react. It was like looking at Jesse all over again." Months ago I'd watched my former partner get bitten and turn into a Halfie in front of my eyes. Watched him murder our other partner, Ash, then look at her with a sick fascination born of passion and confusion. Disgust and bloodlust. And then I shot him in the heart.

"And then Felix smiled," I continue. "Smiled like he'd just discovered the ultimate secret to joy and wanted to share. He looked at me, and even though I could see the madness, for one brief moment he was perfectly lucid. He was Felix. And do you know what he said to me?"

Wyatt shakes his head, eyes suspiciously bright.

"He said 'it doesn't hurt anymore, Evy.'" My voice breaks just as my heart broke earlier on the bus. "He wasn't holding tight. I probably could have gotten my arms free, reached up, and snapped his neck. Kept him from an existence in half-Blood hell, but I didn't."

"You let him go." His voice is so quiet. Not the quiet of calm or intimacy. No, this is furious-Wyatt's quiet voice.

"Yeah." More tears escape, tracking down my cheeks.

"You let a Halfie go."

"I did. I let Felix go."

"No, Evy." Anger flushes his cheeks. His shoulders tremble faintly. "Felix was gone. You know that wasn't him anymore. You let a Halfie go free, and not just any goddamned Halfie, but one with Hunter training and knowledge. One who knows where the Watchtower is and can use all of that against us."

He's livid. Angrier than I've seen him in a long time, and it's my fault. Letting Felix go was wrong and stupid, and a decision made in only a few tense seconds. I can't even defend myself, because there is no defense for my actions. I allowed emotion to control me, and I ignored my training.

Wyatt is not done spearing me with words. "Jesse was your partner for four years. He was infected right in front of you, and you still freed him. Alex was an innocent, and he was Chalice's best friend. And you still put a bullet in the back of his head to free him. You've killed dozens and dozens of Halfies over the years, Evy. They don't get a stay of execution, they get put down with extreme prejudice."

"I know!" The two shouted words come out like vomit—unexpected and bitter. My throat hurts, my chest hurts, and I'm afraid I'll turn inside out from all the emotion churning inside me. "I fucking know that, Wyatt!"

"Then why?" He's finally shouting back, giving in to his temper. "Why Felix? You should fucking know better, Evy!"

I don't want to keep fighting, but say it anyway. "Because he wasn't in pain anymore. I know better than anyone what it's like to spend hour after hour, day after day, in agony, just praying the pain will stop. But it doesn't. It's always there, even when you're asleep. You can't get away from it. The goblins tortured me, Thackery tortured me, and both times I'd have given anything for it to stop. Even if it was for just a few minutes. And all I had to look forward to was death."

Wyatt's eyebrows pull together as he puzzles something out. "You told me with Kelsa that you never stopped hoping for rescue."

"I didn't." Fucking hell, I said too much. My cheeks are hot, my hands are cold, and I'm fairly positive I'm about to pass out. Or maybe spontaneously combust. "I didn't give up with Kelsa." I catch his stony gaze and try to hold it through a film of tears. "But I didn't think I could survive that again and come back whole. I didn't want to."

He blinks hard, fighting his own tears. He knows. He won't ask me to stop talking, but he knows what I'm about to say—the agony in his eyes tells me so.

"So," I say, choking on the words, "I made Thackery promise to kill me when he was finished with me."

All the anger he exuded before disappears, replaced by a kind of miserable grief mixed with disbelief. His eyebrows arch up, his mouth drops open. He's so stricken it's almost comical. But not really. Not at all.

By his own admission, my strength and tenacity are two of the things he loves most about me. Now I've just shown him how very weak I can be. How weak I am still. How completely unlike the old Evy Stone I've become, and just how far I've fallen.

A tear trickles down Wyatt's cheek, and he brushes it away with an angry swipe. Then he rediscovers his lost anger and the mask is back on. Somehow putting his guard up around me, when we've shared so many painful parts of ourselves in the past, hurts more than anything else.

And I'm not even finished breaking his heart. "I knew what Felix was going through, living with that agony," I say, even though the look on Wyatt's face should shut me up. Might as well spill my guts before he decides he never wants to speak with me again. "Agony he was in because of me."

Wyatt inhales sharply. "You didn't attack him, Evy."

"He was at the cabin because of me. The hounds were there because Thackery wanted me." I wipe my cheeks with the back of my hand, exhausted and nauseated and just ready for this to be finished. Somehow. "So when he said it didn't hurt anymore, Wyatt, something in me broke."

"And you let him go," he says coldly.

I swallow back a rising tide of tears and square my shoulders; he can't possibly think less of me than he already does. "No," I say, the words sticking in my throat like barbed wire. "I *told* him to go."

Five words. One final betrayal.

Chapter Twenty-one

"Wyatt?"

The word didn't seem to mean anything to him. He stared, eyes flickering slightly, as if taking me in. Measuring me up. Deciding if I was friend or foe. And then the betrayal winked out in a flash of recognition. His hands dropped away from his mouth, and I choked.

His upper canine teeth had lengthened to an unnatural point, and both had pierced his lower lip. Blood oozed from the wounds, smeared his chin, and stained the neckline of his twisted gown.

The Lupa are bi-shifters.

Someone behind me moved, and Wyatt tensed. The soft growl raised the short hairs on the back of my neck. He narrowed his eyes. I moved forward a few inches, stealing his attention back.

"Evy?" Phin asked.

"It's okay," I whispered. To Wyatt, I asked, "May I come closer?"

He nodded slowly, wary.

One, two, three steps took me to the foot of the bed. It still provided a barrier between us. I wanted to rush to his side and hold him close, and it hurt to go so slowly. Hurt to see him like that, changed so horribly by the

Lupa bite, so unsure and afraid of everything around him.

"Wyatt, do you remember what happened?"

He blinked hard. Unfocused. Went away as he fought to answer my question. "The lot. Jeep. Wolves." The words had a slight lisp as he fought to speak through the barrier of those longer teeth. His voice hadn't changed, its familiar cadence marred only by the terror he was working so hard to suppress.

"That's right," I said. "You were attacked by a Lupa. A werewolf. It bit you."

He looked at his arm and plucked at the loosened medical tape barely securing the bandages. "I remember."

I circled to his side of the bed, slow and measured steps. He looked up sharply but didn't growl at me again. "It infected you. You got really sick."

"Hurts."

"Your arm hurts?"

"Everything. My head . . . burns."

"You may still have a fever."

"Stomach . . . so hungry."

"I'll ask the doctor about some food, okay?"

He closed his eyes and inhaled, nostrils contracting, then flaring as he exhaled hard. His tongue darted out, ran over his incisors once. When he looked at me, shock was mixed with hunger. "I can smell you."

As much as I wanted to blame that on my dunk in the river water, I knew it wasn't what he smelled. He smelled *me*.

"Evy," Phin said, his voice a sharp warning.

"I'm fine," I replied gently, holding Wyatt's gaze the entire time. "He won't hurt me."

"How do you know?"

Wyatt snarled, head snapping toward Phin. "Mine."

Oh boy, that wasn't good. We'd discuss possessive declarations at a later time, though. Wyatt and Phin were both, by their very natures, alpha males, and with Wyatt's newfound Lupa-gene boost, I did not need them getting into a fight. Especially if it led to either of them injuring the other.

"Wyatt, look at me."

He did, those unfamiliar silver eyes blazing with an anger born of fear. "I heard you. Before."

"Before what?"

"Before the wolf woke me. Heard you talking."

My admission before the ferry invasion. My pulse quickened. "You were in a coma."

"Couldn't move. Couldn't talk. But the wolf wouldn't let me sleep. Prowled. Heard you."

To see him, a man so full of strength and fire, reduced to fragmented thoughts and lisped words through nightmarish teeth physically hurt me. I wanted to run away and pretend it wasn't happening. Only I'd never do that. I'd given up enough for one afterlife. I wouldn't give up on him.

We'd deal with this. Period.

"What did I say?" I asked, hoping he'd heard the most important part of that ramble.

"Said you love me."

"I do."

He touched his mouth, fingertips running over those long canines. "Still?"

"Of course." I took a tentative step forward. When he didn't react badly, I closed the distance between us, then squatted down to eye level. He watched me come, as curious as he was scared. "My body changed once, and you still loved me. Underneath all of this, you are still you. I know it."

"I think the wolf is stronger than me, Evy."

"It isn't stronger than us, though." I held out my hand, palm up and open. Tried very hard to keep it from trembling. "Not stronger than we are together."

He eyed my hand, then met my intent stare. "You really believe that?"

Without hesitation—"Yes. I didn't come to a personal epiphany this morning just to lose you to some were-wolf bite, so deal with it."

A spark of humor made the corners of his mouth quirk, and the horrific sight of those fangs and the blood seemed less awful. The Wyatt I knew and loved was still there, fighting hard to stay in control. He reached out. Our fingers brushed, and then he pulled back. Stared at the blood staining his hands.

"Did I hurt someone?" he asked.

"Of course not. You cut your lip."

He tongued his wounds, noticing them for the first time. "I don't want to be like this. I feel like I might hurt someone."

A commotion behind us—voices, scuffling feet, someone grunted—ended with a sharp, "What the hell?" from Dr. Vansis. *Terrific.*

Wyatt shrank back against the wall, growling, a glare both deadly and terrified directed over my shoulder. All of our progress was erased in three seconds of sheer idiocy.

"Stay out," I said. I turned my head toward the doorway; Vansis was three steps inside the room.

"Are you insane?" Vansis asked as he took another step closer.

My head was spinning from its impact with the wall before I fully registered the fact that Wyatt had yanked me behind him. I landed sideways on my hip, braced on one hand. He crouched in front of me, ready to spring up like an attentive attack dog. The snarling increased in volume.

"Evy?" Phin asked.

"I'm fine, and stay back for fuck's sake," I yelled.

"Someone get my bag from the other room," Vansis said. "I need a sedative."

Wyatt shifted his weight to his legs and dropped his shoulders. He was going to attack. The wolf, as he called it, was taking over. Making him act completely on instinct to protect me and himself.

I scrambled forward, heart pounding, and tackled Wyatt before he could jump. It wasn't graceful. We ended up in a tangle of limbs, each grappling for dominance. His teeth snapped uncomfortably close to my left ear. "Wyatt, stop!"

His struggle ceased when he seemed to realize I was the one who'd attacked him. He went limp beneath me, on his stomach. I held his wrists against the floor, my knees braced on either side of his hips. He was panting, still growling, but no longer fighting me.

A shadow moved in my peripheral vision. "Don't come near us," I warned, and I fucking meant it. The look I gave Dr. Vansis could have melted steel. "Get the fuck out right now."

"If he bites you—" Vansis began.

"I'll deal with it. Out!"

"Leave them alone," Milo said. "Let Evy do this."

I would have kissed him if I didn't think it would get him flattened by my half-werewolf boyfriend. And the simple fact that the thought of having a half-werewolf boyfriend didn't send me screaming for the hillside (or racing for the nearest sharp object) felt like personal progress. I was finally growing up.

Once the source of Wyatt's stress moved out of sight, I climbed off and scooted back. Knelt an arm's reach away to allow him the room he needed to sit up. He gave me a sideways look. An assessing look tinged with fear. I still couldn't reconcile those silver eyes in a face I knew so well.

"Did I hurt you?" he asked.

"No."

"Not this time. You should kill me before I do."

A flash of anger that he'd even suggest such a thing ripped through me so fast that my hand jerked. "Not going to happen."

"I'm not me anymore."

"Yes, you are. You are Wyatt Truman. I don't care what's happened to you physically. You are the same."

"I don't feel the same." He cast about the room, as if he could divine answers from the stark white walls. "I feel like a stranger in my own body."

"Funny, I kind of know what that's like."

He held up his hand, bloody fingers facing me. "You didn't become a monster."

"No, I didn't," I said. "Because I was already a monster."

"Not like this."

"I was a worse kind of monster because I let myself be made into one. I killed anything you told me to kill, and I never asked questions. I killed a girl my age to get out of Boot Camp, and I never asked questions. I never let myself think there might be a better way. A black-and-white world was easier to live in."

I scooted closer to him and reached for his hand. He withheld it a moment, then grasped my wrist tightly. His pulse thrummed, and heat radiated from his skin. "Six months ago I'd have killed you just as you asked me to, because this is wrong. It's unnatural. But you know what? So am I. I live in the body of a dead girl. I can teleport, I can heal from almost anything, and I can survive a Halfie bite. I'm exactly the kind of scary, ubermagical creature we always feared and hunted."

"And now," Wyatt said, "I'm a scary, magical were-wolf half-breed."

"See? We're perfect for each other."

He smiled. Those teeth scraped his tender lip, and he winced. Closed his eyes. "God, it still burns."

"What burns?"

"Everything. The wolf is in my head. He can smell you." His grip on my wrist tightened. "Wants to claim you."

Oh boy. I swallowed hard, working to stay calm and not show the sudden flash of nervousness such a statement caused. Wolves sensed fear. I touched his cheek. "The wolf isn't allowed to have me," I said. "Only you, Wyatt."

He opened his eyes, and for a moment they weren't human. The animal had come out. Silver overtook most of the white, and the pupil became less distinct. Then he blinked, and while still the wrong color, they were human again. He pressed into my hand. Inhaled.

"I don't think it's going to be that easy," he said.

"What has ever been easy for us?"

A puff of air that might have been a soft chuckle crossed my wrist. "Good point. How is this happening?"

I had no clue. Therian history said that infected humans were killed or went bat shit from the fever. Wyatt had transformed. Two explanations came to mind. The simplest was that Wyatt's connection to the Break, being Gifted, affected the change. His tether to magic kept him from being consumed.

The other explanation was far more sinister—Amalie or Thackery manipulated this group of Lupa somehow, altering the way the infection worked. To what end, I couldn't begin to guess, and I was done underestimating the lengths to which either Thackery or the Fey would go in order to meet their goals.

Not that I was going to share that particular theory with Wyatt. "I wish I knew," I said. "But it's happening and, in some ways, I'm grateful. What's that saying about a gift horse?"

"I suppose. I want—"

"What? What do you want?"

"To taste your blood." With a cry that echoed what I felt in my heart, Wyatt scrambled back and away. He hit the far wall and stopped, curling tight into himself and covering his face with his hands. "Fuck!"

I left the chasm of distance between us, too stunned to think properly. Certainly nothing had ever come easily for either of us, but we'd never faced anything quite like this before. An enemy we couldn't fight physically was not my forte, and much like a human infected with the vampire parasite, the Lupa virus was changing Wyatt from the inside out. No one had experienced a Lupa infection in centuries. And certainly not the infection of a Gifted human. No one knew what to expect.

Could he beat this?

"Wyatt, tell me what you're feeling," I said.

"Angry," he said, the word slightly muffled but no less powerful. "Aroused. Hungry."

The perfect trifecta of emotions. "Okay, angry. What do you want to do with that anger?"

"Hunt. Fight. Eat."

"What do you want to hunt?"

"Anything." He raised his head, that animalistic glint back in his eyes. "God, your blood smells so sweet, Evy. I don't think you should stay in here."

The room suddenly felt twenty degrees cooler, and a chill ripped down my spine. It was a warning as much as a statement, and I felt the horror of it in my bones. "I trust you, Wyatt." Somehow my voice didn't shake.

"I don't trust myself."

Logic shooed me toward the door. My heart kept me still. "Then trust me."

"I don't want to kill anyone."

"You won't."

"But I want to. The wolf wants to. He wants blood."

"Wyatt, you're in control. You can control the impulses of the wolf, I know you can. You've done it so far."

"He's stronger than I am."

"Bullshit."

He moved faster than I'd ever seen him—across the room in a blink of time. He knocked me backward and straddled my waist. His hands held my wrists by my head, and his face hovered just above mine. The glinting silver eyes and drying blood created a grotesque mockery of the man I loved. My guts twisted into knots of fear and panic, but I forced myself to not struggle. To stay perfectly still beneath his hold, even though my body screamed at me to fight back. To get away, get out from under, get to a safe distance.

"Is this bullshit?" he asked, breathing hard through his open mouth. "No, it's a fucking nightmare, Evy, and I can't wake up from it. I can't shut it off. Please kill me before I hurt someone."

Promise you'll kill me when you're done.

I hadn't thought I could survive Thackery's torture with my soul intact, and I had. Wyatt didn't think he could survive this, beat back the wolf, and be whole again. Be himself.

But he could. And I knew he could.

"Make a deal with you?" I asked, echoing those fateful words spoken to Thackery nearly two months ago.

Wyatt blinked. Started to shake his head, then stopped. He pressed his forehead to mine, the intense heat making me sweat. This close I smelled his own fear—the sour scent of perspiration, mixed with something even more primal. He inhaled deeply through his nose, held it, then expelled it hard through his mouth. Blood-scented breath brushed my lips, and I shivered.

I hated every fucking thing about this, and nearly jumped out of my skin when he said, "What?"

"I want a week. At least a week to help you. Isolation,

chains, whatever you want, but I want you to try with me. Try to beat this."

"Why?"

"Because I love you, you jackass."

He raised his head and gazed at me with a chaotic mix of pride, love, terror, and pain. "I thought I was a dumbass."

"Dumbass, jackass, any kind of ass."

He smiled. "I love you, Evy. I'm sorry for turning my back on you."

"You had every reason. I was a coward."

"No, I was wrong."

"It doesn't matter now."

He seemed to realize his exact position over me and made a surprised sound caught somewhere between a grunt and a squeak. He climbed off and scooted back until he could lean against the wall. The thin gown had twisted immodestly, but he didn't seem to notice the draft. I sat up slowly, careful not to show my utter relief at being free. I hated being held down like that, by anyone.

Wyatt traced a finger across his teeth. "How can you look at me and not see a monster?" he asked.

"Because I didn't fall in love with your black eyes and straight teeth, Wyatt Truman," I said, recalling his own words to me so many months ago. "I fell in love with your confidence and your loyalty and your ability to piss me off in five words or less. In the way you can see the logical side of things that I usually can't. All of that is still there, Wyatt. It just has to work a little harder now."

He gave me a wry smile. "I'm not you, Evy. I won't heal from this."

"You don't know that."

"You'll risk it?"

"Yes."

"I don't—" He cleared his throat, eyes suspiciously

bright. "I don't know if I can live like this. Or if I want to."

Goddammit, I was not going to cry. "Give me a week. Please."

"What if they don't give me a week?"

"They who?"

"The Assembly."

A blast of anger flushed my cheeks. "Fuck the Assembly, if they think they get to dictate your fate. Their decision to eradicate the Lupa centuries ago is what led us to this. They don't get to decide if you live or die."

"Don't be so sure, child," a deep, vaguely familiar voice said behind me.

Wyatt froze, tensed, hands splayed against the wall on either side of him. I twisted around and onto my knees, one hand automatically reaching for the knife still strapped to my left ankle. I stopped before I actually grabbed it, once I recognized the faces standing in the doorway.

Flanked on either side by Astrid and Marcus—each wearing identical expressions of disgusted surprise—was Elder Marcellus Dane of Felia. He was the one who'd spoken.

Chapter Twenty-two

"Don't be so sure of what?" I asked as I stood up. Kept myself between Wyatt and the door.

Elder Dane ignored my question, his attention on the man crouched behind me. He seemed more fascinated than upset, but I'd learned a long time ago to never underestimate the poker face of a Therian. "Remarkable," Dane said. "There has not been a recorded human infection by a Lupa in centuries."

"Yeah, no shit."

"Stone," Astrid said sharply. A warning to stop being so snippy with a Clan Elder. One who'd just indirectly threatened Wyatt's life, and that was not okay with me.

"Wyatt's broken no Therian laws," I said. "His life isn't up to you to save or end."

"On the contrary," Dane said, "his infection by a Lupa makes this an Assembly matter by default."

"Because the Assembly ordered the extinction of the Lupa Clan five hundred years ago?"

"Yes. They were a destructive, bloodthirsty Clan then, and their habits have obviously not changed. Your human now carries their genes in his blood, and it must not be allowed to spread."

"You don't know that he can spread it."

"Half-Bloods are just as infectious as full-Blood vampires."

"He's not a vampire, and neither was the bastard who bit him."

Astrid and Marcus shared a look behind their Elder's head. I didn't know what it meant, but at least they weren't rushing to Dane's defense.

"You would take the risk of him infecting other humans?" Dane asked.

"I would take the risk of him infecting me," I replied. "He's fighting the effects of the wolf, and he's strong enough to beat it. We just need time."

"Time is in short supply of late."

"I've noticed."

He quirked a bushy eyebrow. He was either annoyed at being talked back to, or amused at the novelty of it. I imagined most Elders were used to the whole "I say jump, you say how high" method of giving orders.

"Look," I said, "let Dr. Vansis run some tests, at least. In the meantime, I will keep him isolated."

A moment passed, and then Elder Dane nodded. "I admit, I did not come here prepared to pass judgment on this matter," he said. "In the absence of an appointed voice of the Assembly, I have volunteered to act in that capacity."

Fancy way of saying that with Jenner dead, Dane got the job. "So you're here about Thackery." And considering the fact that both Astrid and Marcus were here, instead of down the hall, meant only one thing.

"You're done questioning Thackery?"

"The exercise proved fruitless, even with the administration of Sodium Pentothal," Marcus said. "He gave up nothing of use, despite the loss of three fingers."

Ugh. Instead of a sense of poetic justice, the knowledge disturbed me. "So we still don't know where he's keeping Ava and Aurora?"

"No. Just that they are with the three surviving Lupa children."

"What about the vampires? Did anyone—"

"Phineas informed us of the vampire Isleen's theory. We're looking into the name Matthew Goodson and any connections to Thackery."

"Nothing from Thackery on that?"

"Just gloating over how perfectly his plan to infect them worked."

Fucker.

"Don't assume," Wyatt said. His interjection stole everyone's attention. He was concentrating on the floor, conjuring up the words. Keeping his thoughts together. "Don't assume he's finished."

"He's in custody," Elder Dane said.

"The hybrids at Boot Camp. The sinking ferries."

"He means that Thackery likes redundancies and backup plans," I said. "Just because we have him here doesn't mean there's not something out there waiting for a signal. Something bigger."

"Something capable of infecting the other vampires?" Marcus asked.

"Exactly." The thought of it chilled me. I also couldn't believe that I hadn't thought of it sooner. "He has three Lupa soldiers left who could be out there doing anything for him. Even flipping a switch on a countdown. He said that something was already in motion that we couldn't stop."

"It's an interesting theory," Elder Dane said, not convinced.

"We've dealt with this psycho before," I said. "He doesn't do anything half-assed, and he doesn't walk into a room without an exit strategy."

"We should inform the royal Fathers," Astrid said. "If they decide there is a threat, it might be safer for them to evacuate the city. At least for the short term."

"Agreed," Marcus said.

One more outcome I was helpless to directly affect. If

Thackery had a redundancy in place, he wouldn't tell. Or he'd tell us just in time for us to watch it kill every vampire who'd ever used Matthew Goodson's sunscreen.

"Did the Assembly reach a majority regarding Jenner's death?" I asked.

Elder Dane gave me one of those looks usually reserved for stuff you scrape off the bottom of your shoe. "Assembly decisions are not your concern," he said.

"The hell they aren't. I work here, too, and Michael Jenner was a friend of mine. Not to mention the fact that Thackery's pups are holding on to my goddaughter and her mother, and killing Thackery too soon means they die."

My spiel seemed to throw Dane for a moment. He frowned at me. "You aren't arguing to spare Thackery's life?"

"Hell, no, I'll dance on the bastard's grave when he's finally in it. One man's death cannot replace the loss of Michael Jenner, to both his Clan and to the Assembly. All I ask for is time. Time to find Aurora and Ava, and to find the three Lupa children before Thackery is killed."

"And you believe you can do this?"

"I have to try."

"How much time do you require?"

Please, oh please, let this be a yes. "Well, Thackery's deadline for reporting back to the Lupa is seven o'clock tonight. If he doesn't, the last child of a nearly extinct Clan dies."

Something in Elder Dane's face softened. I'd hit a nerve. "To ransom a child is the mark of a true monster," he said. "I can give you until seven-thirty. After that, the Equi Elder will demand his justice."

"Thank you, Elder Dane."

"Just find the child and her mother." He glanced past me. "And contain him. The Assembly will rule on our position on his status at a later time. Too much else is of greater concern to us."

I didn't care if we ranked below his laser wart removal—I'd bought us time. Both to find Aurora and Ava, and to help Wyatt get a handle on his new dual nature before it drove him bat shit crazy. Or worse.

Elder Dane left with Astrid close behind. Marcus lingered in the doorway, his gaze on the man behind me. "Can you handle him?" he asked.

"Yes," I replied. "Where's Gina?"

"Awaiting word. Shall I send her in?"

"Yes. Get her up to speed, then have her come with Dr. Vansis so he can draw some blood."

"All right."

"Three fingers, huh?"

Marcus smiled wickedly. "Two fingers and a thumb. Right hand."

"Damn." I glanced at my left hand and the smooth bump where my pinkie used to be. This time I felt a tiny nudge of satisfaction.

"Small comfort to Jenner's widow and children."

"True."

Marcus slipped out.

"Evy?" Wyatt asked.

I turned. Squatted in front of him. His mouth was pinched, the tips of his canines peeking out beneath his upper lip. Eyebrows furrowed, deep in thought.

"What is it?" I asked.

"Jenner is dead," he said in such a way as to be convincing himself.

Uh-oh. "Yes, he is. We killed the werewolf who attacked you, and then we trapped and killed two more. Thackery was angry, so he killed Michael Jenner as payback."

"You killed two more."

"Yes."

"I'm so confused, Evy." He rubbed his eyes with his

fingertips, then squeezed the bridge of his nose. "My mind is racing with so many thoughts. Not all of them mine, I don't think. I'm angry about Jenner, and I'm angry at you for killing the Lupa. I shouldn't be angry at both. The Lupa are our enemies, but I'm one of them."

"No, you aren't one of them," I said. "You are still a human being in all of the ways that count."

He bared his teeth. "I want to hurt you for hurting them."

"But you won't." And there was no way in hell I'd tell him that Phin was the one who'd actually killed two of them. I'd rather have Wyatt angry at me than at one of the Lupa's natural enemies. Truman versus el Chimal was not an epic showdown I had an interest in witnessing.

"All of this anger, Evy, it burns. I want to release it, but I don't know how, except to fight or hurt, but I don't want to do that."

"What about exercise? We can go to the gym or to an empty store so you can run and burn some energy."

"Maybe. It might help. Oh God, you smell good."

Any other day, I'd have thought that a compliment. Right now it was just creepy as hell. "Don't think about what you smell. Tell me what you see."

"I see you." His gaze traveled over me, around the room. "White walls. A bed. A monitor. But it's different. Sharper. It all seems . . . brighter. Are my eyes different?"

"Your sight's definitely improved. And your eyes kind of changed color."

"Silver?"

"Yeah."

"Will they change back?"

The plaintive sorrow in his voice made me ache for him. "I don't know. I hope so. The Lupa are bi-shifters. Maybe once you get a handle on the wolf, you can control the change."

"Maybe." He didn't sound convinced.

A hand knocked softly on the door frame. If Wyatt had been a wolf, his ears would have perked and swiveled toward the sound. Instead, he sat up a little straighter, attention fixed on the door where Kismet and Dr. Vansis stood. Kismet's face was blank, collected and calm, even though her left hand shook slightly. "May we come in?" she asked.

I looked at Wyatt, who seemed to defer the decision to me. "Yes," I said. "Slowly, please."

She took a few steps in and stopped. I really didn't blame her.

Vansis put a small tray down on the foot of the bed. "Mr. Truman, may I draw some blood from your arm? I'd like to run a few tests."

"You smell strange," Wyatt said. "I don't like it."

On a list of absurd ways to answer a question about drawing blood, that definitely ranked at the top.

"I'm Ursia," Vansis said, sounding completely unperturbed by the response. "Is that perhaps what you smell?"

"I don't know. Do Ursia smell like tar?"

Tar? I glanced at Kismet, who was making a valiant effort to maintain her composure.

"It's possible we smell like tar to a Lupa. To me, you smell earthy, like wet cardboard."

Wyatt blinked. "Evy stays?"

"Yes, she may stay. It will only take a moment."

"Okay."

He held out his right arm while Vansis prepared his needle. I sat down next to Wyatt and held his left hand tightly in mine, ready and able to block him from attacking Vansis if he was startled or accidentally provoked. I didn't doubt that Vansis could handle himself in a fight, but I didn't want Wyatt living with the guilt of attacking *anyone*, much less his doctor.

"Look at me," I said.

He did, and he didn't look away. Vansis described

what he was doing in detail before doing it. He worked with a light touch, tying the tourniquet, swabbing the interior of Wyatt's elbow, finding the vein. Wyatt winced only once, when the needle first pierced his skin. Vansis carefully attached the first vacuum tube, and it began to fill with red.

He collected three vials of blood, and with each one Wyatt gripped my hand tighter. Perspiration appeared across his forehead and upper lip. He breathed harder through his mouth. He hadn't once blinked. His control was slipping.

"Almost done," I said.

Vansis placed a cotton ball over the site and pulled out the needle. "Please bend your elbow."

Wyatt did. Once his physical contact with Vansis was over and the doctor had moved away with his samples, Wyatt shuddered. His grip on my hand loosened; my bones ached.

"One more small request," Vansis said. He held up two cotton swabs. "May I swab your mouth?"

Wyatt blinked hard a few times, as if reminding himself of what exactly that entailed. I'd never seen him so muddled, not even when he was falling-down drunk. "Why?" he asked.

"I would like to measure the amount of the Lupa virus present in your saliva. I'd like to know how dangerous it is if you happen to bite someone."

Wyatt considered that. "I think I'd like to know, too." He opened his mouth without further prompting.

Dr. Vansis worked quickly, dropping each swab into its own test tube and capping it with a rubber stopper. "When you're up to it, Mr. Truman, I'd like to do a complete physical."

"Maybe later," I said. He'd had enough. I could see it in the way he'd curled into himself and wrapped his arms around his middle.

"Of course." He collected his tray and left.

Wyatt stayed huddled on the floor. Kismet hadn't moved from her spot by the door. I was at a bit of a loss as to my next step. I needed to get out there and do something to find Ava and Aurora, but I couldn't just leave Wyatt like this. He needed me.

I crossed to Kismet, who had yet to lose her shell-shocked stare. "Do you have any weapons on you?" I asked.

Her left hand reached around to the small of her back. "Gun, why?"

"Just checking."

"Why is she here?" Wyatt asked. He didn't sound suspicious or upset, just curious.

"She's my backup," I replied. "I figured if someone had to kill you for killing me, you'd want it to be a friend."

"Oh."

Kismet's glare left little doubt that she was not pleased with my logic.

"Evy, please tell me what's going on," he said.

I sat down across from him, keeping us on even ground. "We captured Thackery and we found most of the kidnapped Therians. He was using their blood to stabilize his half-Bloods. It's why Felix was so rational."

"Therian blood. Seems so simple."

"It does, only he says they didn't drink it. He injected them with it, which is what made the difference."

"But he killed Jenner."

"Yes. Because we killed his wolves."

Annoyance flickered across his face. "Right. But you're still looking for Aurora and Ava?"

"Yes. Thackery had them in a different location. His three surviving Lupa have them, and he says that they'll be killed if Thackery isn't released by seven o'clock. And we can't do that."

"Seven o'clock today? What time is it?"

"Getting close to three, I think."

"Damn."

"They could be anywhere. Thackery isn't talking. The Assembly is going to want him dead no matter what, and my goddaughter is out there, Wyatt." My voice cracked. "I don't know what to do."

He closed his eyes and pressed both palms against his temples, like someone warding off an impending headache. "Part of me is glad the Lupa have the Coni women, and I hate that, Evy. Shit!"

I hated hearing him say those words. "But I know the stronger part of you wants them returned safe and sound. *That* part of you would never wish harm on a woman and her child."

"Don't be so sure." He looked at me with haunted eyes. "Don't forget Rain. Don't forget the people I've hurt to make the Triads work."

Rain had been a terrible mistake. Four and a half years ago, the young were-fox had been ordered executed for falling in love with a human. A human Hunter who'd been one of Wyatt's. Wyatt had taken the execution order to protect the other Triad Hunters from knowing such an order had been placed, and her death still haunted him. Her only crime—falling in love.

Sometimes we all commit that particular crime.

"You didn't want to kill Rain."

"Maybe they don't want to kill Aurora and Ava."

My mental brakes ground to a halt on that one. It had never occurred to me that the Lupa would be anything except loyal, ready to agree with anything Thackery said and to do his bidding, no questions asked. "But they will, unless he tells them to stop."

"Yes. They're his. They'll listen."

"Not by choice."

"No."

"The Lupa are fiercely independent," Phineas said, his voice an unwelcome interruption. He'd scrubbed himself of the black paint, remaining shirtless in his blue jeans and sneakers.

I expected Wyatt to growl or snarl, maybe even jerk to attention. Instead, he gave Phin a cool glare, then nodded. "Yes," he said. "I feel that, a rebellion against rules. Against order. An embrace of chaos."

Embrace of chaos—the very opposite of Wyatt Truman in every way.

"Is that why the Lupa were hunted?" I asked. "Their independent nature meant they'd never submit to the rule of the Assembly, and they created chaos everywhere they went, and so were ordered to be executed?"

"Yes," Phin said. "Thousands of human lives were saved."

"By killing Lupa," Wyatt said.

"Yes."

"My people."

"You are more human than Lupa, Wyatt Truman," Phin said. "With a human woman who loves you very much. Do not allow the Lupa in you to drive her away."

And then came the growling I was hoping to avoid. "I thought you'd be cheering me on to embrace the wolf," Wyatt replied.

"Why is that?"

"You want her."

I would have laughed at the absurdity of his logic if I didn't think it would piss him off even more. He was actually jealous of Phin. My temper flared to life. "You asshole," I said.

Wyatt blinked, stunned into silence by my challenge.

"After everything we've been through," I continued. "Four years in the Triads, losing Jesse and Ash, my resurrection . . . after Olsmill and Call and Thackery and getting blown up twice—no, three times . . . after what we did in that cabin with our combined Gifts and falling in love with you—you asshole!"

Maybe it was my tone, maybe the short trip down Memory Lane tripped something in his mind, but Wyatt's entire expression softened. Shards of black flickered behind the silver in his eyes, and his elongated canines seemed to shrink just a hair. His humanity was peeking through, and I wasn't even done yelling.

"You really think that you dying would send me running into Phin's arms for comfort? You think his master plan is to see me completely shattered by your death, so he can be there to pick up the pieces? You think that little of both of us? Fuck you!"

Wyatt shut his eyes with a pained whine and turned away, covering his face with his hands. I wanted to scoot closer and hold him, try to comfort him—but something kept me still. Allowed him to work through the storm of emotions churning inside so he could battle the wolf. So the human side of him, the side I loved and wanted back, could rise to the surface.

We waited, silent, as he shuddered and shook. And finally went still, save the rise and fall of his shoulders as he breathed deeply.

He looked up, hands falling away from his face. The canines were back to normal, though the puncture wounds in his lip remained. His eyes had returned to their mostly black shade, with a faint ring of silver around the outside of the iris—a potentially constant reminder of his new dual nature. He blinked hard, gazing around, both curious and chagrined.

He ran his tongue across his teeth. "My vision is still different."

"Well, your eyes aren't completely normal," I said. "How's the wolf?"

"Subdued for now. I'm so sorry, Evy."

"Forgiven. I'm just glad that yelling snapped you out of it, instead of making it worse."

"She was unlikely to make it worse," Phin said. "If memory serves, the Lupa were a matriarchal society, the Packs led by an Alpha female and her chosen mate. If Wyatt's wolf understands that Evy is his mate, he'll obey her instinctively."

What was it with Therians and the word "mate"? I hated that word, and I hated what it implied about a relationship—that it was about reproduction, not love. Phin's admission about his late wife was proof enough that it was much more than simple biology for Therians. They were just as capable of great love as humans.

"The wolf still doesn't like you," Wyatt said to Phin. He used the sleeve of his gown to wipe the blood off his lips and chin, wincing as he scraped the twin cuts.

Phin nodded. "For good reason."

"I apologize for my insinuations."

"They were understandable, under the circumstances."

"You mean my split personality?"

"So to speak. My intention in coming here was not to fight with you, despite its mood-altering benefits."

That got my attention fast. "What is it? Thackery?" I asked.

"Sort of. I have an idea about how to find those three missing Lupa, and I need Wyatt's help to do it."

Chapter Twenty-three

"To do what exactly?" Wyatt asked.

Phin took a few steps forward, putting himself near the foot of the hospital bed. Over his shoulder Kismet remained silent and steadfast, listening and watching everyone involved in the conversation. "I had a chance to speak with Elder Dane a few moments ago, regarding his knowledge of the Lupa," he said. "As you've already been told, the Lupa were once one of the most powerful of the Therian Clans, and not just because of their bi-shifting abilities. They were also the most magically sensitive of the Clans."

"What does magically sensitive mean?" I asked. "They're Gifted?"

"No, not in the sense that you use the word to describe humans and their Gifts. Consider the ability to sing. Most of us are average, many awful. A select few are extremely talented, and once or twice in a generation there is a truly magnificent voice."

Okay, I got that he wasn't saying the Lupa were all opera stars, but the rest of the analogy wasn't quite working for me.

"Therians are considered magical by most because of our shifting abilities," Phin continued, probably prompted by my blank stare. "However, unlike Gifted humans, we do not require contact with the Break in order to shift.

We can travel from here without ill effects. From my experience, all Therians are like this. I would assume Lupa, as well."

"Then what makes them 'a magnificent voice'?" I asked.

"They possess, within a Pack, a sort of telepathy among their members. It is especially strong among siblings, and strongest if they are the offspring of the Alpha female."

"They talk to one another with their minds?" It was my clearest understanding of telepathy, even though I'd met a handful of Gifted telepaths with quite varied talents. Brett Lewis used his psychometry skills for us on a freelance basis (it was hard to believe that it was just last night when he'd identified Thackery as Aurora and Ava's kidnapper). Claudia Burke had been a Hunter, and she'd used her telepathy to sense the truth in people's words—until she was killed in the field last week by a trio of Halfies.

"Not quite. Elder Dane described it as more of a proximity sensor. Siblings can sense the distress of other siblings, and the Alpha female can often sense all members of her Pack."

"So you think they'll sense Wyatt?" Kismet asked.

Phin nodded. "Or he'll be able to sense them. He shares their genetic traits now, so it's possible he'll be regarded as a fellow Pack member. If they can sense his current distress, they may already be seeking him out."

"Even though Thackery ordered them to guard Ava and Aurora?"

"They are Lupa first, trained dogs second."

Wyatt grunted.

I absolutely hated the idea of taking Wyatt out of the Watchtower and making him a target, especially with his emotions on such an uneven keel. But I saw Phin's point. It might be our only chance to find the Lupa before seven o'clock. I wasn't going to speak for Wyatt, though; this was his decision.

"The Assembly won't like it," Kismet said.

"You're right," Phin said. "In my limited experience as a member of the Assembly, I'm fairly positive they would rather execute Wyatt, see the last of the Lupa dead, and sweep this entire incident under the metaphorical rug."

That comment earned a deep-chested growl from Wyatt.

Unperturbed, Phin continued. "Many Elders still see the Lupa as a blight on our collective history and their removal as a cleansing of evil. It's what they learned from the Elders before them, and I can only guess at my own Clan Elder's thoughts on them. But none of them likes talking about it, and it's why the information isn't known among the general Therian population."

"I have a question," I said. "If the Elders don't like talking about it and would rather forget, why bother passing down the information? They thought the Lupa were killed off centuries ago."

"To learn from the past, I suppose. You still teach your children the evils of wars fought long ago, in countries thousands of miles away. The Lupa are part of our collective history. A dark chapter, probably the darkest, but it isn't something we should forget."

"Just something to hide from the general population?"

Phin's mouth twitched.

"Sounds like it works well as a boogeyman story, too," Kismet said. "This is what happens when a Clan gets out of line, so make sure you and your people play by the rules."

Phin angled his body to face her, his expression blank. "That sounds oddly familiar and not a little ironic, coming from an ex-Handler."

She frowned.

"Okay," I said, "so what exactly is your plan? Put

Wyatt in a car, drive him around the city, and hope his werewolf radar goes off?"

"In a nutshell, yes," Phin replied.

"Really?"

"Unless you have a more specific starting location in mind."

It sounded like a great way to waste our entire afternoon. Unfortunately, unless they managed to get something out of Thackery besides more fingers, it was also the only plan we had.

I looked at Wyatt, whose lips were pressed tight, eyebrows furrowed in concentration. He glanced at me with those eerie, silver-rimmed eyes. "This is our only real option, isn't it?" he asked.

"It's the only good one," I replied, "since none of us is about to sit around and do nothing."

"You'll bring weapons?"

"Of course."

"No, Evy, for me. If I lose control out there—"

My heart beat just a little faster. "You won't."

"But if I do, you need to be prepared to kill me before I infect someone. And I mean kill me. You know I won't be able to live with myself if I do."

"I know." I swallowed hard against the lump in my throat. He was right. Taking him into the city while the infection was still fresh, before we'd had any real practice at keeping his wolf under control, was beyond risky. It bordered on suicidal. And yet, as with every other major decision in our lives lately, what fucking choice did we really have?

"Promise me, Evy."

"I promise."

He held my gaze a moment, resolute and angry, then glanced past me. "You, too."

"I promise," Kismet said.

He didn't bother asking for Phin's word.

"Elder Dane won't like us taking Wyatt out of here," I said.

"The Watchtower isn't exclusively run by the Therians," Kismet said. "I'll tell Adrian the plan. He won't say no."

"How do you know?"

"Because he might be a foot taller than me, but he knows I can kick his ass."

Impressed with the implied threat, I smiled. "Works for me. Wyatt's going to need clothes." We'd have to get food for him before we left, too. I could use a snack myself, after all that teleporting.

"I'll get them," Phin said. "As well as some weapons. We'll return in ten minutes."

"Okay."

They left together, and Wyatt and I were alone. We sat in silence for a moment.

"Think you can stand?" I asked.

"Yes."

Using the wall for support, he slid up it until he was on his feet, the gown still twisted awkwardly around his hips. I'd asked him before how he felt, and one of his answers had been "aroused." Standing up, it was obvious he still was, although he didn't seem aware of it. He'd also said "hungry" and "angry," which meant he was likely still those things, as well, deep down below the wall of calm he'd built to contain the wolf.

I wanted to reach out and tug the gown down, but was too afraid of startling him. So I stood up slowly, careful to avert my eyes. "Wyatt, you're kind of hanging out."

He blinked, confused, then looked down. He pulled at the gown so quickly he almost ripped it. Red spots flamed his cheeks. "Dammit," he said.

"Should I be flattered?"

As soon as the teasing question passed my lips, I regretted it. Instead of smiling, Wyatt only looked more miserable. He adjusted the gown, but wouldn't look at me. "Don't be," he snapped. "Considering the circumstances, it's pretty fucking inappropriate."

"What circumstances? The fact that you didn't die today, like everyone was telling me you would? That you're alive, and you haven't hurt me, and you're sane enough to beat this?"

"There's no beating this, Evy. It's part of me now. I can feel the wolf prowling around. It wants to fight. It wants to fuck. It wants you."

Something in my chest tightened, as much at the implicit threat as the misery in his voice. "I don't care what the wolf wants, Wyatt. All I care about is what you want."

"I want to be able to trust myself alone with you."

"We're alone now."

His eyes flickered toward me, then back to a spot on the floor. "Why do you think I'm staying over here?"

Oh boy. "So you're saying what? If I walked over there and touched you, you'd lose control, throw me to the floor, and rape me?"

He flinched, and his entire body seemed to wilt. "I don't know."

God. The fact that he was entertaining such a scenario knocked the wind out of me. He knew what I'd been through—seen the results with his own eyes as he watched me die my first death. The idea of doing what a goblin had done to me, what a pùca had tried to do, had to be killing him inside.

I was desperate to prove him wrong, to show him he could control the raging instincts of the wolf, but what if he was right? If he did hurt me before someone stopped him . . .

Fuck no. I had to believe in him, or no one else would. He absolutely didn't believe in himself, and no one else had as much to lose as I did.

"Did you or did you not sacrifice your free will to bring me back to life?" I asked.

He didn't respond right away. He didn't look at me, either. Finally, he said, "I did."

"Did you or did you not take a bullet for me and die for your trouble?"

He still paused, but the second reply came a bit faster than the first. "I did."

"Did you or did you not save me from an exploding Halfie in a parking garage, love me no matter what bullshit you learned about my past, support my decision to save Phin by going with Thackery, and combine your Gift with mine to create a truly impressive display of human magic by summoning half a car through a wall?"

His head turned in my direction, gaze still on the floor. "Yes. I did."

I took a chance on two steps forward. He tensed but didn't draw away. Three long strides separated us. With my heart in my throat, I said, "You know I used to fuck around, Wyatt. I was no angel. I liked sex and I had a lot of it. Mindless, emotionless sex. Even, for me, our one time before I died."

His entire body flinched, and I hated that, but it was true. As nice as it had been, sleeping with him three months ago had meant a lot less to me than to him.

"But that morning in the boys' apartment, before I went to Thackery, was different. It was beautiful and it was real. So did you or did you not become the first and only man I've ever *made love* to?"

That got his attention. His head snapped up, eyes meeting mine. Wide with surprise and understanding, he opened his mouth, but didn't speak. He shifted until his body angled toward me, hands loose by his sides. I wanted to leap across the space between us and pull him into my arms. To feel him around me, holding me again.

Physical proof that he was alive, heart beating, blood pumping.

I stayed still. He had a question to answer.

He took a step, then another, tentative and calculated. Three more small steps and he was in front of me, breathing hard, eyes brimmed with unshed tears. He raised a trembling hand; I forced myself to relax, let him do this. He brushed the pad of his thumb across my cheek, down my jaw. Warm breath gusted across my lips, and I breathed him in—the unfamiliar scent of earth, a tang of blood.

He closed his eyes and pressed his forehead to mine. His skin was damp, hot, almost feverish. The hand on my jaw loosely cupped my cheek. He didn't kiss me. He simply stood there, touching me, breathing me in. Working whatever inner demons he was fighting into a rational calm, despite our proximity.

I almost didn't hear him whisper, "I was."

"You are," I said.

"I want to be, always."

"I want that, too."

He turned his head and pressed his cheek to mine, breath tickling my ear. His skin was rough with stubble, his hair damp. The sweet hint of cinnamon I'd always associated with Wyatt was gone, replaced by something else—foreign and still somehow familiar. Our bodies remained apart by a few meager inches. It was too far . . .

"I love you," he said.

"Me, too."

He nuzzled my cheek, and I broke first. I turned my head until our noses touched, mouths aligned. The cuts on his lips terrified me on one level, but deep down I knew I'd be okay. I'd survived the bites from Wolf Boy a month ago; I'd survive a kiss from Wyatt. But he needed to initiate it.

The hand on my cheek slid around to the back of my neck, a loose hold.

Please . . .

The gentlest brush of his lips sent my heart galloping. It was all I needed to capture his mouth in a desperate kiss. All of my love and need tried to show itself, and he responded in kind, kissing me hard. Nothing existed except our questing mouths and our bodies pressed together, hearts beating, hands holding and pressing. Somehow I ended up with my back against the wall and I didn't care, because it was Wyatt holding me there.

I wanted him in a way I'd never thought possible, and I didn't care that it was the wrong time, place, circumstances—wrong everything. He was hard against my hip, my jeans the only real barrier between us. It had been almost two months since we'd been together in any meaningful way. Hard, fast, and dirty had been part of my old life, but goddamn I'd take a little of that right now.

Except Wyatt was my gentle. Wyatt was my slow and nice. If we had sex like this, up against a wall in a haze of desperation, he might regret it after. Might blame the wolf for his lack of control. He did self-hate way better than I did, and I wasn't about to give him another excuse.

I also wasn't about to drag him into the city without taking the edge off, first.

My hand slid between us, beneath the gown, to grasp his erection. He gasped into my mouth. I managed an awkward stroke, and my own arousal surged at the deep (and very human) growl that it elicited from Wyatt. He thrust into my hand, mouth still working mine. My lips tingled; our kiss tasted faintly of blood. Harder, faster.

With a choked cry, he pressed his face against my shoulder and came, spilling warmth over my hand and wrist. He shuddered and gasped. I worked him through it, my free arm tight around his shoulders, holding him close until both of our heartbeats calmed to a reasonable pace.

I wiped my hand on the hem of his gown, then threw that arm around his waist. Our clinch became a hug—an embrace of souls I never wanted to end. The outside world wasn't allowed to invade the little bubble of peace we'd created for ourselves—only I couldn't stop it.

A shadow in the doorway reminded me of our deadline and, with regret, I gently squeezed Wyatt's neck. "You okay?" I whispered.

He loosened his hold and pulled back. His eyes were red, cheeks streaked with tears, but he smiled. Nodded. "Thank you."

I pressed my left palm flat against his cheek and looked right into his silver-rimmed eyes. And I smiled back. "You don't have to thank me. I'm being pretty selfish this time." At his curious look, I said, "I can't lose you again."

He leaned closer and kissed my forehead. As he pulled back, his nostrils flared and he tensed just a little. "Phineas is outside."

"How do you know?" His back was to the door.

"I can smell him."

"Oh." That was going to take some getting used to.

"Dare I ask what I smell like?" Phin said as he stepped into the doorway. He had a bundle of clothes in one hand and a knapsack slung across his chest, likely holding our weapons. His expression was unreadable.

"I wouldn't ask, no," Wyatt said without turning around. "Gina's not back."

"She's meeting us in the garage." He put the clothing bundle down on the foot of the bed. "I'll wait down the hall."

"We'll be right there," I said.

The clothes he'd brought were Wyatt's, right down to the black sneakers. I handed the items to him one at a time—boxers, jeans, polo, socks—as he dressed. I didn't know how we were going to get him past Dr. Vansis, or anyone else who didn't like our plan. Hopefully no one would be dumb enough to try to stop us from leaving the compound.

Wyatt peeled away the last of the bandages on his arm and neck. The wounds had scabbed over and looked nowhere near as raw and infected as they had only a few hours ago.

"You want me to rebandage those?" I asked.

"They're fine."

"Ready to go?"

"No, but I suppose we don't have a choice."

Did we ever?

I heard Phin and Dr. Vansis arguing before we reached the outer office. I squeezed Wyatt's hand and held tight, as much for his courage as for my own.

"—still don't know how infectious he might be to others," Vansis was saying. "You're putting thousands of people at risk."

"We're only putting me at risk," I said, earning their collective attention. "I'll be at Wyatt's side the entire time we're out there. Even if he bites me, I don't think it'll do anything other than bleed. I've been infected before and beaten it."

Vansis scowled. "And if he's not finished changing? If he attacks someone who isn't you?"

"Phin has weapons. We're all prepared to use them."

"You'll shoot your lover dead to save an innocent?"

I couldn't seem to say yes.

"She knows that's what I want," Wyatt said.

"That didn't answer my question," Vansis replied.

"No, it did," I said. "And I don't plan on having to find out."

"No one ever does." He glanced at Phin, whose expression remained frustratingly neutral. Phin could make a fortune at high-stakes poker with that face.

"This might be our only chance to save Ava and Aurora."

"I know. I won't stop you, but please be cautious with him."

"We will. The vampires?"

Vansis shook his head. "Three of their own healers are on their way with some specialized equipment. Maybe they'll be able to find something I can't."

"We need to go," Phin said.

We had a long walk from the infirmary to the garage and absolutely no way to hide Wyatt from sight. The Therians lingering in the corridor would smell something odd about the man with us, no matter what we dressed him up in, so we chose to walk with our heads high. Humans and Therians stared at us. A few texted messages. Someone even growled.

But no one was dumb enough to get in our way.

At the entrance to the garage, two figures lingered in our path, arms crossed over their chests like a pair of silent sentries. Milo and Marcus were certainly the last two people I'd expect to try to interfere.

"Astrid couldn't be bothered to stop us herself?" I asked as we drew near.

Marcus frowned. "She's choosing to not acknowledge that this is happening. She can't condone Truman's leaving the premises, but she does believe your decision is correct."

"So why are you here?"

"To help."

"Really?"

"We want to go with you," Milo said. "Since we're both technically wounded and not on duty, no one will look too hard if we aren't here."

The show of solidarity planted a little seed of pride in my chest. To Marcus (who'd lost his walking cast at some point in the day) I asked, "You're defying your Elder?"

"Technically, no," Marcus replied. "Not unless he finds out you've removed Truman from the premises and I'm assisting you and he orders me to bring you back. Then I'll be defying my Elder."

At that moment, I really, really liked Marcus. "Terrific. Then let's go."

We left the mall parking lot without incident or alarms. Kismet drove, with Phin riding shotgun. Marcus and Milo took the rear bench seat of the SUV, while Wyatt and I sat together in the middle. Without being asked, Kismet pulled into the first burger joint she passed and ordered a bunch of food off the value menu.

Wyatt worked his way through a bag of cheeseburgers with all the grace of a stumbling drunk, devouring three in the time it took me to choke down a grilled chicken sandwich.

"All right," Kismet said after we'd settled lunch and gotten back on the road. "It's three-twenty. Anyone have a thought on a good place to start?"

Looks were exchanged, but no one spoke.

"I do," Milo finally said.

I twisted around in the process of unwrapping a second sandwich. "Where?"

"Amalie's avatar was also the lawyer handling the property where the Lupa lived, right? Isn't her name Edwina Fair?"

Damn, I'd actually forgotten about that connection during all the chaos around Wyatt's infection. "Right."

"Where does she live?"

Next to him, Marcus pulled out his cell phone and

checked something. "A development called Forest's Edge. 345 Applewood Lane."

It sounded familiar.

"Forest's Edge?" Phin repeated.

"Yeah, somewhere northwest of here. Why?"

Phin made a rude noise. "Because that's the neighborhood where Michael Jenner lived."

Chapter Twenty-four

Forest's Edge was aptly named for its proximity to the mountains that surrounded the valley's sprawling city. It was several minutes west of the up-and-coming neighborhood of Parkside East (my new body's former address), and it took us twenty precious minutes via the bypass to even get there. It was polar opposite of the Watchtower's location, and miles north of the historic district.

A fancy white gate announced we'd arrived at the community of condos. Dozens of freestanding buildings, with simple, modern architecture and between four and six homes per, dotted long, intersecting streets. They'd been built around existing trees, so decades-old and hundred-foot-tall oaks and maples lined many of the streets, giving the five-year-young development a homey, lived-in feel.

I wondered how many other lawyers called Forest's Edge home.

We rolled down all the windows in the SUV. Community signs announcing "Children Playing" and "Slow Please," right at the gate, were a perfect excuse to trundle along toward our destination. Wyatt slid closer to his door and leaned his face out the window.

I didn't know what I could say to encourage him, so I kept my mouth shut.

As we drew closer to the sign for Applewood Lane, Wyatt closed his eyes, eyebrows furrowed, nostrils flaring. All I smelled was fast-food grease, so I hoped he was having better luck. Phin and Marcus were both intently sniffing the air out their respective windows in a way that was almost comical.

Soon after Kismet turned onto Applewood Lane, Edwina Fair's home appeared, a third-floor condo in a building of six. Kismet parked across the street. Some nearby residences had cars parked, but many residents didn't appear to be home. Good for us. The middle of the afternoon on a hot summer Saturday wasn't prime time for folks to be hanging around the house.

"Anything?" I asked.

"Not the Lupa," Wyatt replied. When he looked at me, more silver had crept into the black of his eyes. "But I sense magic. There's a Break around here, a Sanctuary."

Terrific. Was I that exhausted from my early-morning teleportation session that I'd fried my Break sensor? I barely felt the level of magic I was used to and hadn't really missed it until Wyatt mentioned the increase. Would I even be able to teleport if I needed to?

"Well, now what?" Kismet asked. "Are you going to ring her bell and ask if she's harboring fugitive werewolves?"

"Might as well," I said.

"Evy—"

"If Amalie is in her avatar, then she knows we're here. Before she died, Jaron told us that Amalie can sense anyone who's been in her true presence, which Wyatt and I both have."

"Sense how?"

"I'm not completely sure. At the very least, she knows we're both alive. At the most, she knows we're practically on her doorstep right now."

"If she's still using her avatar," Marcus said. "Edwina

Fair has not been to work in several days. Her employer stated she requested a brief leave of absence."

"How brief?" I asked.

"Through the weekend. Apparently, she's due back on Monday."

I glanced at Wyatt. "Ready to knock on an old friend's door?"

"As I'll ever be," he replied.

We climbed out our respective sides, and I met him by his door. A yellow sports car drove past, its music blasting bass even though the windows were all up, keeping in the air-conditioning and the worst of the noise. Walking across the street toward 345 Applewood Lane, with Wyatt by my side, felt right for so many reasons—solving a mystery, impending danger, a possible fight. I had a knife by my ankle, a gun at my waist hiding under my T-shirt, and a blast of adrenaline setting my heart pounding.

It was an old, familiar buzz, and I'd kind of missed it.

We took the stairs quickly to the third floor. The curtains were drawn in all the windows, and a brightly colored floral doormat decorated the stoop. The door had a silver knocker and a bell.

"Anything?" I asked.

Wyatt closed his eyes and inhaled deeply, held it. On the exhale, he looked at me. "I smell death."

Terrific.

"Do you sense the Lupa at all?"

"No. I'm not sure what I'm supposed to feel, but I don't feel any different."

Awesome.

I rang the bell. Twice.

"Maybe she's out getting her nails done," I muttered, then banged on the door with a closed fist. "Ms. Fair, are you home?"

Wyatt grabbed the knob. It turned, and the door creaked open. "I'll be damned," he said.

"This isn't good."

My nose verified my trepidation as I stepped inside. Humid, hot air carried the odors of human waste and decay. The air-conditioning was off, the windows were sealed, and the room was stifling hot even with the shade. Something had died in here.

The condo was tasteful and expensive, with chrome lighting fixtures and a black-and-white color scheme, and very little in the way of personality. It was an odd contrast to the colorful doormat. And despite the stink, it was clean and extremely tidy.

We found the source of the smell in the master bedroom. Edwina Fair lay on her bed surrounded by deep purple pillows and an empty pill bottle. She'd been there a couple of days and her face was badly swollen, but I couldn't mistake that hair—bright red ringlets, long and thick.

The irrational side of my brain expected the dead woman's sunken eyes to snap open, blazing with blue energy, and for Amalie's voice to lay some vague threat on us like a creature from a horror movie. But I knew that wouldn't happen. Sprites could inhabit only living bodies.

Then again, almost everything I'd once believed about the Fey turned out to be wrong, or badly skewed.

"So either Edwina Fair was a very, very disturbed and lonely woman," I said, "or Amalie helped her avatar commit suicide."

"Could be both," Wyatt said as he inspected the woman's dresser. "Losing hours of your day, not knowing why, probably took its toll. Do you remember Jed Peters?"

It took a moment for the name to click. "Jaron's avatar?"

"When the Triads cleaned out his apartment after his

death, they found migraine medication and prescription painkillers and a lot of unpaid bills. Apparently he suffered crippling headaches and blackouts, which made it hard to keep a job. Doctors were unable to diagnose his illness, so they just kept him doped up."

"Jaron did that to him?"

"I think so."

The truth of it disgusted me. The sprites had been recklessly using those humans to communicate with us, with no regard for their health or mental state. Being a sprite avatar had been slowly killing Jed Peters long before his death at Token's hands. Just as it had likely been killing Edwina Fair long before she swallowed that bottle of pills.

"Un-fucking-believable."

"This scares me, Evy."

I turned to face him, surprised and concerned by the admission. "That Amalie's avatar is dead?"

"Yes. My money is on Deaem's avatar being dead, too. The brass collectively killed themselves last month. The Fey are pulling out of the city."

"It does seem like it." Deaem had been Jaron's replacement as Amalie's second when the latter died almost two months ago. Like Wyatt, I wouldn't be shocked if a look at recent suicides listed an Asian man of about thirty years old.

The implications of the Fey cutting their ties to the city were staggeringly bad. They lived and breathed the magic of the Break, and they protected a doorway to the place where that magic originated. A place where demons existed.

"Do you think they'd leave First Break?" I asked.

"I don't know. I guess it depends on what happens next. I feel like we're trying to cross a frozen river that's cracking to pieces under our feet, and Amalie's standing over us with a rock, waiting for the right time to drop it and shatter the ice."

"Chaos."

"And a lot of death."

The enormity of the situation threatened to smash me into the ground. It was too damned much, and I hated it. But hiding wasn't an option, and it never would be. Looking at the big picture made our task seem impossible. I had to keep us focused on things we could affect. Things that were not beyond our ability to control—like two Coni who needed us.

"I'm scared, too, Wyatt," I said. "Terrified, in fact. But I can't think about whether or not Amalie's dropping that rock. Right now, only two deaths matter to me. The deaths of Ava and Aurora, and those are deaths I can't let happen. I need to save them. The rest has to come after."

He was quiet a moment, then looked at me with a familiar and comforting expression of sheer determination. "You're right."

We left the apartment as we found it, careful to wipe the few surfaces we'd touched. Without the protection of the brass (a hilarious concept, now that I knew just what the brass had been), we needed to be extracautious about not leaving fingerprints. Our report on the apartment was greeted with similar reactions of surprise and dread from our companions in the SUV.

"I don't get it," Milo said. "If all the Fey want is mass chaos and to see humans and vampires and Therians fighting one another, why all the subterfuge? They're insanely powerful."

"But they are also, by their very nature, pacifists," Marcus said. "They suggest and whisper in your ear, and they provide certain means, as they've done for centuries, without direct interference. They will not raise

their hands to strike directly, nor will they order someone to do it for them."

"So they have both the ability and the desire to see
this city in ruins, but they won't just do it because . . .
they're too nice?"

"Something like that. Sprites could no more raise their
hands in violence to me than you could shift into a
jaguar."

Milo's face screwed up into an epic frown, and he
turned his head to glare out his window. Marcus reached
over and gave the younger man's shoulder a tentative
squeeze. Milo impressed me by not shrugging off his
touch.

"So option one was a bust," I said. It was four o'clock.
Three hours and counting. "Now what?"

"While you were inside," Kismet said, "Reilly came
through with some information on Matthew Goodson."

"Alias?"

"Yep. Reilly stumbled across the name in his earliest
research into the city's vampires. He has a surveillance
photo of Goodson meeting with an unidentified vampire
female, and he's traced him to an herbal tea shop in
Mercy's Lot owned by a man named—"

"Brutus Longfellow," Wyatt said. His fists were clenched
in his lap, his eyes narrowed.

I knew that name. "Why do I know that name?"

"He's a mage I've done business with before." A low,
deep growl filled the SUV. "Bastard."

Then I got it. "The invisibility spell."

Wyatt had traded with Brutus for the enchanted or-
ange crystal that briefly rendered me invisible to the eye,
so that I could attend Alex's funeral service. I never met
Brutus, but I knew that Wyatt had done business with
him in the past for various things. I guess Brutus didn't
discriminate with his customers.

"Old World Teas," Wyatt said. "It's in Mercy's Lot, corner of Adler Road and Cottage Place."

The drive took less than ten minutes. Cottage Place was a block north of Wharton Street, and Adler Road intersected it two blocks east of the Black River in a busy little slice of the Lot popular with college students and wannabe hippies. About six blocks farther east, my old neighborhood crept up like a dirty little secret. Lined with loft apartments and dozens of shops and unusual restaurants that sold everything from used records to chipotle ice cream, the trendy area was bustling with business this Saturday afternoon.

Old World Teas was situated in a narrow building between a beeswax candle shop and a tattoo parlor, with a simple, painted-wood sign the size of a mailbox. If you weren't looking for it, you'd probably wander past it. A parking spot didn't look likely, so Kismet drove half a block down and stopped.

I climbed out with Wyatt, Phin, and Marcus. The SUV pulled away.

A trio of girls sitting in an outdoor café giggled and pointed at us, and it took me a moment to realize they were admiring my male companions. All three were incredibly handsome in their own ways—something I probably didn't stop to appreciate often enough.

Wyatt led the way back down the sidewalk. We followed single file, with Marcus in the rear. We didn't have time to plan this carefully, and none of us knew what to expect from Brutus. So Wyatt barged inside the shop door, which rang with the jingle of a happy bell.

The shop was long and narrow, with polished wood shelves lining both walls and filled with dozens of jars of teas. Two small tables with mismatched chairs filled the front window, and a three-foot counter sported an antique register, an antique balance, and an electric kettle. Teacups hung on hooks behind the counter. The entire place had an air of magic, rippling just below the surface like water trapped in the desert. Just waiting for someone to tap into its potential.

A teenager was browsing a row of teas halfway down the shop. He saw us and left, either assuming we were cops or intimidated by the glares he was likely receiving. The bell dinged as the door shut.

"Be right there," a voice bellowed from the far rear. I noted the beaded curtain, and what was probably a storeroom beyond it.

Marcus locked the front door and turned over the Out to Lunch sign.

Wyatt didn't wait. He stormed down the length of the shop. A shadow moved behind the beads and a meaty hand reached through to brush them aside. Wyatt grabbed the hand and yanked Brutus into the shop, hard enough to send the larger man crashing into a shelf of teapots. Several broke; Brutus yelped.

"There's cash in the register," Brutus said.

Snarling, Wyatt crowded in and grabbed the front of Brutus's shirt, making sure Brutus got a good look at his old client. Brutus went pasty white. His lips parted and his eyes widened. I pulled my gun and took a position opposite the pair, giving me a good line of sight on both men—just in case one of them did something stupid. Phin and Marcus flanked me.

"Mother and Earth, Truman, what happened to you?" Brutus asked.

"Seen anything with eyes like this lately?" Wyatt said. Brutus swallowed hard.

"I smell them," Marcus said.

"Go," I said.

He and Phin disappeared behind the beaded curtain.

Brutus started to protest. Wyatt shoved him hard against the shelves.

"You sold a sunscreen to the vampires three years ago on behalf of a human named Walter Thackery," Wyatt said.

Brutus shifted from surprised to annoyed in a single breath. The magic around us felt denser, as though it was crowding in. Our resident mage was not a happy guy anymore. "Yes, I did," he said.

"Why?"

"I'm a businessman, Truman. I've done jobs for a lot of people in the thirty years since I opened this shop, yourself included. I stay in business and I stay alive because I keep my blessed nose out of things and don't rat on my clients."

I snorted. "Which means he paid you a lot of money."

Brutus tried to look at me, which earned him a firm shake from Wyatt. "Money buys monthlong vacations in warm, tropical climates."

"Money also signs death warrants for entire races of living beings," Wyatt snapped. Even from his profile, I saw the solid silver color of his eyes. His canines had grown just enough to hang below his upper lip—far enough for Brutus to notice the change.

"What in the name of Mother Earth happened to you?"

Wyatt bared his teeth. "Werewolves."

"Werewolves don't exist."

"Try telling that to the one who bit me. Are they here?"

"Are who here?"

Another hard shake sent a ceramic teapot shattering to the floor. "The Lupa. Teenagers. They work for Thackery."

Brutus started to shake his head, then stopped. Thought about something. "Wait, those kids were werewolves?"

"They were here? You saw them?" I asked.

"A few hours ago. They paid me a grand to babysit a pair of caged birds until six-thirty."

My heart leapt into my throat and my hand jerked.

"Go," Wyatt said. "I'll watch him."

I didn't like leaving Wyatt alone with Brutus, but the idea that Ava and Aurora were so close, almost safe, propelled me forward. I'd just crashed through the wooden beads when Phin shouted my name. I peered through the gloom of the back room, past stacked boxes and a tiny desk that served as an office. A single open door was tucked away behind a row of storage containers, and it led to a rickety staircase.

Up I went, into the odors of bacon grease and patchouli. Halfway there I sneezed. The stairs led into an apartment—kitchen and living room, two other doors. One door was open and obviously a bathroom. The other door would have been my destination, even if I hadn't heard the unmistakable sounds of a kestrel keening.

"Phin?" I said, charging at the door.

He and Marcus were inside a cramped bedroom. Two metal cages stood atop an old wooden dresser, and inside of them, the two most beautiful things I'd ever seen—Ava and Aurora in their true forms. One was an adult, the second a miniature version of her mother. Phin stood in front of the cages, hands out and palms up, both crisscrossed with weeping red welts.

"The cages are silver," Marcus said. "They can't shift and we can't break them."

"We need a key," Phin added.

"Something tells me the Lupa have the key," I said. "Maybe Wyatt can summon off the locks?"

"Where—?"

"Downstairs with Brutus."

Marcus left without being asked. I moved closer to the cages holding my friends, so relieved to see them that I wanted to weep. Ava was crying constantly, her kestrel scream indignant and frightened, even with her mother close by.

"We'll get you out," I said to them.

Aurora screeched at me.

I lifted one of the cages—heavy, but not impossible to move. Phin grabbed a pillow off the bed and shook it out of its case. He ripped the case into strips and began wrapping them around his hands. I caught on and helped until we'd created a pair of makeshift mittens.

As I pulled the last knot, Phin's head jerked toward the bedroom door. "Something's happening downstairs," he said.

"Come on."

I grabbed Aurora's cage. Phin took Ava's and followed me into the living room.

The floor in front of the stairs exploded upward, and a big black shape was flung toward the ceiling. It bounced off and landed in a heap next to the kitchen's miniature fridge—Marcus in jaguar form.

Shit.

Chapter Twenty-five

Marcus lifted his head and blinked at me, dazed, before putting his head back down. Anything that had sent a two-hundred-pound cat through the floor wasn't something Wyatt needed to be fighting alone.

I put the cage down, leapt over the hole in the floor, and landed on the first step with enough grace to twist my left ankle. I stumbled down the steps two at a time anyway, pulling my gun again, all to the sounds of Wyatt's deep-chest growling. Something else crashed and thumped in the shop below. Then it went quiet.

The beads were down. Wyatt was crumpled on the floor in the doorway, conscious but stunned. I hopped over him, into the shop, stupidly blind as to what awaited me.

Brutus stood in the middle of his shop, clutching a leather cord. Dangling from it was a blue crystal, about four inches long, tapered at one end like a nail. Power crackled around the room, caressing my skin and urging me to tap into my Gift. I didn't know much about mages, but I'd seen crystal magic at work, mostly as some sort of blocking spell. Blocking a person from sight, for instance, or blocking their ability to tap into the Break. It was organic magic, requiring proximity to the crystal for it to work.

Brutus glared at me, his eyes swirling with a faint hint

of light and power. "I won't be bullied by you people. I took a blessed job, nothing more!"

Rationally, I understood that. He was a businessman. He sold exotic tea, and he enchanted crystals if you could pay him enough money. He'd helped us out a few times in the not so distant past.

Emotionally, I didn't give a shit. He'd hurt Wyatt. He'd held people I cared about in tiny cages made of a material that injured them if they touched it. He'd taken money from my greatest enemy.

"Please, try to take me down, little girl," Brutus said.

As much as I loved the idea of breaking his nose with my fist, I knew I'd get bounced into a concussion by that crystal in his hand. I couldn't get through. But I bet a bullet could.

"If you insist," I said. I raised my right hand, steadied it quickly across my left wrist, aimed my gun at his fist, and fired.

He screamed loud and long as his hand exploded, and the crystal fell. It shattered against the concrete floor, releasing a blast of power not unlike a faint electric shock. He fell to his knees, clutching his wounded hand against his chest. I walked over and kicked him in the face. He toppled over, unconscious.

"Little girl, my ass," I said.

"Evy?"

I turned at the sound of Phin's voice. He stood just behind Wyatt, one cage in each hand. I holstered my gun and squatted in front of Wyatt. His eyes remained wholly silver and his canines long, but he didn't snap or snarl. He let me help him sit up.

"How's Marcus?" he asked.

"Stunned," Phin said. "You?"

"Same. That crystal had a pretty good punch."

"Can you walk?" I asked.

"Yeah, I think so."

"Awesome."

I found Marcus's discarded clothes and took them upstairs. He'd pulled himself into a sitting position, but hadn't changed back yet. His copper eyes watched me, a little too wide, and he didn't move when I knelt down and touched his head. The fur at the base of his skull was damp with blood. My fingertips brushed a knot there and he hissed.

"Sorry," I said. "Brutus is down. We have the girls; we need to go."

He lurched to his feet, then promptly flopped back down. Whined.

"I know, pal, you've got a good-sized goose egg on your head. Can you shift back into a man, at least?"

He whined again. Downstairs, the doorbell dinged.

"Come on, Marcus." I felt strange talking to a giant black cat. But manhandling a human down the stairs would be easier, so I needed him to shift.

Feet pounded the steps. Unsure who was coming, I said, "Watch the hole."

"The what—? Oh." Milo leapt gracefully over the hole in the floor and crouched on the opposite side of Marcus. "Is he okay?"

"Concussion. Brutus tossed him through the floor."

"Ouch. No wonder he's lying there like a stuffed animal. Big, bad mage beat him up."

Marcus lifted his head, and I swear he glared at Milo. Yawned. Then he closed his eyes. Magic sparked around him in the faint way it always did when a Therian shifted near me. Black fur melted away, paws lengthened into fingers, pads into palms, and his face blurred as the cat gave way to the man. The sound was similar to sticky tape peeling away from skin.

His long black hair was loose around his shoulders, making the goose egg hard to see, but I still noticed some blood on his neck. Milo and I each took an arm and helped him stand. He wobbled a little, so Milo acted as a human crutch while I assisted Marcus in stepping into his jeans.

Me dressing a naked man—I could just imagine the possessive, overprotective reaction this would get out of Wyatt's wolf.

By the time we got his shirt over his head and settled properly, Marcus seemed more alert. Just enough floor remained along the edge of the hole for us to slide around, backs to the wall, and over to the stairs. Milo and Marcus went down first, the former still supporting the latter, and I couldn't help smiling at the friendly rapport that had developed between them.

Down in the shop, Brutus was being tied up none too gently by Phin. Kismet had one cell phone in her left hand and another pressed to her ear. She read telephone numbers to whoever was on the other line.

"Those are all the numbers he called or called him today," she said. "No, he's unconscious."

I glanced at Phin, who mouthed "Astrid" back at me. "He" had to refer to Brutus.

"He said the Lupa paid him to watch their birds until six-thirty, that they'd be back for them then," Kismet said. Paused. "I doubt it. They'd see the shop's closed, or they'd smell that we'd been here and run." She walked toward the street window, probably looking for a good surveillance spot.

Wyatt was sitting cross-legged in front of the two cages, and he waved me over. I squatted next to him, relieved to see the canines gone and the silver in his eyes reduced to a single circle of color. Pride swelled my chest—he'd done that without me.

"I can summon off the locks," he said. "I didn't want to try without you."

"Okay."

His ability to summon inanimate objects to himself

had come in handy dozens of times in the past. But he hadn't attempted it in the few hours since his infection, and I appreciated his need to be cautious. The kestrels had crowded as close to the backs of their cages as they could get without touching the silver bars, probably unsure exactly what Wyatt was now.

"It's okay, we're getting you out," I said to them.

Wyatt closed his eyes and turned his right hand palm up. His fingers twitched, and I felt the shift in the Break as he connected to his tap. The silver padlock on Aurora's cage shimmered, disappeared, then reappeared on his open palm. He hissed and dropped it. I turned the latch and opened the door.

Aurora exploded out of the cage with an excited screech and a blur of feathers. She flew the length of the room twice before settling on a high shelf, far out of reach. She screamed again, as if to say to hurry the hell up.

He summoned the second lock as easily as the first, but when he opened his eyes the silver glow was back. I unlatched and opened Ava's cage, then pulled Wyatt away. Once we'd given the cage a wide berth, Aurora coasted down and landed on the floor. Ava crept forward in the cage, blue eyes gleaming, then hopped out. She huddled beneath her mother's chest.

Phin approached slowly, the relief and joy on his face heartbreaking. He knelt in front of them and held out his hand. Aurora tilted her head, blinked, then pecked at his fingertips. "I'm so sorry you were taken," he said. "Forgive me?"

She screeched at him, then began to shift. Feathers smoothed into creamy skin, and long, thick spirals of brown hair sprang from her head. As if prompted by her mother's magic, Ava shifted as well. Soon mother and daughter were in each other's arms. At only two months old, Ava was the size of a child four times her age, with a crown of brown curls just like Aurora's. She sobbed as only a baby can, her face pressed against Aurora's chest, terrified and uncertain.

Aurora looked up, her doe eyes full of falling tears. "It wasn't your fault, Phineas," she said.

He choked, then collected his family into his arms and held them tight. I looked away, eyes stinging, but incredibly happy to have them both back.

Wyatt and I stood and moved away, giving them a moment. We stepped over to where Milo and Marcus were leaning against the counter. Kismet was still on the phone with Astrid, working out some sort of plan.

"I didn't think Therians could shift so young," Milo said quietly.

"It's possible, but unhealthy," Marcus whispered back. "We prefer to wait until they're at least eighteen months old, so they're better able to understand the shift and the stress it places on the body. The electricity used to tame them on the ferry may have forced Ava's shift."

A blast of hatred swept through me, directed right at Thackery, for doing such a thing to a child. It was worse than any other crime he'd committed, and it made me pray that I was there when he was executed.

Kismet snapped her phone shut. "Okay, so Sharpe's on his way over with a squad to watch the place, just in case the Lupa do come back to collect what they left. Humans only, so scent doesn't tip them off."

"Our scents permeate this place," Marcus said. "It will take longer than a few hours for them to fade."

"I know that and so does Astrid, but we need to take the chance. Those Lupa lost their master. We need to catch them so they're not running free to infect anyone they get mad at."

Wyatt flinched.

"Did she give Thackery the happy news?" I asked, jacking my thumb over my shoulder at the trio.

"No, Astrid thought Aurora might like to give him the big fuck-you in person."

"I'd pay money to get in on that."

"Take them back, then." Kismet handed her keys to Milo. "I'll stay here, sit on Brutus, and wait for Sharpe."

I nodded, then eyed the busy street out front. "Is there a back door to this place, you think?"

"If not, we'll make one," Marcus said.

There was, indeed, a rusty back door hidden behind a stack of boxes. Milo and I wrenched it open, then he dashed out into the smelly, oil-stained alley to fetch the car with a promise of "back in five." I went inside to collect our passengers, more than ready to get back to the Watchtower and rub this little victory right in Walter Thackery's face.

Joseph was waiting in the parking area when we got back, along with a small crowd of happy and relieved faces. Aurora climbed out of the SUV with Phin's help, holding her sleeping daughter tight to her chest. Ava had cried herself to sleep during the ride back, her young face pinched and blotchy, her rest anything but peaceful. Joseph pulled all three of them into a tight group hug—the last of their kind, reunited.

The sight clogged my throat; I looked away.

"How's your head?" Astrid asked, stepping around the quartet.

"Fine," Marcus said.

"How's his head?" she asked me.

"He was dazed and confused for a while," I replied.

"Doctor. Now."

Marcus scowled, but didn't protest. Not even when Astrid added, "Gant, make sure he gets there."

Milo sighed at the assignment, but something in his

face hinted that he wasn't as put out as he wanted us to believe.

The pair wandered off; Astrid gave Wyatt her full attention. He stared back, standing straight, more confident now than when we'd sneaked him out. "I should probably yell at you both for leaving the grounds at all, especially without knowing your ability to infect others," she said, "but I can't argue with your results. Nice job."

I'd prepared for an ass reaming when we got back. Praise for a job well done was unexpected. "Did Gina tell you about Edwina Fair?" I asked.

"Yes. And she was right about Deaem's avatar. He died last week, anaphylactic shock from accidentally consuming shellfish, which he was allergic to."

"Accidental, huh?"

"That's what the medical examiner's report said. The Assembly also ruled on the Equi Elder's request for justice."

"Which was what?"

"That Walter Thackery die before sunset today. And now that Ava and Aurora are safe, there are no on-record objections to the ruling."

"The Equi are satisfied with that?"

"Fortunately, yes. The Elder was convinced that Thackery was acting out of grief for the loss of his own family, and that his actions did not speak for the whole of humanity. So only Thackery is to be punished."

Thank God for that.

"And me?" Wyatt asked.

Astrid was quiet a moment. "Elder Dane was furious when he found out you'd been taken off the premises. But I think your assistance in identifying the tea shop, as well as your restraint in confronting the owner, will go a long way toward swaying them toward leniency."

"As opposed to what?"

"Execution for carrying the Lupa gene."

I shuddered. "The Elders realize we'd never let that happen, right?"

"Chances are good it won't come to that," Astrid said, not acknowledging my implied threat.

"If the Lupa don't return to your trap in the tea shop today," Wyatt said, "I may be the only person who can draw them out."

Not a fact I liked bringing up.

The quartet behind us had disentangled themselves. Ava slept on, but Aurora looked worn out, beaten down, and too damned tiny in a set of Brutus's oversized sweats. But she stood straight, determined to look her kidnapper in the eye and show him the evidence of his defeat. In the two months I'd been dealing directly with him, Walter Thackery had always been three steps ahead of us.

Today, we'd finally beaten him.

All of the recovered kidnap victims were standing outside the storefront where Thackery was held—Dawn Jenner, Leah de Loew, and Lynn Neil, with Kyle and Jackson by their sides. Joseph walked with us and joined the group, everyone as overjoyed to see Aurora and her daughter as we had been. Baylor was there, with Elder Dane and a second gentleman I didn't recognize. By his long, narrow face and tall, slim build, I guessed him to be the Equi Elder.

Turned out I was right. Elder Joshua Dannu was the youngest Elder I'd ever seen, maybe at his half-life point, and very pleasant considering the recent murder of one of his own. Both Elders went inside with us, escorted by Baylor and Astrid. I followed with Wyatt by my side and Phin close behind. After him came Aurora and the rest of our rescued Therians.

Thackery was still chained to his chair. A drying puddle of blood surrounded his feet, mostly around the rear of the chair. Marcus had mentioned the loss of three digits, and evidence of other torture dotted his bare chest and arms. They'd physically broken him, and yet, as he raised his head to see who'd come inside his private prison, some keen intelligence still glimmered in his eyes. He tracked our movements, his face revealing nothing.

We created a wall of sorts, momentarily blocking the grand surprise from view.

"It's a party," he said. "What's the occasion? Letting me go?"

Phin laughed.

"It is a celebration, actually," I said. "And we even brought party favors."

"Oh? Paper hats and plastic whistles?" Thackery asked.

"Even better. Proof of life."

His expression shifted from bland interest to confusion. I stepped to the side, angling so Aurora could come forward, Ava tucked close beneath her chin. She glared at Thackery with murder in her eyes. His mouth fell open; his face went blank. The others moved in and circled around us, each person a testament to his failure.

"No," he said.

"You lose," Aurora said, her voice sharp as a blade.

"Anne. Oh my God, Anne."

His late wife—the woman who'd been six months pregnant when she was infected by a Halfie. The woman for whom Thackery had sold his life's work and cashed out his savings in order to save. The woman who'd ultimately been put down by a Triad because Thackery hadn't been able to help her or to find his precious cure.

I'd seen a photo of Anne Thackery. She didn't look much like Aurora, but I could see how Thackery could mistake them—he'd lost blood, been injected with massive doses of drugs, and endured a lot of pain in the last few hours.

Smart cookie that she was, Aurora played along. "Oh Walter, what have you done?" she asked in her soft, songbird voice.

"I did it for you," he said. "For you and our son. All for you."

"No, not for us. We're dead. You did this for you, not for us."

"I can find a cure, Anne. I just need more time."

Aurora took half a step closer. "How many more people will you hurt in my name? How many will die in William's name? How can you make this our legacy?"

His face crumpled, and in that moment I almost felt sorry for the son of a bitch. When faced with all of his mistakes and all of the lives he'd ruined for the sake of research, he finally understood. The zealot who believed wholly in the need to eradicate the vampires from the Earth was gone, replaced by a grieving husband and father who'd lost everything to a single, tragic bite.

"I'm so sorry, Anne," he said.

"It's too late."

"No, it's not. Please. I love you. You and William, you're my life."

She shook her head, and I saw the tears in her eyes. "The half-Blood infected us, Walter, but you—you chose to become a monster. You *chose* that."

"Anne . . ."

Aurora turned and slipped back into the group, over to where Joseph waited to wrap her into a hug. Thackery pulled against his restraints, eyes glistening with tears, breathing hard.

"Anne, please," he said. "I'm sorry, please. I did it for you . . . I'm so sorry . . ." He was lost in his grief and memories, finally understanding how wrong his path had been. "Oh God, my boys . . . my boys . . ."

He was worried about the remaining Lupa teens. Once he was gone, they'd have no one. It was a card we could play. I glanced at Astrid, who mouthed "Wyatt" at me. I nodded, glad she was on the same page. Wyatt seemed to be with us, too, because when he looked at me, he'd pulled enough of the wolf to the surface to once again color his eyes and elongate his canines.

I squeezed his wrist. He held my gaze a moment, then stepped forward without prompting. He stopped an arm's reach from Thackery's chair, so tense I thought he'd spontaneously sprain something. My angle gave me only a quarter of Wyatt's profile, but I had a good view of Thackery's face when he finally looked up and saw the man invading his personal space.

Confusion came first—with the puckered eyebrows and pursed lips—followed quickly by a horrified understanding. "I should know you," Thackery said, "but I can't seem to recall your name."

"You don't need my name," Wyatt said. "Just take a good look. You say everything you've done is to preserve humanity, but look at the scorecard. You lost yours, and you stole mine."

"You were bitten."

"Yes, and not by a vampire. By one of your boys, who are now out there, unsupervised, free to infect more humans. Free to create more . . . whatever it is I am now. Is that how you preserve humanity? By destroying its protectors and by protecting its destroyers?"

"They're just children."

"Angry, abandoned children, raised by you to hate. Without help, they'll continue to destroy until they've been hunted and killed." The anger and regret in Wyatt's voice stunned me. And I realized he wasn't speaking just for the wolf inside him; he was speaking for himself and the furious teenager he'd been when his own family was ripped away. His emotional weakness had been exploited by the Fey, and he had become a perfect tool for them for ten years.

Wyatt didn't want to kill the Lupa. He wanted to save them.

"They were just pups when Edwina brought me to them," Thackery said, distant, reliving as he recalled it. "She told me what they were, how special and rare. She said they needed a father. All I wanted was their blood. Until the first time Charlie looked at me and said Da-da." He swallowed hard, Adam's apple bobbing, and real tears tracked down his cheeks. "They killed Charlie this morning."

"You exploited them for your experiments, and you dare be upset that they're dead?"

"You don't have children. You can't possibly understand."

Wyatt growled, low and deep. "I don't have children, but I know what it's like to lose someone you love. I've felt that glacial emptiness inside, when you're certain your heart will never beat again. You'll never feel warm and you'll never look at the world with anything except contempt. I've lived it, too, more than once, so stop using your grief as a fucking excuse."

Thackery jerked as if slapped. He looked past Wyatt, right at me, and in his haunted eyes I saw something surprising—regret. Exactly what he regretted I don't know, and in that moment I didn't care. There was no forgiveness in my heart for Walter Thackery. Just pity.

So much intelligence and so much potential, lost to madness and vengeance.

His gaze wandered around the room, taking in the faces of those condemning him, until his attention returned to Wyatt. "Their names are John, Mark, and Peter. They look like their brothers did. I don't know where they're hiding until seven o'clock. I told them not to tell me."

"Where were you supposed to meet them?" Wyatt asked.

"Grove Park."

The place I'd gone to meet Thackery, only to be whisked away on the back of a Lupa. It was in Mercy's Lot, about eight blocks east of Brutus's tea shop. At a sudden rustle of movement, I glanced behind me. Astrid had moved away from the group, cell phone at her ear, presumably getting a squad over to Grove Park, ASAP. As soon as the Lupa realized the Coni prisoners had been compromised, they were unlikely to go to the park, but we had to follow every lead.

"Please don't kill them," Thackery added.

"I can't promise that. But I'll do my best."

Astrid grunted.

"If you were intelligent enough to save my laptop from the ferry," Thackery said, "the keyword is 'height.' Do what you can with the research."

"Thank you," Wyatt said.

"I did have the best intentions, you know."

What was that saying? The road to hell . . .

Wyatt returned to my side, and I slipped my hand into his. He squeezed tight. I held on.

Elder Dane stepped forward, hands clasped loosely in front of him, back straight. "Walter Thackery, you have been condemned to death for the crimes of kidnapping, conspiracy, and murder. There is no plea, and there is no clemency. There is only justice. Are you prepared to meet your god?"

"No just god will welcome me into his heaven," Thackery said.

"Very well."

Dane stepped back into the circle of witnesses. Phin took his place. He'd stripped off his shirt and revealed his majestic wings. The Coni blade glinted in his right hand, an ancient symbol of an old order in which an entire race of people had been mercilessly hunted at the whim of another.

Phin paused. He turned far enough to look at me, an unasked question in his eyes. A few months ago, I'd have relished the idea of executing someone like Thackery— a man who'd caused me untold heartache and who'd hurt people I loved. Thackery deserved punishment, and I would not grieve his death. But I didn't want to be his executioner.

I wasn't that person anymore. I shook my head.

With a slight, acknowledging nod, Phin turned to face Thackery. Thackery looked up and didn't blink. For a brief moment in time, only those two men existed. United by very different kinds of grief and hatred, two players in this final act of justice.

And then Thackery closed his eyes. Phin struck fast and true, driving the double blade deep into Thackery's heart. He twisted once, hard to the left, and Thackery's head fell forward. He was dead.

It was over.

Kind of.

Chapter Twenty-six

Something warm and damp gusting across my face woke me from a deep, dreamless nap, and I blinked my eyes open. Twin blue orbs gazed back at me, so close I went a little cross-eyed trying to look at them. The owner crawled away with a sharp giggle and climbed onto the opposite bunk, where her mother sat, dressed in clothes that fit, watching us sleep.

At my back on the narrow cot, Wyatt didn't stir. We'd returned to my quarters to rest after hours of waiting (the Lupa didn't show up at either Grove Park or Old World Teas) and then grilling, courtesy of several members of the Assembly. Together and then privately, I'd paced the floor in front of Operations while Wyatt was questioned, not settling until he exited—with more confidence than I'd seen in him for weeks.

The Assembly had agreed to let Wyatt try to capture the three remaining Lupa as long as we found no evidence that they'd infected anyone else. He'd bargained for their lives and won. It was a small victory, but it had helped calm the wolf still raging inside of him.

"I'm sorry she woke you," Aurora said.

"I'm not," I said, sitting up and bracing on my elbow. "How is she?"

"Time will tell how the early shift has affected her. But she seems joyful again."

"I wish it hadn't happened."

"I wish many things had not happened. But you saved her, Evangeline, and I don't have the words to thank you."

"You don't have to." I looked around and realized that my little room didn't have a clock. "What time is it?"

"A bit after midnight."

Damn, it had been a fucking eventful twenty-four hours.

"Phineas is taking us back to his condo for now," she said. "Until the Lupa are found, our country home isn't safe. I thought you'd like to see Ava before we left."

"Thank you." Ava didn't really know me yet, but seeing her again now, awake, aware and smiling, lifted a heavy weight from my chest. "As long as I'm able, I'll always protect her."

"Thank you," Aurora said, beaming a grin at me that made me smile in kind.

I eased off the bunk and hugged her. She collected Ava, who tolerated a forehead kiss from me, then headed out into the maze of corridors that made up the sleeping quarters. I was often surprised that I could find my way back to this room each time.

The eerie sense of being watched tickled the back of my neck, and I turned around. Wyatt blinked at me from the bed, looking relaxed for the first time since he'd woken up in the infirmary.

"Hey, sorry," I said.

"I've been awake for a while," he said. "I just didn't want to scare them."

"They'll get used to your new look. We're a package deal, you and me."

His mouth quirked. "You aren't pissed at me for wanting to save the Lupa instead of killing them?"

"No." Might as well be honest. "I don't know if I agree with your decision, but I do understand it, and I'll help you."

"Thank you."

"Phin, on the other hand, is pretty pissed about the Assembly's allowances."

"The allowance on my life, or on the three Lupa children?"

"The Lupa, dumbass."

He smiled. "Jackass?"

"That, too." I stretched my arms over my head, a little stiff from our impromptu nap. "I don't know about you, but I'm hungry." His smile got so broad that I couldn't help asking, "What?"

"Just glad to see your appetite back."

"Me, too. Buy you lunch?"

"It's the middle of the night."

"Good, the cafeteria won't be crowded."

He joined me in the doorway, hair sleep-tousled and chin badly in need of a shave. Except for the telltale ring of silver around his eyes, he looked like my old Wyatt. The man I'd fallen in love with, pushed away, and yanked back harder than ever. And this time, I wasn't letting him go.

I wrapped my arms around his waist and leaned close, feeling the heat of his skin and the thrum of his heart-beat. He clasped my hips in a gentle grip and sought out my mouth. Our lips brushed—a quiet kiss that lingered awhile, until I wanted more. I licked inside his mouth, needing everything he had to give, and he returned in kind. Possessive, wanting, taking—I wanted more, but we needed a much bigger bed and more privacy than these sheetrock walls and doorless cubicles provided. My lips tingled—that same faint sensation that Dr. Van-sis hadn't been able to account for.

His tests had determined that Wyatt's saliva didn't

carry enough of the Lupa virus to infect another human through a bite. His blood, however, could potentially infect someone if enough came into contact with an open wound. It made fieldwork more dangerous, but it was a risk I could live with.

A faint commotion caught my attention, and our lips parted reluctantly. I strained to hear, unsure what was happening or where.

"Come on," Wyatt said.

He grabbed my hand and we jogged through the maze of quarters, toward the exit. At least a dozen people had gathered just outside, in the main corridor. Wyatt and I eased through to the front, and I gaped at what was happening.

Two large white trucks, similar to what movers use for furniture, were parked in the middle of the corridor, angled slightly so their back ends faced the entrance to the vampires' quarters. Vampire pairs dressed in familiar black warrior gear, their white hair pulled back or braided up, took turns carrying unconscious vampires up the ramps and into the trucks. After I watched the third vampire being taken up, arms dangling, head lolling, I realized that it wasn't just the sick ones who were being carted off.

Standing nearby in a small cluster were Astrid, Baylor, Kismet, and two vampires who exuded royalty. They wore deep purple robes, so dark they were almost black, and had purple jewels embedded in their foreheads. One was male, the other female. Tall, thin, and pale, they watched the proceedings with an intense quiet.

Kismet spotted us. Instead of waving us over, she jogged to our side of the hall.

"What's going on?" Wyatt asked.

"The royal Father of Isleen's family has persuaded the other Fathers to remove the vampires we've quarantined here. Sick or healthy, they're all going."

"Where?"

"They won't tell us. He says it's a vampire illness and his people will deal with it. Without our help—he was sure to reiterate that several times."

I watched them drag an unconscious Quince out of the quarters and up the ramp. Kismet put a hand on my shoulder, and it kept me from bolting over there. "Shit," I said. "Will they all be killed?"

"I don't know, Evy," she said. "They have their own doctors, and we copied them on the information we took off Thackery's laptop. If there's a cure to be found—"

"This is a mistake."

"Astrid already tried arguing that. A lot of us did, but the Fathers are insisting on containing it themselves."

Vampire after vampire was loaded onto the trucks, all of them allies, some of them friends. Eleri was one of the last to be taken, her skin blotchy and cracked and oozing blood.

Someone nearby inhaled hard; it was a loud, angry sound that earned my attention. I spotted Paul standing near the wall with Crow—Eleri had been their squad leader. Paul was glaring at the vampires with a kind of disgust I didn't recognize at first. Then I understood. He clearly didn't agree with Eleri's removal or her treatment. His support for his nonhuman squad mates shattered the last of the dislike I'd always felt toward him, and it allowed a hint of something brand new—respect.

Even Isleen, daughter of a royal Father, was carted out the same way—like a fresh carcass. She was barely recognizable beneath the ravages of the unknown disease that I felt certain would kill her before the sun rose.

Even if it didn't, she and her fellow infected vampires would never be the same again.

The truck doors were slammed shut, then they backed out slowly the way they'd come. Astrid and Baylor escorted the vampire royalty on foot, until they turned the corner and were gone. One-third of the Watchtower forces were depleted in minutes.

"Did the vampires pull their support completely?" I asked. "Of the Watchtower and what we're doing here?"

"They pulled out temporarily," Kismet said, making air quotes around the last word.

"What about the Sanctuary?"

"One of the Fathers set a magical lock of some sort. He said if anyone tries to enter, we'll get blasted."

I'd felt magic blasts before; they sucked.

"Our greater concern is the Fey," she said. "We have no way to anticipate their next move, no way to prepare for or prevent it."

"We also have the possibility of more intelligent Halfies out there," Wyatt said. "Plus at least three Lupa teenagers."

"Not to mention the everyday crazy street-thug Halfies and a whole horde of goblins who haven't been seen or heard from in long enough to make me really nervous."

Goblins. They hadn't been a real threat since Olsmill. But that battle was three months ago, more than enough time for them to regroup and come up with a new plan. The only enemies I underestimated anymore were the dead ones—and even then, it could be iffy.

I didn't want to think about it right at that moment, though. "You know what we're going to do?" I said.

"What?" Wyatt asked.

"We're going to get something to eat. Then I'm going back to bed."

He stared. Kismet looked at me like I'd grown a second head.

"I think this has been the longest damned day of my life," I said. "If the world doesn't end before I wake up tomorrow morning, we'll work out a plan. Until then, all I can really deal with is food and sleep."

Wyatt slipped an arm across my shoulders, and I leaned into him. "Food and sleep sound fantastic," he said.

"Says the man who spent half of yesterday in an induced coma."

"Hey, only a few hours of it."

"Whatever," Kismet said, throwing her hands up. "You two find me when you wake up and we'll see what's what, okay?"

Wyatt and I mumbled our agreement.

The corridor was clearing out, leaving only a handful of loiterers. Leaning against the nearby wall, Paul was still staring at the now-empty vampire quarters. I used to look at him and feel a surge of anger, seeing only the boy who'd shot and killed Wyatt. Now I saw a young man, hardened by the worst job he'd ever had, sharpened by anger and loss. I saw someone so much like my former self that my heart ached.

"Paul?" I said.

He jumped, casting about for the source of the voice. "Yeah?"

"You hungry?"

Wyatt gave me a curious look that was perfectly matched by Paul. "I could eat," Paul said.

"We're heading to the cafeteria. Why don't you come with us?"

Paul's curiosity shifted from me to Wyatt, then back again. He smiled. "Okay," he said, and the three of us set off in search of food.

Chapter Twenty-seven

On Monday afternoon, a memorial service for Michael Jenner was held in the city's high school gymnasium. Someone called in a favor and, with school still out for the summer, the request was granted. Hundreds (if not close to a thousand) Therians filled the bleachers—more than I'd ever seen gathered in one place at any given time. The majority were Equi, but every Clan was represented—either in the audience or by their Elder.

At one time, fourteen Elders sat on the Assembly; now the Stri were extinct and only four Coni remained. Thanks to an early-morning tutoring session with Kyle, I knew the names of the remaining twelve Clans represented by the Elders seated together on a dais. Six I knew on sight because they had members in the Watch. The sorting of the remaining six remained a temporary mystery, and it was difficult to imagine that one of them could shift into a Komodo dragon.

The only person missing from the group of Elders was Phineas, who'd chosen to sit down among the other Watchtower representatives—everyone except for a skeleton crew had come. A dozen people separated us, including Tybalt, Sharpe, Milo, Marcus, Astrid, Leah, and Jackson. Even Autumn showed up, her throat impressively wrapped in white bandages, upright if a little stoned from painkillers.

I hadn't managed to ask Phin why he wasn't on the stage with the other Elders, and as the first person rose to speak, I lost the chance to find out. Kismet and Baylor sat on my right. Wyatt was on my left, my constant companion. I was even getting used to his new silver-rimmed eyes.

When we'd first arrived, some Therians whispered; others bared their teeth. No one was dumb enough to directly threaten either of us.

The service was brief—more of a reflection on Jenner's commitment to the Clans and the Assembly than a memorial to his life. Considering Therians' relatively brief life spans, I imagined they rarely had elaborate funerals. Unlike the human rituals meant to comfort those left behind. Few faces in the massive crowd seemed comforted. Mostly they looked angry.

After the service concluded, I cornered Phineas to find out what was going on. He shocked the hell out of me by saying, "I resigned my position as an Elder."

"You . . . why?"

"There are too few of us left, Evy. Ava, Aurora, and Joseph were taken because I was too far away to protect them. I cannot serve as an Elder if I can't even protect three. We're all that's left."

"So what are you going to do? Guard them twenty-four-seven?"

"No. Elder Dane has graciously allowed them to live in his home temporarily. Because he shares a rather large, security-heavy house with the Felia Pride's Alpha, they'll be more than safe there."

"While you do what?"

His expression softened, becoming almost sad. "I'm going away for a while."

"What? Why?" My heart pounded harder.

"To be certain that we're alone. Therians live across the globe, but many have chosen to live as outsiders, as animals. My people, the Coni and Stri, embraced our lives among humans. There may be others out there like us. I have to know." He swallowed hard, his blue eyes glistening. "I have to know if the last of my people will die with Ava."

I understood, and my heart ached for him. "When?"

"Tonight."

That hurt like a fist to the eye. "Were you going to say good-bye?"

"Astrid knows my plans, but no. It would have been easier to simply go."

"You're coming back." It was not a question.

"Of course." He smiled warmly. "My family is here, my friends are here. Just try to not get into too much trouble while I'm gone."

I snickered. "Trouble follows me like a shadow."

"Even so."

He looked at Wyatt, and whatever they shared in that silent communication seemed to each satisfy the other. I reached back, and Wyatt slipped his hand into mine. We both squeezed tight.

"Good luck," Wyatt said.

"And to you both," Phin replied.

"Maybe try to refrain from getting kidnapped or killed," I said.

"I'll do my best."

Someone called his name, and Phineas melted into the shifting tide of people, both human and Therian. We'd come together to honor a fallen friend. Now it was up to us to remain united against several common enemies— and with those enemies quickly stacking up, it was more important than ever. Especially with the vampires sequestered in their private facility in the outskirts of the city. They'd broken all communication. I had no idea if Isleen, Eleri, and Quince were alive or dead. No one did.

Wyatt wrapped his arms around me from behind, and I leaned back against his chest. His familiar scent was there, just a hint of soap and cinnamon, but beneath it was something new. Muskier, more feral. More proof of how much he'd changed in these last twenty-four hours . . . and how much remained the same.

"What are you thinking about?" he asked.

"The future."

"Anything in particular about the future?"

"Just glad to have one." I brought one of his hands up and kissed his knuckles. "With you."

"Me, too. So much."

I smiled.

"Anything you want to do with that future right now?" he asked.

"I did kind of have one thing in mind."

"Oh?"

"Yep." I twisted in his arms to face him and rested my hands on his shoulders.

He was smiling, too, but beneath it lay curiosity and caution. "Will I enjoy this thing on your mind?"

I tilted my head and leaned in just a little, close enough to smell his breath and feel it on my face. "I think you'll find the results of time spent and energy exerted to be quite rewarding."

"Then I'm all for it."

"Fantastic." I planted a quick kiss on his lips, excited at the prospect of getting started. "Let's go track us some werewolves."

He sputtered, and then it turned into laughter. "Yeah, let's do that."

"Together."

Wyatt brushed my cheek with the back of his hand, love shining in his eyes more vividly than if he'd said the words out loud. "Always."

Given our line of work, *always* could as easily mean an hour as a lifetime. But as long as I had him, I planned to love him—him and his grumpy, possessive inner wolf. We'd fought every twist and curve thrown at us since my resurrection. We could deal with Wyatt being part werewolf.

"I just have one condition," I said.

He quirked a dubious eyebrow. "Oh?"

"If you ever come home with fleas, I'm dumping you."

Only Wyatt could do incredulous indignation with such precision, and the comical expression made me double over with laughter. He held me patiently until I got it all out of my system, probably fielding a lot of curious stares along the way. Once I had my breathing back under control, I wiped tears from my eyes and stood a little straighter.

"Do you really think I could get fleas?" he asked, perfectly serious.

I lost it all over again.